City of the Queen

MODERN CHINESE LITERATURE FROM TAIWAN

CITY

OF THE

QUEEN

A Novel of Colonial Hong Kong

SHIH SHU-CHING

translated from the Chinese by
Sylvia Li-chun Lin and
Howard Goldblatt

COLUMBIA UNIVERSITY PRESS

NEW YORK

Columbia University Press wishes to express its appreciation for assistance given by the Chiang Ching-kuo Foundation for International Scholarly Exchange in the preparation of the translation and in the publication of this series.

Columbia University Press
Publishers Since 1893
New York   Chichester, West Sussex
Copyright © 2005 Columbia University Press
All rights reserved

Library of Congress Cataloging-in-Publication Data

Shi, Shuqing, 1945–
  [Xianggang san buqu. English.]
City of the queen : a novel of colonial Hong Kong / Shih Shu-ching ; translated from the Chinese by Sylvia Li-chun Lin and Howard Goldblatt.
    p.   cm.— (Modern Chinese literature from Taiwan)
    ISBN 0–231–13456–8 (cloth)
  1. Hong Kong (China)—Fiction. I. Lin, Sylvia Li-chun. II. Goldblatt, Howard. III. Title. IV. Series.
PL2899.H279   X5313   2005
895.1′352—dc22   2004061754

∞

Columbia University Press books are printed on permanent and durable acid-free paper.
Printed in the United States of America
c 10   9   8   7   6   5   4   3   2   1

City of the Queen

PART
ONE

1

Huang Deyun was thirteen that year.

Dressed in a faded short jacket with loose sleeves, she came out of Dr. Zhou's Herbal Pharmacy on West Corner, a bamboo basket hanging from her arm. Her prematurely born baby brother had spent a restless night. Saying the infant was frightened, Deyun's mother had told her to drop by the Temple of Mazu for an amulet to exorcise the evil spirits.

Passing a stand of sandalwoods by the river, Deyun headed toward the temple, the tips of her worn cloth shoes kicking the yellow dirt under her feet and sending tiny specks of dust dancing in the early morning September sun. For generations the villagers of Huang Deyun's hometown had lived on that yellow soil. Since the late Ming or early Qing dynasties, they had abandoned their fishnets and stayed ashore to grow sandalwood, which thrived in the hard soil, and produce Dongguan incense.

Fragrant incense destined for export was first transported in sampans to a port called Stone Raft Bay on a small island in the South Sea, where it was transferred to cargo junks and shipped back to Canton and the large cities of Jiangsu and Zhejiang. At some point, Stone Raft Bay was renamed Hong Kong, or Fragrant Port. Over time, the name was used to refer to the whole island.

Deyun was worried about her brother, and was thinking about things that concerned every thirteen-year-old girl, unaware that the moment she reached the last step on the flagstone stairs leading up to the temple courtyard, her life would be forever changed, that barely an hour later she would be on her way southward, following the route of the fragrant wood on which generations of her kin and neighbors lived, all the way to Hong Kong. Stepping over the high threshold of the temple, she entered the courtyard, now quiet since Mazu's birthday had just passed. Still a child at heart, she played hopscotch on the flagstones and jumped onto the temple stairs, sending her red copper earrings jangling as a tall figure ducked behind a dragon column on the south side and a light perfume rose from the rustling cassia flowers beneath the stairs. Deyun thought it must be some of those roughnecks from a neighboring village who sneaked into the temple to prey on stray dogs that wet the temple walls with their urine. Every autumn, the season for restorative nutrition, none of the dogs around the village, fat or lean, was spared.

Before she had a chance to look up, Deyun felt darkness descend around her as a burlap sack, like a deep well, dropped over her head. She was about to shout when a large hand clamped over her mouth through the burlap sack. With a twist of her neck, she bit down on the invisible hand; her mouth filled with putrid, salty burlap soaked in seawater. As she was lifted up by the waist, something fell off and rolled across the ground. It was a copper earring, the only thing she would leave behind in her hometown.

Now wearing a single copper earring, Deyun was tossed into the dark hold of a ship, where a heavy sea sent her rolling around in her own vomit. She lay in a daze for a long time before she finally saw the sun again. Brought up onto the deck, she gazed around with eyes like those of a frightened animal, unaware that she had arrived in Hong Kong, Queen Victoria's city.

In 1839, half a century before Huang Deyun landed at Pedder Wharf, the Daoguang emperor in Peking sent an imperial commissioner southward to ban opium. At the time the opium-smoking population in China had reached two million. Armed with his imperial edict, Lin Zexu arrived in Canton, where he forced the foreign opium merchants to turn in twenty thousand cases of opium, to be destroyed at Tiger's Mouth Beach. This act by the imperial commissioner would decide both Hong Kong's fate and his own.

The Daoguang emperor subsequently signed the first unequal treaty in modern Chinese history, ceding Hong Kong to British opium merchants, who could see that the geographical location made it one of the finest ports in the world. But Queen Victoria believed that the British Empire had got the worst of the Treaty of Nanking: except for an indemnity and five ports opened for trade, the empire's new territory was a desolate island without a single brick building. Following Lin Zexu's exile to the hinterland by the Qing government, his British negotiating counterpart, Captain Charles Elliot, was banished to the new Republic of Texas in North America as punishment for his incompetence.

But this was ancient history by the time Huang Deyun, hands tied behind her back, was shipped to Hong Kong on September 25, 1892. The Union Jack, under whose protection the British opium smugglers flourished, fluttered in the wind. Long forgotten were the words of England's conservative MP, Sir James Graham, who passionately denounced the Opium War as "unjust."

Now, under the flag that had shamed Graham, heads bobbed amid the shouts of rickshaw coolies and street vendors. Queen Victoria's desolate island had transformed itself into "the pearl of the British Crown." The busy Victoria Port had fulfilled the British Empire's dream of controlling the seas, with opium merchants setting up a permanent transfer port there. Thatched huts and bamboo sheds had been replaced by opium warehouses and godowns for firms such as Yee Woo and Tai Koo. A port city at the foot of Mount Taiping rose up out of the water like a miracle. Queen's Road was lined with banks, family associations, churches, stores, and British firms, all in the neoclassical architectural style of the Victorian era. Perhaps because the colonial government wanted to flaunt the maritime hegemony of an empire where the sun never set, or because the conservative, ill-adjusted Britons were incapable of changing their lifestyle outside of England, scenic Hong Kong, surrounded by mountains and water, had become a city much like Bombay, Calcutta, and Singapore, except that the bricks, tiles, granite, and marble all came from China, along with the bricklayers, stonemasons, and carpenters.

As she stood on the deck, Huang Deyun had no idea where she was. Queues coiled atop the heads of coolies in short jackets and wearing cloth shoes were a familiar sight, but the red-bricked clock tower, a colonial symbol, on Pedder Street told her she was in an alien land.

Suddenly a commotion erupted on the wharf. Beneath the clock tower, a group of smartly dressed Chinese in black silk gowns and brocade satin jackets struck an interesting contrast with the European clock tower, a strange harmony, like the mingling of Chinese and westerners on the wharf, a sight one gradually got used to if one stared at it long enough. This group of prominent Chinese gentry was about to set off for the Taiping Theatre, where they would call for a ban on the evil custom of keeping and abusing slave girls in Chinese families.

As early as 1880 Governor Hennessy had raised the issue of slave girls with the colonial administration. Twelve years later, under the rubric of Western humanitarianism, these Western-educated Chinese bigwigs launched an unprecedented campaign. Waving the banner of the "Anti-Slave Girl Society," they distributed leaflets to fight for the rights of Chinese women who were being sold as maids and abused like animals.

If not for this impressive demonstration by the Chinese gentlemen as soon as the sampan docked, the frightened slave trader who had kidnapped Huang Deyun would have sold her like a beast of burden to a rich family, where she would have been worked to death. Had that happened, many years later, sociologists would have found the record of Huang Deyun's suffering as a slave girl among a vast collection of historical documents stored at the Rehabilitation Board.

As it turned out, Deyun would in fact be linked to the Rehabilitation Board, not because she had sought shelter at this humanitarian organization, but because a large sum of money would be donated to the board in her name. Even now, a large color portrait of her as an old woman hangs above the stairs of a local orphanage. Wearing a traditional Chinese dress with a long emerald necklace, she had been granted an honorific title as a result of her son's achievements.

But all that would happen much later.

2

On the deck of the sampan, the slave trader grabbed Deyun by the hair and examined her for the first time—thin eyebrows over brown eyes that, reflected in the afternoon sea, were much lighter than those of the average Chinese. Her single-fold eyelids, long and narrow, slanted upward, and her eyes reminded him of the prostitutes on Lyndhurst Terrace, most of them mixed bloods from Macao. So Huang Deyun did not become a slave girl, after all. Instead, she followed in the footsteps of a different group of girls kidnapped from inland China to an even worse fate—she was sold into prostitution.

Unloaded along with boxes of cargo, Deyun climbed the stone stairs toward Mid-Level in Central District. Only a few days earlier, her strong, still growing legs had been mounting the last stone step of the Mazu Temple when darkness fell before her eyes. Now, when she reopened them, she was facing a black-lacquered bed, as big as a house. Thick smoke floated in the air like dust with a pungent smell that scratched her throat. Someone lying on the bed facing the wall was smoking. By then, Hong Kong was suffocating in this white acrid smoke; the person in bed, like millions of Chinese, was curled up in the fetal position in a fog, as if dead. Even if the westerners' cannons were splintering their doors, they would satisfy their craving before getting up.

The feet resting on a footstool belonged to a woman. The soles of her black embroidered silk shoes looked brand new, as if they had never stepped on solid ground.

Yihong, the woman in bed, stirred and sat up lazily. Her hair was unkempt, her short, green-edged jacket open at the neck, exposing peach-pink underwear. Without raising her puffy eyes, she listened as Huang Deyun was dragged over by a maid, who rolled up the girl's sleeves.

"The skin is fair enough," Yihong said, as if buying livestock. "Let's see her teeth!"

The manly hands of the maid pried open Huang Deyun's mouth, exposing a mouthful of white, pearl-like teeth. The woman in bed snorted.

The maid went out to bargain with the slave trader.

Yihong, once the concubine of a Happy Valley tea merchant, had been lured into prostitution. Eventually, she opened her own brothel, Yihong Pavilion, on Hollywood Road, populated with girls bought from poor families or kidnapped from inland China; she took them all in as her own daughters. She also sent pimps out for abandoned baby girls in Hong Kong and Kowloon orphanages, and bought illegitimate girls born to cloistered women in Chinese nunneries. She trained them all herself, teaching them a variety of skills, musical and sexual, and calling them her little "lute girls," then sold them for good prices.

Upon Deyun's arrival, Yihong got up off her opium bed to attend to the new girl personally. To keep calluses from forming on her hands, Deyun was not allowed to do anything for herself, not even wring out a towel after washing her face. Relying upon a girl's natural love of beauty, Yihong taught her how to apply makeup, to match colors in clothing, and to conduct herself like a lady. She hired tutors to teach her how to play instruments and sing, even some English conversation, leaving nothing to chance. Within two years, the girl had learned how to play finger-guessing games, had become a capable drinker, and was a talented musician. But the moment Yihong turned her back, Deyun would sit by the window, lost in thought.

One day, a fellow they called Fatman, who had not been around for a while, called on Yihong with a shipment of Yunnan opium. Wu Fu, the right-hand man of Comprador Wang of the Yee Woo firm, had just returned from inland provinces where he collected opium revenue for the firm. After welcoming him in a side room reserved for special guests, Yihong sent for a servant best known for her opium preparation skills to wait on them. With her head propped against a high porcelain pillow, Yihong finished a pipe of opium without coming up for air, then took a cup of hot tea in both hands and relaxed.

At that moment, Deyun's maid came in to report to Yihong that Deyun would miss today's English lesson, because her teacher, Miss Young, had not shown up. Wanting to ingratiate herself with Wu Fu, Yihong said to the servant, "Bring Deyun in. We've a teacher right here in our midst." Then she added, "Remember to deduct a day from Miss Young's pay."

A soft breeze transported a lovely figure up to the opium bed. She was dressed in everyday clothes; her hair, now much longer, was coiled into a bun. But the face below the bangs was exquisite under the flickering lamplight. Fatman sat up quickly.

"I've been to Yihong Pavilion so many times I've nearly flattened the threshold, but somehow you managed to hide this beauty from me."

"Fatman, don't pretend you don't know the rules here. I'm making an exception today because you know the barbarian tongue. I would like you to test her English, so I'll know if I've gotten my money's worth from Miss Young."

With her eyes cast down, Huang Deyun sat up straight, appearing distant and reserved. Sensing that the girl was far too good for the likes of him, Wu Fu did not bother arguing with the madam, proceeding instead to test Deyun's English with a string of simple questions. When she heard that Wu Fu was also from Dongguan, she quaked. Staring at the flickering lamp, she was silent for a moment before mustering the courage to ask him about her hometown. At that point, Wu Fu had used up nearly all the pidgin English he had learned from the taipan. Scratching his head, he scrambled a few phrases together. Meanwhile, Deyun bent forward, her fingers clenching the silk skirt draped over her knees, beseeching Wu Fu with her eyes to tell her more about her hometown. Wu Fu cocked his head, searching for tidbits to tell her, finally produc-

ing some fragments he'd heard a month earlier, when he was in Dongguan collecting opium money. Deyun smoothed her rumpled skirt as her
face gradually lit up. Yihong, sitting off to the side, was secretly pleased
that the tuition had not been wasted and that her foster daughter's fluent
English would undoubtedly drive up her price.

But the madam was no fool, either. Knowing that anything could happen if the conversation went on too long, she waved Deyun away. For she
had plans for the girl. Even if guests filled up Yihong Pavilion, only a
handful of her clients could claim a status higher than Wu Fu's. High officials and rich tycoons spent their gold and silver elsewhere, in licensed
brothels.

So she went to see the madam at Heavenly Fragrance Tower.

"My foster daughter is a rare beauty who can sing and can play a
musical instrument," she boasted. "She also speaks fluent English, personally taught by the comprador of a foreign firm."

Following a round of negotiations, the two women agreed to split the
fees paid for Deyun's first night, although the final sale price would have
to wait until the madam at Heavenly Fragrance Tower saw Deyun in
person.

After Yihong left, the madam at Heavenly Fragrance Tower was
occupied by different thoughts. On the previous New Year's Eve, a
group of foreign women had come to Lyndhurst Terrace as part of an
Australian theatrical troupe. When the performances were over, the
actresses stayed behind to take up residence on a street corner a block
from Heavenly Fragrance Tower, where they opened a house of prostitution directly opposite the clock tower of the Roman Catholic church
on Wellington Street. Clients who went there in search of foreign beauty
reported that the brothel was decorated like an imperial palace, extravagant and luxurious. All the foreign beauties had skin like snow that
would melt at the slightest touch. And they exposed half of their buttery
breasts for anyone to ogle for free. The mattresses were so thick you sank
in as soon as you lay down. Who would want to leave a place like that?

Not long after the Western owner, Madame Randall, placed a witty ad
about sweethearts in an English newspaper, her place of business was

packed nightly. British soldiers thousands of miles from home were easy prey when they read about "women dressed like fresh flowers, lying in bed waiting to be picked by men."

As she thought of Deyun's fluent English, the owner of Heavenly Fragrance Tower rubbed her chin and had a brainstorm.

In the meantime, Deyun was dressed according to Chinese standards of beauty: a red brocade blouse, an emerald green crepe skirt sprinkled with tiny flowers, and a headful of ornaments. Walking out of her "home" for the first time in two years, she held the arm of the woman who served her. Several times, she opened her mouth to say something, but nothing came out. Eventually she turned and climbed into the curtained sedan chair that would take her to Wellington Street. When she stepped down from the sedan chair, a drinking party had just begun in the east wing of Heavenly Fragrance Tower. A stream of prostitutes summoned from other brothels were standing behind clients, pouring wine and serving food.

The patron who bought Deyun's first night, a crossed-eyed, uncouth tax collector, treated money like dirt, for his income came mainly from loot his lackeys plundered on the ocean. The decorations he displayed for Deyun's first night provided an eye-opener for everyone in Heavenly Fragrance Tower. All sorts of foreign curios filled the room, where a foreign golden coin was tied to the tassel of each hand towel.

The colonial government's policy on prostitution had an interesting history. In the beginning, prostitutes were expelled from Hong Kong. But during Governor Davis's tenure, a "prostitution tax" was collected each month, since the prostitutes were the ones who infected lonely seamen and British soldiers. The prostitutes were also required to set up a hospital for patients with venereal diseases. Later, a "Venereal Testing Regulation" was implemented and licenses were granted to brothels, thus contributing tax revenue to the colonial government.

In 1903, when the first land reclamation project was completed, the area around Shek Tong Tsui was still barren and desolate, and prostitution appeared to be the best way of bringing prosperity to the place. So the government, under the pretense that there were too many brothels in the crowded Possession Street district, relocated them and issued more licenses.

But this, too, would happen much later.

The owner of Heavenly Fragrance Tower had not given up on the idea of earning foreign currency through Deyun. Speculating that Madame Randall could not guess the age of a Chinese girl, and would probably treat Deyun as a novice, she looked forward to bringing in a tidy sum in a deal with the foreign brothel. But that was not to be, since she lacked the necessary connections, and had to settle for second best, selling Deyun to Southern Tang House next door, a haven for Western patrons, whom they called *guailow*, barbarian.

It was on the seventh day of the seventh month, the Chinese Valentine's Day, that Deyun moved to Southern Tang House. It was raining—the separated celestial lovers, the Cowherd and the Weaving Maid, who were cursed to meet but once a year, were shedding tears.

Deyun sat by the window, hands clasped around her knees. Her fingers were painted bright red with Western nail polish given to her by a patron but lacking the fragrance of touch-me-not, which Chinese girls used to color their nails. It was still drizzling; the celestial lovers seemed more sorrowful than usual this year. Deyun sighed softly. This house, her third in Hong Kong, had a more alien feeling than the previous two. The Western-style Southern Tang House, which had been built on the side of a hill, seemed to hang in midair, and each time the porters strained to climb the hill, her sedan chair would turn nearly vertical; Deyun, feet sticking up in the air, would be thrown into a terror.

Confined to an attic room, she was like an exile on a remote island. Surrounded by water so blue it seemed demonic, there was no way for her to escape. Yet even if she could, she had no place to go, for she had by then given up hope of ever returning to Dongguan and her parents. For a while she had asked heaven to take pity and send a benevolent patron to buy her out. She would willingly become a maidservant, a slave even. But now that she had been resold to Southern Tang House, hope died. How could she entrust the remainder of her life to some barbarian, a *guailow* with crimson eyebrows and red hair?

The prostitutes at Southern Tang House, which catered to western-ers, all wore Manchu dresses to show off their Chineseness. Holding embroidered handkerchiefs and swaying in high-heeled Manchu boots, they looked like royalty. With delicate fingers they would lift a Suzhou curtain embroidered with a hundred birds paying tribute to a phoenix, and there, behind a gilded screen, was hidden a China that indulged westerners' imagination: imitations of old paintings of mountains and rivers hung on the wall, vases in famille rose from the town of Jingde stood in the corners, drum-shaped stools with blue inlay and hardwood tables intermingled with sofas and silk chaise lounges; antique curios were piled everywhere, and of course, there were the ever present opium couches.

This concocted China had nothing to do with Deyun. When she stood up, walked in Manchu boots that seemed to lift her into the air, and gazed past the steeple of the Roman Catholic church outside the window to the north, above Victoria Harbor crammed with sails and masts, she saw a red brick wall encircling the western corner of Kowloon Penin-sula. Shaped like the Great Wall, this barrier surrounded a six-acre land called Kowloon, an isolated territory with family shrines and local tem-ples familiar to her. Farmers there lived in tile houses and worked the land following the changes of the four seasons. There was even a private school designed like an imperial college.

Why would a miniature of old China be hidden in an island port open to foreign trade? After the first Sino-Japanese War, when the British colonial government expanded its foreign concession into the New Ter-ritories, the Manchu Imperial court, in order to save the last vestige of face, retained the right to rule Kowloon. So banners embroidered with yellow dragons rippled on either side of the city gate, as sounds of stu-dents reciting the Chinese classics drifted out of the school, and the offi-cial appointed by the Manchu court sat in his little enclave daydreaming about how to subdue the barbarians, totally oblivious to the fact that the foreign powers were biding their time before the next assault.

3

This alien land was a bleak and barbaric hostile island, not just for Deyun but for the early colonizers as well; it was a frightening place with barren mountains and unruly waters. Britons considered it an insidious form of exile to be sent to the queen's most backward city in the Pacific. Even ambitious young civil servants did not accept their posts without qualms, let alone view them as stepping-stones for future promotion. British sailors who planned to make careers in the Royal Navy had a rude awakening when they were sent to the Western Garrison. The well water decimated their ranks, and taipans, who engaged in smuggling by sea, found the terrible weather on land unbearable. Every winter, snow covered Mount Taiping, which was not even two thousand feet high, and as soon as May arrived, the humid, stuffy summer took hold before anyone had a chance to change out of their woolen undergarments. They ate fly-specked meat, then spent half the summer seeking medical treatment for stomach ailments.

Then came an unknown fever, and members of the Western Garrison began dropping like flies. Malaria spread from the marshes eastward, and a quarter of the artillery troops quaked in their beds like leaves in the wind, hot one minute, cold the next. Those who died so far from their homeland were buried in a cemetery called Happy Valley, which years later would become a racecourse.

During the Dragon Boat Festival of 1894, hordes of rats appeared in Chinese residential districts, gnawing on rice stuck to bamboo leaves used to wrap holiday rice dumplings, their never-ending chittering sending shivers down the spines of those who could hear them. When people went out at night, they felt gentle squirmings underfoot, like wading through water. When they shone their lanterns on the ground, they ran off in terror, dropping their lights, as high-pitched squeals rose around them, making their skin crawl. Rats swarmed out of ditches, caves, and basements. Packs of them materialized in hallways, on staircases, in kitchens, in corners, on roof beams, and in attics, twitching violently several times, balletlike, before rolling over and dying, blood spurting from their mouths, like red flowers.

Every morning, refuse carts from the Sanitary Board rolled from one end of the street to the other, their wooden wheels clattering on the flagstones. Uniformed workers walked in line, like a funeral procession, carting away the dead rats for cremation. So many rats dying in droves could not be cleared away immediately, so by the afternoon, the bloated rodents stank horribly in weather that abruptly turned hot around the time of the Dragon Boat Festival.

The bloating soon spread to human bodies, with hard lumps appearing on necks, under arms, and in groins. Afflicted men and women, their limbs splayed grotesquely, ran fevers of 102 degrees, with intermittent heavy breathing, amid the whimpering of the dying rats. The city of the queen had become a bubonic plague zone, and drugs to combat the disease had yet to be discovered.

A dozen years earlier, the colonial government, concerned about overcrowding in the Chinese districts, had limited the number of residents on each floor of all buildings. Officials checked the areas at night, giving illegal residents no chance to escape. But after the outbreak of the plague, the Chinese managed to hide these illegal residents, some infected, in the homes of relatives, and the plague spread unchecked. As the number of dead increased, fearful families dumped the corpses outside at night. Every morning, workers from the Sanitary Board carted the dead away to St. Mary's Hospital to await dissection by medical students.

One must admire the foresight of the tenth governor of Hong Kong, Sir William Des Voeux, who legislated against the intermingling of Chinese and Europeans in order to prevent the expansion of Chinese business. The colonial government even implemented laws forbidding the Chinese from residing in Mid-Level and on the Peak of Mount Taiping, so as to "keep the Europeans out of harm's way." But even segregating the Chinese at the foothills did not ease the concerns of the governor, who then established a Sanitary Board, second in size only to the Police Bureau, which was charged with preventing violence against the colonial government. One of the duties of the Sanitary Board was to enforce hygienic standards in the anthill-like Chinese colonies, whose residents were ordered to disinfect their bedding and furniture and keep their streets, kitchens, and ditches clean.

Following the onset of the plague, the director of the Sanitary Board, Mr. Dickinson, authorized his Chinese interpreter, Qu Yabing, to lead a cleaning crew to saturate the plague-infested areas with disinfectant. Soon, white globules covered Hollywood Road, the smell of disinfectant lingering for days. By then Mr. Dickinson was so caught up in paperwork that he no longer had time to swagger into the Chinese districts, his white-gloved hands clasped behind his back, ready to order a rewash for areas that failed his inspection.

As the plague raged, afternoon tea was served as usual at Dickinson's home on the mountain peak. Standing on a porch lined with marble columns, he welcomed his guests as they walked up a garden path. If not for the sedan chair beside the gate and the gardeners' Hakka straw hats peeking out here and there amid the bushes, lending the place an oriental flavor, his guests would surely have thought they were back in London as they passed the Romanesque fountain and entered the crowded Victorian living room to sit on walnut chairs with green silk cushions.

More than any of the others, Adam Smith, a pale-faced young man with green eyes, freckles, and a pug nose, who worked for Mr. Dickinson, was deceived by the illusion, for he was a newcomer to the city of the queen.

Mr. Dickinson was a bearded man with a ruddy face and a booming voice, especially when he laughed. Born into the middle-class family of a general store owner in Edinburgh, he was not eligible for postings in

India, a magnet for British aristocrats, or Shanghai, a city of adventure, nor even Canton, the "London of the Orient." Because of his background, he had been sent to this barren backwater to sit in his office at the Sanitary Board, surrounded by green walls, swallowed up by paperwork in the dull, monotonous life in the colony.

Two weeks before the plague outbreak, Dickinson had received the latest yearbook of the East India Company. On the inside cover of the gilded volume was a portrait of a British aristocrat, a patrician in tails and a stiff white collar. Oh, how he wished for a similar portrait of himself, standing in front of his Romanesque columns.

Sometimes, when he could contain himself no longer, he would put aside the difference between himself and Adam Smith, his subordinate, and complain about how others who had begun their foreign service at the same time as he were being promoted regularly and enjoying themselves immensely in Calcutta and Shanghai.

"Think about it, Adam. This godforsaken place was opened for trade at the same time as Shanghai, and more than two hundred foreign firms are already operating on Shanghai's Bund. Here, it seems, our only industries are natural disasters and man-made calamities, rampaging pirates, gamblers, and opium smugglers. It's worse than Macao!"

At dusk that afternoon, Smith, the last to leave the tea party, walked down the flagstone steps and entered the garden, where a black furry thing stumbled through a gardenia grove and jumped into a sedan chair by the path. He later realized it had been a staggering, infected rat whose faint squeaks were swallowed up by the deepening evening air.

The next morning, a liveried servant, holding a silver teapot, stood in the dining room, with its spotless cabinets and dining table, waiting for Mr. Dickinson to come whistling down the stairs for breakfast. But when Mrs. Dickinson opened the velvet curtains in the bedroom, she found her bedraggled husband slumped by the window, his limbs splayed, his face crimson, breathing heavily.

"A wall . . . should've built a wall, damn it!" he mumbled before losing consciousness.

Dickinson had sent more than one request to the governor to build a wall to keep the Chinese out, so as to protect the tranquility of life of the British expatriates inside, advice considered extreme by the governor. For the British residents, this subtropical island was little more than a stopping-off point for ships. The treaty the British had drafted granted legal rights to opium-laden British ships from India to enter Victoria Harbor, one of the finest deepwater ports in the world, and they got exactly what they wanted. Yet, half a century after Hong Kong was opened for trade, the colonial government still had no intention of developing the island. That was not what they had in mind. They had set their sights on the population and resources of China's inland cities, a huge market for the British to dump their consumer goods. The most they would do in Hong Kong was to ensure that their transit port was clean by decreasing the number of people who had contracted fever, malaria, or cholera.

Except for the issue of sanitation, the governors of Hong Kong historically could not have cared less about the Chinese, who were left to fend for themselves. That included Governor Hennessy, who, on the premise of respecting the Chinese lifestyle, turned a blind eye to such problems in the Chinese residential areas as poor ventilation, a scarcity of drinking water, and no underground drainage system, all the prerequisites for a sanitary environment. The Chinese, who made up 90 percent of the population, were squeezed by the colonizers into the western corner of Queen Victoria's city, with a total space of half a square mile to serve as their business, entertainment, and residential district. It was overcrowded even before refugees fleeing the Taiping Rebellion arrived from the mainland. Added to that were farmers and fishermen from Southeast China who took up temporary residence before setting off for North America and the South Pacific. At the time, Hong Kong had the highest population density in the world.

Upon hearing the news of Mr. Dickinson's death, the colonial government, as a last resort, ordered that the infected areas be torched and the residents to be relocated within seven days. Responsibilities at the Sanitary Board fell to Adam Smith precisely when the terrified governor issued his order to quarantine all victims of the plague and seal up their houses.

Rest in peace, Mr. Dickinson! Adam Smith vowed to avenge his supervisor. He bowed deeply before Dickinson's casket. With a strange glint in his eyes beneath their silvery brows, he raised his face, which had been baked red by a blazing sun, balling his fists in hands empowered by the order to seal up plague-infested houses. As acting director of the Sanitary Board, he had now become a warrior, armed with orders issued by the governor himself to crush the ubiquitous plague demon. He would hold high his torch and fling it into polluted corners; the plague, hiding in the dark, would squeal and scurry amid the raging fire and turn to ashes.

Final victory would be his!

Wearing a helmet and an oilcloth protective suit, and accompanied by his Chinese interpreter, Qu Yabing, Adam Smith walked toward the plague area on Ice House Street, followed by a gang of sanitation workers carrying wooden planks and hammers. Climbing the hill, he stood facing Hollywood Road, the first street to be developed after the queen's city was opened for trade. The normally bustling, chaotic street was deadly quiet under the blazing noonday sun; abandoned rickshaws and sedan chairs were strewn everywhere.

As he stood on the deserted street corner, Smith felt forsaken by the world. Unlike the young people he had grown up with, he had chosen not to stay in his hometown to inherit the family mill by the little creek, where, on summer afternoons, he would have rowed and sung with the neighbor's daughter, Annie. One day he had discovered a diary among a pile of magazines in the attic, and it had changed his life. The yellowed pages of the diary recorded the travels of his uncle, and so, on an early November day, as snow fell on Britain, a ship crawled through the narrow waterway of Carp Gate, carrying Adam Smith and a letter of employment for foreign service from the British colonial government. In the eyes of the twenty-year-old, Victoria Harbor had looked like a lively seafaring port.

Mount Taiping Street was inhospitably steep. Early visitors had predicted that the stony island, with its rugged geography, could not possibly develop into a metropolis. But it had. The streets, narrow as shirtsleeves, were crammed with stores on both sides, their signs hung so closely together they were an unbroken tableau. A dazzling array of shops and services, from foreign goods to money exchange, to rice shops, grocery stores, soy sauce plants, and teahouses and, of course, authorized opium retailers. With the sun blocked by all the store signs, the street was forever dark, as if in the shadow of a solar eclipse.

It was afternoon nap time, and the doors were closed. Smith was uneasy, for the street seemed to have been seized by the plague demon, its terrifying ghosts snickering behind closed doors. Most of the residents had left. Shop owners infected with the plague had boarded ships on dark nights, returning to Canton in hopes of finding a cure. Their employees, fleeing the plague, had also returned to the countryside, in defiance of laws prohibiting anyone from leaving Hong Kong.

Mount Taiping Street had been cowed into silence by the plague demon, all but the shop at the end of the block with the sign proclaiming Top Quality Legal Opium. As advertised, the odor of burning opium hung in the air, deeply intoxicating. Adam Smith inhaled twice, despite himself. He felt like a man wandering in a wasteland, never expecting to see another living soul, and the unexpected smell of opium, a scent from the world of the living, sent a chill through his body.

As he left the business district, his nostrils were assailed by the smell of incense, so thick it overpowered the burned odor of opium. The few Chinese who remained had gathered outside the Temple of the Guanyin Bodhisattva to pray for protection from the plague. Ashes from paper spirit money and papier-mâché, in all sorts of colors, filled the sky above them; offerings to the deities—chickens, ducks, fish, eggs dyed in red, and a braised suckling pig—were piled high. Devout believers who could not find a place to kneel crowded against each other outside the temple, all holding joss sticks.

Back when the plague had first erupted, an herbal doctor practicing medicine on Hollywood Road had set up a stand next to the temple, displaying a banner proclaiming him to be the "Reincarnation of Huatuo," the magical physician of Chinese legend. Even on hot days, he wore a felt top hat adorned with yin and yang hexagrams; a red mark between his brows looked like a third eye, and his spittle flew as he touted magic pellets and divine oil, which he claimed had been passed down in his family.

On this day, he was again out hawking his wares, drawing crowds of people to his stand, which prompted Adam Smith and Qu Yabing to do the same. Suddenly an old man in a white robe sprang out of the temple. With a sword in his left hand and a duster in his right, he darted around the courtyard. Acting as if the true god had arrived, the believers, men and women, knelt and kowtowed, a sight that drew away those buying divine oil.

The old man was the incarnation of the legendary Immortal Tan, who, he said, had given him a secret formula to cure the plague. Qu Yabing translated the legend for Adam Smith, adding, "The Immortal Tan, the patron saint of fishermen, was actually a little boy. His image in the temple shows that he was barely twelve years old. They say he controls the weather, which is why fishermen worship him."

"It seems that the young boy has yet another talent. Those who worship him can be free of plague!"

Qu silently considered the sarcasm in the Englishman's comment.

Qu Yabing had completed the fourth form at an English school, but the color of his skin dictated that he serve under the younger Adam Smith, who had arrived in Hong Kong barely four months earlier. Carefully and respectfully maintaining a distance between himself and his British superior, Qu walked one step behind and cast his eyes down, holding his arms tightly along the seams of his pants when he spoke. His mother had been a maidservant in the Qu household, a family of wealthy landowners. Sired out of wedlock by the licentious Master Qu, Yabing had been expelled from the Qu family, along with his mother, by the mistress. Raised in a church-run orphanage, Yabing had seen his fill of the hypocrisy of the church people. Commingling their respect for Queen Victoria and the will of God, the pastor and his flock systematically oppressed the Chinese. Yabing hated yet feared them. But he could not stand the barbaric nature of his own people either.

Following Adam Smith, Qu passed the Guanyin Temple and arrived at the marketplace. His face, gloomy after the eruption of the plague, now turned red in shame. It was not what one might imagine a plague-infested area to be. Bare-bottomed children rolled in the mud with pigs; hens expelled green excrement alongside the mud holes. A shoe repair-man looked on coolly, smoking his pipe. At one of the stalls, salted fish hung from bamboo poles, while squid and raw oysters lay drying on the ground. Flies swarmed up with a loud buzz as soon as someone came near. The thatched awning of a food stand, blown over by the last typhoon, was propped up with rocks and ropes; droves of customers kept the owner too busy to make repairs. Bamboo poles strewn with laundry poked out from Chinese-style houses. Water dripped through the holes in the awning, but the customers didn't notice. Mostly men with queues coiled atop their heads, they squatted barefoot on bamboo stools, stretching their necks to gobble down fried crabs, Chinese sausages, and cow innards. One cent per earthenware bowl. Soup min-gled with their sweat and ran down their chests, but they were like starv-ing animals, too busy slurping down their food to wipe it off.

Squatting on the dusty ground, this group of diners paid no heed to the strangely dressed Adam Smith. Except to make important proclama-tions, the fair-skinned Englishmen rarely showed up here. But a woman selling fruit, spotting his helmet and oilcloth protection suit and thinking he was a demon from hell, fainted dead away on a pile of sugar cane.

Smith's instincts told him he should not have set foot in a place like this unarmed. If attacked, he would not have been able to fight back. The colonial government had warned police and officials to be armed when entering Chinese districts. But these ordinary citizens, shoulders and backs laden with saleable items, were too intent on eking out a living to bother, while the beastly diners appeared incapable of sparing the energy to harm him. Smith was shocked by the voracious look on the Chinese as they wolfed down their food. In his homeland, religious beliefs and a system of education regarded gluttony as one of the deadly sins. Even as a plague raged around them, and as their relatives dropped like flies, in the midst of this unimaginable horror, these people knew only how to satisfy their desire for food. They ate as if there were no tomorrow. What kind of race was this?

Sunlight that had originally given him a feeling of rebirth now bore straight down like needles, piercing his helmet. Sweat drenched his silvery eyebrows and blurred his vision. He felt that his life was threatened even before he had time to adjust to this desolate island, with its barren mountains and unruly rivers, and was distressed that he had not been assigned administrative duties. As he stood under the blistering sun, he thought of his superior, who had lain in the hospital, blood spurting from incisions on the buboes in his groin. Smith had been left to combat the omnipotent plague demon alone, and soon he would follow in the other man's footsteps. He had yet to encounter any of the mysteries recorded in his uncle's arcane oriental diary, and already he was on the brink of death. If he took another step forward, the demon would set him ablaze, weaken his pulse, and swell his chest with fever and black splotches. But could he just turn and walk away, leaving behind this group of ridiculous-looking Chinese workers with queues hanging limply down their backs?

The Chinese customarily rang bells to scare away demons when plagues erupted. Now Adam Smith longed to hear the sound of a bell, which he associated with the lepers of medieval Europe: a cluster of afflicted wretches swathed in cloth from head to toe, exposing eyes that were beginning to fester, and ringing bells to warn off others. The ringing of the bells, at least, was a sign of life, no matter how debased and putrid it might be.

Ahead of them, where Hollywood Road met Lyndhurst Terrace, finally emerged the sounds of humanity. Those who had stayed behind were awakened from their naps to protest the sealing up of their houses. A mere block away, Lyndhurst Terrace and Wellington Street were strangely full of life, in total disregard of the encroachment of the plague. People were lying low in opium dens, gambling houses, and brothels, waiting for the shroud of sunset to disappear before they swarmed out to earn dangerous money, wagering their lives. More and more rigid corpses were being carted away, replaced by people creeping up onto the salty, smelly shore. Newly opened stores run by compradors on Lyndhurst Terrace displayed a neat array of goods to challenge the plague demon. Long rows of cask-aged brandy stood behind dozing shopkeepers who were struggling through the sweltering afternoon to welcome the arrival of extravagant evenings.

Soft music seemed to drift out from Madame Randall's beauty den. Two days earlier, in a public toilet, Adam Smith had overheard two policemen whispering salacious tales about their weekend. An unknown anxiety raged in his body; there was so much empty space to fill, especially at a time when there might not be a tomorrow. The suppressed passion accumulated over the past few days was in urgent need of an outlet.

The sun was still baking his back. To escape from the burning heat, Smith opened a door he mistakenly thought belonged to Madame Randall. By thus accidentally entering Southern Tang House, he would alter Huang Deyun's life completely. She, of course, had no premonition of what was about to happen. Sitting in the same chair she'd sat in the year before, when she'd first arrived, she had just awakened from a nap. Wearing a loose dress with wide sleeves, her bright red undergarment unbuttoned, she was lazily waving a cattail fan—the one that had hung from Yihong's opium couch. Her embroidered shoes were softly kicking the edge of the bed, either because she was bored or to pass the time before night arrived. Her shoes, dimpled by the kicks, showed signs of movement, unlike Yihong's, which had stuck out of the opium couch and rested on the footstool. Deyun had not yet given up on herself.

Just before her door was thrown open, Deyun noticed that the cross atop the clock tower of the Roman Catholic church was nearly melting under the blazing sun. Then a shadow crept into the corner of her eyes and hesitated before pitching forward into the room. Professional training prompted her to cast a sideways glance before turning to look, her lightly painted eyebrows showing no sign of surprise. All men were free to enter her room, anyway, particularly now, as the plague raged. Clients had lost all sense of propriety, coming to her without regard for day or night. And the brothel servants failed to announce the clients' arrivals, since they themselves had already gone into hiding.

But the sight of the helmet and the oilcloth protection suit Adam Smith wore so shocked Deyun that she quickly stood up. The newcomer rushed toward the dark shadow—his eyes had yet to adjust to the darkness—before his legs buckled and he fell to his knees. Grabbing Deyun's waist, he buried his head between her legs, sending his helmet rolling to the floor and revealing a head of curly chestnut hair. He was exhausted, having just climbed out of the plague demon's pit. Never before had he been so close to death; he felt the demon howling around him, dragging him toward a bottomless abyss, deeper and deeper. . . .

Barely recovered from the fright, Smith tremblingly returned to the world of the living. His protection suit, treated with oil and dried by the sun, cracked and rustled as he trembled. Now that he had seized a body—the warm, soft body of a woman—he felt safe.

"Let me hold you. Let me hold you a while."

Caressing his protruding ears, which stuck up helplessly, like those of a deer, Deyun assumed that Adam Smith was another boy far from home who had come to seek a moment of comfort from her. The cold glint of a sneer flickered in her experienced eyes over his misfortune. And as her lips curled slightly, she held up the head in her arms, the loose sleeves of her purple satin dress dipping down to reveal a naked shoulder. Smith looked up and came face-to-face with the bright red undergarment of a prostitute. He froze at the redness, like a bloody flash. Flinging away the caressing hands in disgust, he stood up and ran out, not giving the woman a chance to see his face clearly.

Smith dragged his weary body back to his government flat, where he had been spending so many lonely dusks in the colony. Lighting a cigarette, he thought of his faraway hometown and of Annie, until the urge for whisky overpowered him.

But then the dying sunset in the ocean sky called out to him, and he found himself walking along the steep flagstone steps leading back to Southern Tang House. There he downed the glass of whisky handed to him by the bartender, but the alcohol failed to revive him; instead, fatigue blurred his eyes and lent his face a shrouded expression. Holding onto the banister of the spiral staircase, he walked upstairs, nearly falling several times when his hand slipped. Alcohol surging in his empty stomach filled him with a hollow feeling. He kicked open Deyun's door and saw her playing solitaire under a lamp, his helmet resting beside her. The sound at the door had not startled her, for she was waiting for him, certain he would return. The cards in her hands opened and closed like a fan, but she paid no heed to the man standing there. The shadow on the wall grew and grew, until it enshrouded her. Like a thief, he snatched his helmet and held it to his chest.

"I came . . . came back for this," he said, backing away until his body was up against the door. "I need it for tomorrow morning. Mr. Dickinson fell ill, infected, ill . . . I must take his place."

His shoulders slumped. The woman put down the cards in her hands and stood to face him. Tonight would be her night; she had carefully made herself up, colorful and dazzling.

Outside the nearly dark window, the cross of the Roman Catholic church was obscured. The beautiful woman, as if inlaid on the screen like dark night, began to move, gracefully walking toward the man pressed to the door.

"My poor child!"

4

Officially, the plague of 1894 took 2,552 lives, but the actual figure was far greater. Some victims were buried privately, others were never reported, and still more deaths occurred after the infected sneaked back to die in Canton. On June 7 alone, on Mount Taiping Street, where the plague was most rampant, 107 people died in a single day, with 60 more infected.

At first, the doctors at St. Mary's Hospital, unable to find the cause, were mystified by the number of corpses piling up. Later the London government sent Professor Pearson, a bacteriologist, to investigate. Wearing a white surgical mask and rubber gloves, he retrieved a curled up, stiff rat from an infected house for testing. Then he wrote to the governor of Hong Kong to request the assistance of eight bacteriologists from Japan. In the end, they were able to prove that the plague had come from the fleas carried by dead rats. There was no cure.

The colonial government posted announcements in the slum districts of the Chinese quarter, listing anti-rat measures. Thus began the reign of an animal with a long, pointed mouth, sharp teeth, and a thick tail with a wiry tip over the lives of more than a hundred thousand Chinese, who realized that dead rats were even more fearful than live ones. Workers from the Sanitary Board entered infected households and swept out piles of dead rats, which were not only the cause but also the victims. Residents of the infested areas lived in terror; at night they kept their eyes open in the dark, sweeping their hair behind their ears to listen to the soft rustle of rats on the beams, in cabinets, in closets and dressers; to the gnawing on ropes of oil bottles; or to the hungry squeals, comforted to know that the rats were still alive. In the mornings, when they opened their doors, their greatest fear was of seeing a warm body fall from atop the doorframe onto their heads before hitting the ground. For when they looked down, they would see blood smearing the pointed mouth, as if the rat were holding a red flower between its sharp teeth. Then it would twitch a time or two before stretching out its paws and dying before their eyes. A tingle would rise up on their scalps, immobilizing them and keeping them from touching the spot hit by the falling rodent.

They then had to force themselves to sweep dark corners with a long-handled broom. Whenever they touched a hard object, their first impulse was to throw down the broom and run away. But this was their home, so they gritted their teeth, closed their eyes, and swept vigorously. No need to look, for they were certain it would be blood-curdling dead rats, and not just one but several of them.

Governor Robinson urged the residents to raise cats, and installed oil-filled metal boxes on lampposts, at street corners, on trees, and against the pillars of street overhangs. The residents were asked to drop the dead rats inside for future inspection.

It was a time when rats ruled over humans.

Waving its bloody sickle, the plague demon pressed forward, from Hollywood Road to Lyndhurst Terrace, leaving scores of victims in its wake. Gone were the lantern-toting men who visited brothels; so too the throngs of foreign sailors, who had just entered port, waving their tattooed arms like troops to be reviewed. The blue cloth curtains outside opium dens, which only two weeks before were being parted constantly, now hung quietly. Dead silence loomed over the gambling houses; no more shouts to entice gamblers dreaming to get rich quick. Goods were strewn atop the counters of compradors' shops; no more whisky, no more brandy, for the smugglers, fearing for their lives, no longer climbed up the salty, smelly shores.

At first, it seemed to be business as usual at Madame Randall's beauty den from early morning till noon, for soft music drifted out from the partially closed door and echoed on deserted streets littered with empty liquor bottles and trash. Chinese imperial-style carved lanterns made of copper still burned bright. But, unable to contain his curiosity, a beggar sleeping on the steps quietly pushed open the door, with its blue and red stained glass, only to find that the interior was empty. Madame Randall and her prostitutes had disappeared overnight, leaving behind a floor strewn with clothing and makeup, a house stripped bare of curtains and drapes. Their departure had been as sudden as their arrival. Like soldiers striking camp, they had vanished without a trace.

A stifling wind blew over the ocean, sending the strong odor of sulfur rushing like lava toward Southern Tang House. The rotten-egg smell meandered along a winding path, from the drinking room to the opium beds, hopping onto the red-lacquered staircase to bang on the door of Deyun's attic room. She had no idea that Madame Randall was gone. With her door shut to block out the plague, she sat behind a beaded curtain in her dark room, her mind clear. She was no longer a prisoner in the attic on the besieged island. Three days earlier, the deity worshipped by prostitutes had finally answered her prayers, sending a savior down from the clock tower beyond her window. As the plague raged, a white, slender figure with velvety hair had entered her life.

Her maid brought up a three-legged, red-lacquered bathtub and filled it with water warmed by two hours of sunlight. This would keep Deyun free of heat rash. After ordering the woman away, Deyun bent down to test the water. For three days she had been washing her prostitute's body with this tepid well water, over and over, washing off the breath, saliva, and filth left there by countless clients before the appearance of Adam Smith. The sun-warmed water opened thousands of little mouths to suck on her skin, a tingle like mild electric shocks, like the soft lips of a lover, kissing her passionately as he wrapped his arms around her.

Stepping out of the tub, she walked barefoot on the red tiles. Her cleansed, orchidlike fingers lifted a red embroidered silk that covered her dressing mirror. Not wanting to get her hair wet, she'd pinned it up with a white jade hairpin, which she now removed. She ran a red, crescent-shaped lacquered comb though hair that had not been trimmed since the day she was sold to Yihong Pavilion. Soon, the prostitute in gaudy clothes and tinkling ornaments vanished from the mirror, replaced by the Huang Deyun of old, carrying a bamboo basket to the Temple of Mazu to pray for an amulet. Thin bangs lined her forehead; copper earrings dangled from her ears. She was the sandalwood-harvesting girl of Dongguan, who, on early autumn mornings, went to Fragrant Mountain with neighbor girls to dig up the roots of sweet, ancient sandalwood. All the greedy young girls would cut off small portions from the finest sandalwood and wait for the best offer from out-of-town merchants.

But now Deyun didn't have her sandalwood, except for a black leather case, gilded with a phoenix, which was hidden in her dresser. Besides the strings of pearls, silver hairpins, and jade bracelets she'd been given, she had put away money from her clients and kept it hidden from the madam. She now had enough to buy herself out. Contented, she sat back. Everything was ready, including the red satin bedspread and the neatly creased new bedding beneath it. With her hands crossed, she waited for the slanting sunlight to stream through the curtain, when her lover would rush toward her, his helmet in hand, leaving his protective suit by the door, just like the day before.

In a short while, she would be caressing her lover's beard, which he hadn't had time to shave since assuming the position of acting director of the Sanitary Board. She would beg him to stay the night, for then the plague demon howling outside could not harm them. She would protect him; he would be safe.

All Huang Deyun wanted now was to have her lover stay on this island with her.

5

After Governor Robinson declared Hong Kong a plague port, the Western businessmen began leaving, taking their families with them. On an afternoon with chilling winds and icy rain, Adam Smith went to bid farewell to Mrs. Dickinson. Before she lifted her black widow's skirts to board the ship, she turned to cast one last bitter look at Victoria Harbor. How many lives had already been sacrificed for this port amid the smoke and dust of guns and cannons? And the disaster wasn't over yet. Her husband had given his life in an effort to maintain a sanitary space in the South Sea for British citizens. Mrs. Dickinson resented this gray, misty seaport, shrouded in the gloom of rain, and vowed never to set foot on the place again as long as she lived.

Clustered among those who came to see off the ship, Smith waved listlessly. The long, loud whistle from the soon-to-depart ocean liner nearly tore his insides apart, for once Mrs. Dickinson was gone, he would be abandoned on this remote island, a stranger in a strange land, facing the plague all alone. When kissing him good-bye, she had mentioned Annie. Unable to understand what was keeping him here, she was afraid he'd end up like her poor husband if he didn't leave soon.

Without waiting for the ocean liner to get under way, Smith folded his umbrella and walked down the pier, cluttered with crisscrossing ropes and fluttering flags. Coolies were loading coffins onto a ferryboat, followed by wailing family members in mourning clothes. Governor Robinson had finally relented, allowing the victims of the plague to be transported back to their hometowns for burial. Those who clung to life were also permitted to leave Hong Kong to seek cures elsewhere. The dying lay on stretchers placed alongside the coffins, waiting to board the ferry.

The sampan that had carried the kidnapped Huang Deyun three years earlier was also moored there. The colorful bunting on its bow had faded in the sun, and the slave trader had been replaced by moaning patients. Smith knew nothing of Huang Deyun's past. Oblivious, he walked to the end of the pier to take the Peak tram to his two-story government flat at Mid-Level, feeling as drenched inside as his wet overcoat. The outside wall of his quarters was painted light green, its wooden blinds shut tight the year round to keep dampness from seeping through. The upstairs balcony, encircled by iron bars, faced Victoria Harbor. On a clear day he could see the undulating mountains of Kowloon.

As he stood on his balcony, Smith smoked gloomily, the sight of luscious banyan trees in the rain reminding him of the moist green lawns of his home in Brighton. He missed kindly old England. At the far end of the lush vegetation of the Mount Taiping foothills, Victoria Harbor lay quietly like a giant gray ribbon. Mrs. Dickinson's ocean liner had by then sailed for England, to pass through the South Pacific, the Malacca Straits, the Indian Ocean, and the Red Sea, arriving in Liverpool two months hence. His hometown was now beyond his reach; maybe he would never again lie on its velvety grass.

Smith had not come to the Orient to nurse a wound. In scenic Brighton, he had longed for adventure. As a little boy, he had fantasized about leaving home to join wandering gypsies who sailed the open seas. In his veins flowed the wayfaring blood of his uncle. If he had been born half a century earlier, he imagined he'd have been among the first to land in Hong Kong after it had been ceded to the British Empire. Enthusiastic over Queen Victoria's policy to expand the empire, he'd have jumped off the British multimasted sailboat onto a rocky cape, sending naked natives scurrying in fright before this band of armed, strangely clad and equipped invaders, seemingly descending from the sky.

But when he actually set foot on the small island, he understood why Queen Victoria had complained that her empire had gotten the worst of the Treaty of Nanking. Half a century after the British government took over, Hong Kong was no longer the desolate fishing village it had been when the treaty was signed, but there was still so much to be done. Even something as basic as drinking water was a huge problem. Infectious diseases caused by unclean water from mountain streams and wells went unchecked. No sooner had Smith assumed his position than he was confronted by the worst plague to hit the port after it opened for trade. He prayed that he would not follow his boss as a sacrificial victim to the expansion policy of the British Empire.

His servant Yafu walked up, a white towel draped over his shoulder, to inquire about dinner. Smith changed out of his half-dried coat, hastily combed his slightly mussed curly hair, and went downstairs. Tonight he was in no mood to dress for dinner. Now that Mrs. Dickinson was gone, the social etiquette he had learned from her would be of little use, unless the wife of the police chief invited him to afternoon tea. And there was little chance of that. From now on, his only opportunity to show that he was a gentleman would be the annual party at the governor's residence to celebrate Queen Victoria's birthday. The rest of the year he would have to content himself with playing pool with bachelors working at the Hong Kong and Shanghai Bank. The governor's residence, Happy Valley, and the Hong Kong Club would provide the limits of his social circle. He never dreamed he would live such a confined life.

Sitting under the dim candlelight, he dined on Portuguese curried chicken, a dish that was popular in Macao. The candlelight illuminated a mammoth oval dining table occupied by him alone. It had been brought there by his predecessor, from a government warehouse. When he took over the position, he inherited everything from his predecessor—from the furniture to the knife and fork in his hands, from the plates in front of him even to the servants. It was like staying in a hotel.

The feeling that this was not his home was particularly strong this night. The empty rooms of the flat were locked up in darkness. So would the dining room be when Yafu, who was waiting outside, quietly came in to clear the table and blow out the candles after Smith pushed his chair back and left the table. He dragged himself up the stairs to smoke in the parlor. Then he wandered into the study, where many of his suitcases stood unpacked, before returning to his bedroom. Shadows cast by candlelight following him from one room to another seemed to be everywhere, but they were all his own.

This was not his home. To the east of the foothills was his secret residence, a place much more like home. There his woman awaited him with tenderness, painstakingly outfitted in colorful clothes and makeup, gracefully moving from behind the gilded screen toward him. On that first night he quaked uncontrollably, for he had just climbed out of the valley of death. Fear twisted his sunburned face. As his silvery eyelashes fluttered, he spread his arms in search of human comfort. Climbing up onto the prostitute's bed, he surrendered himself completely, afraid that his days were numbered. Perhaps when he woke up the following morning, his pulse would be weak, black splotches would have appeared on his skin, and he would feel heat deep down in his chest. Then terrifying swellings would materialize behind his neck and in his groin before his blood turned tar black. His life would be over before it had hardly begun.

Poor child, my poor child! Huang Deyun's head struggled out from under his body, all wet and clammy, as if dredged up out of water. My God, you really are just a child! Another traveler far from home who has lost his virginity amid the red undergarments of a prostitute. Deyun sighed over how he had poured out his passion, over his clumsy movements, over how he was too ashamed to face himself, let alone look at her. She could not forget the night she had lost her virginity to the scruffy tax collector. With red candles burning bright, she had sat at a mirror putting on her makeup, trembling inwardly. Her sisters in the brothel had described to her the splitting pain of the first night. Feet trembling with excitement, the man who bought her first night had clamored for the ritual wine drunk by newlyweds. She had wanted to fling open the door and flee, but the madam had grabbed hold of her to change her girlish hairstyle to that of a married woman. Maids had then entered to place pink folded towels under the sheets and a bucket of water behind the bed. All these ritualistic actions were signs that she was about to begin the life of a prostitute.

From then on, every night passed in the same way. Before she went to bed with yet another client, she would reapply makeup to make her face dazzling and fetching. Unwilling to muss her hair, she would place a leather pillow under her head, in order to maintain a dignified appearance while the client stripped her to do whatever pleased him.

But on the night after Adam Smith showed up at her door, she did not call the maid to make up her hair. She knew that the man would return, so she braided her waist-length hair and waited. Seeing her bangs in the mirror, she felt as if she had returned to her last night as a virgin. She sat under the lamplight, guarding the helmet of that alien young man, who had worn such odd clothes. And that face—Huang Deyun had never seen such a look of desperation in her life. His legs buckled and he held her, as if grasping the last rock on a cliff. He was no client coming for a night's pleasure. If he returned, it was because this attic had become his shelter, his refuge.

He would be back, Deyun believed tenaciously. And when he appeared at her door, she would slowly lead his fingers, trembling in hunger for human contact, through the thick hair at her temples, leaning gently toward him so he could feel the breath of a living human being. Smith would open his eyes, his white brows wet with perspiration, and, in the dim candlelight, gaze into the disarmingly lovely face he held in his hands. Butterfly, my yellow-gossamer butterfly.

Squat black trees fill a verdant valley, a windless valley. Caterpillars wriggle in their cocoons, noisily announcing their imminent entry into the world, reborn as butterflies, rustling all the leaves of the trees. Pop! Tens of thousands of butterflies are born. They circle the squat black trees and create a golden panorama. The yellow butterfly is reborn in the arms of a foreigner.

Huang Deyun took out a handkerchief and cleaned him carefully. She was glad the maid had not followed the usual practice of placing a pink towel on the bed and filling a wooden basin behind the bed with water for those who entertained overnight guests. The rules at Southern Tang House had fallen into disuse with the rampage of the plague.

6

The day before the Sanitary Board torched the plague area near Mount Taiping, Huang Deyun stepped over the unconscious body of the pimp and, suitcases in hand, climbed into the sedan chair that would take her away from Southern Tang House. She was dressed in flowery silk clothes, a far cry from the wedding procession she'd dreamed about as a little girl.

The stained-glass doors of Madame Randall's beauty den stood open, but the place was stripped bare, except for burn marks from disinfectant on the floors and the stairs. The red silk lanterns offered by Southern Tang House to deities had been flung to the ground. The doctor hawking magic cures for the plague had disappeared without a trace. Earlier, when she had heard him peddling his magic elixir, she had sent a maid down to purchase some, for she could not afford to fall ill. Thoroughly exhausted, she wondered how it could take so much energy just to love someone. When Smith had closed the door behind him and left in the middle of the night, his smell had lingered on the bedding and on the mattress. Reluctant to close her eyes and go to sleep, she inhaled the pillow's fragrance to relive again and again those tender moments. She needed to feel that she was in love and was being loved; she needed all her strength to nurture a romance that was more important than her own life. She could not afford to fall ill.

The new place Smith found for her was a Chinese-style building with a vaulted ceiling in Happy Valley. The first thing he bought was a large four-poster bed, nearly new, with a coiled spring mattress. He had found it at an auction on Queen's Road. Formerly owned by an opium shop comprador, it had copper posts, and with the curtain down, it created its own small universe. Huang Deyun lay down flirtatiously.

Adam Smith's hand, which had wielded a torch to burn the plague areas, now held a white candle, which he moved around to gaze at the languid body before his eyes. It was red with intoxication, longing to be controlled, and he was its master. Huang Deyun said he was a sea lion, holding and embracing a woman who was delicate and fragile, yet an expert in sex. Butterfly, my yellow-winged butterfly. He rested her legs on his shoulder, sensing that he was her ruler and that she would submit to his control.

This wasn't love, Smith told himself, but a form of conquest. If he wanted, he could bend this pliant body backward, like a circus acrobat, turning it into a ball of flesh; with her face pressed against the bed, he could thrust around and play her like a toy. She could also be a soft snake coiling around his neck to arouse him once more. This former prostitute from Southern Tang House was the incarnation of sexual desire; the Chinese-style building was his harem, which he decorated based on the images of the Orient he had known: palace lanterns in red silk, carvings of soaring dragons, bamboo chairs, high tables, porcelain vases, complete with serving women dressed in white silk blouses and black silk pants. And his woman, wearing cheongsams with loose sleeves, crawled on the floor to serve him submissively.

This harem was his harbor, to which he would always sail. He would let the onetime prostitute of Southern Tang House hide him in a different world, one he would never leave.

The twenty-two-year-old being could no longer sustain the burdens of the outside world.

7

The plague had finally passed.

On a morning after the Mid-Autumn Festival, Adam Smith stood on his balcony to watch the sea after his morning toilet. A soft breeze with the light fragrance of cassia brushed over and slipped into the open collar of his pajamas, so comforting. Long-tailed birds flew in and out of the banyan trees beyond the fence. When he took a closer look, he saw bright yellow stripes alongside the beaks and around the eyes.

It was a pleasant Sunday morning. The steeple bell of the Gothic St. John's Cathedral was summoning the faithful to Sunday mass. Only those who believe in God can gain eternal life. Rubbing his clean-shaven face, Adam Smith waited to put on a snowy white, stiff-collared shirt, laundered and ironed by his servant, Yafu. Later he would sit with a Bible in his hands in a church pew, listening to Pastor Thomas's sermon. Organ music would fill his heart with reverent happiness.

Standing on the balcony, Smith luxuriated in this beautiful Sunday morning. Bright sunshine fell upon a rational, conscious world on the day God rested after six days of creation. And yet, he felt lonely. He didn't want to go to church alone. But he went, and when others went home with their families, he returned alone to eat the lukewarm food Yafu had set out for him before leaving for his day off.

He had nowhere to go, except for one place, that secret spot in the foothills, his harem. Agitated, he paced back and forth on the balcony, waiting for the last rays of sunset to disappear from the evening sky, longing for the arrival of night. Darkness was an abyss; as usual, he would walk down the mountain and tumble all the way to the very bottom of that abyss. The lamplit house in the foothills was calling out to him. There his angel sat beneath a lamp in a cloud of Dongguan fragrance. She was his night sibyl, a night-blooming flower.

He never stayed the night. When the effects of alcohol wore off, he would return to his Mid-Level flat with its fireplace and balcony, no matter how late it was. After playing her three-stringed lute for him, she would lie down seductively and, displaying her most bewitching profile, entice him with the skills of a prostitute. He'd bend her pliant body at will while she changed positions to please him, positions a normal woman could not achieve. He ruled over her as the two of them enjoyed a feast of carnal pleasure, the joys of degeneration.

Then she would lie at his feet, like a cat curling up, catching her breath between waves of sexual desire. After the ecstasy of his climax had subsided, Smith lay spread-eagled on the bed, shocked at the extent of his sexual desire. How could he have such strong cravings?

This time, unable to resist her pleas to spend the night, he stayed, falling asleep in the arms of his sibyl. The next morning, he opened his eyes in their pleasure bed, to see the reality that had been hidden by candlelight and darkness: the red-tiled floor was littered with her underwear; in a corner stood a pagan alcove with ashes from incense piling up like a small tomb. A bizarre sight rose from the carvings of soaring dragons, the red silk palace lanterns, and the bamboo chairs and tables that represented the China of Smith's imagination. They were mingled with Western items bought by Huang Deyun in Wan Chai—lace curtains, green velvet cushions, and tasseled tablecloths.

Then he discovered that the bed they were lying on stood in the middle of the living room. The bedroom was upstairs, but the undernourished coolies had left it here when they hadn't the strength to carry it upstairs. A solemn room used by Chinese to worship their ancestors and deities had become the scene of carnal appetites. Only a prostitute ignorant of propriety would do something like that.

Smith gave the woman lying at his feet a vicious kick. He wanted to leave immediately. Rummaging for his clothes in the disheveled bedding, he was grabbed tightly by the waist from behind and pulled back to bed. The woman, whom he'd just kicked, straddled him with the glint of desire in her eyes. Feeling violated, Smith tried to free himself, but she bored into his flesh and became part of him. She touched him, using all her bewitching skills. Thousands of tiny ants clawed and crawled through his veins. Unable to resist the seduction, he was aroused yet again. Then, after the evil, wanton deed, he lay there feeling even lonelier than before. He sensed that a part of his body no longer belonged to him, was beyond his control. He had sold off his senses and was no longer his own master.

A loathing for the woman rose from the depths of his heart. He cursed her, the sibyl who had bored into his body. He turned away, unwilling to face her inscrutability, trying to forget how he'd run his fingers through her thick black hair, the physical sensation of holding another life in his hands. He vowed to forever stay away from this body that so eagerly came to him. He would not respond to her nuzzling, nor would he succumb to the temptation to devour and be devoured. After what seemed like an eternity, he heard her satisfied sighs, then collapsed on top of her, feeling a void blanketing him, body and soul.

Now that he was sated, he rolled over and climbed off the bed, making all sorts of excuses to leave; he wanted to return home, where he would stand on the balcony, his hands thrust into his pockets, looking out at the dark, indistinct Victoria Harbor.

8

The plague had passed.

The Chinese in Hong Kong who had escaped from the demon's clutches erected stages with thatched roofs in front of temples throughout the island to thank the gods for their protection. Cantonese opera troupes touring China boarded sampans with props and costumes and sailed down the Pearl River. From late November through the end of the year, gongs, drums, and firecrackers sounded continuously, from the Tam Kung Temple at A Kung Ngam in the north to the Man Mo Temple on Hollywood Road and the Goddess of Mercy Temple on Mount Taiping Street in the west, from the Temple of Mazu at Stanley in the south to Dawang Temple on Wan Chai Road in the east.

Every night after dark, gas lamps in every temple on Hong Kong Island illuminated dazzling stage displays, turning them into lustrous, resplendent diamonds against backdrops of black velvet.

Sitting next to her maid, Ah Mei, Huang Deyun looked over the heads of the audience to the stage, which was lit up like daylight. The performers were acting out the scene of "Xue Pinggui Returns to the Kiln" from the opera *Red-Maned Steed*, the story of Wang Baochuan, who lived in a kiln for eighteen years, waiting for her husband, Xue Pinggui, to return from a frontier battle, without knowing that he'd married the daughter of his captor king.

Few women came to night operas, let alone one dressed so fetchingly. Naturally, she attracted a great deal of attention, particularly from young men sitting up front, who kept turning to look at her. But she paid no heed; she was too busy cracking sunflower seeds from the lacquered tray held by Ah Mei.

A sunflower seed cracked in two with a crisp sound between her teeth. Things that had been bothering her for at least half a month were finally clearing up. There on the stage they were acting out her story. She was like the poor Wang Baochuan, who lived on wild grasses while her Xue Pinggui found his princess. The Xue Pinggui up on the stage was gone for eighteen years, but what about hers? Deyun choked on a sunflower seed, thinking that Smith must have found someone else. Her foreign lover had another woman! Bitterness welled up in her throat and tears streamed down her face. Oh, how she wished she could choke to death. She should not have loved him so much.

How long had it been since he'd run his fingers slowly through the hair at her temples and held her disarmingly lovely face in his hands? Butterfly, my yellow-gossamer butterfly. He'd also stopped shining a candle on her, starting at her wavy black hair, then moving down past the slender porcelain neck, all the way down. The look in his bright green eyes would gradually soften as they followed the contours of her figure, until, with a sigh, he'd fall upon her pink body and they would become one.

He looked down into her face, a lock of sweat-soaked hair covering his forehead. Lovingly, she reached up to brush it to the side, but he pushed her hand away roughly. Her fingertips stiffened, and she didn't dare caress the folds in the nape of his neck, as she'd done so often in the past. His green eyes, shielded by those white brows, glinted like cold glass, bereft of any expression, so she could not see into his heart. She could not enter his world; he'd become a stranger, and she did not know what to do about the lover in her arms, whose heart was so far away.

Over the past couple of weeks, Smith had come less frequently, and his arrival times had varied wildly. She'd often had to wait until late at night before he pushed open the door and entered, eyes bloodshot, reeking with alcohol. Stumbling toward the four-poster bed, he'd then pass out in a drunken stupor.

In order to please the unpredictable Smith, although Deyun continued to get up at noon, she spent longer at her mirror. So as to look her best when he showed up, she resumed the habit of making up three times a night, as if she were once again the prostitute at Southern Tang House. She fetched the black leather, phoenix-gilded case from her dresser and put on her pearl-inlaid combs and jade hairpins. She sighed deeply at the return of the gaudily dressed prostitute, in jangling pearls and dangling jade. On the day Smith had sent the sedan chair for her, she'd thought she had finally cut herself off from that kind of life, and so had buried the case at the bottom of her dresser, a private treasure that lessened her feelings of insecurity.

In fact, Huang Deyun had no worries about getting by. The Englishman had always been generous to the woman he kept in his Happy Valley harem. Even though he came less frequently, before he left he never forgot to leave the monthly stipend they'd agreed upon. When her sisters from Yihong Pavilion and Southern Tang House saw how elegantly she was dressed for the stage performances, they envied her fortune in finding a good man. Deyun responded to their comments with a wry smile.

But her lover's visits had now grown so infrequent that she could no longer wait for him by the lamp and play solitaire. Now, before it got dark, she would move her chair to the window facing the path Smith would take, anxiously awaiting his appearance, hands clasped around her knees. When footsteps echoed around the corner, out of sight, she would anxiously bend forward to grab the windowsill, then slowly relax her fingers as the footsteps moved away. She waited every afternoon until the last glimmer of sunset vanished, the path became indiscernible, and chilled air seeped up through the bricks under her feet. Her maid brought out the lamps, under whose light Huang Deyun would then reapply her makeup. Every evening she waited until the light turned dim, but she was reluctant to let down the curtains. Wrapped in a blanket, she'd sit in bed holding her three-stringed lute, feeling her eyelids growing heavier, but trying not to fall asleep, lest he suddenly appear. Mistaking every sound of the wind as a knock at the door, she summoned her maid to open it, only to admit a gust of cold air that forced her back to bed. She loathed his heartlessness.

In recent days, Smith had been frequenting an orphanage, where the children gathered around to hear him recite idyllic poems by Tennyson. He was deeply moved by his own rhythmic voice and the captivated, worshipful expressions on the children's faces. Touching the braids on a little girl's head, he thought about how life would have been so much simpler if he'd chosen a different path and become a missionary in Africa. He would walk out of his thatched hut at night and stand beneath the boundless evening sky, clear as a mirror. The stars would hang so low he could reach out and pluck one. He'd have felt close to God under the evening sky, and spiritual happiness would have filled his heart.

After evening prayer, Smith said good night to the children and walked home under a moonlit sky. Fate had played a cruel trick on him by sending him to this desolate, plague-infected island, with its barren mountains and unruly rivers. To seek human comfort, he had tremblingly climbed into a prostitute's bed, and he could never forgive himself, the acting director of the Sanitary Board, for hiring a sedan chair to move this prostitute from Southern Tang House at the same time that he was torching the plague areas. Oh, how he regretted that a colonized prostitute had become his kept woman.

Smith had once read a book on customs of the South Sea Islands. The shamans of Bali, in order to eliminate male desire, would ritualistically file their canines with a sharp rasp. Desire disappeared as soon as the teeth were smoothed. He could be rid of Huang Deyun and her Chinese-style house, with its foot-long centipedes, its poisonous black widows, its hordes of roaches, as well as the fleas that hid in dark corners and the termites living inside wood pillars. And, of course, the epileptic maid, Ah Mei, who curled her body around the well, foaming at the mouth, each time she had a seizure.

At this moment, geckos with transparent bellies were climbing the green plaster walls of the Chinese-style house. On the four-poster bed, so filled with rampant desire and filth, his yellow mistress, breasts bared, lay in bed waiting for him, bejeweled with golden hairpins and jade pendants. Her heavily made-up face was like a mask. He would never be able to guess what lay behind that mask. He could smell the greasy scent of

her powder and the pungent odor of touch-me-not that she applied to
her fingernails. Mingled with all this was the heavy aroma of Shatin
incense coils, combining to emit a nauseating, nightmarish smell.

The woman on the four-poster bed is a trap, a cunning vampire with
long, sharp teeth. She lives off my body and, with her inexhaustible
energy, will suck dry every drop of blood in it. She will drag me down
to the hell of wanton filth.

When the plague had passed, the new director of the Sanitary Board,
Charles Windsor, finally arrived in Hong Kong to assume his new post
as Mr. Dickinson's replacement. Rumor had it that Mrs. Windsor had
aristocratic blood, and as soon as she took up residence in the mansion,
she stripped everything from floor to ceiling, eradicating Mrs. Dickinson's "gaudy bourgeois tastes."

A new group of guests came with the new interior. Smith was
removed from the afternoon tea guest list, which made him miss Mr.
Dickinson even more. On Christmas Eve, Sir Philip, minister of colonial
affairs, came to the Orient on an inspection tour, and Mrs. Windsor, a
distant relative of his, was eager to show off her newly remodeled home.
She sent out invitations for a formal dinner party, an official banquet for
Sir Philip, who had been sent by London to inspect Hong Kong in the
wake of the worst pestilence since opening for trade. Adam Smith, who
had been partly responsible for wiping out the plague, was invited. During cocktails, he was introduced to the guest of honor, a silver-haired,
starched-collar aristocrat who could have stepped out of a patrician oil
portrait. Dressed in a formal dinner jacket and wearing white gloves, Sir
Philip would have been an object of veneration for Mr. Dickinson.

Holding his breath, Smith gathered his legs tightly together to salute
Sir Philip, then cast his eyes downward, not daring to look above the
man's starched collar. Pretending to be lost in thought, he sipped a glass
of champagne taken from the silver tray held by a circulating waiter,
sensing that nervousness was turning his lips blue.

Sir Philip repeatedly interrupted Smith as he reported on the process
of eliminating the plague. The true purpose of the London patrician's

visit, it became apparent, was to probe the attitude of the colonized Chinese. He was eager to know if Governor Robinson's decision to torch the plague areas had stirred up rebellion among them and whether or not they were plotting an insurrection.

Smith kept switching the champagne glass from hand to hand. Breaking out in a cold sweat, he could only stammer, "Couldn't allow the Chinese to use herbs, had to close Tung Wah Hospital. I believe—"

Sir Philip waved him away without letting him finish. Like a pardoned miscreant, he bowed deeply, backing up four or five steps before daring to turn around.

At dinner, Smith was seated between two ladies, one old and one young. The old woman to his left, who wore a corset under her evening gown, looked as if she was being tortured. She turned to him and blurted out, "I hate Hong Kong. It's a wretched place."

Smith, who was still recovering from his panic-stricken interrogation by Sir Philip, was even more shocked by this naked display of resentment toward life in the colony.

To his right sat the daughter of an admiral, the colony's ranking military man. Displaying an overtly contemptuous indifference, she guarded herself carefully, not deigning to talk to him even once. After dinner, she held her head high and trailed other female guests as they followed Mrs. Windsor to the bathroom to powder their noses.

The men were invited to a smoking room, where they talked about James Matheson of the Jardine, Matheson Company, a man who had made a vast fortune in the opium trade and had bought the Scottish Isle of Lewis on his return home. Newspapers in London praised him as an adventurous business tycoon, a true hero.

"What a bloke, buying off the whole Isle of Lewis!" the gentlemen exclaimed, begging the guest of honor for more news from London.

Sir Philip rolled the cigar handed him by the host alongside his ear and took a prolonged look before reluctantly lighting it.

"Gentlemen, have you heard of a book called *The Origin of Species* by a botanist named Darwin? This bloke sailed the world in the *H.M.S.*

Beagle. To prove a theory of his, he went to South America to record the evolution of birds and beasts. Can you guess what happened?"

Sir Philip took a leisurely puff on his cigar.

"He reached a conclusion that all closely related species, be they animal or plant, come from a single origin!"

Sir Philip smiled at the puzzled looks on his enthralled audience.

"He, Darwin, said that men are but a species, and that we have evolved from an earlier species. Gentlemen, listen carefully to what I'm going to say next—no, what *Darwin* said. Since men are similar to apes, then men and apes share the same original species."

"Sir Philip, who does this Darwin think he is? How dare he utter such heresy? No, men are the only sentient beings created in God's image." Pastor Thomas's waxen face was flushed with anger. "Men evolving from animals like monkeys? That's utter nonsense! It's blasphemy!"

"I agree with you, Pastor." With one hand on his hip, Sir Philip leisurely blew out another mouthful of smoke. "Before leaving London, I attended a party where people were discussing Darwin's theory of evolution. One of the guests was so frightened when she heard that she was a descendant of apes, she actually grabbed someone and begged, 'Please don't let it come this way, this ape.'"

The gentlemen all laughed at his humor. Then the subject changed to the human species. Sir Philip the blue blood believed that the English aristocracy belonged to a species all its own, genetically different from the lower classes. He openly declared himself to be a disciple of a certain duke, the Aryan author of *Theory of Inequality Among Species.*

"If the aristocracy were abolished and the government handed over to the hybrids, European civilization as we know it would come to an end."

Sir Philip detested intermarriage most of all.

"Think about it, gentlemen, crossing a superior species with an inferior one can only impair the superior one. That is common sense. The children of mixed marriages are fit only to be ruled by the white people, to be their slaves."

Sir Philip rolled his eyes, as if searching for prey at a hunt. Casually, he decided to sacrifice Adam Smith. He pointed at him with his cigar, so close it nearly touched Smith's eyes.

"Just imagine, gentlemen, I'm just saying imagine, this person—uh, Smith, right? What kind of child would be born of him, with his green eyes, if he married an Oriental woman with dark brown eyes? A child with clouded eyes and neither white nor yellow skin. His intelligence would be like the yellow race, with its slow movements and lack of vitality. But, eh, of course, you're more familiar with the Chinese than I am. They know only how to reproduce, yearning for throngs of children and grandchildren!"

The gentlemen echoed his statement loudly. Sir Philip solemnly raised his cigar in warning:

"You must never underestimate the yellow race. Even though the sweltering heat saps their energy, they are hardworking and resilient. The enemy at the door of the European continent are the yellow Asians, are you aware of that? They are the colonized Indian and the semicolonized Chinese of the British Empire. If the Europeans really believed in the heresy of human equality, as promoted by the likes of the Frenchman Rousseau, it would give the yellow race lurking at our borders an opportunity to conquer and rule us. We must never close our eyes to the yellow peril!"

Adam Smith suffered through the party, and when it was finally over, he held his head in his hands and left the Windsor house. On the way home he felt sick. From that evening on, he had the same dream every night. He was sinking to the bottom of the ocean, where the water was pitch black. Green seaweed entangled him, dragging him down, as odd-shaped sea creatures surrounded him. One of them, a fish with a terrifying face and, on both sides of its belly, four oarlike fins, reached out to grab him. . . .

"Don't look at me. Turn your head!"

After the dinner party, Smith went to the house in Happy Valley, which he entered for the last time. It was past midnight when his fists banged on the door. Thinking that pirates had come ashore to rob her,

Huang Deyun was scared out of her wits. She held her three-stringed lute and got down to crawl under the bed when an icy hand grabbed her by the nape of her neck and lifted her up. The lute dropped to the floor with a thud; all the strings snapped. Before she had a chance to grope for it in the dark, she was flung down on the bed. In the darkness, her eyes were opened wide, like those of a blind woman.

"Don't look at me. Turn your head!"

His words were accompanied by action, as he twisted her neck as if trying to snap it. Then, without undressing, he forced his way into her. Shocked yet pleased, she held on to him, but he violently swept her hands away.

"I hate you," Smith shouted hoarsely. "I hate you! I hate you, you yellow whore! I'm going to destroy you! Destroy you!"

He spat in Huang Deyun's face.

9

The colonial government's curfew kept Huang Deyun in Hong Kong.

One evening in 1894, after having lost the favor of her English lover and grown tired of waiting for him, she went out to watch some Cantonese opera. Prior to that, she had attended seven consecutive daytime performances, captivated by a martial arts actor.

Seven days earlier, a renowned Cantonese opera troupe had sailed down the Pearl River and arrived at the Dawang Temple on Queen's Road in Wan Chai, where they set up a stage with a thatched roof. Their premiere performance opened on a chilly winter afternoon. Huang Deyun, accompanied by her maid, had gone to the temple to burn incense and pray for her lover to change his mind and return to her side. It had been two weeks since he'd left without saying good-bye, after treating her so abusively. Tears welled up in her eyes as she thought about that night. She bit her lip and forced back the tears. How could he treat me like that? What was I to him? I did nothing to provoke him like that!

A flurry of rapid gong- and drumbeats interrupted her painful recollections, and she turned just as the performance began on a stage across from the temple. The troupe was performing a worship rite, asking the mythical White Tiger to exorcise evil spirits from the temple grounds, its traditional opening. Each time the sun peeked out from behind a cloud, its warmth comforted Deyun, who could smell the pungent odors of egg roe and cuttlefish cooking at stands beneath the stage. She could think of no reason to return home, only to sit alone in a cold room, so she fell in behind her maid, Ah Mei, who had joined the crowd thronging toward the stage. This was the sort of thing Deyun had done as a child in Dong-guan. The two women found seats in the fourth row.

Up on the stage a martial arts actor with his face painted black and wearing a black helmet, black armor, and a black cape played the role of Zhao Gongming, who would subdue the White Tiger. Zhao descended from a cloud, and the battle was on. As he spun around, a portion of wil-low green lining showed beneath the legs of his black pants, a sight that made Deyun's scalp tingle. The White Tiger leaped, kicked, and vaulted, sending sand and gravel flying on the stage. Then the rhythmic clappers stopped abruptly; the White Tiger flicked its tail, turned around, and stood up like a human, and as it bared his teeth, its bulging, fluorescent green eyes sent a terrifying glint directly at Huang Deyun. Each time her English lover had leaned toward her at the height of pas-sion, his eyes had emitted the same green glimmers, brightening and darkening as his excitement peaked then tapered off. The sight had always aroused Deyun, until her whole being seemed to be on fire.

The drums and gongs started up again, louder and louder, like a herd of galloping horses, as the fight between Zhao Gongming and the White Tiger reached the point of white heat. The White Tiger, whipping its tail back and forth, began to show signs of defeat; finally it pawed the ground helplessly and collapsed. Zhao Gongming wrapped a chain around the dejected tiger's neck, then straddled it and rode triumphantly off the stage. A piece of cloth draped over the tiger's face hid its eyes from view. Forgetting herself, Deyun clapped excitedly and shouted, "Bravo," as an indescribable pleasure filled her heart. The stage was quickly taken over by actors and actresses as the main performance got under way, but Deyun saw nothing but the tiger-subduing hero.

She returned the next day and the day after that. Following the per-formance on the third day, she veiled her face with a handkerchief and went backstage with her maid. It was a surprisingly warm afternoon. Under a cotton tree, stagehands in charge of props and costumes were shouting back and forth; older women were helping the actors and actress into their costumes. Smoke drifting out of a makeshift kitchen filled the air with the aroma of stir-fry.

No one paid any attention to Deyun, who looked like one of the actresses. She had left her fur shawl at home, and her bright yellow jacket with its rolled hems over a peach pink velvet pleated skirt, which had caught the eyes of people in the audience, paled in comparison with the colorful costumes. The feeling of blending in pleased her.

An old master of the two-stringed fiddle, his face weatherworn, sat on a costume chest tuning his instrument, turning discord into silky smooth notes. Homeward-bound swallows soared gracefully in the dusky sky, with its drifting clouds. Huang Deyun kicked the hem of her peach-colored skirt, as images of earlier days returned to her. She thought of the opera stage in her hometown of Dongguan, where, under a thatched tent, three colorful sets, with pavilions, towers, and the mansions of emperors, generals, and ranking ministers were erected, looking real through the greedy eyes of a child. Standing there in the sunlight, which illuminated her extravagant beauty, she imagined herself on the hometown stage.

Ah, home, her Dongguan hometown, with its famous Dongguan incense!

She found her tiger-subduing Zhao Gongming, Jiang Xiahun, the mainstay of the Cantonese troupe, beneath a cotton tree that stood as proud as a dragon. He was leaning against the tree, arms crossed, wearing a four-color short jacket over a snowy white shirt and green silk pants that rippled in the winter afternoon, seductively inviting glances toward it. Pretending to talk with her maid, Deyun observed him out of the corner of her eye: above the heavily rouged cheek of his broad profile, a bushy eyebrow slanted upward toward his temple. His body seemed even more imposing now than onstage, creating a powerful aura.

But the itinerant actor was thinking about home, which, like Huang Deyun, he had been forced to leave. His last recollections of home were of hatred and blood. At the time he had not been called Jiang Xiahun, which was a chivalrous name given to him by the owner of the operatic troupe.

It was the year that Hong Xiuquan's soldiers of the Taiping Heavenly Kingdom had stormed into his hometown of Nan'ao like rampaging locusts, leaving a trail of dead bodies in their wake. The survivors pulled together to harvest ripening rice grains from fields trampled by the invading troops. Ruthless though the soldiers had been, at least the villagers still had their land. But when the "foreign brothers" came from the sea, they brought disaster and destruction with them. It had been a spring day, and Jiang Xiahun, along with his father and his brother, was planting new stalks in the soft soil when a loud boom from the ocean shattered life in sleepy Nan'ao village.

The foreign devils swarmed off the fire-spitting ships they had used to transport opium and built houses where they wished, without ever treating Nan'ao as home. The village became a center for opium smugglers, who seized Jiang Xiahun's family land and turned it into a pasture, with stable and paddock, to raise thoroughbred horses imported from England. His father and brother were then kidnapped by American slave traders when they went out to collect firewood. He alone escaped and left his hometown, his desperation tempered by hatred. After surviving by doing odd jobs here and there, he finally reached Canton, where he looked after the props of a Cantonese opera troupe whose owner later trained him to be martial arts actor.

This would be his first visit to Hong Kong, and as he sailed down the Pearl River, he felt that the world was his to conquer. The Dawang Temple grounds, where they set up their stage, were but two blocks from the Wan Chai brothels on Spring Garden Lane and Sampan Street. Whenever a merchant ship came into port, throngs of prostitutes in gaudy makeup appeared, seemingly out of nowhere, bellowing and fighting for the favors of the sailors, who exchanged imported goods from their ships for the bodies of the girls; they in turn sold the goods to shops on Spring Garden Lane, whose shelves were filled with all sorts of strange Western merchandise.

Balling up the fists he'd used to fight the tiger onstage, Jiang Xiahun vowed to burn down this sinful city on the night the troupe left town. He still regretted not having flung a torch into the stables the Englishmen had built on his home on the night he left.

Now, as he leaned against the cotton tree, thinking his own thoughts, out of the corner of his eye he caught a glimpse of peach pink—it was

Huang Deyun's skirt. Without turning to look, he could tell it was another female fan coming to see him. Judging from what he could see of her clothes, she was either the bored concubine of a wealthy man or a prostitute who provided pleasure to foreign sailors. Having seen enough of both over the past few days, he merely raised one eyebrow in disdain.

Huang Deyun, on the other hand, was gazing at the cotton tree, her head filled with fanciful thoughts. If her hero knew that she'd been mistreated by that green-eyed sea lion, he would swell with righteous anger and come to her aid. Deyun knew she needed a man, that she couldn't live without one.

Only a few months had passed, and already Smith had cast off his tenderness and patience. Reeking with alcohol, he'd stumble through the door. He no longer wanted to hear her play her three-stringed lute; instead, he'd climb on top and ride her like a green-eyed beast, no different from the sailors who came ashore in Wan Chai. She had become the Deyun of the Southern Tang House days, before meeting this man, who would become her lover and, later, her nemesis, when she would serve one *guailow* after another—different nationalities and indistinguishable faces, they were clients and she was a whore. Butterfly, his yellow-gossamer butterfly. But he had stopped coming, leaving her sitting and sleeping alone, to suffer terrible loneliness.

Huang Deyun asked the woman in charge of costumes if she knew which Cantonese opera troupe the popular hometown female lead Xin Yanmei had joined. She had been Deyun's childhood idol. As she folded a python robe, decorated with sea dragons, the woman said she'd never heard of Xin Yanmei and couldn't say which troupe she might have joined. Tucking the sleeves of the python robe under her chin, she looked Huang Deyun up and down before deciding that she had a desire to join the troupe and had merely mentioned Xin Yanmei as an opening gambit.

"There," she pointed with her pursed lips, "go talk to the owner. He's the one walking this way."

As if her intentions had been revealed, Deyun turned to walk off and avoid the troupe owner, a literate-looking man who was coming in her direction. She could feel Jiang Xiahun's eyes on her, which made her uncomfortable; she quickened her pace on her way out from backstage. Not until she reached the exit did she turn to look at the cotton tree, where Jiang stood with his back to her, his willow green silk pants rippling in the windless dusk and recapturing her attention.

Biting her lip, she fantasized about the hard bones and powerful muscles hidden by his shirt, the result of martial arts training, and could almost hear his joints pop as he wielded his sword.

And, as she reflected on her own life, she was caught up in fanciful thoughts of laying her bedding out on the stage and nestling up against his broad chest. At that moment, she made up her mind to run off with the performing troupe.

After rushing back to her dark, lonely house and sending her maid away, she picked up a lamp and removed the loose red brick on the floor—the new hiding place for her black leather case. She quickly took off her hair ornaments and tossed them into the case, then packed her clothes and other personal belongings. Placing the mirror that had recently chronicled her fading beauty on the top of a suitcase, she wondered whether or not she should take a wool blanket imported from England. She had spent a fortune on it. As she held up the blanket, unable to make up her mind, a loud boom sounded in the distance. Her hands shook. It was the curfew signal. It was too late to get out; she could not get away now.

The colonial government's curfew kept Huang Deyun in Hong Kong.

In the wake of the Opium War, the colonizers had restricted the people's freedom of movement, strictly forbidding Chinese to be out on the streets after ten at night. Violators were to be arrested on the spot. The implementation of a curfew had stemmed from the government's fear that the Chinese would conspire against them, that they would make trouble and engage in thievery at night. Soon after the curfew went into effect, a British lawyer was robbed in his carriage on the way up to his mountaintop home. So the colonial government then required all Chinese to carry a lantern between dusk and ten o'clock, to distinguish them from the British. In the meantime, the government also issued a "Code for Maintaining Public Security," stipulating that, after nightfall, all Chinese must hang a lantern inscribed with their family or store name by their door for the benefit of patrolling police. If required to be out during curfew, they were to obtain a pass.

Yet even with such comprehensive regulations, the colonizers remained so uneasy that every foreign firm was assigned a soldier to guard the place during the day. At dusk, cannons were deployed for protection, while squads of eighteen policemen were dispatched to patrol the streets. When they reached areas generally considered dangerous, they fired shots in the air before pressing forward. Out at sea a pair of steamboats policed the shore day and night, firing cannons at night to keep up the soldiers' morale.

When the curfew cannon sounded, Huang Deyun dropped the half-folded British wool blanket and fell back onto the bed, her escape plan foiled. The night would quickly deepen once the curfew was in force. Stray dogs on the mountain slopes howled the nights away. Later, when she thought back to how she had nearly run off with an itinerant martial arts performer, her eyes were shocked wide open by her audacity.

Until 1894, Happy Valley, which was part of the village of Wong Ngai Chung, was still considered a desolate, remote area. A City Limits stone marker had been erected at the entrance. The English taipans, who had made their fortunes from the opium trade, turned the scenic valley into a racecourse and built stalls with bamboo and cattail leaves to house the horses imported from England. Before the valley was developed, it had been called "Elysium," since it was the burial ground for British soldiers who had died like falling leaves in this inhospitable land, rife with malaria and other feverish diseases.

In addition to the Happy Valley graveyard, the horses, and the annual spring racing season, some of the Englishmen installed women like Huang Deyun on this spot outside the city proper. These English taipans of the opium trade, with their lower-class backgrounds, had responded to Queen Victoria's expansion policy for maritime hegemony by sailing eastward for adventure. After making their fortunes and building mansions adorned with giant Romanesque columns on top of Mount Taiping, they began to be concerned about social status. Yet, unwilling to give up or to share the prostitutes they had visited before becoming respectable merchants, they set up love nests in Happy Valley, a clutch of harems of yellow-skinned mistresses. A tiny percentage of their opium profits was more than enough to feed and keep both their mistresses and their horses.

As the sun set, the taipans would leave their firms in Central District and drive horse-drawn carriages against the ocean breeze and setting sun, passing by the City Limits stone marker. Enjoying thoughts of how their lovers would be wringing their handkerchiefs anxiously, awaiting their arrival, the taipans would flick their whips and congratulate themselves on their success at keeping this little secret, thus preserving their rising reputations. Assistant Director of the Sanitary Board Adam Smith had followed suit by installing Huang Deyun in a Chinese-style house in Happy Valley, and had thus sealed her fate.

It was getting late. Even if she had the courage to retrace her footsteps and return to her martial arts performer, she did not have the nerve to violate the curfew. So, hugging the black leather case tightly to her chest and not bothering to take off her fur-lined jacket, she fell asleep on the spring mattress, covered only by the wool blanket she had planned to take with her. As soon as the curfew was lifted in the morning with the first cannon shot, she could leave.

Early the next morning, not trifling with makeup, Deyun walked out of the house, suitcases in hand. Misty fog shrouded the end of the long street. Gripped by anxiety, she hurried through the mist, looking back constantly to see if she was being followed. When she turned back to face the street after one last look, she discovered that the stage and everything else were gone, as if by magic. Letting go the suitcases in her hands, she reached out to part the mist, gasping like a fish out of water. At that moment, the first ray of sunlight pierced the mist and lit up the sky, only to expose the cruel sight in front of her eyes. The yard, now stripped of the stage, was empty except for smoldering firewood rising from a temporary stove. The aroma of boiling white congee and stir-fried vegetables of the past eight days had been replaced by the acrid smell of doused ashes. A solitary cotton tree stood in the middle of the yard; gone was the martial arts performer, who, only the day before, had sat beneath this tree to smoke, like a common peasant. The look in her eyes had told him she'd be back. Now here she was, but he had not waited for her. He'd left with the troupe, gone as quickly as he had come.

Holding her head in her hands, Deyun could not believe her eyes. She stumbled toward the cotton tree, knocking over her suitcases and dropping her black leather case, littering the ground with its gold and pearl ornaments. She stepped on them, as if wading through water; they meant nothing to her now.

Many years later, when Deyun thought back to that morning, what came to mind first was not the tree, against which the martial arts performer had leaned to smoke his pipe, but a barren spot in the weeds on that deserted spot. It was where the troupe had left a pork offering to the White Tiger spirit. No grass grew there, just as predicted in legend.

As time went on, whenever Deyun thought about that spot in the weeds, shaped like a long strip of pork, she invariably shuddered.

After the Cantonese opera had completed its last, and most famous, performance, *Red-Maned Steed*, the night before, the owner had the stage dismantled so they could immediately return to Canton on the Pearl River. Women folded costumes for Xue Pinggui and Wang Baochuan, still warm from the bodies of the actor and actress who had worn them. A crew took down the palace and tower and packed them in trunks, along with swords and spears. The cook gathered up his pots and pans, the clanging noises awakening the sleeping children who traveled with the troupe.

While the backstage was filled with postperformance chaos, Jiang Xiahun stole away to the pier at Wan Chai, still wearing the four-color jacket that revealed the willow green linings of his pant legs. The pier was deserted, since the sailors who had arrived earlier that evening were now sleeping in the arms of the prostitutes in the cheap inns of Spring

Garden Lane. All of Wan Chai was slumbering lustfully. Jiang Xiahun, a onetime farmer and first-time visitor to Hong Kong, squatted by the water and smoked his pipe. Smudges of makeup clung to his sunken cheeks, especially around the corners of his staring eyes; his expression was as unfathomable as the blackish water.

Feeling a numbness in his legs after squatting for such a long time, he stood up. Still staring at the water, he was thinking about his father and his brother, who had disappeared without a trace. Another shadow appeared at some point during his reveries. It was a stranger dressed in traveling clothes darker than the night. His pant legs were tied around the ankles and he was wearing a straw hat, like those the Hakka used to block the sun, a black veil covering half of his face.

The stranger moved closer, like a shadow, to watch the ocean with Jiang Xiahun for a while before he took out a pipe.

"Got a match, brother?"

The pipe was lit and the stranger fell back into silence as he smoked.

Jiang Xiahun did not return to Dawang Temple to join the departing troupe that night. The owner had, through the intervention of the Dawang Temple secretary, obtained a special permit from the colonial government to travel after curfew. When the troupe arrived at the Wan Chai pier, Jiang Xiahun and the dark shadow had disappeared. As they waited on the sailing ship, cold and tired, the performers urged the boatman to set sail. Finally, he had no choice but to give up on Jiang and agree to set off on the journey upstream to Canton.

As for what happened to Jiang, several versions circulated for years. One told of him taking off his costume, sticking his pipe into his belt, and boarding a foreign freighter as a stowaway, vowing to find his kidnapped father and brother, no matter how long it took or where his search led. According to this version, he set out on a journey, whose destination he himself did not know, and disappeared in the ocean.

The second version was also related to the ocean. Jiang was said to have been so filled with national pride and indignation that he joined a band of pirates who plundered British freighters. Some said he was killed on one of the voyages, others that his pirate ship had been sunk by a

British fleet during a typhoon and that he had surrendered along with the pirate leader. He later returned to Nan'ao as a farmer and died an old man.

The third version had him joining Sun Yat-sen's anti-Manchu revolutionary cause, vowing to expel the Manchus and reestablish Han rule. Apparently, Huang Deyun was not the only one who had been impressed by Jiang's performance in the tiger-subduing scene. A mysterious, middle-aged, simply dressed man with determined eyes had gone backstage to see Jiang after that performance. The stranger returned the following day, and the two of them had a long, amiable talk. In fact, they had several long talks, during which the stranger instilled anti-Manchu revolutionary thoughts in Jiang. By then, Dr. Sun had already formed a society in Hawaii that would one day become the Kuomintang, and the stranger was raising an army for a Canton insurrection the following year. Jiang was said to have finished his pipe and, in defiance of the curfew, followed the stranger to join the revolution. The strategy of Dr. Sun, who returned to Hong Kong a month later to plan his attack, was to blow up the governor's office on the day Cantonese returned from Hong Kong to sweep their ancestral tombs. Jiang was rumored to be one of the revolutionary comrades who smuggled munitions from Hong Kong into Canton. But the plot was discovered by the colonial government, which notified the Canton governor, and Jiang, along with forty other revolutionaries, was arrested. The Manchu government tried to torture information out of him, but he died a martyr, taking his secrets to the grave.

The fourth version had it that the onetime farmer could not have become a pirate, for he lacked courage and was unfamiliar with life at sea. Nor could he have become a revolutionary, since the nationalist ideology was too profound for him to grasp. Most likely he joined a tong, one of China's secret societies. This version also had him being tortured to death. His first assignment was to post street signs to warn Chinese merchants against doing business with the British devils under the threat of having their houses in the countryside torched and their relatives taken captive. The profit-oriented merchants were indifferent to nationalism but complied to save their ancestral homes and relatives—all but one, a shop owner surnamed Xu, who continued to sell provisions to British ships, despite the fact that one of his shops had already been burned down by the tongs. The legend had Jiang bribing a bakery worker to lace bread with arsenic, which poisoned four hundred people, including the Hong Kong governor and his wife. Fifty-one workers were arrested, but no evidence could be found against Xu, who later moved with his family to Annam. The bribed bakery worker was tortured until he gave them Jiang's name, and the onetime farmer died before he turned twenty-four.

10

Deyun's last thread of hope was severed.

She had no recollection of crossing the mountain and following the country road on her return to Happy Valley. She recalled only sobbing before the image of Mazu. When she opened her eyes again, she was lying in bed, covered by the British wool blanket. Everything remained the same: the broken three-stringed lute lay against her chair, incense still burned in the little red corner alcove, and curtains made of imported cotton fabric fluttered at the window. She did not know if it was dawn or dusk outside.

Sitting up in bed, Deyun wondered if she had been dreaming. She looked down to see that the brick floor was neat and orderly, and there was no trace of her suitcases. Quickly getting out of bed, she found them where they were supposed to be. But both were empty. So it must have been a dream, since her clothes and other personal belongings, all neatly folded, were still in their drawers. She suddenly thought about her black leather case and all her personal treasures inside. At that moment, her mind cleared. She recalled carrying the leather case under her arm and going out back to lock the door of the shack where Ah Mei slept. Planning to run away in secret, Deyun feared that Ah Mei might inform Adam Smith, who would send the police after her. This bought her enough time to be safely at sea by the time Ah Mei managed to free herself.

Her leather case! She had nothing now. The two men in her life, Adam Smith and the martial arts performer, had both left her, and she could not afford to lose the case on which her existence now depended. She rummaged through her dresser and closet, tore the wool blanket off the bed, searched amid the sheets and the pillows. She even looked under the bed. Nothing. Except for that one place, the most secret place, known to no one but herself. She alone knew about the loose brick in the corner. She crawled over and removed the brick. Her outstretched hand touched a hard object and felt the rough surface of lacquered leather. With a trembling hand she took it out, but did not have the courage to open it. Instead, she weighed it in her hand, trying to recollect its original heft.

From that moment on, Huang Deyun understood the depth of the enmity that existed between her and her maid, Ah Mei, who now knew all her secrets.

Also born into a poor family, Ah Mei lacked Huang Deyun's beauty, so the slave trader had sent her on a different path, as a slave girl to a rich family in Wong Ngai Chung. She never knew her real family name. Her earliest memory was of standing barefoot in front of a curtained bed, holding a basin of water, waiting for the third wife to get up. From that day on, she did not enjoy a moment's rest: fanning, massaging, serving tea, cooking. Whenever she provoked the slightest displeasure from the third wife, she would be forced to kneel on the floor—if she were lucky. If not, she would be tied to the bedpost, not allowed to eat or use the bathroom, and gagged so that she couldn't cry out.

One cold winter, Ah Mei stood barefoot on the red brick floor, massaging the third wife's shoulder. Bone-chilling air seeped in through the bricks and through her skimpy clothes. Her nearly frostbitten hands trembled violently; agitated by her slow movements, the third wife turned and hit her in the face with a copper hand warmer. Red-hot coals scorched Ah Mei's forehead and sent blood dripping down her face. The scar from the wound looked like a centipede curling up on her forehead. Afterward, she suffered more and even worse abuse at the hands of the mistress, who was upset over the fact that Ah Mei, whose scar ruined her fair compensation, could not be sold to another family as a concubine.

Unable to endure the abuse any longer, Ah Mei escaped one night and was found by police at the gate of the Happy Valley graveyard. Before being sent to wait on Huang Deyun, she worked for the mistress of a taipan who had made his fortune in the opium trade. But, barely half a year later, the mistress, also a onetime prostitute, died under suspicious circumstances, and the taipan sent Ah Mei, bundle in hand, over the mountain to see Adam Smith. Finally she had found refuge in a storage shack by an old well in the Chinese-style building, and, out of gratitude, she saw to Smith's every need.

Huang Deyun's instincts told her to be wary of this maid. So that day, after taking out the leather case from its hiding place, she locked her door before counting the case's contents three times. To her amazement, nothing was missing. Ah Mei was a puzzle to her, but she told herself that she must never let her guard down with the woman—the maid who now knew all her secrets.

Clasping her hands, Deyun was considering her next move when a strange thing happened. She felt a cramp in her abdomen, and feminine instinct told her that she was pregnant. It must have been that last night, when Smith, reeking with alcohol, called her a yellow whore and spat in her face. On that shameful night, when she endured worse abuse than a prostitute, the last night she wanted to remember in her life, he had left his seed inside her.

Deyun caressed her still flat belly. After losing her virginity to a coarse tax collector at the age of fifteen, she had been lucky to remain free of any venereal diseases. A woman who had spent most of her life in the red-light district once told her that she would never be pregnant if she did not have a baby by the first three clients, since their mixed seeds would poison her womb and make her sterile. But now, it seemed, she was indeed carrying a child.

To guard against a miscarriage, Deyun lay in bed all day long with the leather case safely under her pillow. With nothing better to do to pass the time, she counted the jewelry in her case, every piece bartered with her body. She was often choked with emotion when she pondered her life as a prostitute. The thought of that first night, when the trembling, innocent Adam Smith had climbed into her bed, also saddened her immensely. But soon she had no more tears to shed.

Deyun glumly turned over in bed. Beds defined her life. She had moved from the bed in Southern Tang House, where any man could climb in to sleep with her at any time, to this four-poster bed bought at an auction in Happy Valley. Even when she was devoting herself to Smith, her life was confined to a bed. And if she had been able to run away with the martial arts performer, a bed would still have constituted her whole life. Memories, painful and sweet, were intertwined with beds in which she had either slept or dreamed of sleeping, but the tenderness was gone. She would never forget how Smith had violated her on that last night, and now she was doomed to carry the scar of his abuse throughout her life.

She was trapped in bed, slowly tortured by memories.

Deyun's only outlet was Ah Mei. Symptoms of early pregnancy turned her into a mean-spirited, irritable woman who abused her maid at the slightest offense. Nothing Ah Mei did pleased her. The soup was either too bitter and too salty or too bland and tasteless, worse than dishwater. She would fling the bowl at Ah Mei, sending hot soup dripping down her face. And she would not allow her maid to walk away. Instead, she would order her up to her bed, where she would grab Ah Mei's long braid in one hand and lash out at her with a rattan whip with the other. Deyun amused herself by abusing her maid, thus relieving the boredom of lying in bed all day with nothing to occupy her.

When Ah Mei wasn't toiling at all the unreasonable demands of Huang Deyun, she would be sent to the well to kneel down and carry a laundry stone on her head, not allowed to put it down without permission.

One day at dusk, when Ah Mei was at the well, carrying the laundry stone, a black object shot into Deyun's room, so startling her that she leaped out of bed. It was a battered old crow, which whirled and flew right back out, landing on Ah Mei's shoulder, where it cawed in her ear, as if giving her a message. Ah Mei, motionless under the weight of the stone, raised a hand slightly to calm the bird, which tucked in its wings and perched on the maid's kneeling leg, as if hypnotized. In the dim light, the crow's black lacquerlike feathers reflected an eerie, cold glint.

Later, in her bath, Deyun discovered a bruise on her thigh. She felt no pain, but the bruise grew larger over the next few days, and she began to suspect that Ah Mei was performing some sort of sorcery against her. First, Ah Mei had summoned the crow to frighten her, then she had recited an incantation to send little demons to pinch her leg when she was asleep. Both frightened and enraged, Deyun forgot all about her pregnancy as she ran over to the storage shed and kicked open the door. She searched the room, convinced that her maid was trying to murder her with witchcraft. But she found nothing. To vent her anger, she turned to her rattan whip. The blows fell like rain. Covering her head with her hands, Ah Mei cowered by the well; she had no place to run. Caught up in a frenzy, Deyun beat her maid even harder, until the woman dropped her hands, revealing a scar on her forehead in the shape of a centipede, normally covered by her bangs. In the eyes of the pregnant Deyun, the scar was a telltale sign of witchcraft.

It was also by the old well where Deyun repeatedly witnessed Ah Mei's terrifying seizures. It was always the same: Ah Mei would slip and fall with a loud thud. Her eyes would roll back in her head and her neck would be stretched like that of a marionette, pulled taut by a puppeteer. Then her head would twist to the side, as her arms and legs twisted and twitched spastically. An old Chinese herbal doctor in Wan Chai had determined that Ah Mei had epilepsy and told her to avoid salt. But she wouldn't listen; her room was filled with vats of pickled mustard greens and strings of salted dry fish hanging from the beams.

Convinced that she was living with a sorceress who was waiting for the right moment to exact her revenge, Deyun knew that her days were numbered. Something was stirring in her belly, forcing its way out, like the centipede on Ah Mei's forehead. Unable to hold it down any longer, she retched violently, as if she were throwing up her intestines. She thought she was going to die.

But she didn't. The symptoms of early pregnancy slowly disappeared and she found a new purpose in life—to find the father of the baby in her womb. As her belly began to swell noticeably, Deyun ventured out of the house and traveled the streets in search of her English lover, the man who had abandoned her. For three weeks, she wandered over half of Hong Kong Island, asking everyone she met for news of the Englishman from the Sanitary Board who had worn a steel helmet and white gloves as he led workers in disinfecting the plague zone. Everyone she stopped thought she was crazy, and none was willing to talk to her.

But Deyun refused to give up. And as she continued her journey, she thought back to the conversations she'd had with Smith. Recalling that he had mentioned that he could hear the tram bells from his Mid-Level flat, she now asked everyone she met about the Peak tram station.

For four days she rushed about searching for the station, stopping from time to time to cock her ear and listen for bells. Smith had said that the bell always sounded before the tram entered a station. When it stopped, the conductor would pull two long bladelike brakes, and the tram would lurch to a stop with a loud creak, sending passengers careening backward as the tram parked nearly vertically on the slope. It was both scary and exciting. From Smith she had gotten a picture of his two-story flat at Mid-Level. The light green building came into view when you got off at the second stop and walked past a grove of trees. It had an upstairs balcony. He told her that on clear days he could see the undulating hills of Kowloon on the other side of Victoria Harbor.

"One glimpse of those hills and you'll know where Kowloon, 'Nine Dragons,' got its name."

He also told her that his living room was crammed with furniture brought over by his predecessor from the government warehouse, and that he spent little time in it. In his second-floor bedroom, he had moved his bed to face the ocean and opened windows originally sealed to prevent humidity from seeping in. In the mornings, sunlight crossed the doorframe and crept onto his bed, moving up his body inch by inch. He said, playfully, that it was sort of like lying on the beach and slowly being buried in the sand.

Not quite catching the nuances of his language, she had listened to him prattle on. That was back when they had just met and their passion for each other was at its peak. Deyun was so filled with curiosity about her lover's unattainable Mid-Level flat that she cradled his head, with its curly chestnut hair, and begged him to tell her again and again about the interior, leaving nothing out, not even the potted plants at the end of the hallway and on the landing. Having committed the place, inside and out, to memory, she felt settled whenever she thought about it, as if it were her own home.

In the evenings, when she sat under the lamplight, playing solitaire to pass the time until Smith arrived, she would think about the flat at Mid-Level. In the dark, the green exterior would become indiscernible; a fire would flicker in the living room, where her lover, following the custom of upper-class Britons, would glide down from his dressing room in a dinner jacket. His servant, Yafu, a snowy white napkin draped over his shoulder, would wait respectfully by the dinner table to pull Smith's chair out for him. Then he would light the candles in the silver holders before retreating outside the dining room to wait. Smith would loosen his bow tie a bit before clearing his throat as a signal for Yafu to bring in the soup. And the candlelight dinner would begin.

For Huang Deyun, it seemed perfectly natural for someone to sit alone at a dining table intended for twelve. Now if she moved into this official residence—she knew she was dreaming but could not help it—where would she sit? At the far end, facing Smith, as mistress of the house? No, she was not born with that kind of good luck. How about sitting on a stool behind Smith to wait on him? The custom in local brothels required the prostitutes to serve their clients this way. But that would not be considered proper conduct in an official residence. They might carry on any way they wished behind a closed bedroom door, but must be proper and respectable in the living room, especially in front of the servants.

But this was all wishful thinking.

"The Peak tram station is located on Cotton Tree Drive," a Sikh in a purple turban told Deyun. But before she could ask directions to Cotton Tree Drive, an armed police patrol turned to stare at her, sending her running in fright into the teeming marketplace at the Western Garrison, where she roamed aimlessly.

11

At that moment, the person Huang Deyun thought about day and night was kneeling before a cross in deep penance at St. John's Cathedral on Garden Road. The Sunday mass was nearly over, the organ was playing a hymn, and sunlight streamed in through the stained-glass windows. The cathedral was ablaze in golden light. Smith prayed that the light would turn into angels, who would ride the waves of music down to carry him up into the sky under their white wings, away from the miseries and entanglements of this mortal world.

"May God in all His mercy forgive you," Pastor Thomas said meaningfully, gently patting his shoulder. Smith did not dare meet the pastor's gray, keen, knowing eyes. Brought to his knees in this holy sanctuary, Smith was sure that his sins were beyond redemption. He wondered if the Lord Jesus would forgive and bring him salvation. In order to resist temptation, he filled his hours with work. In the evenings, after leaving the Sanitary Board, he went straight to an orphanage, without stopping off at home first. There he led the children in reciting psalms, and taught them English till midnight before walking home under the moonlight, fingering his rosary and reciting prayers. Then, before going to bed he kissed the crucifix hanging at the head of his bed, praying to fall asleep with God's blessings.

But regrettably, the corrupting devil managed to sneak into his heart whenever he let down his guard. In an instant he would find himself back in Happy Valley, as if sleepwalking, where the sibyl of carnal desire waited on the other side of the window, tempting him to jump through, straight into her arms. Smith's inner struggle turned his already pale face ashen, like a sheet of white paper.

Dark clouds shifted in the starless sky and blotted out the moon; Smith felt darkness descend around him. He could not believe he had fallen so low, having brought shame to the island's colonizers. Hadn't the aristocratic Mrs. Windsor, the wife of his superior at the Sanitary Board, preached that the English needed to maintain the reputation of colonizing authority on this oppressive, dusty foreign island? If one day she somehow got wind of his behavior and learned that he was a whoring wastrel who kept a yellow-skinned prostitute in a rented house in Happy Valley, she would humiliate him and order him out. Or she might walk past him as if nothing had happened and keep her distance until the party was over, then close the door and solemnly order her husband never to allow that fellow to enter her house again. Being seen as an equal to a miller's son, a strange phenomenon that could occur only in the Hong Kong colony, was the limit of her tolerance. She would never permit Smith, who had lain with a member of the colored race, to sit on her velvet chairs or finger her silverware. It was a sign of moral corruption, and it had nothing to do with racial discrimination. Mrs. Windsor regarded herself as open-minded and free of prejudice, although, in her mind, a superior race must resemble her: blue eyes and blond hair on the outside, surpassing intelligence on the inside.

"May God bless us and keep our intellect from withering away in this sweltering heat."

Mrs. Windsor was proud of her enlightened, democratic attitude, particularly when she heard that the Brahmins of India, for fear of spiritual contamination, never took food from the hands of the lower castes. Except for her personal maid, whom she had brought with her from England, Mrs. Windsor hired Chinese to take care of the household and wait on her family, something that brought her enormous pride. In her eyes, Chinese were officials who were yet lackeys to the westerners, compradors in the opium firms, prostitutes who served Western men in Wan Chai, or sedan chair carriers, gardeners, and other servants who crowded her kitchen. After reading a letter from an American in an

English-language newspaper that suggested the implementation of a policy of segregating Chinese and westerners on Hong Kong trams, Mrs. Windsor wondered why the American could not take her lead and go about in a sedan chair. Why would he want to crowd onto public transportation in the first place? What sort of white person was he?

On the last night they spent together, Adam Smith had kicked open the door of the Chinese-style house, thrown his whore on the bed, and spat in her face to vent the hatred welling up inside him. But even that hadn't been enough. He needed to smash windows and destroy the harem he had built with his own hands, his China. He would crush the red silk palace lanterns, the dragon carvings, and the blue flowered porcelain vases. But he would reserve the most violence for the little alcove in the corner, where a red candle burned day and night beside a clay idol, the pagan's god, Pastor Thomas's "satanic icon."

If Pastor Thomas of St. John's Cathedral had known what parishioner Smith was involved in, he'd have demanded, "Torch, my son, raise the torch in your hand, and this time, cast it down upon the demon-inhabited cove of that pagan with its sordid soul, and incinerate the heretical sorceress!"

Christianity, the religion of fire. The God Jehovah is a raging fire, as the Old Testament tells us. Over the centuries, Christians had punished countless heretics and pagans with their holy flames. But to the pastor's chagrin, the holy fire of Christianity had yet to be ignited on an island filled with the spirit of Satan.

Jesus had sent Pastor Thomas to the colony twelve years earlier. "Go," the Lord had said in a dream. "Say to your superiors, 'Please send me to China, to that wondrous place where I can spread the word of God!'" But he had arrived too late to participate in the early efforts to translate the Bible, and was placed in charge of St. John's Cathedral, East Asia's first Anglican church. Applying himself diligently to spreading the teachings of Christianity, he chose Timothy Richards, a British Baptist missionary, to translate his writings into Chinese for publication.

Pastor Thomas, his wife, Pandora, and his only child, Emily, lived in a luxurious mansion far more extravagant than Mr. Dickinson's hilltop residence. After the plague, Adam Smith visited the pastor and was astonished by the luxury, which was in stark contrast to its occupant, a short, pallid man who dressed simply. Invited into the luxuriously appointed study, with its exquisite antique tables and walnut desk, he sat across from the pastor in his rich, red leather chair.

"Stay for lunch, my child. Tell me, have you any news of Mrs. Dickinson?"

"She arrived safely in England and wrote to tell me that once she settles down—I'm sure you've heard that she went to live with an aunt in York—she'll help me get in touch with Annie."

Pastor Thomas averted his keen, all-knowing eyes, paying no attention to things that weighed on the young man's heart, reflecting instead on how, as the plague was spreading outward from Hollywood Road the year before, he had donned his holy vestments to deliver a sermon at the cathedral in his singsong cadence: "Disaster has befallen them. The pagans who have not accepted Jesus as their Lord are reaping the punishment they deserve."

Yet, when Governor Robinson ordered the plague zones put to the torch, Chinese residents dragged their sons and daughters to kneel outside the missionary Timothy Richards's house. Banging their heads on the ground, they pleaded with him to ask the government to rescind the order. Richards stormed out of his house and headed for Pastor Thomas's residence on Garden Street. Upon hearing Richards's report, Pastor Thomas rolled his eyes and clasped his hands to thank the Lord for his blessings. God had answered his prayers to punish the island's sinful, unrepentant idolaters, even though he believed that God was being too benevolent, since torching the deserted plagued-infested houses was little more than a warning to the Chinese, slight punishment, indeed.

Following the plague, Governor Robinson had adopted strict measures to improve the drinking water in the Chinese districts and accelerated work on the sewer system. He had also issued a new building code that angered the Chinese community, for 10 percent of the Chinese buildings were deemed unfit for human habitation and were to be demolished.

Irate citizens had hurled rocks at the sedan chairs of leaders of the Chinese community, venting their anger over the fact that their representatives had not conveyed their concerns to the colonial government. One of the rocks had struck Timothy Richards as he emerged from his sedan chair; hiking the hem of his robe with one hand and rubbing his bruised forehead with the other, he had whirled around like a spinning top, momentarily at a loss as to where he should go to plead on behalf of ordinary Chinese. The wretched people whose homes had been destroyed were now crowded into temporary residential areas with even worse living conditions. He had relatives living there but didn't dare go see them, afraid he might be stoned again.

But he was, nonetheless. And this time the news was even worse. He could hardly believe his ears when he heard that the colonial government planned to turn the razed area into a park. Over two hundred thousand Chinese were crammed into the west side of Victoria City, an area less than one square mile, to the point that people were stepping all over each other. It was incomprehensible that the government would make a park out of land that was more valuable than gold.

Timothy Richards prayed even harder now, but was increasingly perplexed.

Things went from bad to worse for those Chinese who had barely survived the plague and who now watched their houses torn down. These humble, conservative, common citizens, who wanted nothing but food on their tables and a roof over their heads, were dirt poor. And now even their shelter was about to be taken from them. Passive and incapable of resistance, some twenty thousand of them decided to give up life in the colony, where they were always at the mercy of others. They packed up what little they owned and boarded ships to return to the countryside in the interior. Thus began an unprecedented exodus from Hong Kong.

Pastor Thomas could not have been happier, convinced that God had finally begun driving the loathsome pagans out of his colony.

12

After Huang Deyun asked the Sikh for directions to the Peak tram and was frightened into fleeing by an armed policeman, she aimlessly climbed uphill and arrived at a temple on Elgin Street. The small temple, a Mecca for prostitutes from Shui Hang Hao's Hollywood Road, was nearly enveloped by the giant canopy of a banyan tree. Recently remodeled, the temple, including the altar and tablets, was painted bright red, blinding red, bloodred.

Deyun knelt at the altar. Only the patron saint of prostitutes could understand what was on her mind, things she could not share with anyone else. She begged her patron saint to change the mind of her English lover and make him return to her. But deep down, she knew better, knew that her plea would go unanswered. For as long as he lived, Smith would never again set foot in that Chinese-style building. And without him she didn't know what to do, for she was engulfed in sexual desire. Often she would toss and turn in bed, panting and trembling all over. Over the past two weeks, when she was most desperate, all but convinced that she was doomed to the life of a prostitute, she had even thought of returning to Southern Tang House to resume her former profession. She would kick out her despicable maid, Ah Mei, lock up the house, and hire a rickshaw to transport her and her suitcases back onto the path she'd taken eight months earlier, before the plague had cut a swath through the colony.

Nameless birds called out from the shadowy banyan tree. Unconsciously, Deyun caressed her slightly swollen belly, wondering what to do with the bastard fetus inside. Back when she was living at Southern

Tang House, she'd come to this place with Autumn Shadow, also a prostitute, to pray to their patron saint. Deyun had heard that Autumn Shadow had suffered more than one terrifying pregnancy:

"That silly girl takes things too seriously," one of the brothel maids had said. "She says she wants a child to rely on, so she won't have to be a prostitute forever. That sounds fine, but she wasn't born with that kind of luck. The monster in her belly was prematurely born with one freakish foot out first. Besides webbed feet, it had half a brain, soft like jelly and nearly transparent. Now she's pregnant again, from the evil seed of another *guailow*, so no wonder she doesn't want it—"

Huang Deyun's pregnancy had not been a smooth one. The old Chinese herbal doctor on Spring Garden Lane felt her pulse and told her that the fire of pregnancy was sapping her yin; with insufficient yin in her kidneys, her liver was too weak to keep her blood pressure down. So she felt dizzy during the day and shivered from cold sweats at night. The old doctor prescribed a concoction of ichthyus grass, skullcap, indigo, dandelion, and gourd melon seeds to ease her shortness of breath and relieve the heaviness in her chest.

Then he felt her pulse again, this time with a grave expression, and listened to the position of the baby when Huang Deyun said that she'd been gripped by searing abdominal pains the night before. But he found nothing. Maybe it was too early. "We'll wait a few months. Once it develops into a human form, we'll decide what to do," he said. But rather than suffer through the full term, only to face a monster with part of its head missing or festering feet, she would rather pray to the patron saint for a potion to abort the baby.

But as she stared blankly at the patron saint's spirit tablet, Deyun vacillated.

Had Pastor Thomas realized that during the migration of twenty thousand Chinese, Huang Deyun was among those who had decided to stay—was, in fact, lying in bed in Happy Valley—and had he discovered that his young, able parishioner, Adam Smith, was wandering, as if possessed, outside the window of the wicked house, unwilling to leave, he'd have stepped forward boldly, the holy Bible in one hand and a holy fire in the other, to set up an altar of religious judgment and condemn that evil, licentious sorceress to immolation. In the name of Christ, he'd have exorcised the evil spirit from Smith and warned him of the consequences.

But while Adam Smith dared not argue with Pastor Thomas over the issue of moral corruption, he knew deep down that what drew him to the window at midnight was not just feverish carnal desire but also his futile tenderness toward the woman inside. She had been his first. They had found each in the valley of death as the plague raged around them, and as long as he lived, he would never forget the consolation of finding another pair of tear-filled eyes as terrified as his own. After he had crawled to her, they had held each other tight. The woman's soft, warm body had made the blood flow again in hands numbed by sealing up disease-ridden houses. They had been the only couple on a plague-infested, destitute island, and were fated to be together. It was their unyielding union that had enabled them to triumph over the plague demon and creep out of the valley of death. And it was tender concern that had made him think of nothing but Deyun's safety when he was about to torch the most gravely affected area around Mount Taiping. Smith had told his Chinese interpreter, Qu Yabing, to hire a sedan chair to move his lover from the Southern Tang House to a safe haven, ignoring the look of surprise and objection in the man's eyes. It had been a sign of his love for Deyun to place her safety as his highest priority.

Shrouded in darkness, nights in the lonely colony after that had been particularly long, the lamplit Chinese-style house in Happy Valley the only bright spot. Standing on the balcony of his Mid-Level official residence, Smith could look down and see the light, the only warm place in the dark, drawing him to it to melt in her soft, sweet, tender love.

His futile tender love.

After bidding farewell to the patron saint, Huang Deyun hesitated before finally accepting the packet of herbal medicine from the temple caretaker. She walked along Elgin Street, weighed down by her tangled thoughts, and before she knew it, she had arrived at the red-light district.

She was struck by immense sadness when she thought back to the times she'd returned to the brothels with her sisters, all giggling, after paying tribute to the patron saint. Everything looked the same to her, with gaudily festooned signs still hanging in front of restaurants famous for their pleasure-quarter banquets. On both sides of the street were the money pits for potential clients, brothels with swallowtail eaves, green window frames, and red thresholds. The area now basked in the lazy sunshine of late spring, no sound emerging from behind the beaded curtains. Clients who had lingered at the restaurants and their prostitutes were still in bed; but once night fell, the place would take on a different look, with red-sleeved hands pouring wine, and tipsy diners toasting one another.

As she stood on the street corner, Deyun reminisced over her days as a prostitute: splendid clothes and dazzling makeup, the embodiment of charm and glamour. Maybe she was fated to be a prostitute for the rest of her life, living off her body. Otherwise, why did she feel that if an old acquaintance from Southern Tang House, even a gardener, had walked up now, she'd have rushed forward with open arms, as if greeting a long-lost relative?

If she saw no old friends, she had another plan—she would return to Yihong Pavilion. She could strike a deal with Yihong to become a non-indentured prostitute. Although Yihong had taught Deyun the trade, she had sold her once, and Deyun felt she owed the woman nothing. She could then find a place in the brothel, where Yihong's maid could serve her, and she would give Yihong half the money she earned. She was confident that the clients she attracted, old and new, would keep her busy once she resumed her old profession.

Indulging in the past glory of a life in the flesh trade, Huang Deyun imagined herself returning to Southern Tang House, where she would raise the handkerchief in her hand, part the Suzhou curtain, embroidered with a hundred birds saluting a phoenix, then climb the black-lacquered stairway and return to her attic room, a place that had made her feel like a captive upon her arrival, with no hope for escape; now she missed the large bed, with its brocade cushions and a bedspread decorated with cop-

ulating mandarin ducks. When it was dark outside, the window facing
the Roman Catholic church would be transformed into a large, black
screen. Deyun, carefully made up, would slowly rise in front of her mirror and, like a beauty walking out from a painted screen, gracefully move
forward to spend the night with a lustful client.

Turning off Hollywood Road and looking down Lyndhurst Terrace,
Deyun was filled with emotions. On the night she'd gone to the performance by the temple, she'd suddenly been seized by the panicky
thought that the madam and pimps from Southern Tang House might
sneak up on her, tie her up, and return her to her old trade at the brothel.
So, without waiting for the audience to disperse, she had dragged her
maid along as she pushed her way through the crowd. It was then that the
thought of running away with the troupe had entered her mind. Now a
mere three months had passed, and she couldn't wait to return to Southern Tang House. She had to laugh at her mercurial moods.

The red silk lantern flung to the ground on the day of her departure
had been taken away; only the hook remained, dangling beneath the
eaves in an imperceptible breeze. The plague was long over, so why
hadn't a new lantern replaced the old one? Deyun was puzzled. She
pushed open the door, which gave way with a creak, and drew the
Suzhou embroidered curtain aside. Specks of dust invisible to the naked
eye rose up and dissipated in the air. Southern Tang House was deadly
silent, slumbering on this late spring afternoon. Like the restaurants in
the red-light district, this place also belonged to the night.

When she entered Southern Tang House, she sighed, as if she'd finally
come home. The plague had swept over the brothel, but miraculously the
place seemed to be intact, with everything still in its original place: the
opium bed, the curio cabinet, embroidered cushions, pillows, gilded
screens. In the dim light, the silk and brocade embroidery appeared
faded, giving it a look of dying glory. Deyun walked on the floral-
patterned Tientsin carpet, each step launching clouds of dust, but she was
completely oblivious. With some difficulty, she climbed onto the stool by
the bar, where she rested her elbows on the counter and stroked her hair
coquettishly, relishing the memory of drunken clients ogling a thigh

revealed by the slit of her cheongsam. She held her head with one hand and laughed at the thought of all those men who could not wait to swallow her up.

Breathing the lingering smell of sulfur from the disinfectant, Deyun began to sense after a while that something was wrong. The more she looked at this familiar place, the stranger she felt. In her memory, the bar, once swimming in liquor, had never been so neat and tidy. She picked up an empty beer glass, which was covered with a thick layer of dust. The bar, long out of use, was also blanketed with gray dust. The colorful vases on tall stands in the corners looked murky, no longer nearly transparent porcelains. She got down off the bar stool; the tips of her fingers came away coated with dust. She felt as if she'd broken into an abandoned house buried underground for a very long time, and that she would sink with it if she stayed any longer. She needed to go to a familiar, safe place.

Holding the black-lacquered banister, she walked up one step at a time, convinced that only when she had returned to her attic room, with its beaded curtains, would she feel she was truly home. On the day she'd left, suitcases in hand, she'd stepped over the dying pimp and climbed into a sedan chair sent by Adam Smith. She recalled that on her way out, the chair was leaning against the window, seemingly waiting for her to return and sit down to daydream again. What would she be thinking if she sat in it once more?

The attic door was locked. Deyun, suddenly intimidated, lacked the courage to knock, afraid that, unprepared, she might be shocked by what she saw inside. She took a deep breath and quietly sneaked up to listen through the door. It was silent inside, not a murmur. She thought about the things she'd left behind: her embroidered slippers, an ingenious music alarm clock, the oval mirror. Her concern for personal belongings removed the last vestige of inhibition, and she banged on the door; her action was met with dead silence. The idea of not being able to return to her own place angered and prompted her to kick at the door, but to no avail. A door that once could be opened freely by any man now refused entrance to its mistress.

Resentfully and reluctantly, Deyun went back out onto the street. The stained-glass door of Madame Randall's was wide open, revealing something stirring under a pile of stinking filthy curtains. Apparently the low-class, illegal prostitutes from the coast had taken over the evacuated brothels on Lyndhurst Terrace at the height of the raging plague. Now they were conducting their business in broad daylight. Deyun spat at the stirring shadow and turned away in disgust.

Finally, Deyun had to admit that the red-light district had yet to recover from the plague. The restaurants, with their beaded curtains, and the deathly still brothels she'd seen along the way weren't taking an afternoon nap; they were closed for business. She surveyed the sight before her and realized that there was only one more place for her—Yihong Pavilion. She hoped that Yihong would still be there, puffing on her opium pipe. Four years earlier, when Deyun was first brought before Yihong's opium bed, the acrid smell had scratched her throat; later, when she suffered from menstrual cramps during her first period, Yihong had ordered one of the maids to pry open her mouth and make her swallow some opium to ease the pain. Never had she thought that one day, in the Chinese-style residence in Happy Valley, she would follow in Yihong's footsteps and become acquainted with opium, the Hibiscus Fairy. In order to satisfy her raging sexual appetite, brought on by the pregnancy, Deyun had taken up opium smoking to relax her tense body and dissipate her dejection over Smith's desertion and the fear of an unknowable future.

With difficulty, she leaned against the door of the Wellington Street store where she'd once bought rouge. Drenched in cold sweat, she moaned and turned to face the mirror on the wall. There was a time when she'd looked at herself in that mirror wearing a pair of new gold earrings. The shiny luster of gold had made her face sparkle, a sight she could never forget. Mechanically, she moved closer to the mirror, only to see broken images of herself on the cracked surface. She screamed and backed away. The face in the mirror was splotchy, with puffy eyes, jutting cheekbones, and sunken cheeks. That withered face, glossy with black grease, wasn't hers; it was the face of the madam, Yihong, who had disgusting blackened teeth and a skeletal neck showing above the peach-colored underwear. And those shoes. Deyun recalled seeing the black satin embroidered shoes resting on a stool at the foot of the opium bed, where she stood the very first time. The soles were spotless, as if their owner had never stepped on solid ground. Purple phoenixes were embroidered on the tops of the shoes. She imagined she saw a funeral procession with a skeleton dressed in colorful grave clothes appear before her eyes. Was it Yihong's funeral, or her own?

No longer able to withstand the violent quaking of her body, Huang Deyun slid down the wall. Squatting on the ground, she buried her face in her hands. Her reflection gave rise to shame and despair. At that moment, she had to fight the urge to bite down on her tongue and end her life. She had reached the end of her rope; there was no way out. Her natural, flowerlike beauty had been destroyed by opium, and the plan to resume her profession was shattered like the cracked mirror.

Deyun's teeth were chattering. She pried them apart and stuck her tongue between them, trying to muster the courage to bite it off and end her miserable life. She closed her eyes, obliterating both the scene around her and her dying beauty. A surge of well-being rose slowly in the wake of her struggle. No longer fearing death, she clasped her hands and bowed in the direction of her hometown.

Just then a stampede of clattering footsteps roared over like crumbling mountains and surging oceans, thundering down the street and bursting into Deyun's suicide plan. Bolting upright, she rubbed her eyes, thinking it was another opium hallucination.

Huang Deyun was witnessing the 1895 migration of twenty thousand Chinese leaving Hong Kong for their Canton homeland in protest against the colonial government's new housing policy. People swarmed down from Mount Taiping Street, carrying their belongings on their shoulders and herding flocks of chickens, ducks, and pigs ahead of them. The men, rage and indignation written on their faces, strode purposefully, vowing to never again set foot in Hong Kong under the damnable British rule. The women, carrying children in their arms and on their backs, wiped away tears while constantly looking back at homes they had been forced to abandon.

They were taking their families and livestock to the coast to board ships that would take them back to their ancestral homes. Deyun had a hometown too—Dongguan, the place to which she'd knelt in farewell moments before. It had been nearly four years since she'd been kidnapped, when the late autumn fragrance of cassia blossoms permeated the air, and she wondered if her baby brother had ever reclaimed his wayward soul. After she was taken away, there would have been no one to pedal the waterwheel, since consumption had prevented her father from working in the field, which must now lie fallow. Several reincarnations of a girl's life in Dongguan paled in comparison with her four years in Hong Kong. But in the end, she had wound up with nothing; it was all an empty dream. Time to go home.

Following the homeward trek, Deyun negotiated the flagstone steps. When she reached the bottom, she turned to look back, struck by the feeling that her years in Hong Kong had indeed been a dream. In a mere four years, she had come full circle. So she dusted off the hem of her skirt, symbolically putting all this behind her. She would say good-bye to the flagstone street one last time. As long as she lived, she would never return to this place.

She could go home, she could return to her homeland in Dongguan!

13

A battle for land between humans and nature was waged the moment Hong Kong opened for trade.

In 1841, after the Royal Navy landed, they first leveled the craggy coast. Then they hired Chinese coolies to carry dirt and pave a road, paralleling the long stretch of coastline; this was Queen's Road, the colony's first thoroughfare. When the prototype city of Victoria first emerged, it lacked the potential of a downtown, since it was shaped like a belt, leaving too great a distance between its east and west ends. But level ground was rare on this hilly, rocky island, and the only plausible solution was to extend the city toward the ocean, to snatch land from Mother Nature. To that end, reclamation projects of leveling hills and filling up the ocean were undertaken simultaneously.

But not immediately. The first few governors talked about plans but were unable to carry them out, since the coastal areas had already been carved up and occupied by opium dealers and taipans, whose power far exceeded the governor's authority. They treated as private property the piers and godowns they had built without authorization, and others, including the colonial government, had no right to interfere. The ninth governor, Sir George Bowen, who wished to finally realize the dream of reclamation, ordered possession of the seabed taken from the opium dealers and taipans to move the coastline outward. But his order was met with opposition, and trouble erupted when the foreign merchants jointly protested to the minister of colonial affairs in London.

Governor Bowen, forced to concede, was outraged.

"It's unthinkable for merchants to have that much control over local government."

And the taipans did not stop there. A year after the midsection of the coastal embankment was destroyed in a powerful typhoon, Governor Bowen ordered the business owners along the coastline to pay for the repairs, but the taipans ignored the government's policy on land leases. So the governor pursued legal means, an unprecedented instance of a government actually suing its citizens. In the end, a special court was convened to try the case; incredibly, Governor Bowen lost.

During the early days of Hong Kong's colonial history, the power pyramid was topped by the opium dealer Jardine, followed by the Jockey Club, and finally the governor.

But the battle for land had to be waged. Research and investigation by experts showed that Hong Kong's coastline was dotted with numerous bays that slowed the flow of water. Reclaiming land in shallow waters would increase the usage of the deepwater area without disrupting the water flow. The colonial government realized that reclamation would be a profitable business, for not only could it buy private land cheaply, it could then turn around and reap tremendous profits by selling off the reclaimed land.

Finally the tenth governor, Sir William Des Voeux, reached an agreement with the foreign merchants, and land reclamation projects got under way during his tenure. In 1862, the first colonial paved street, Queen's Road, gave way to a new street on reclaimed land, named after Des Voeux.

Decades later, after the 1894 plague, which cost at least 2,547 lives, Governor Robinson ordered the construction of reservoirs to improve the quality of drinking water in the Chinese sector, while accelerating the building of a sewage system. But his order of 1895 to tear down Chinese houses that fell below sanitation standards, nearly 10 percent of the total, triggered a historical migration. Throngs of angry Chinese abandoned their homes and showed up at the pier to board ships that would take them back to their hometowns on the mainland.

Following this sad procession was a slovenly dressed woman with a bulging belly. She walked slowly, alone and empty-handed. Amid this migrating convoy, the woman seemed out of place.

Huang Deyun, who had finally given up the search for her English lover but was pregnant with his child, had changed her mind about resuming her profession as a prostitute and had decided to return to her hometown, Dongguan.

The migrating crowd moved slowly toward Sai Wan, where sampan sails were set to take them back to where they'd come from. But Huang Deyun was moving against the flow, heading in the opposite direction. She was looking for Pedder Wharf, where she'd first set foot in Hong Kong four years earlier. She recalled the scene at the wharf: the big, strange-looking houses in the foothills of a mountain that seemed to rise up out of the water, the red and blue flags flapping above the houses, and the coolies. She also recalled seeing ships that were bigger than houses; the rusted, salty odor from water-soaked chains mingled with the disagreeable smell of fish roe and squid coming from food stands along the pier. Holding her belly with one hand and grabbing her throat with the other, she forced herself to stop thinking, fearing that her pregnancy could not withstand the agony of retching.

When she came to the intersection of Queen's Road and Pedder Street, she was relieved to see that the clock tower was unchanged. The wharf shouldn't be far now, and she'd have no trouble identifying the skiff that had brought her to Hong Kong among the sampans, ferries, and ships crowding together. She would then beg the owner to take her home. She recalled its brown, patched sails and the faded red paint on the bow, with its yellow triangular flag. It seemed such a long time since she'd gone to pray for an amulet for her baby brother.

Deyun quickened her steps, eager to find the skiff whose thatched canopy had been blown askew by a typhoon. The yellow flag must have faded after all these years.

As she stood in front of the red-bricked clock tower, she was confused by the sight before her. The original azure ocean was now shrouded in roiling yellow dust; the stinking Pedder Wharf, with its panorama of bobbing heads, was gone. Flying dust and airborne gravel covered everything. Coolies unloading cargo and shouting vendors and rickshaw pullers had been transformed into road-construction laborers in conical bamboo hats, carrying baskets of yellow dirt on their shoulders. They had joined the battle between man and nature, driving back the ocean inch by inch. Looks of single-minded determination showed on their sweaty, mud-streaked faces. After dumping a load of dirt, they straightened up and stomped down fiercely in their straw sandals. This fight was for their children and grandchildren, for generations of families that would build homes on land wrested from the ocean.

Stumbling around in the yellow mud, Deyun searched in vain for the familiar wharf. If she was serious about going home, she still had time to turn back and head for the coast at Sai Wan. Suddenly regretting her decision to leave the procession, she lifted one foot from the sticky yellow mud and turned around, when an earth-shattering explosion set the ground trembling under her feet. Billowing smoke rose from the bay to the north, followed by a hailstorm of stony rubble. Covering her head and squatting down in the mud, she thought the end had come.

"Hurray—another mountain has come down!" men shouted excitedly.

The colonizers had found another purpose for the cannons they had used to blow open the door of the Manchu court; one had just demolished a small hill blocking the road by the navy pier. It took the dumbfounded Huang Deyun, who was shielding her belly with her hands, a few minutes to regain her senses. When she opened her eyes, she realized that she was squatting in yellow mud. In front of her lay a tiny paper packet, which apparently had fallen out when she went down. It was the herbal abortion medicine for which she'd prayed at the temple of her patron saint. Tied with string, it was now floating in a muddy puddle. She could make out the magic symbol of the patron saint—crossed swords that seemed aimed at her belly. With a shriek, she fell to the ground, stretching out her foot to stomp the packet into the mud, until it was no longer visible. For in that instant, she had changed her mind about leaving. The wharf was gone, and she could no longer go home.

Suddenly fearless, she stood up from the muddy ground. She and the baby inside her had each other to rely upon; she would build a home on this reclaimed land for them both.

It was dusk when Huang Deyun returned to the house at Happy Valley. When she saw light from the setting sun in the open doorway, she assumed that the place had been ransacked by pirates who had come ashore. She crouched at the base of the wall and listened for a while, but it was quiet inside. So she crept into the house, where there were no signs of pillaging or disturbance. The parlor, now used as a bedroom, with its curtained four-poster bed, looked just as it had when she'd left that morning. The opium paraphernalia on the bed was like a grave mound, waiting for her to lie down and crawl into the cave of darkness to spend the rest of life, until she breathed her last.

She drew the curtain aside and was immediately assailed by the lingering odor of the opium she'd smoked the night before. She shouted out for her maid, Ah Mei, but got no response. The clothes she'd washed that morning hung by the well in the backyard, rippling silently in the evening breeze. The door of the storage room was ajar, but there was no sign of the woman.

Ah Mei, finally fed up with Huang Deyun's abuse, had fled the house when she was out. But before leaving, she'd broken the water vat to vent her anger. Now water that had spilled out from the kitchen wetted Huang Deyun's cloth shoes. Every step left a footprint, from one end of the house to the other. This place was hers, every inch of it covered with her footprints. Three months earlier, her English lover, Adam Smith, had left and never returned, and now her maid was gone. Alone in this large house, she could start anew by preparing a clean, warm place for herself and the baby in her belly.

She began by removing the curtains around the bed and the pillows embroidered with mandarin ducks. No longer was this to be a love nest in which she twisted her hair into a tantalizing bun or removed the pins to let it fall to her waist. Nor was it to be a tender trap to imprison her. She snatched up the opium pipe that had helped her through so many lonely dawns and dusks, and, along with the little gilded teapot, tossed it into the back yard. She then rolled up the window curtains that blurred the difference between day and night, so that moonlight and tomorrow's morning sunlight could shine in. Finally, with water she boiled herself, she sat down in a wooden tub to bathe. With her chin resting on her knees and hot water rising up to cover her neck, she washed the filth from her face and body.

The next morning she would go to Spring Garden Lane and ask the old Chinese herbal doctor at Evergreen Hall to prescribe a tonic to sustain her pregnancy.

14

Once the plague had passed, Royal Navy doctors and a fair number of others in the colony jointly petitioned Governor Robinson to shut down Tung Wah Hospital, arguing that its doctors treated their patients with Chinese herbal medicine. Suspicious of the therapeutic effects of Chinese medicine, the doctors complained that the Chinese herbal practitioners knew nothing about human anatomy and were ignorant about bacteriology. During the plague, not only was Tung Wah Hospital powerless to adequately treat patients, its doctors did not even perform autopsies on those who had died in spite of their herbal treatment. Most were buried before the cause of death could be determined.

The petition recommended that the hospital be converted into a public clinic to treat civilians with Western medicine. Forced into action, Governor Robinson ordered the formation of a five-member investigative committee, whose recommendations would then be used to decide the fate of the hospital.

Back in 1872, philanthropic Chinese elites, enlightened by the Western notion of humanitarianism, had collected donations to found Tung Wah Hospital to treat Chinese who could not afford doctors. Free herbal medicine was distributed three days a week. The hospital was equipped with a large kitchen, where dozens of stoves and kettles cooked up herbal preparations. The poorest patients, who had no means of boiling their own medicine at home, could take medicine prepared for them by the hospital before they left.

But herbal medicines passed down and used by generations of Chinese over thousands of years met their first challenge in the colony.

Doctors trained in Western medicine had been rare ever since Hong Kong was opened for trade. Not until the 1880s did Macao-born Portuguese and Caucasian doctors from the South Pacific begin practicing medicine there. Their patients were all westerners. In light of insufficient Western doctors, the colonial rulers, under the pretense of respecting Chinese customs, had allowed herbal doctors to treat the sick with homemade ointments, pills, tablets, powders, even unprocessed herbs. But they were not addressed as doctor, and their status was much lower than the physicians who treated westerners.

The five-member investigative committee included a token Chinese, a typical tactic of the rulers. On one bitterly cold, rainy April morning, four committee members arrived at Tung Wah Hospital, accompanied by the assistant director of the Sanitary Board, Adam Smith, and his Chinese interpreter, Qu Yabing. The Chinese member, citing a conflict of interest, given his familiarity with herbal medicine, was absent. Early that morning, the hospital's director and duty supervisors, dressed in long gowns beneath short jackets, stood respectfully at the gate to welcome the committee; determined to accede to the recommendations of the more capable Western doctors, they expected to be asked to leave their positions. Even knowing they were powerless before the will of the rulers, and that the committee's investigation was bound to be perfunctory, still they bowed humbly in welcome.

The first stop was the storage room for medicinal herbs, where piles of withered but still potent herbs reminded the committee of weeds pulled out by Chinese gardeners in their hilltop houses. Except that the weeds didn't smell as bad. The Chinese interpreter explained in his inadequate English that, according to the *Bencao Gangmu*, a medical book compiled by a Chinese during the Ming dynasty, thousands of efficacious cures were hidden in this pile of weeds. The committee members smiled; Qu Yabing smiled back deferentially. Then they were drawn to the process of drying and frying. Workers, stripped to the waist, stood in front of a gigantic iron cauldron, stirring the plants inside.

The preparations gave off pungent and repulsive odors that forced the committee members to leave the processing plant and move to the pharmacy next door, which was also an eye-opener. Above a table with red candles and coiled incense hung a portrait of Shen Nong, the mythical father of agriculture. The Chinese interpreter explained that he was also the founding father of Chinese medicine. Esteemed by the Chinese, like Pan Gu, who created the universe by separating heaven and earth, Shen Nong taught the early Chinese to till the land and harvest the five grains. Legend had it that he beat hundreds of grasses with his omnipotent red whip to determine their medicinal nature. The committee members smiled, but the disbelief and disdain in their smiles only deepened the fantastic and mythological nature of the legend. Qu Yabing also smiled. The director and duty supervisors understood only too well the meaning of those smiles. Their faces reddened; how they wished they would be permitted to quote the classics and inform these men that Shen Nong had tasted seventy different kinds of plants in a single day. But, like chickens talking to ducks, they could not possibly get their ideas across, so they simply looked away in silent anger.

The committee next focused its attention on the gigantic medicine cabinet standing against the wall, noticing that every drawer was inscribed with Chinese characters indicating the names of the herbs inside. Qu Yabing asked the director to pick some herbs and define their therapeutic natures: Ma huang, or *Herba ephedrae*, is used for coughs with bronchodilative effects; Chang shan, or *Radix dichroae*, consists of several antimalarial agents; Ku lian, or *Cortex meliae*, is effective in expelling tapeworms; Shi gao, or *Gypsum fibrosum*, alleviates mild symptoms of high fever and thirst; Dang gui, or *Radix Angelicae sinensis*, promotes blood circulation and regulates menstruation; Wu tou, or *Radix aconiti*, helps alleviate stomachache and chest pains; Chai hu, or *Radix bupleuri*, also helps with fever associated with common colds, and so on. The rows of porcelain jars painted with blue flowers, and the copper and tin cans on top of the medicine cabinet, what are those for? To store even more rare and more valuable herbs. Someone standing alongside the black-lacquered counter was holding a tiny scale used to measure dosages prescribed by the Chinese doctors.

Imagine, the Chinese weigh the dosage of their medicine with a scale!

Then they came to the boiling room, where windows were open on three walls. The stove looked as big as a house. On each of the round openings of the honeycombed surface was a kettle. Female workers, cooking prescribed medicine at temperatures as high as the inside of a burning oven, were drenched in sweat. The committee members stuck their heads inside to watch the workers pick up kettles of boiling liquid, black as ink, a nauseating odor permeating the steam. For thousands of years, the poor Chinese had drunk this black herbal soup when they were sick! The committee members sighed. For them the national hospital located in the Western Garrison was a true hospital, a place where one saw nothing but whiteness—snowy white sheets; glaring white walls; clear, sparking glass pots and thermometers; shiny scalpels—with the smell of disinfectant filling the air.

On the previous Sunday, Adam Smith had gone to visit Pastor Thomas's daughter, Emily, who was hospitalized for acute chest pains on Good Friday evening. Three days later, the Easter breakfast held at St. John's Cathedral to celebrate the resurrection of Christ was joyless. Children dressed in their holiday best quietly searched for Easter eggs in the bushes, stifling their happy shouts of discovery, while the adults sat in church praying with more devotion than usual for Lord Jesus to bless Emily with an early recovery.

After the worship breakfast, the women came to the pastor's residence to comfort Emily's mother, Pandora.

Normally, these women would have been gossiping about what the high officials' wives had worn to church that day, or criticizing the outdated pattern and color of the hat worn by the governor's wife, or complaining about the weather and the boredom of life in the colony, or bragging about their own husbands. Then they would lower their voices and cover their mouths to whisper about some of the men and their mistresses. They were the wellspring of rumors in the colonial social circle.

"Did you see that carriage? The one by the church gate?"

"That's Emily Thomas's wagon. So what?"

"If you want to know who's a frequent passenger, that's what."

"Who is it? Tell me!"

Wanting to keep them in suspense as long as possible, the wife of a whisky merchant criticized Pandora, Pastor Thomas's wife, instead:

"Ladies, I'm sure you noticed Pandora's dress today—orange. My God, she looked like a volcano, an erupting volcano—"

"She is, after all, the wife of a pastor, and should not dress like that!"

"Louise, don't be so catty. Are you still upset because she didn't invite you to her Christmas party?"

The wife of the secretary to the director of the administrative bureau snickered, "Who cares about her party? People who went said it was a terrible party, the music, the cocktails, everything just horrible. They couldn't wait to leave. The pastor's wife knows nothing about social etiquette, inviting only those who toady up to her!"

"You can't blame her, given her background. Now, Mrs. Dickinson knew all about Pandora's past. So when poor Mrs. Dickinson left, there went Pandora's mortal enemy, and now she's free to do whatever she wants."

The gossiping women watched one another like hawks, full of pent-up hostility.

The wife of the whisky merchant gathered her parasol and handbag, as if to leave.

"If you ladies aren't interested in the person in Emily's carriage, then let it be. I'm off, see you next Sunday!"

"Well, earlier I saw Pandora leave with a young man. Was that—"

"Marianne, who was that man, anyway?"

Now that she had their attention, the wife of the whisky merchant sat down smugly.

"That man, I've asked around, his name is Adam Smith, the second son of a mill owner in Brighton. He arrived last year to serve as assistant director of the Sanitary Board. He works for Mr. Dickinson—"

"Worked," a schoolteacher corrected her. "Now the director of the Sanitary Board is Mr. Windsor. His wife—"

The other women sternly shut her up before turning back to the wife of the whisky merchant and begging her to tell them more.

"That poor young man! I think Pandora's planning something. Did you see how she nearly pushed him into the carriage—"

"But, where's the carriage taking him, that Smith?"

"Who cares? It was Emily's carriage, and that's enough for me."

The women exchanged knowing winks.

"Someone saw it with her own eyes. Emily kept that young man at the orphanage," the wife of the whisky merchant said with a singsong voice. "Every night, till midnight."

"Every night—"

The gossiping women covered their mouths with their handkerchiefs, silenced by shock.

"That young man, so skinny and pale, he doesn't look healthy to me—"

But all that was forgotten now, as the women came, their eyes moist, to see Emily's mother, Pandora, and to inquire about hospital visiting hours.

Adam Smith did not join the entourage of women visiting Emily's mother. Instead he walked past St. John's Cathedral and came to the Botanical Garden, where he stood in silence under a subtropical palm tree. Gently brushing the tag on the tree trunk, he was weighed down by his emotions.

After returning from the Tung Wah Hospital inspection trip, Adam Smith went to report to the director of the Sanitary Board.

Mr. Windsor had a visitor, a young man in formal dress and sporting a handlebar moustache. Smith apologized softly and turned to leave, but was stopped midway by his superior.

"Come in, Adam. This is Mr. Dent Jr., the nephew of a dear friend of mine. James, you don't mind, do you?"

The visitor shrugged indifferently, not saying a word.

"Adam, you've heard of the famous Dent & Co., haven't you? It belongs to James's uncle."

Smith was awestruck. Dent & Co. was one of the oldest firms in the colony. Its oceanside Victorian building in Central towered over the harbor, signifying the fruits of the British Empire's maritime expansion It was a symbol of veneration for adventurers who sailed the seas. One of the Dent & Co.'s businesses was the coolie trade, in which the company profited from kidnapping Chinese from southern China and shipping them like swine to South America for sale. Only a year before, one of their ships, the *Calvin,* had shipped 298 Chinese coolies to Cuba. En route, 45 percent of them had died of neglect, attracting the attention of the British government, which ordered an investigation. The verdict by the Hong Kong Supreme Court was predictable: "The deaths of a large number of Chinese were not caused by human error. It was God's will." The shipowner was fined 50 pounds, and the case was closed.

With God on the side of Mr. Dent, the Chinese were doomed to be sacrificed. But to everyone's astonishment, even Dent & Co. suffered losses. The arrogant young Mr. Dent Jr. had come to the director with bad news. A riot had broken out on a ship named after his Aunt Caroline, and the ship was pillaged in the South Sea. The coolies locked in the hold were thought to have broken down the iron bars, overcome the armed seamen, and joined forces with pirates preying on the Canton coast. The company had lost contact with the *Caroline,* its whereabouts unknown.

"They're worse than animals. If they're caught—and they will be caught—I am going to personally oversee their punishment. I shall have them tied together to the railing by their ridiculous queues, in groups of ten, and flogged to within an inch of their lives . . ." Junior's face, distorted by anger, looked savage and terrifying." Then we shall pour saltwater on their backs, and see if any of those animals ever dare to run away again."

"I've told your uncle many times that slave trading is a risky business. His old profession was safer." Mr. Windsor slowly blew out some smoke. "The opium trade is a safe, gentlemanly enterprise."

Then Mr. Windsor pointed his pipe at Smith, who, not having been asked to sit, was standing by deferentially. "So, you've been to Tung Wah Hospital. We sent some gentlemen to enlighten these ignorant people about their barbaric ways of treating illness, James. Drinking black weed soup, indeed. How disgusting! Did you take a gun with you, Adam? When you go to the Chinese shantytowns, you must arm yourself in case the natives decide to attack you."

"Yes, Mr. Windsor, I took my gun along."

"But who knows, perhaps the natives were afraid to provoke you. James, this fellow put a torch to the plague zones, in forty-degree heat. He entered the most severely affected areas and came out alive," Mr. Windsor mumbled. "The plague couldn't touch him."

Twisting his handlebar moustache, Junior smirked at Smith, not saying a word; it was clearly beneath his dignity.

That afternoon Mr. Windsor invited Smith along on a bird-watching outing he had arranged for Sunday. Smith's superior's extravagant outing took him by storm. After stepping down from his sedan chair, Mr. Windsor leisurely selected a vantage point to watch the birds, then took a pair of high-powered binoculars from his slavish manservant. When he tired of standing, a folding chair was gently placed under him.

The picnic was equally impressive. With a snap of Mr. Windsor's fingers, a giant umbrella materialized, as if by magic, above a dinner table covered with a snowy white tablecloth. As if they were serving a party in his hilltop house, the maids brought up a plate of cold, boneless chicken and Scottish smoked salmon. Then a male servant, a white towel draped over his shoulder, uncorked a bottle of Moët champagne and poured it into mirrorlike crystal flutes. The picnic ended with pudding and a fruit medley of grapes and apples.

This outing to Mipu awakened Adam Smith's determination to imitate and learn from the upper class. From now on, he would study Mr. Windsor's every move, using him as a model for appropriate social etiquette and manners. Smith was confident that, given time, he could transform himself into a proper gentleman and act with dignity in front of his Chinese employees. The authority of the colonizers—Mrs. Windsor's favorite phrase. His commanding style would gain respect from the Chinese. The life of an aristocrat on an English estate was beyond his reach, of course. So he took the view of the government officials and taipans, who said they needed to start anew in this remote colony, enjoying the gentleman's life behind closed doors: four consecutive days of horse racing in Happy Valley in February, boating races in the spring and winter, polo on three-acre lawns, and bird-watching in the countryside on weekends.

The following month, a Gilbert and Sullivan musical was scheduled for the concert hall. Smith had already ordered two tickets, but hadn't decided whom to invite. Then there was the celebration for Queen Victoria's sixtieth year on the throne the following February, for which Mrs. Windsor had already begun worrying about what to wear. If that weren't enough, the image of the arrogant James Dent Jr. in his formal attire flickered past Smith's eyes. So he decided to make oblique inquiries into the best tailors.

Smith returned to the Chinese-style building one last time, only to see that the place had changed beyond recognition. He knew everything on the other side without having to look through the cracks in the wooden window frame, for on long, sleepless nights, his mind's eye had roamed through every corner of the house, his hands touching each table, every chair. He was the master of that house; everything inside it belonged to him, including the woman who had turned her back to show her displeasure at his long absence, and the maid, Ah Mei, who, with her downcast eyes, was always ready to kneel down to serve him. Even the smells, a mingling of powder, rouge, the grassy odor of touch-me-not, the coiled mosquito incense, and the fragrance of jasmine nectar, with which she later covered her body to seduce him—it all belonged to him.

As he sought out the smells, he opened his eyes, a glint flickering in his dimmed irises. A new lamp appeared to have replaced the old one, for the other side of the window was brightly lit. This was not the shadowy harem he knew. There, he would hold up a candle to shine on the naked female body, starting from the mysterious long black hair that cascaded like a waterfall. Every spot highlighted by candlelight brought immense surprise and pleasure. Then he would put down the candle and lower himself onto the bed to become intertwined with that naked body. Shifting shadows on the plaster walls were indistinguishable; there was no way to tell which was his and which was hers.

But the shadows were gone now. The house was much brighter than before, which provoked a strange, alien feeling in Smith. The mirror she'd used to make herself up so alluringly, taking him hostage, still stood by the dresser in the corner, but now it was covered by a piece of nondescript cloth. The three-stringed lute that used to rest on the chair was nowhere in sight. Finally, Smith let his eyes drift to the spot he'd been avoiding the whole evening. The bed on which he'd spent countless bewitching nights seemed to be in a different place. The silk curtains and drapes he'd personally chosen to increase the romantic feeling of a harem had been replaced by a white mosquito net that sealed the bed off, protecting the person inside—if there had been someone in there.

It was this mosquito net that had brightened up the house. Wiping the cold sweat beading his white eyebrows, Smith felt his forehead with his hand. Was the sight before him merely an illusion caused by delirious fever? This pure, white mosquito net could not belong to the woman he knew, the former prostitute at Southern Tang House on Lyndhurst Terrace. Unless the place had changed owners. Could Huang Deyun have moved away, after waiting for him by the door for so long? Had she finally disappeared from his life?

Could it be that God had finally answered his prayers to end this karmic relationship, expelling from his heart the woman who had led him into licentious corruption? He promised to return God's grace with faith and sacrifice and to resume his past life of spirituality. He couldn't wait to erase his ignominious past, so that when he faced Mrs. Windsor, he would no longer be shamed by his whoring ways. His self-loathing would vanish. At dance parties on Sunday afternoons, he could hold his head up as he chatted with her about the music of the Calcutta Military Band. Better yet, he might even play a minor role in the amateur drama performance at the concert hall in the fall, to pass the long, monotonous days in the colony.

And yet, as he faced the white mosquito net, he did not experience the relief he'd hoped for. For too long he had submerged himself in the passionate suffering of loving a woman he should not have loved. Endless conflict and struggle had enabled him to feel the substance of life, a full life. Hopeless love had weakened him, but at the same time, his longing for illicit pleasure and the resultant happiness of breaking faith with his upbringing had made him feel that he was truly alive.

He removed his sweaty forehead from the windowpane. What did his future hold now, except for emptiness and ennui? He felt a heavy sense of loss. He had signed a three-year lease, so he should have been the first to know if there had been any changes.

If the taipans of Happy Valley got wind of this, they would thrust out their bulging, well-fed necks and burst out laughing, mocking the inexperienced Smith, who had spoiled his woman. These wealthy opium merchants had their own way of rewarding the women they kept: they tossed newly minted coins to the floor to enjoy the sight of their women down on all fours to retrieve them. They would surely shake their heads in disgust if they knew that the shy Adam Smith had stuffed the monthly expenses and an extra gift under a pillow before dressing and leaving in the mornings. They would say that the mill owner's son still had a lot to learn.

When he returned from Happy Valley, Smith summoned his Chinese interpreter, Qu Yabing, and handed him an onionskin envelop that bore no signature.

"Take this to Happy Valley," he ordered officiously. "Give it to her. No need to report back."

Taking the heavy envelope, Qu Yabing could tell from the touch that it was filled with twenty-cent and ten-cent silver coins, perhaps also some copper pennies.

"Of course, sir, don't worry. I'll take care of it, sir."

Qu Yabing stood for a moment with his feet together, before lowering his eyes and walking out deferentially.

Adam Smith stood up at his desk and walked over to the window. The flame tree was covered with new leaves, like an open umbrella, and it was easy to envision the fiery red flowers that would bloom in the summer. As his glance moved downward, Smith noticed that the ground was littered with tender young branches, blanketed by twigs and fresh, saw-toothed leaves, like a grave mound. There had been no wind during the night, so someone must have cut them down and hacked them to pieces. Smith's cheek began to twitch. Unnerved by the sight outside his window, he took a deep breath and turned away, content to have the entanglements of his youth buried with the twigs and branches that had been ripped from the tree before they'd had a chance to mature.

Following his superior's instruction, Qu Yabing said nothing about the task he'd been given. The former prostitute of Southern Tang House on Lyndhurst Terrace may have disappeared without a trace, but only to her English lover, Adam Smith. The chronicle of her days with Qu Yabing, Chinese interpreter for the Sanitary Board, was about to begin.

PART

TWO

1

On his thirtieth birthday, the Chinese interpreter Qu Yabing picked up a newly arrived copy of the magazine *London Hunter* at the English-language bookstore on Queen's Road and returned to the Sanitary Board, where he presented the magazine to Adam Smith. After handing it to him with both hands, he stepped back and lowered his hands to his sides, asking his superior respectfully if there were anything else required of him. As he flipped through the pages of the magazine, Smith waved the man away without so much as looking up. On the latest bird-watching outing to Mipu, the Sanitary Board director, Mr. Windsor, had shared a piece of exciting news with him. The hunting rifles he had left at the manor of his aristocratic uncle had been packed up and put in the mail that should arrive in Hong Kong with the next liner. Mr. Windsor, who had a nose for the hunt, judged that the rugged hills ringing Kowloon Harbor would offer excellent hunting grounds, and he was already making arrangements to test his theory. Adam Smith, who summoned up the courage to volunteer his services to assist Windsor, sent in a subscription to the hunting magazine as soon as he returned home, in hopes of adding to his meager knowledge of the sport.

"If there is nothing else, Sir, thank you."

With a low bow, Qu Yabing turned and tiptoed out of the office, softly closing the door behind him. He heaved a sigh. Adam Smith would be settling in for the rest of the afternoon to read his new magazine, absorbing its wisdom like a sponge, and would not have any more errands for Yabing until the end of the day. On most days, Yabing sat in a chair in Smith's outer office with his arms crossed, in a state resembling combat readiness. At the first sign of movement inside, he sprang to his feet and stood respectfully at the door, awaiting orders from his superior. There was little to do at the Sanitary Board once the plague had passed, except for the brief period of frenetic activity during the monthly cleaning. Some of the time, Qu Yabing sat there bored, counting the red bricks on the floor, over and over, just to pass the time. The bricks to the right were lighter in color than the others, since they were in the path of direct sunlight. The green paint on the window was peeling, which was an eyesore at the Sanitary Board. No one, not even the second in command, Adam Smith, had the courage to bring the cockroach-infested men's toilet to the attention of the director. The first thing Mr. Windsor had done upon taking charge of the board was to have his office renovated.

"My God," he had exclaimed with an exasperated sigh, "get rid of all this vulgar, disgusting bourgeois trash!"

Not only was the paint peeling but also the area beneath the eaves was probably filled with cobwebs, Qu Yabing was thinking, as if it were of no consequence to him. He just sat there day in and day out, his arms crossed, watching the sky change colors, frequently gazing up at the clock to confirm the passage of time. His guesses were more often right than wrong, and today was no exception. The hours seemed to crawl by until quitting time, when he could softly open the door to his superior's office and stand in the doorway, his head bowed meekly.

"Sir," he'd murmur, "if you no longer require my services, is it all right for me to leave?"

Then he would bow to his superior, who wouldn't even deign to look up, and back out of the room, to return to his bachelor's quarters next to Victoria Prison, in the manner of an animal burrowing into its cave as night fell.

Over the past two weeks or so, Adam Smith had gotten into the habit of going home early, leaving Qu Yabing to guard the fort until quitting time, when he would, by force of habit, softly open the door and ask the empty office for permission to leave for the day. Today was his thirtieth birthday, a significant milestone in a man's life, and no one but he had remembered it. He felt very much alone, a man with neither family nor friends, the only person with whom he had been close now lying in the cold ground. After handing over the magazine, Qu Yabing sat in the outer office, his arms crossed, listening to the sound of pages being turned on the other side of the door. It was an oppressive afternoon, but that didn't keep the hands of the wall clock from moving along. Time was passing more quickly than usual, causing Yabing's heart to beat faster. The past twenty-nine years had slipped by in silent obscurity, and there was no need to try to relive them. Today constituted a new beginning, so why was he sitting there with his arms crossed and letting time pass him by without a sound?

To commemorate this special day, he had rummaged through his bureau to take out clothing he wore only once a year, at New Year's. His cotton trousers were still nicely creased, and his cloth shoes were so new he stepped lightly as he walked to keep them that way. He had shaved his head for the occasion, and his forehead glistened. He couldn't sit where he was until the shine faded and the pallor returned, and now that the sky was darkening, he was eager to get away from this lifeless office and out on the town to celebrate his birthday. The teahouses at the Central Market were still open, and there was time to enjoy a pot of thick, fragrant Pu'er tea and a plate with his two favorite snacks: shrimp pot stickers and buns stuffed with barbecued pork. And since it was his birthday, he had to have a bowl of longevity noodles. Right, I'll order a bowl of beef noodles. Picking up the long noodles with his chopsticks, he would recite the phrase "Long Life—Good Luck" before shoveling them into his mouth. If extravagance was called for—he jiggled the coins in his pocket—he might wave the waiter over and shout, "Bring me a plate of piglet and roast goose slices and a small bottle of double-distilled Zhujiang rice liquor. It's a special occasion, and I'm going to drink to my heart's content!"

At this thought, Qu Yabing could no longer sit still. He jumped up from his chair and, in high spirits, opened Smith's door a crack. But his courage failed him; clearing his throat softly, he said, "Sir—"

His superior ignored him from behind the desk. His face turning ashen, Yabing froze with his hand on the doorknob. After a moment, Adam Smith waved impatiently, without looking up, as if he were chasing away an annoying fly.

"Close the door and go."

Thus scolded, Qu Yabing felt as if he had received a pardon. Walking out of the Sanitary Board, arms swinging, he was drawn to the Western Garrison Market by the imaginary aroma of roast piglet. As he had anticipated, the Minru Teahouse was still open for afternoon tea. Braised pork, fried chicken, piglet, and roast goose hung in the window, lightly charred and dripping oil, making his mouth water. This teahouse was famous for its delicious dim sum and excellent tea. Every time he walked by, he lingered before the newly roasted meat, thinking that one day he'd jangle the coins in his pocket and swagger into the teahouse, where the waiter, in white shirt and black pants, would walk up with a long-spouted aluminum kettle, remove the lid of his cup, and pour him some tea.

But now, squeezing the coins in his pocket, Qu Yabing stood outside, unsure if he should go in or not. A gust of wind hit him from behind, as two gentlemen in silk-embroidered, padded robes swaggered into the shop. One of them, who was holding an ivory fan, appeared to be the owner of the pawnshop next door. Qu Yabing instinctively reached out to hold open the door that was about to close and stuck his head inside. His eyes first fell on the spittoons on the floral tiles, one at the foot of each black-lacquered table. A waiter, aluminum teakettle in hand, his queue coiled on top of his head and his pant legs tied for ease of movement, immediately set down his kettle and bowed, inviting his guests upstairs.

"The best seats are upstairs, waiting there for you."

Fancy satin shoes, one pair following the other, climbed the stairs to the left, the embroidered silk robes billowing in tiny gusts of wind. As Qu Yabing let go of the door and looked down at his idiotic black cloth shoes, the coins in his pocket promptly lost their weight. He gave up on the idea of having tea inside and walked out from under the portico, where he joined the crowd of pedestrians. A porter, carrying a bundle of firewood over his shoulder, was banging into people, but they didn't seem to notice or slow down on their way to their destinations. All except for Qu Yabing, who rubbed his chin and ambled aimlessly amid the torrent of humanity. This particular street was lined with stores—Deren Ginseng and Exotic Herb Shop, Zhaojihao Money Exchange, Xinglong Soy Sauce Store, Hengxinghao Grocery, Deyue Bakery, Guangzhou Hualong Silk Shop, Zhengjiyuan Papier-Mâché Shop—but he couldn't enter any of them. Standing beneath one of the porticos, Qu Yabing silently faced his own forlorn shadow. On this special day, he wanted to grab hold of something belonging to him, something he could savor over and over when he was old, gray, and toothless.

"Xingchang Photos and Portraits." An ad on one of the pillars caught his eye. Since when had British photo studios started to appear in the Chinese section? He'd been to Victoria Photo and Portraits on Queen's Road to pick up a photograph for the former head of the Sanitary Board, Mr. Dickinson. But that was long before Mr. Dickinson had fallen ill with the plague.

Qu Yabing had followed Mr. Dickinson's directions in search of the place, which was a dark room on the second floor, with black curtains hung on all four sides. Light streaming in through the stairwell enabled him to see a wall filled with black and white paper on which there were small human faces. A bearded Englishman was covering a box with a piece of black velvet, exposing a tripod underneath. Even though it was the middle of the day, opposite the black box was an English gentleman in a formal Mandarin gown, complete with white gloves and a top hat. Qu listened absent-mindedly as the bearded *guailow* complained about how Hong Kong's humidity had ruined the chemicals he'd shipped from London. He also said something about silver-plate photography and wet-glass plate negatives—a process entailing the smearing of fresh egg whites and other ingredients on a glass plate prior to exposure, something not made for photographers traveling long distances.

"I use bright lights on dry plates," the bearded man added, "instead of egg whites. That way I can reduce the exposure time."

Qu Yabing understood only the word "lights." When the bearded *guailow* wasn't looking, he reached out and touched the sheets of paper on the wall. They were flat, but the faces on them looked just like those of shrunken heads, some of which were smiling at him. These photographs were altogether different from the pictures at the Yuxingtong Terrace on Wellington Street. Mr. Dickinson had once sent him there to pick up an oil painting of a boat with raised sails. He saw the painter, with rolled-up sleeves, adding color to the canvas with a long brush as he stood on a desk.

The bearded *guailow* took down a picture from the wall; it was a portrait of Mr. Dickinson, his jaw squeezed square by the starched collar. He was sitting shoulder to shoulder with a long faced, curly-haired woman, probably his wife. Behind them was an embroidered Chinese screen with orioles flying toward swaying willow branches. Did the Britons on the Peak have screens like that in their houses? Qu Yabing had yet to find an answer to his question, for after poor Mr. Dickinson died from the plague, his wife must have taken that photograph back to England.

Originally operated by the Britons on Queen's Road, the many photo studios had now spread to the Chinese district in Central. Since he couldn't bring himself to enter Minru Teahouse, Qu Yabing felt the coins in his pocket and considered having his picture taken at the photo studio. He'd never have another thirtieth birthday. He even mapped out the pose and smile: his hands on his knees, legs spread, looking straight into the black box—now he knew the source and function of the flash. Everything had to be perfect, eyes and ears showing and no shadows around his nose.

The thought of having his photo taken reminded Qu Yabing of his poor mother, who had coughed up one last mouthful of black blood before dying of consumption. He'd been so overcome with filial grief that he'd even forgotten to have a charcoal picture drawn of her by a painter who set up his stall by the Tung Wah Hospital gate. If he'd had her likeness by the spirit tablet, his bachelor dorm next to Victoria Prison would not have seemed so lonely and bleak.

At her grave site, he made a silent vow that when he'd saved up some money, he'd have a papier-mâché shop craft a cushioned sedan chair, some servants, and a fully furnished Chinese-style building, so she'd have everything she needed in the netherworld. He looked up and saw that he'd arrived at Zhengjiyuan Papier-Mâché Shop; he took out the coins, still warm from his hand, to fulfill his promise to his deceased mother. Then, with the change he received, he bought two eggs and a small batch of noodles, before glumly returning to his room next to Victoria Prison.

After cooking the longevity noodles in the yellow light of the setting sun, he picked them up with his chopsticks, but his stomach felt bloated and his throat tightened up after only a few mouthfuls. Unable to swallow any more, he touched his wet face, unsure if it was sweat or tears. Putting down his bowl, he stared blankly at the lime wall, feeling his face get wetter and wetter. It was tears, but he didn't feel like wiping them away; he just sat there weeping quietly.

Dusk surged into his room, but he remained sitting there, not getting up and going out until it was so dark he could barely see his fingers. An evening wind dried his tear-streaked face, turning it taut and sore, as if covered by a transparent membrane. It still wasn't completely dark outside. Even in broad daylight, the prison area was an unlucky place that people tried to avoid; now it was more deserted than ever, like a ghost town, where even the turbaned Sikh guard was nowhere to be seen. Standing beneath the crude stone prison wall, Qu Yabing looked up but couldn't see the top. For the prisoners inside, each day must seem like a year; they too probably grumbled about the boredom of life. The prison gate was locked, of course, but there was a small door to the left for visitors. While he was watching, the door opened for a woman with a black scarf over her head. She emerged in a crouch, carrying an empty bamboo basket. Her prison visit over, the latest parting in her life—probably from her husband—she was drained, physically and emotionally, and walked off unsteadily. Yet even a convict gets food and sympathy from his kin, and as he watched the woman stumble off, Qu Yabing reflected on the fact that he'd had to buy his own birthday noodles.

With his forehead pressed against the coarse wall, Qu Yabing longed for someone to talk to before his thirtieth birthday was over. There was, he recalled, that lonely woman in Happy Valley. On the first of each month, his legs carried him down the hill to the prostitute who had been kept and then abandoned by his superior, Adam Smith. He would toss a packet of new coins onto her table, telling her it was her monthly allowance from the *guailow*. On his first visit, the woman had shouted, "Is the *guailow* dead or have his feet rotted off? Why send a slave like you?"

The following month, she had received the charity with a cold face, not uttering a word of thanks. Rebuffed and feeling totally redundant, Qu Yabing wondered why he hadn't simply handed her all the packets at once. That way he'd only have needed a single visit to carry out his duty. On his most recent visit, the woman had opened the door as soon as she'd recognized his voice. With a frown on her ashen face and a swollen belly, she'd moved with difficulty, eliciting Qu Yabing's sympathy. He'd offered to help her with the heavy housework, such as chopping firewood and drawing water from the well. She'd sat there in her rosewood chair, resting her elbows on the table, her belly pushed up tight under her breasts, biting her lip, as if finding it hard to speak, and she had merely shaken her head slowly. He'd had no choice but to leave, as she struggled to her feet, swaying dizzily. Startled, Qu Yabing had gestured for her to keep her seat.

"I can let myself out," he'd said as he backed up. "Please don't get up."

"But I have to close and lock the door. The woman from the herbal store told me that trouble has been brewing out at sea in recent days."

The knowledge that someone had come to look in on her had eased Yabing's concern. After walking outside, he had turned for a last look at Huang Deyun, who had followed him to lock the door. He could sense her fear, the sort of crippling dread of someone who had no control over her own fate.

But today was only the fourteenth, two weeks before he was due to give her the allowance. He arrived at her door, still trying to dream up an excuse for his visit. The door was slightly ajar, and his heart skipped a beat as he recalled her comment about pirates causing trouble. Suddenly, a tortured scream, more animal than human, tore through the crack in the door; with a stagger, he burst in through the door.

"Let me die. I don't want to live anymore!"

Spread out on the four-poster bed, Huang Deyun was clutching the headboard behind her, her body wracked by convulsions. Sweat had soaked her hair and stained her blouse. More ear-piercing, terrifying screams forced Qu Yabing to steady himself by grabbing hold of the table. He stood there stunned in the flickering candlelight, not knowing how he'd gotten involved in such an appalling situation. His original intention had been quite simple: unwilling to spend his birthday alone in that bachelor's dorm, he'd thought of the woman in Happy Valley, with whom he shared a similar fate. If she didn't want to talk, he thought, he'd sit quietly with her under the candlelight, which would be better than being alone. Little by little, Huang Deyun's wariness and animosity toward him had lessened, and he was fairly confident she wouldn't send him packing.

But now he'd gotten himself into a hellish situation, assaulted by inhuman screams that tore from the woman's body. He had to escape. But as he was moving to the door, it was pushed open from the outside, and two women rushed into the room. The one in front, a midwife, laid down the cloth bundle she was carrying and climbed up onto the bed to feel the pregnant woman's belly. The other woman dragged Qu Yabing into the kitchen to help her boil water.

"The birthing room is no place for a man, what with all that blood," the woman said as she started a fire. "You work for that *guailow*, right? She told me everything. Ai! Talk about karmic retribution! She didn't take any precautions when she was with that *guailow*, and who knows what kind of monster she'll give birth to? Our old Chinese doctor is a nice man who feels sorry for her now that she's pregnant and the *guailow* and her maid have both left. He told me to check on her every few days. She seems okay. Says she's from Dongguan, kidnapped at the age of thirteen and sold to a local brothel.

"It's fate. That beauty mark on her cheek has ruined her life."

The woman picked up a basin of hot water, walked out of the kitchen, and turned to remind Qu Yabing to stay out of the room. With the glare from the stove, he could see the untouched dinner on the table: a bowl of soup, a plate of stir-fried leeks and half a bowl of soupy rice noodles that had soaked up the liquid and turned into a sticky mess. She'd probably just sat down and picked up her chopsticks when the contractions sent her running into the other room. He smirked, without being aware of it. This daughter of a Dongguan sandalwood-harvesting family ought to be running up Fragrant Hill with her girlfriends to gather incense, hoarding the best of it to sell on their own. The renowned Dongguan Girls' Incense. How had she come to Hong Kong and let a green-eyed, high-nosed *guailow* plant his awful seed in her and then cruelly abandon her, leaving her to face the greatest terror in life, except for death itself, all alone?

The agonizing screams from the front room were getting worse. Covering his ears with his hands, Qu Yabing tucked in his head and sat down. The fire in the stove had died out, dimming the light in the kitchen. His thirtieth birthday was nearly over, and his only company was the cold, uneaten dinner. Darkness quickly enveloped, then swallowed him up. Darkness, his constant companion. In his bachelor's dorm, he'd walk around in the dark, too lazy to light a lamp. He had nothing to look forward to, no emotional entanglements; his heart was shrouded in darkness even during the day. Throwing up his hands, he followed orders like a zombie, toiling at his superior's behest. When he wasn't being ordered around, he'd sit outside his superior's office, staring with dead-fish eyes at the clock on the wall, waiting for the hands to move to five o'clock, when he would drag his feet, like an animal returning to its den at night, and hide in his dark room. Over and over and over.

He did not belong here. Out in the front room, three women were working, each carrying out her duty, to bring a new life into this world. Drenched in sweat, they were exhausted from their battle with death. Through their combined effort, several times they dragged the two lives in one body back from the gate of hell. Two women kneeling on the messy, filthy, muddy straw mat wrestled with the one lying down. Her shouts rattled the roof tiles, but he was blocked from participating in the drama. He stood to leave, after remembering to throw some kindling into the stove. The fire flickered a few times and began to burn brightly.

By then the front room, on the other hand, had sunk into an inauspicious silence. Qu Yabing stood still and pricked up his ears; suddenly, a loud baby's cry broke the deadly silence.

"Hurry, go tell his daddy," the midwife said, holding the newborn baby in her arm as she poked the younger woman with her elbow, "that it's a boy. My, what a big nose!"

The other woman wiped her sweaty face with her sleeve and whispered something to the midwife, who, with a doubtful look, held the baby up to the candlelight to scrutinize him. What the other woman had said now made sense.

"No wonder he's so big, six or seven kilograms. I'll take a closer look when he has his first bath on the third day."

The other woman carried the basin back into the kitchen. The man had left, but the fire was burning brightly.

"I'm glad he's gone. It's not his baby," the other woman said.

2

Whenever someone from the royal family visited Hong Kong, everyone in the colony, from the governor down to the last civilian, created an extravaganza to welcome the honored guest; lanterns and festoons were displayed everywhere, starting at Queen's Pier. When the queen's son, His Majesty the Prince, stopped in Hong Kong on his return to the United Kingdom after visiting India, the governor led the local Chinese gentry in their formal robes and fancy vests to greet him at the pier. That night the Chinese leaders pooled their money to entertain the prince with gourmet Chinese food. As he was leaving, they presented him with an embroidered screen as a memento. On the screen were the words "God Save Our Prince."

Queen Victoria's Golden Jubilee in 1887 was celebrated in the colony with three days and nights of festivities, to which the citizens of Hong Kong were forced to contribute. An awesome display of peace and prosperity, an unprecedented grand occasion. Countless relatives of local residents came from Canton by boat to enjoy the spectacle. Ten years later, four continents around the globe took turns celebrating her sixtieth year on the throne of an empire where the sun never set. Hong Kong had begun planning a year before the event: the Administrative Department for Chinese Affairs called meetings of all professional guilds, selecting representatives to form a preparatory committee for the celebration for the queen's jubilee, which would last three days and two nights, an extravaganza that would cost millions of Hong Kong dollars.

On November 9 Governor Robinson dressed formally, complete with medals and feathered top hat, to inspect the army and navy. Then, following a brass band, he led a procession to pay tribute to the queen's statue before heading a parade along Des Voeux Road and Queen's Road. The local Chinese gentry also had their parades, taking different routes each day. Lion dances and dragon dances were performed to music outside the governor's office.

As the jubilant air of festivity spread to all corners of the island, Huang Deyun finally convinced Qu Yabing to go watch the celebration in Central with her. From their viewpoint at Wan Chai, they saw that Queen's Pier was brightly lit and enveloped in gleaming auras. The brightness seemed to push the dark sky higher and farther away. A lantern procession came down from the governor's office and slowly formed a cordon at Central to salute the queen's statue. The flower- and fish-shaped lanterns, with their large candles, looked real, so delicate and colorful that the spectators sighed in awe. The papier-mâché fruit plates and flower baskets also drew loud applause.

Without being aware of it, Huang Deyun, pumpkin lantern in hand, leaned against Qu Yabing as they joined the lantern procession. When they turned onto Des Voeux Road, a green light flashed before their eyes—it was a Qilin, a Chinese unicorn, made of silk. It seemed to drop from the sky, the golden embroidery on its body so dazzling it nearly blinded the parading crowd. Then a commotion broke out, disrupting the parade. People rushed forward like a tide, sweeping Huang Deyun along with it. She stumbled, and when she turned to look, Qu Yabing, who had been walking beside her holding a banner, had been swallowed up by the crowd.

She darted to the side of the road, where she held her pumpkin lantern high over her head, waiting for Qu Yabing to find her. But the crowd surrounding the green unicorn passed her by, wave after wave of people, and she didn't see Yabing anywhere. Not knowing what else to do, she let her feet take her back into the crowd as it headed toward Central, the Chinese business district, where the celebration took on an unusual flavor. On the street was a puppet platform decorated with a pavilion, a balcony, and a tower. Hidden from sight, the puppeteer played out a drama with his wooden figures.

Hong Kong's first Chinese commercial establishment, North and South Hong, had erected a magnificent celebration arch, spanning the shops on the east and west sides of the street. A golden glitter emanated from its carved beams and painted pillars, illuminating the red silk lanterns with long, golden tassels hanging imposingly above the walkway. Sikh guards stood by the arch, but curiosity got the better of Huang Deyun, who reached out to touch a column, with its carved dragons and phoenixes, when the guards weren't looking. To her surprise, it was made of paper over a bamboo frame, not carved wood, as she had thought. She sighed aloud over the exquisite workmanship, and her praise was echoed by a Western couple who had just come from a garden party. The woman, wearing a pink gown and elbow-length gloves, brushed her fingers against the upturned feathers of a phoenix. "How lovely . . . oh, it's made of bamboo and colored paper . . . impossible . . . it's so beautiful. . . ."

Huang Deyun nodded to the lady, and as she did, her glance fell on the profile of her male companion. For a moment she thought it was Adam Smith. Could it be really him? A year and a half earlier, she had tramped across every inch of the city, looking for the lover who had left without saying good-bye, the father of her child. But she never found the green building on the hill.

Afraid of being recognized, Huang Deyun stepped behind a column, heaving a sigh of relief in the dark. With her hand pressed down on her pounding heart, she stole another glance at the man, who was wearing a black top hat. A handlebar moustache rising stiffly above his upper lip made him look reserved and sober. Framed by the bright yet warm light of the red silk lanterns, the side of his face she could see wasn't pale as it had once been; now it was a pudgy, smug face. He was quite attentive, talking and laughing with his female companion, a sight that made Huang Deyun's heart ache. The father's name on the birth certificate of her month-old son, home asleep in Happy Valley, remained blank, and no baptismal record would ever be found in St. John's Cathedral. Even if her son were to be baptized in the church, the colonial government stipulated that, owing to the color of her skin, her name would not be recorded. Moreover, mixed-raced children were not allowed to use their Caucasian father's surname. They could, on the other hand, use his given name, such as George or Peter, as their surname, but that would require the natural father to come forward and openly admit paternity in front of his compatriots. These children would have great trouble finding a suitable match for marriage, and even when they did marry, their fathers would shy away from the humiliation of attending the wedding ceremony.

Oblivious to such discrimination, Huang Deyun felt that she could not let this moment go, that she must stop him before he held out his arm to the woman and left with her, that she had to take him to back to that Chinese-style building to rock his son, his own flesh and blood, in the cradle. When the father picked up his ugly and yet somehow lovely baby for the first time, she would step over to the window and, with her sleeve, shed dry tears over this reunion scene. But now she was frozen behind the column, agonizing over her inability to walk out into the open; she was shaking all over, as if wracked by malarial tremors. Holding her head in her hands, she leaned against the column, and in a matter of seconds, the couple had left. The red lanterns were still there, but their light had dimmed. Leaning her forehead against the column, she wondered if it had all been a dream. Adam Smith could not have been wearing a top hat, nor would he have had a moustache; and surely his cheeks would not be so pudgy. Was she simply eager to find a name for her illegitimate son, or had her feelings for Smith still not died?

Only the man who was now turning the corner and walking toward her was real. If he would let her—up till now he never had—she would go up and touch the loosely braided queue behind his head or the dirty shirttail of his gray shirt, its bamboo pattern displaying a special kind of softness, since it hadn't been washed for a long time. He was a bachelor who did not know how to take care of himself, but at least he was free, unlike the westerner, whose woman was by his side. The man's sleeves and trouser cuffs flapped as he walked, creating anxious gusts of winds, his black cloth shoes kicking up clouds of dust. Cold sweat beaded his shaved forehead, which had a greenish tinge. He had been looking frantically for the woman from whom he'd been separated, yet could not see that at that very moment she was standing just beyond the lights, waiting for him. Huang Deyun could not tell if she was happy or sad, but there was fullness in her heart. From the darkening center of the street, the man was walking toward her. Under his green-tinged forehead a gloomy face, as always, the dull skin scarred by scabs from smallpox, which were most prominent around his cheeks. His dark, purple lips were tightly closed. He was a thirty-year old, inarticulate bachelor, a Chinese interpreter who had no influence and no connections in the colony. He rarely looked into her face and did everything possible to avoid the sadness in her self-pitying eyes.

Huang Deyun smoothed her clothes to greet the man walking toward her. She had no choice; her life was like the lights, dimming with each passing moment. She was not concerned about her own future; it was all for the nameless son asleep in the Chinese-style building. The sacrifice was worth it. Finally Qu Yabing spotted her, and a light flickered in his gloomy eyes. Or did it just seem so in the fading lamplight? He rushed toward her but slowed down as he drew near.

She held out her hands to him, feeling the excitement of reunion. But rather than take her hands, Qu Yabing looked her over carefully to see if she was all right. For tonight's outing, she had put on clothes she'd worn before her pregnancy; the light green wool jacket with ruffled sleeves wrapped tightly around her full body was obviously too small. Surprised by his own discovery, Qu Yabing quickly lowered his eyes.

"It's getting late, and everyone's gone home. Let's head back."

3

"You've taken my virginity. It's all your doing."

Qu Yabing groused at Huang Deyun, who lay beside him. He'd been a thirty-year-old virgin. Since childhood, his mother, a devout Buddhist, had admonished him that lust was the greatest evil. Even on her deathbed, she had reiterated her caution with her last breath. Never once going against his mother's wish, he'd remained chaste, until he met the former prostitute, Huang Deyun. She had skillfully guided and instructed him. Slightly anxious, owing to ten months of abstinence, she had grappled with him as if engaged in a wrestling match, employing tactics she'd used on older, wealthy clients, but with double the effort. Unable to hold out, he'd fallen for the first time into the dark, damp interior of a woman, dizzy, chilled. He felt as if his body had been utterly discarded. His dead mother was turning over in her grave, glaring at him with angry eyes, the black hole of her mouth opening and closing silently, cursing his betrayal. Cold sweat coursed down the back of his neck, and he felt as if he'd been dredged out of water. He was swimming on a seemingly boneless female body; the sweat on his lashes blurred his vision, which he mistook as a sign of retribution and thought he'd gone blind. The shock forced him to pull out of the female body that was stuck to him like an octopus. He covered his eyes. I'm finished. A mother's punishment.

He turned and jumped off the prostitute's bed, opening his eyes a tiny crack, only to see the red bricks under his feet, which made him think of his own virgin blood. "You've taken my virginity. It's all your doing." He hurried back to his dorm room, where he swallowed three raw eggs as a tonic. On the following day, after work, he stopped by Lam Kwai Fong and bought a bouquet of withering purple daisies before going to see Huang Deyun. But when he was face-to-face with her, he lost his courage and was unable to hand the flowers to her as a westerner would. He dropped them on the table when she wasn't looking, then sat hugging his knees, as if nothing had happened. Stealing a glance at her, he saw she was wearing indoor clothes. Her arched breasts had dampened her blouse with milk, a sight that had him salivating. The woman he'd held in his arms the night before was there in front of him, and she would come to him if only he would reach out for her. But he held back, unwilling to surrender yet again.

Huang Deyun laughed inwardly. In her experienced eyes, a man like him, with his head tucked down between his shoulders, back arched, and droopy eyes, would not have been worth a second glance from her. Even if he could afford it, he would not likely have had the chance to touch her.

The night before, just as she was about to give herself to him, she was reminded of the Western couple who had taken in the sights with her by the celebration arch at North and South Hong. As nonchalantly as possible, using words she'd rehearsed countless times, she asked about the whereabouts of the heartless Englishman.

"Transferred to Calcutta," he answered casually. "He went on an East India Company ship. Britons were needed to put down some riots there."

Afraid she might not believe him, he added, "I saw him off myself. He left last month, on an East India Company ship."

Huang Deyun sighed and closed her eyes. That's it, then. For the sake of the poor baby in the cradle, she slowly unbuttoned her blouse. The man-child curled up on the bed, terrified at the prospect of losing his virginity, yet aroused to the point of uncontrollable tremors. With an air of wickedness, she winked at the thirty-year-old man-child. When the last button was undone, she held the blouse open like a flag, exposing her body to him. Taking his sweaty, clawlike hand, she rested it on the milk-filled breast of a new mother. The hand uncurled to cup her breast, followed by an unexpected squeeze. She tossed her head back and released a moan that had nothing to do with the pleasure of being caressed.

Tonight she would be a martyr, offering up her body to this inarticulate man, the tragedy of motherhood. Her body, it was all she had. Back at the brothel, she had used that supple body in exchange for money spent to buy her favors. She had then let her foreign lover run his fingers through her hair and cradle her disarmingly lovely face in his hands. A foreshortened moment of tenderness had left in its wake a child without a name. The space for father on his birth certificate remained blank, waiting to be filled in.

Let it be him, then. But this time it wouldn't be for just a night. The bodies that lay together would be those of a couple united forever; she would give herself to him and become his wife. As she struggled to move her face out from under the drenched body pressing down on her, she could not help but think about another pale, sweaty body, that of a young traveler far from home who had become a man atop the red vest of a prostitute. The same awkward movements, the same look on the face, turned away in embarrassment. The difference was that the other pale body had been given to her unconditionally, pouring all his passion into her, until they had melted into one. She would never forget that love; she had no regrets.

Beginning on the night of the festivities, Huang Deyun never again wore her light green blouse, with its ruffled sleeves, not because it was too small to accommodate her nursing breasts, but because she did not want to be seen again in the green and blue colors of a prostitute once she had decided to give herself to Qu Yabing. Although they were not formally married, she secretly promised her heart to him; in her mind, she was a married woman, no longer a prostitute. After shedding the colors of a prostitute, she dressed only in plain house clothes. Combing her hair into a loose bun at the back, she wore no makeup, even though her eyes were still fetching under her sparse brows. Tending to Qu Yabing like a wife, she darned his clothes and made his shoes. She followed the change of seasons and prepared tonics, with frequent trips to the Longevity Herbal Shop for herbs such as tuckahoe, angelica root, and wolfberry fruit, until Qu Yabing's dull face began to brighten; even his pockmarks glowed.

Qu Yabing no longer returned to his room each afternoon after work; instead he went straight to the house in Happy Valley. On this particular day, he noticed cooking smells wafting from the kitchen. With the baby on her back, Huang Deyun was stir-frying Chinese broccoli, while his favorite spareribs with bitter melon were stewing in a clay pot. The baby howled when drops of hot oil spattered on his tender skin. Without a word to the woman, Qu Yabing deftly took him from her and carried him away from the kitchen, where he stopped crying. Out in the courtyard, his clothes, freshly washed and hung out to dry, flapped in the evening breeze. A half-finished shoe sole lay on the bamboo chair, the uneven stitches showing that they had been done by someone who had yet to master needlework skills. She was making him a pair of cloth shoes. He freed one arm to pick up a handful of rice from a vat to feed the chickens by the well. Then he noticed that the firewood in the shed was nearly gone, so he put down the baby and found an ax. Rolling up his pant legs and coiling his queue atop his head, he split firewood in the dying light. He knew too that the water in the vat was low and that he must remember to fill it later.

Just the day before, Huang Deyun had asked him where in the courtyard to put up a trellis for the gourd vine. By the wall, so it can climb up? Or above the old well, so the gourds will hang down like lanterns? Straightening up, Qu Yabing leaned on his ax and looked around before deciding to put the trellis over the well. That way, on sweltering summer days, the adults could cool themselves in the shade, while the child rocked on his hobbyhorse. The boy was just learning to walk, and this would tickle him no end. Qu Yabing had thought of everything.

Huang Deyun came out to tell him that dinner was ready. Holding a half-filled washbasin and a soft towel over her arm, she waited as he washed up. He dried his hands and wiped his face before sitting down. She turned up the lamp wick, dusted the wood shavings from his shoulder, and, holding the baby in her arms, watched him eat the spareribs with bitter melon. The tip of his nose and his forehead shone under the lamplight as he ate heartily. There was nothing more she wanted from life. Back at the brothel, a rich client would spend a huge sum for a feast, at which bird's nest soup and shark's fin were common fare. When the parties began, each guest would have a prostitute standing behind to wait on him. Whenever her client was the host, she would be the hostess, standing behind the table and refilling the guests' glasses. When the shark's fin arrived, she would serve them. A sumptuous feast. Now, as she watched her man—at least that was how she regarded him—slurping the soup she had made, she felt that the nights of drinking, singing, and illicit sex belonged to another lifetime.

Everything was fine where the daily routine of firewood, rice, oil, and salt was concerned. But after they put the baby to sleep and climbed into bed naked, problems arose. Qu Yabing, still acting like a man tormented by the loss of chastity, would cross his arms and lie with his back to her. It was always Huang Deyun who had to play the role of seducer. She would reach out to tease him until he was aroused and reluctantly turned to face her. Angry with himself for not being able to resist, he was surprised to find that she also had her back to him. The difference was that her back was naked except for the thick, glossy hair lying against snowy white skin, so lovely it was nearly demonic. Her hair was silky to the touch. She was a naturally licentious woman who exuded lust, even from her back, and he wanted to devour her. When she sensed he was aroused, she rolled over and spread out seductively before him, like a blooming flower waiting to be plucked. Instinctively Qu Yabing closed his eyes, then opened them with his hand over his pounding heart. How could she expose her private parts in the light? What a shameless woman. He sat up to blow out the oil lamp, but she stopped him. Her cheeks were burning red, her naked body lying there like flowing water, waiting for him. She was turning intercourse in the dark into copulation in full view. She was a prostitute, a woman who made a living selling her body; when she stripped naked under the lamplight, she shed her sense of shame. I'm corrupted again, Qu Yabing sobbed inwardly. But it wasn't too late; he could still get up, put on his clothes, walk out of the prostitute's flat, and return to his bachelor's dorm next to Victoria Prison, where, with a blanket over his face in the dark, he could engage in self-gratification, which he had done often before surrendering his chastity to Huang Deyun.

Sex with the lights on! It must be a habit left over from the days of the Englishman. Resentfully, Qu Yabing spread his fingers and grabbed her breasts, which had swollen so much after childbirth that he could barely hold them in his hands. His ideal breasts had always been smaller ones that he could wrap his palm around, bestowing the pleasurable feeling of conquest. Feeling the pain in her breasts, she raised her head and tried to kiss him, like a hissing snake. He turned away; his bitterness would not allow him to gratify her. She had conquered the area below his neck, where she had total control, and he must thwart her assault on the last remaining territory. The way he twisted his face away from her was both comical and pathetic.

From then on, each time they finished in bed, he told her the story of how the pirate Xu Yabao killed two British officers who had raped a woman in Stanley. The two Britons, who were stationed at Stanley, got drunk one afternoon and broke into a house in a fishing village, where they assaulted a young woman. Her parents-in-law tried to stop them, only to be whipped by the Britons. Xu Yabao heard the villagers' cries for help on his ship and rushed ashore with his armed band, where they killed the two *guailow*. They then carried the bodies on bamboo poles to a cliff and tossed them into the sea. The authorities offered a reward of a hundred pounds for information leading to the arrest of Xu Yabao, but, of course, they failed miserably.

Qu Yabing repeatedly stressed how Xu Yabao, with his superior ability, came and went at will, but never revealed that a memorial was erected at St. John's Cathedral for the two British officers.

4

The second time Qu Yabing was sent by the Britons to deliver silver was in September 1898. It was three months after China and the United Kingdom signed a special treaty to develop and expand the New Territories, which would add 335 square miles to the colony. He was to meet the recipient of the silver, Lu Huan, the Magistrate of Xinan County, on a remote path in Fenling reputed to be frequented by tigers. Qu Yabing had been chosen to bribe an official of the Manchu court because of his background: he came from the most prominent family of Qintian Village in Xinan County.

James Stewart Lockhart, colonial secretary and registrar-general, had decided to collect information on possible resistance waged by residents of the New Territories, who had begun to raise a stink. Hearing that Lu Huan was an ineffectual and greedy magistrate, one who cared for nothing but money and was known for turning a deaf ear to the people's cries for help, Lockhart bribed him in order to be updated on the residents' course of action, which would then guide the colonial government's actions, with inside help, when the time came.

Carrying a parchment envelope stamped "Top Secret," Qu Yabing cowered behind an old banyan tree to wait for Magistrate Lu Huan's sedan chair. A mere courier following orders, he'd never expected that he himself would be betrayed. The calculating Lockhart, with his high nose and deep-set eyes, had informed Lu Huan beforehand that the courier, a member of the Qu clan, had reached an agreement with his clan members to cooperate with the colonial government's plan to take over the New Territories.

It was close to midnight when he heard straw sandals trampling on windblown sandy soil. Suddenly, two flickering red lanterns, like a tiger's half-closed eyes, came down the country path toward him. Magistrate Lu was in plain clothes, riding in a cushioned sedan chair with only two attendants; normally, his outings were an imposing procession, with clanging gongs and shouting attendants. He was two hours late, in order both to satisfy his opium craving and to show up the Britons. Qu Yabing, impatient after his long wait, leaped out from behind the banyan tree and ran toward the official. Dark figures appeared from the shadows like a flash to block his advance. After carefully checking his identity, they let him approach the sedan chair, on which the curtain parted, and the person inside cleared his throat to exhibit his authority. Bent at the waist, with his head bowed, Qu Yabing handed the envelope into the sedan chair with trembling hands.

"Sorry to trouble the magistrate." As soon the envelope was received, a lantern was moved into the sedan. Qu Yabing, still bent at the waist, stood aside respectfully, not raising his eyes. He heard the sound of the envelope being opened and cash certificates being removed. After a while, the magistrate snorted with a pompous, official air before stashing the certificates under the right side of his seat and taking out a paper packet from the left, which was placed into waiting hands, thus concluding the transaction. Holding the packet in his hands, Qu Yabing turned and quickly disappeared in the darkness.

The certificates would be cashed, and half the money would be presented to an official in the capital, a schoolmate of Lu Huan's who was swiftly rising through the ranks. Officials in the capital, serving at the feet of the emperor, were powerful and well informed, and if Lu Huan found the proper channel, he would become an insider and be in line for promotion. No one wanted to rot away in a remote corner of heaven and sea; the foreign devils had already bled the place dry, and he had no way of fattening his purse in an impoverished farm area.

With the certificates in hand, Lu Huan laughed at the foreigners for their poor business sense, since he had the upper hand. It was a simple matter for a magistrate to obtain information recorded in the county annals—population and maps—and the names of twenty-seven prominent figures in Xinan County. The red-haired, blue-eyed foreign devil spent so much money for this—how stupid! Still not satisfied that the mission had been accomplished, Lockhart used Qu Yabing as an intermediary to inform Lu Huan that he would personally call on the official. He took a scribe along, who spent three days copying a detailed land record of the New Territories. Then, alternating between threats and flattery, he sent Lu Huan to persuade and appease the twenty-seven prominent members of Xinan County, so that they would cooperate with the colonial government.

Qu Yabing conducted all his clandestine intermediary work between the Britons and the magistrate in the dark, until late October. One sweltering summer afternoon he was seen leading two Britons along the country path toward Qintian Village. He had recently been transferred to the Police Board, along with his superior, Adam Smith, who was wearing a straw hat to block out the scorching sun; a pair of binoculars hung around his neck. Their new boss, Colonel White, a heavy-handed police chief, admired Smith's courageous performance in incinerating contaminated houses in Mount Taiping at the height of the plague and had requested that Smith be assigned to him to work for the New Territories takeover. The new head of the Sanitary Board, Mr. Windsor, had stayed in London during the plague, delaying his departure for the colony to succeed the late Mr. Dickinson. Knowing he had no power to keep Smith, Windsor had been forced to permit the temporary assignment of his second-in-command to the Sanitary Board's longtime rival department, along with his Chinese interpreter, a member of the most prominent clan in Qintian.

Thirty-nine-year-old Colonel Douglas White came from a middle-class family in Newcastle, where he was to have succeeded his father as a shipbuilding engineer. But he joined the British Colonial Police instead, and had been stationed all over Asia: Fiji, Malaya, Burma, and now Hong Kong. He lived in a white Victorian house atop Mount Taiping, to which he dreaded each return at sunset. The abandoned garden was overrun by weeds and vines, while in the second-story bedroom lay his poor wife, paralyzed, like a doll with a broken neck. Only five years earlier, Colonel White had taken his new bride, Charlotte, by the hand and led her down the gangway at Queen's Pier, placed her in a red sedan chair carried by eight men, and ridden a horse in front of the sedan. He recalled how he had smiled at the bashful way she had stolen glances at him.

After the furniture, part of her dowry, arrived in Hong Kong, Charlotte busied herself with decorating the house, which, as it was built on the Peak, had unobstructed views of the ocean on all sides. She put the heavy oak bed, the chests, and the carved trunks in their bedroom, laid a Belgian shepherd rug on the living room floor, and hung oil portraits of their families along the staircase. She would dress in an embroidered satin, high-collared evening gown and long white gloves before sitting across from her husband in the candlelit dining room, where they would enjoy a dinner whose menu rarely changed: roast lamb, potatoes, and pudding for dessert.

That is how she spent her first winter in the colony.

When spring came, Charlotte displayed her gardening skills, planting rose branches that she had obtained from the garden at the governor's mansion. She wanted nothing less than an English garden at their house on Mount Taiping. The pungent smell of newly tilled soil hung over the garden, where a gardener followed Charlotte around with a watering can. White would sit at the window, cheeks lathered, feeling total contentment as a barber trimmed his beard.

Charlotte quickly became accustomed to life in the colony. On weekends and holidays, she would accompany her husband to Mipu to birdwatch. She enjoyed collecting seashells and broken ceramic pieces on the beach. Once, on their way home from the seashore, she stopped the sedan chair on the damp, shady side of the mountain to dig up some orchids, which grew wild among the roots of big tress, or out from under rocks. There were bamboo orchids with pointed leaves and light purple or pink flowers, crane's head orchids, with four-inch broad leaves and white flowers with a yellow center. Seeing his wife in her full-length white dress brushing the soil in the mountain dampness, a modern-day nymph, he felt he was the luckiest man on earth.

But the wild orchids could not survive the new environment. In that sunlit garden, which faced the ocean, they withered and died in two weeks. All that survived were the wild, aromaless roses, whose pure white flowers grew like wildfire.

She was greatly disappointed.

On the third spring after her arrival in the colony, Charlotte became pregnant. The trials of early pregnancy reduced her to skin and bones. White told her to stop worrying about the garden and begged her to stay in bed. But as soon as he left the house, she would get out of bed, put on her straw hat, and begin working in the garden. Once the rainy season arrived, she spent nearly every waking hour standing on the balcony to watch the never-ending drizzle and worry about the newly planted passion fruit, whose roots would surely rot away if the sun did not come out soon.

But the rain continued from morning till dusk. One evening, the maid tiptoed in the house to turn on the lamp. The rain had just stopped, and the house was the only bright spot as darkness enveloped the mountain. Clutching a shawl around her shoulders, Charlotte turned to walk inside, when a terrifying sight appeared before her eyes.

Tens of thousands of newly hatched termites, flapping their shiny yellow wings, swarmed up from the rotting wood, flying in through open windows and doors as soon as they saw the brightly lit house. In an instant, the house was filled with termites.

The maid heard her mistress's terrified screams and quickly brought water-filled basins from the kitchen and bathrooms, placing one under each lamp. The nearly transparent wings of the termites fell from their bodies and drifted down right before Charlotte's eyes. The wings piled up loosely on the dining table, the chairs, and the rugs, while the now wingless bodies, circling beneath the lights, fell silently into the basins.

The sight of their bodies floating on the surface of the water made her nauseous, and she swooned on the spot.

That night she had a miscarriage. Visions of naked termites swirling in the water floated before her eyes, reminding her of the unformed life in her belly. Knitting her arched eyebrows, painted in the latest fashion, she was deeply troubled. What ensued was a disease that plagued her plants and flowers. Starting with the rose, it spread rapidly through the garden. With her trowel she dug up countless white, squirming worms. She screamed, threw down her trowel, and ran back to her room, from which she never reemerged. For shortly thereafter, she lost the color in her cheeks, like the roses outside her door, which grew increasingly pale.

Charlotte fell into a deep depression. With her head lowered, she rarely spoke, preferring to lock herself in her room, keeping even her husband out.

On one stuffy, humid summer evening two months after she fell ill, she destroyed the garden that she had spent so much time and energy growing. Not a blade of grass, not a single tree escaped the onslaught, razed with strength no one knew she had. Brandishing a pair of shears, she lopped off all the blooming flowers and buds. Then, after uprooting several dozen tall roses, she turned to the Christmas trees along the path. She was discovered after exhausting her strength while trying to topple a small tree. Colonel White carried her into the house; her arms were bloodied by the pricks of rose thorns, her white cotton nightgown covered in mud.

The plague of insects infected the entire colony, with its barren mountains and menacing waters, and destroyed Charlotte in the process. Clenching his fists as his soft blue eyes turned cold, Colonel White vowed to spare nothing in taking over the New Territories, whatever the cost in blood.

Adam Smith's performance during the takeover process greatly disappointed Colonel White. Qu Yabing, on the other hand, performed extremely well. Whether as an intermediary beforehand or as the colonel's fifth column afterward, he climbed the bureaucratic ladder by stepping on the bones of his clan members. He would rise to a significant position—for a Chinese—in the colonial government as a result of his betrayal of his hometown, and earn for himself the obloquy of his clan, who interpreted his behavior to be the greatest shame in family history.

But Qu Yabing had always felt himself to be an outsider in his hometown.

As a child, he had once asked his mother where he had come from. Pointing at the storks walking slowly in a rice paddy, she had said that one of them had carried him in its beak and dropped him through the chimney. He had believed her.

His mother had been sold into the Qu family as a slave at the age of nine.

The poor girl did not even have a contract specially drawn up for her. A large family, the Qu household needed a great many servants, requiring the steward to deal with the human traffickers almost daily. Tiring of all the details, he figured that the Qu household's farm animal contracts would work just fine, since the motive for selling—the girls' fathers were poverty-stricken—was simple, and the demand wasn't all that different. So he had a contract drawn up for buying slave girls by simply changing the item for sale from "oxen" to "daughter." The spaces for signer, birthday, and the girl's name, as well as the price, remained blank to be filled in for each transaction.

After entering the Qu household, the girl was sent into the kitchen to brew tea and peel fruit. She rarely smiled, keeping her lovely teeth hidden from view. During a rare free moment one summer afternoon, she was sitting in the hallway stringing jasmine flowers that she'd picked earlier that morning for her mistress, the first wife, to wear in her hair after her noon nap, thus carrying the fragrance wherever she went. A servant woman in the kitchen waved her over and handed her a bowl of lotus seeds cooked with rock candy, which she was to deliver to the master in the living room. The master's maid had coughed when presenting him a bowl of bird's nest the day before, and Master Zunde, a fanatic about his health, assumed that the maid had consumption and dismissed her on the spot. When the news reached the maidservants in the kitchen, they all made up excuses to avoid going to the front room. But the girl, Xigu, ignorant of the situation, put down the jasmine flowers and picked up the shiny red-lacquered tray, oblivious that the bowl of desert would change her life.

Master Zunde, senior member of the thirtieth generation of the Qu clan, had just woken from his nap. Through the translucent gauze curtain, Xigu saw an old man with a gray beard and long white eyebrows that covered his eyelids, looking very much like the God of Longevity. A practitioner of the Taoist theory of longevity, he believed that sleeping with ten girls each night would recapture his youth. None of the passably attractive maids had eluded his attention.

On that afternoon, he opened his eyes and saw Xigu standing outside his curtain. Her developing breasts rose slightly under her blouse, like a pair of tender white pigeons. The old man was enchanted; Xigu never returned to the hallway to finish stringing the jasmine flowers. She became Master Zunde's new favorite. When he was in the mood, he would sit Xigu, who was young enough to be his granddaughter, in his lap and teach her to read, instructing her in the classics. He dressed her in clothing with sleeves wide enough for him to reach up inside and fondle her breasts. Soon she was pregnant. But once she had the baby, she was no longer fit for Master Zunde's Taoist practice and lost favor. The first wife quickly ordered her to cut kindling and grass on the mountain, where the torturous reeds cut and scarred her arms.

According to custom, when a slave girl reached adulthood, the master's family would find a match, selling her to be the concubine in a rich family or the wife of poor man. Having lost her virginity to Master Zunde, Xigu could not be sold as a concubine, and the loss of that money turned the first wife against her. She suffered much abuse; even her son was not spared. When he was five years old, his father, Master Zunde, slapped him so hard he became partially deaf. That occurred on a day in the hottest summer on record. Like a puppy suffering from heat, Qu Yabing was licking a block of ice on the table reserved for his father after his afternoon nap. His tongue was numb from the ice, and the chilled sensation that went through his heart made him shiver. What followed was a burning hand descending from above and sending him reeling to the floor. He lost all sensation under the assault of heat and cold, including the hearing in his left ear.

That was before man-made ice was possible, and ice was costly as gold. Blocks of naturally formed ice had to be shipped from the American continent; sailboats carrying chunks of ice chipped from lakes and rivers traveled the oceans for months before reaching Hong Kong. Sawdust and chaff were smeared on the ice to keep it from melting, and it was sold twice daily, at five cents a pound. Only the wealthiest and the most powerful families could enjoy ice in the summer to cool off. During the summer when Qu Yabing was slapped by the master, a severe shortage of ice had occurred owing to record heat and unfavorable winds that delayed the arrival of sailboats.

After losing the hearing in one ear, Qu Yabing became the target of jeers and abuse by brothers in the clan. Even the family tutor treated him as deaf and punished him at will. The teacher would raise the discipline ruler and smack the slow-reacting Qu Yabing savagely, leaving bruises and welts on him. Covering his head, he wished he could pack up a bag, leave his mother, and go up into the mountains to study martial arts. Then, once he became a martial arts master, he would come down to exact his revenge, throttling all the brothers who had abused him, knocking down the stone wall around the estate with his bare hands, and take his mother away from that prison house.

He never had a chance to fulfill his wishes. One day, the aged Master Zunde choked to death while eating litchi nuts. The first wife dismissed all the servants, with the exception of Xigu, whom she wanted to sell into prostitution. The clan elders tried to dissuade her, saying that, after all, Xigu had given the Qu family a son, which was recorded in the family lineage book. The clan could not afford the stain on its name. She defended herself by saying she was going to keep the boy, but that the lowly woman had to go. When Xigu got wind of the plan, she bundled up her son and left the house that very night.

Twenty-five years later, Qu Yabing returned to his hometown. As he stood alone on the silent country road, with its yellow leaves and whitening reeds, he imagined how the stone wall had finally been toppled by the powerful guns and cannons of the British army. He'd avenged himself.

To be fair to Qu Yabing, he was not on the ruling British side the whole time during the takeover of the New Territories. He had actually had a change of heart. The villagers of Dapu County, citing *fengshui* as a reason, objected to Colonel White's plan to build a provisional police station at Dapu. On April 3, Colonel White led a group of policemen to check on the progress of erecting tents at Dapu, only to run into the villagers' resistance one more time. He ordered a crackdown. The angry villagers, carrying hoes and clubs, rushed forward and took the hilltop occupied by the Britons, torching the tents in the process. Outnumbered, the panicky Colonel White escaped to Hong Kong on a fishing boat. Qu Yabing retreated with Colonel White and, as he stood on the deck, with an evening wind blowing over him, he felt as if he'd grown in stature, as if he were standing on the hilltop and cheering with his fellow countrymen, invigorated from having beaten back the enemy. Laughing inwardly at the defeated Colonel White, he wished he could give the man a savage kick from behind to vent his anger.

Intoxicated by the thrill of victory, Qu Yabing went to see Huang Deyun around midnight. Thinking whoever was pounding on the door might be a pirate coming ashore to loot her flat, she hid under the bed in terror. Qu Yabing pushed the door open and swaggered inside, where he dragged the cowering woman out from under the bed. Tonight, he would be the master and ravish this woman who laughed at his fecklessness behind his back. His body, swollen in victory, crushed down on her, while in his head, villagers, brandishing spears, swords, hoes, and clubs, formed banner-waving groups amid the din of drumbeats and shouts; they surrounded the huts on the hill, the colonial government's provisional police station. Qu Yabing, who was hiding behind a banyan tree, felt as if he had floated out of his body and landed among the crowd, with whom he shared bitter anger and camaraderie in the fight against the Britons. The gongs and drums were beating faster and faster, as spears, swords, hoes, and clubs assaulted the huts. The doors could not sustain the pounding and were broken down, revealing an ashen-faced

Adam Smith, who stood on the fallen doorframe holding his head in his hands and wondering if he should abandon the police station—symbol of the rulers.

Qu Yabing, who felt himself growing bigger and bigger among the crowd, would not give the Englishman the chance to choose. Tonight, the intoxicating sense of triumph would instill in him the power and confidence to drive the defeated Englishman, his superior, out of the female body the man had occupied and enjoyed. He would destroy the residual lip marks, saliva, and every trace of caresses the Englishman had left on her, eliminate the evil habit of exposing her naked body under the lamplight, and drive his shadow completely out of her heart. As if breaking out of a cocoon, Qu Yabing forced his way in, getting braver with each thrust. Each time he began to fade, the slightest touch had him rising again, as if filled with air, his manhood clubbing out the enemy. A fire raged; thick smoke rose all around. Adam Smith abandoned the hut and fled in disgrace with his fingers pinching his throat.

That night, Qu Yabing did not need to recite the story of pirate Xu Yabao killing the British officers who had raped the village woman, for he continued to rise to the fight, all night long. Holding tight to this new man, Huang Deyun was overcome with joy.

This was his first and, unfortunately, his last moment of masculine prowess. The following day, on his way back to the New Territories, Colonel White was ambushed by villagers throwing firebombs from behind trees. Incensed, the police chief fired off a request to Governor Blake to send troops to quell the Chinese opposition. The warship *HMS Fame* arrived with regular troops and a massive amount of firepower.

After his hometown fell, Qu Yabing walked out into the fields, where rice stalks grew unaffected in the spring breeze. The villagers, even while engaged in meetings and bomb making, had not forgotten their work in the fields. But while the green mountains were the same as always, the windswept fields no longer belonged to the people who tilled them. Looking back, Qu Yabing saw the remaining half of a tree in front of the clan shrine; the top half had been destroyed by lightning the night before his father, Zunde, had died, and the remaining half, with its drooping branches and withered leaves, seemed to indicate that the clan's fortune was nearing its end. The lightning had exposed the rotten, hollow center of the tree, and a *fengshui* master had recommended that it be replaced with bamboo if the seemingly inevitable fate of Qintian Village were to be avoided. But the clan members let the dying remnant of the tree stay in order to retain the ancestral design.

Qu Yabing himself had seen signs. In the winter of the previous year, he was leading two British colonial officials through tree groves that remained emerald green even in the heart of winter and arrived at his ancestral home. Adam Smith had looked around through his binoculars. Qu Yabing envied this new Western invention. He admired the westerners' talents and skills, which enabled them to invent all sorts of things: big ones such as oceangoing steamships and speedy trains; deadly weapons such as artillery and bombs; and small ones such as kerosene lamps, cameras, soap, and clocks and wristwatches. And now binoculars. Their ingenuity was displayed in such novelties.

"Come take a look." Qu Yabing timidly took the binoculars from Smith, and as he carefully grasped the two round barrels, he saw how his yellow fingers covered the spots touched by the Englishman only seconds before, and he felt the warmth of his superior's fingers. It was the first time his body had come in direct contact with Smith's, causing his fingers to twitch. But maybe it wasn't the first time, for on the body of the woman in Happy Valley, he had sensed the Englishman's breath, lips, and saliva everywhere he touched. He was entangled with a woman from whom his superior had taken pleasure and then tossed aside.

"Tell me what you see."

As his gaze scanned the tops of the acres of paddy fields, which were as lovely as embroidered silk, the stone arch bridge at the village entrance, the low-slung Temple of the Earth God, and the flying eaves of the Qu clan shrine, Yabing saw the rotting, hollow tree, its dying leaves swaying in the icy wind. He lowered the binoculars to see if the red cinder path in front of the shrine was still there. He blinked and saw traces of blood on the path leap up through the lenses. The patches of bright red scattered on the ground startled him. He quickly shifted his eyes away from the lenses, at a loss for words.

In fact, the red patches were petals from plane tree flowers that had fallen in the rain the night before. The water-soaked petals stuck to the sandy soil, giving Qu Yabing the mistaken impression of congealed blood. In the days to come, he was reminded of the patches of blood he'd seen through the binoculars whenever he thought about the loss of the family manor. But had he moved the binoculars up and to the left, he'd have seen that the flame tree, which the villagers called a red shadow tree, was blooming out of season.

This inauspicious omen had been fully realized, for the Qu clan members covered the landscape with their blood in a vain attempt to protect their homeland. Qu Yabing, on the other hand, walked away from Qintian unscathed. He was indeed an outsider in his own hometown.

5

Adam Smith's colonial experience had been similar to that of Colonel White, but unlike White, he never wore a mask or played an active role in the British Empire's overseas expansion and oppression, which could have put him solidly in the ranks of white colonial rulers.

Five years after his arrival, during the takeover of the New Territories, he shed the starched white uniform of the Sanitary Board and replaced it with the khaki tunic of the Royal Police. His hands, once sheathed in white gloves, now held a pistol, but since he never pulled the trigger, he could not become a true conquering hero. Even long after the attack was over, he could not forget the bloody battlefield scene. Every time he closed his eyes, he saw the disfigured, bloody villagers rushing toward him. The corpses lay heavily on him, making it hard to breathe. And at the moment when he thought he would die of suffocation, he would wake up, not daring to close his eyes again.

But even that was not the end of his nightmare. Colonel White, an icy glare in his blue eyes, had ordered him to remove his leather belt in front of all the other policemen, demanding that he turn over his pistol, which had not been fired, and take off his police uniform before kicking him out the door. Adam Smith later dreamed that he was standing stark naked outside the door, so humiliated he couldn't raise his head. And that was not the first time he'd been shut outside. After disappointing Mrs. Dickinson, wife of the former head of the Sanitary Board, who had wanted him to send for his childhood girlfriend, Annie, he had walked out of her Peak house for the last time, the wrought-iron garden gate slamming shut behind him. By sending a sedan chair for the prostitute Huang Deyun, he had been exiled from the colonial circle and never allowed back in. Betraying Mrs. Dickinson meant turning his back on social status, the moral values, and the superiority of the white rulers, which she represented. Now this time he had betrayed the grand world-mastery ideals of the British Empire. Colonel White had criticized his spinelessness in the face of the enemy, and lumped him together him with all people who lost their sense of honor. Not even trying to hide his disappointment, Smith handed over his pistol. Being forced to take off his khaki tunic had not been a dream.

Smith had once dreamed of requesting a transfer to the Royal Police Board, which had recently been set up in the New Territories. Quartered in one of the mat sheds on the hill, he would stand each day and watch the Union Jack slowly lowered, as another day ended. But it was not to be.

Having nowhere else to go, Smith took the Peak tram to his residence to continue the life he'd led before the takeover of the New Territories. But the green two-story building was not his home. He had moved in years earlier with two suitcases, much like taking furnished rooms in a hotel. Everything, from pots and pans and kitchen utensils to bedroom and bathroom linen, even the servant, had been left behind by the previous tenant. At first, he'd thought of moving some tables and chairs out of the living room and keeping only the matching sofas and high-backed oak chairs. Then he could light a fire in the fireplace to create an air of domesticity, and send out invitations for a housewarming party. But whom would he invite? A few acquaintances' faces flashed before his eyes: Pastor Thomas with the waxen light on the tip of his nose? Shame quickly quelled this idea when he envisioned the pastor's luxurious house, which was filled with antiques and oil paintings. The gray-haired judge who had praised him for his performance during the plague probably would not deign to visit this shabby place either. Surely he dared not hope that the taipans he often saw at the Hong Kong Club would come, for they were given to ceremony and were in constant competition with government officials for rank and position. Then there were the blustery bankers, with their tailored suits and gold pocket watches, who loudly toasted one another, "Whatever's good for the colony is good for the Wayfoong Bank."

What remained were the low-ranking officers and bank clerks with whom Smith played pool and drank. But they got drunk too often and were far too boisterous, shallow, and laughable for his tastes. And they were shocked to learn that he had been to the dank Chinese market in Central; if they'd known of his visits to the Chinese-style building at Happy Valley, where he drank warmed rice liquor from a tin pot and ate animals' intestines that had stewed for days, they'd have treated him as a freak and never spoken to him again.

So Smith never did throw that party, and his living room remained overfurnished. Not a single guest was ever entertained in his residence. He would always remain outside British colonial social circles and would never be accepted by self-important ladies, even though he'd been willing to learn how to be a gentleman, using his boss, Mr. Windsor, as a model.

After the takeover of the New Territories, Adam Smith returned to his post at the Sanitary Board, while Qu Yabing stayed on at the Police Board. One night, Huang Deyun was giving the baby a bath when he blurted out, "Still think about him? Want him to come back to you?"

It took her a while to understand what he was getting at. Without turning her head, she answered in a flat voice, "Whatever are you talking about? He's not here anymore."

"How do know you he's not here?"

"You told me so. You said he was transferred to Calcutta. You even went to see him off."

"Aha, you remember everything. You must still be thinking about him."

Suspicion turned his eyes gloomier than ever. He curled up in bed with these thoughts on his mind. In order to prove her fidelity, Huang Deyun fondled him, trying her best to arouse him, but he was unable to respond, just as the night before, and the night before that. His performance in bed inevitably followed the rise and fall of the villagers' resistance against the British takeover. His most impressive and overpowering performance ever had occurred on that night when the Dapu villagers had burned down the provisional police station, but that had proved to be short-lived. And when Colonel White turned the tables on the villagers, Qu Yabing's sexual prowess went from bad to worse. Huang Deyun was so anxious that she spared no expense, buying even the most expensive stag penis to improve his situation. Bowl after bowl of herbal tonics that were said to strengthen the *yang* was forced down his throat, turning his belly into an inflated ball, but nothing changed from the waist down. So, putting her clay pot for brewing herbal tonics aside, she went to Longevity Hall to see the old Chinese herbalist. Saying she'd lost her appetite, she lingered at the counter after filling her prescription, blushing and unwilling to reveal the true purpose of her visit. The midwife who had attended the birth of Huang Deyun's child knew that she was involved with the Englishman's Chinese interpreter, and after dragging out the truth from Huang, she smiled and asked the herbalist for a bottle of Rising Yang pills, a miraculous cure for many ailments, including impotence. She told Huang not to give him too much, a comment that elicited much giggling from the two women.

But even a full bottle of Rising Yang failed to produce results, so Huang Deyun took a rattan basket with a piece of sacrificial meat, some walnuts, and some peanuts to pray at the marriage stone on Mount Bowring Street. Before leaving, she thought long and hard over which hairstyle to wear. On the night of her first client, years before, the madam had changed her little girl's style into a married woman's bun, and every night thereafter, a new bridegroom had been ushered into her room; but she was still not a married woman. She'd heard that the marriage stone worked magic: pious men would get a wife and pious women would get a husband, while parents would be granted a son. If she was going to pray for marriage, she ought to wear the double bun of an unmarried woman; but she changed her mind and combed her hair into a single bun when she considered her four-year-old illegitimate son, picked up her basket, and walked out the door.

The stone at Mount Bowring Street rose into the air, like a man's erect penis. With a sad face, Huang Deyun knelt before the stone for a long time, begging the deity to help her man regain his manhood. Every possible medical cure had been exhausted, and her only hope was a miracle from the stone.

6

Qu Yabing had high hopes for the future. Following the British takeover of the New Territories, rather than return to the Sanitary Board with Adam Smith to resume his original position, he began to envision all sorts of possibilities for himself. After being transferred to the Police Board, he learned that the British interpreter to the Police Court had been fired when his scheme to collaborate with pirates was exposed, and the position remained unfilled; Qu Yabing coveted the job.

Yabing's aspirations had changed as he grew older and his fortunes improved. As a youngster he'd dreamed of becoming a missionary one day. But when his mother left Grace Catholic Church, which had taken them in, and decided to live out her days in Baolin Temple in Kowloon, Sister Maria accused her of turning her back on the Lord, thereby bringing an end to Qu Yabing's desire to spend his life amid candlelight, the Psalms, and incense. His passion for reading scriptures shifted to studying English. After leaving the Catholic Church, he pinned his hopes on becoming a court interpreter, believing that his facility with spoken and written English could be put to use interpreting between Chinese and English for the sake of judges, the accused, and witnesses. But the colonial powers did not share his views, convinced that the best English speakers among the Chinese could handle only daily conversation, that they lacked knowledge of the law and had no familiarity with legal terminology, and that they were incapable of dealing with the nuances of the English language; even the most gifted linguists among the Chinese would find it virtually impossible to overcome cultural barriers. And if they could not grasp the essence of these distinctions, how could they convey them in either language?

As a result, the Hong Kong courts handed this supremely important responsibility over to British "old China hands" who spoke a bit of Cantonese they'd learned in childhood from the kitchen help but could not read a word. Qu Yabing, with his yellow skin, was thus not qualified for the post of court interpreter, and had wound up at the Sanitary Board with the title of interpreter, while in fact he was little more than a personal errand boy for his British superior. But his thoughts were constantly on the position of court interpreter, which came with a high salary and a working day that ran from ten in the morning to four in the afternoon, and conferred instant prestige on whoever stood there carrying on a dialogue with the individual in the defendant's box. He had confidence in the musical quality of his voice, thanks to years of singing the Psalms as a child.

Adam Smith had been back at the Sanitary Board less than a month when Qu Yabing was summoned to the police station, with its intimidating reputation. Once there, Colonel White sent the guards out of the room, closed the door behind them, and walked over to the large oak desk. Instead of sitting down, he leaned against the desk with both hands and gazed down at Qu Yabing, who looked like a dwarf by comparison. This frightened informer, who had sold out his own hometown, stood with his arms hanging stiffly at his side, eyes cast to the floor, legs turning rubbery under the piercing stare of two icy blue eyes, until he could barely stand. Colonel White, who was wearing a starched khaki uniform and a shiny leather belt from which a holstered, fully loaded pistol hung, held Qu Yabing in utter contempt for his willingness to climb upward by stepping on the bones of his fellow villagers, but in order to realize the overseas expansionist ideals of the British Empire, he put aside his personal prejudices for the greater good.

Slowly and deliberately, Colonel White sat down at his desk and made it clear to Qu Yabing that his performance had left something to be desired, but that, given his unique background, Colonel White was willing to give him another chance to prove himself in the role of go-between, to serve the empire. He would be given the title of special administrative assistant; in addition to maintaining close ties with the Anxin County head, Lu Huan, he was to prowl the streets and byways, listening for any talk or gossip that presented a danger to the Hong Kong colonial government. He was to keep an ear out for any and all subversive rumors, and report back to Colonel White twice a month.

"The colonial government has an important role for you, and how you play it is critical."

Confirming the prediction of his clan elders, Qu Yabing played the jackal to the tiger, a party to the inevitable misdeeds, thereby becoming a loyal agent of the white rulers, whose backing allowed him to oppress his countrymen.

His long, narrow eyes began to shine, and now, when he looked at a person, he rolled his eyes upward and the cold glint of suspicion emerged. His movements were more relaxed than before, and he began to attend to his appearance for a change: his shaved scalp shone as if oiled, and he dressed in Canton silk trousers and jackets with buttons down the front. He even had a skullcap and a pair of satin high-topped boots made at a famous old tailor shop in Central. That way he wouldn't look out of place if he participated in some grand occasion. On the first and fifteenth of every month, in his capacity as Colonel White's special administrative assistant, he went to the Xinan County headquarters, Lu Huan's *yamen*, setting out after dark to avoid being seen. At the second watch, right on schedule, a yamen runner, lantern in hand, would be waiting for him in one of the dark alleys to take him to the opium bed of a yamen advisor by the name of Wang, a taciturn opium smoker who would take a sealed envelope out from under his pillow and hand it to Qu Yabing. After making sure that Qu had put the envelope safely away, he'd invite him to smoke a couple of energizing pipes before heading back. Qu never got on the road until the moon had fallen to the horizon and roosters had begun to crow.

Qu Yabing was confident that he'd soon have an opportunity to wear his new skullcap and boots. No longer did he rush home to the flat in Happy Valley after a day's work to roll up his sleeves and coil his queue atop his head so he could chop firewood, fetch water, feed the chickens, and put up vegetable trellises for Huang Deyun, as he had in the past. Now he tucked his hands into the wide sleeves of his jacket, his pinkie nails left to grow long and useful, and when Huang Deyun spoke to him, he turned his back on her and all but shut his eyes to keep her melancholy from getting through to him, for that could only remind him of the sham his life had become. Her sole recourse was to serve him even more diligently than ever. After dinner she would mend his clothes and cloth shoes in the light from the lamp while he sipped a cup of tea; hardly a word passed between them—in that regard, they were an ordinary couple. When she stood up to add boiled water to the teapot, he would stretch and yawn, telling her he had to be up early the next day for work; he'd get up and return to his dorm room.

At the end of his first month as Colonel White's special administrative assistant, Qu Yabing spent his increased salary on two things:

First, he went to see the artist who had set up his stall across from the entrance to the East China Hospital, where he described in minute detail what he wanted the man to draw. Over the next several days, Yabing's deceased mother gradually came into view on paper; finally, when it was finished, she seemed to come alive, and Yabing could not keep from reaching out to touch the portrait just below her nose, as if he expected to feel a breath of air. As the artist put away his brushes and paints, he said that Yabing was either a fool or the sort of filial son one rarely found these days.

Qu Yabing told the artist that he had long felt the spirit of his mother here, where she had died, and that this drawing had brought it all back to him, for which he, the man, had earned Yabing's undying gratitude. Once he had the drawing back in his dorm room, the loneliness he had felt there vanished.

The second thing he did with his first month's salary was make up for what he had missed on his thirtieth birthday. Dressed in new clothes, he returned to the Minru Teahouse in Central. Pushing open the door with great fanfare, he was pleased to observe the new crease on his smooth sleeve; with a broad grin on his face and new cloth shoes on his feet, he climbed the stairs to the second floor, holding his head high. On his thirtieth birthday, when he had peeked inside the teahouse through a crack in the door, he'd watched as a pair of satin-topped shoes slowly climbed those stairs; as nearly as he could tell by the lined silk Mandarin robe the man had been wearing and the ivory fan in his hand, it must have been the proprietor of the pawnshop next door. Now, after climbing those same stairs on the invisible prints of those satin shoes, he sat down at an unoccupied table, spread his legs out grandly, and summoned the waiter to pour him some steaming tea from his aluminum pot. He then ordered food, reciting each dish from memory: a plate of piglet and goose strips, some shrimp dumplings and stuffed buns, and a bowl of beef noodles, topped off with a bottle of twice-steamed rice liquor from Zhujiang.

As soon as the liquor arrived, he filled his glass and immediately drained it, followed by a proud smacking of the lips. He then shook his legs and dug into the array of food on the table. When he was done, he splurged by ordering a bowl of dessert. His birthday meal finished, he lovingly stroked his bulging belly as he walked downstairs, swaying from side to side, a toothpick wedged between his teeth and poking out of the corner of his mouth to announce to one and all that he had just polished off a nice meal at the Minru Teahouse.

As he passed by the Xingchang Photo Studio, he made up his mind to have his picture taken with his second month's salary; he'd already decided on the pose: hands on his knees, legs spread, looking into the camera so that both ears were visible and there were no shadows on either side of his nose.

Following his promotion, one of his neighbors came over to introduce herself, the taps on the door of his dorm room from the handle of a goose-feather fan sounding like a woodpecker. It was a pointy-mouthed, pointy-chinned old woman with a black scarf over her head; she looked more avian than human. Apologizing for his cramped quarters, he stepped out into the corridor to see what the woman wanted. She told him she lived in the next lane over, and that Qu Yabing passed by her humble wooden gate every day.

"I hope you'll forgive me for showing up like this," the old woman apologized.

She had a nephew who worked as a janitor in the official guesthouse. "He came to see me the other day, and when you passed by, he said, 'My goodness, Auntie, does that man live around here? I know him. He's had a stroke of really good luck lately. I see him coming and going at the guesthouse in the company of the foreigner in charge.'"

Qu Yabing smiled, basking in the old woman's flattering comment. He was pretty sure she'd come to see him on behalf of her janitor nephew, so he stood there, his arms crossed, waiting. Burning with curiosity, the old woman craned her neck to see through the nearly closed door into the room behind him, more than once barely restraining herself from pushing the door open with her fan.

"And how is your wife?" she blurted out. "Won't you have her come out to meet her neighbor?"

Qu Yabing rubbed his cleanly shaved head.

"I'm sorry to admit that I'm still a bachelor," he replied somewhat tensely. He'd had to care for his ailing mother for so long before she died that the opportunity had passed him by.

The old woman responded with talk of the importance of marriage before turning with a wave of her fan and saying good-bye. Qu Yabing went back into his room, which was barely big enough to accommodate a cot and a chair. There he reflected on his life; they were not pleasant thoughts. Getting married and starting a family wasn't a simple proposition for someone with his unenviable background. If there were a girl somewhere who was willing to hook up with him, given the rowboat size of his room, they'd be bumping into each other every time they turned around. After the death of Master Zunde, his mother, fearing that the widow would sell her into prostitution, had taken her son and fled the manor in the dark of night, imploring a fisherman to ferry them across the water. The following morning Yabing had found himself kneeling before a statue of Jesus, Bible in hand, under the malevolent stare of someone called Sister Maria.

Only the morning before, Yabing had been following his mentor, rocking his head back and forth as he memorized the classics in the Qu Manor private study. In the space of a single night he had been uprooted. Later, as he moved from the Grace Catholic Church to the bachelor's dormitory attached to the Sanitary Board, it was little more than exchanging one bed for another, the only differences being that he now had the privacy of a single room and a door he could close, and he was close enough to Victoria Prison to hear the nighttime moans of convicts being beaten.

7

After paying her respects at the marriage stone, Huang Deyun once more tried to get her man interested in her, but nothing worked. So once again, basket in hand, she made another trip to Mount Bowring Street, where a group of older women was standing under a banyan tree talking all at once in praise of the powers of the marriage stone. Whatever one for wished for, the deity granted. The recipient of the divine manifestation this time had been the prostitute Liu Ruxian from Embroidery Palace on Possession Street. Liu had fallen for one of her rich clients, who had not returned after they'd taken their pleasure together.

"When that lady of the night heard that the Stone God answered all prayers—for husbands, for wives, for children—without fail, she rushed over to offer up her prayers, every day and every night. The god was so moved by her devotion that within a month the rich client had a change of heart and returned to her—"

One of the other women cut in: "I hear that her rich client was lured to the brothel by a fluttering strip of red silk, just when Liu Ruxian was hopelessly love-struck. When she saw him walk in the door—"

"Then what?" Huang Deyun blurted out, unable to silently eavesdrop another second. Ah, then what! Well, the rich client had bought her out of the brothel with pearls and put her up in a nice home, where she started life anew as a proper housewife.

Huang Deyun went up to the marriage stone, fell to her knees, and began to pray, though she wasn't sure at first what she was praying for. Did she

hope that her man would regain his virility and restore to her the pleasure of conjugal union, or did she want the Stone God to bring about
their marriage? If Liu Ruxian, who had rolled about in the world of
prostitution for so long, could be set up in a nice home, then why
shouldn't she too have a future as a lawful housewife? For several years
she had dressed simply and lived the life of an ordinary housewife, rising early in the morning to buy fresh vegetables from vendors who came
to her door, grabbing an extra stalk of onion or slice of old ginger as she
handed over the money. What was she, if not a homemaker?

After lunch, she'd take her four-year-old son to the square in front of
the Heavenly Dowager Temple to see the local herbalist, who would
spread out his medicinal pellets, as well as a container of tiger-bone
liquor, on a filthy piece of cloth. Her son was always fascinated by the
snake stewing in the liquor, but timid enough to hide behind his mother's
skirts and stick his head out just far enough to see. With a laugh, Deyun
would rap him on the head. On the road home, they'd stop at a shop
named Felicitation, where she would buy a bowl of twenty-four-flavors
iced tea, drink half, then force her son to drink the rest as a hedge against
colds and sore throats.

At night, if she knew that Qu Yabing would not be coming over, she
would invite the woman from the pharmacy to go with her to the night
market to listen to storytellers. When the blind musician began singing a
song of sorrow, she'd find an excuse to return home.

In practical terms, if not in name, Huang Deyun was a housewife.

In recent days, pleading a busy schedule at the guesthouse, where he
was constantly being sent off on one errand or another by the foreign
honcho, Qu Yabing was unwilling to stay the night. Huang Deyun
thought he wanted to avoid complications over his lack of performance
in bed, which was why he wiped his mouth after dinner, stood up, and left.
She wished he'd stay, since her place could always use more male energy,
especially late at night. When he coughed deeply, sneezed loudly, slurped
his tea and porridge, it somehow made her feel better. Qu Yabing's promotion brought Deyun a mixture of joy and sorrow. As a consequence of
her increased attention to his needs, in addition to his own sense of self-

satisfaction, even his old pockmarks had a sheen and his shaved forehead had lost its drabness. Grasping his wide sleeves and clasping his hands behind his back, he walked with a swagger, head held high; he seldom had anything to say to her, because he was now a man of substance.

Qu Yabing was supremely conscious of the need to attend to his new social status and protect his reputation, which is why he waited until the sun had set before slipping quietly into Deyun's place; after finishing his meal and after-dinner tea, he got up to leave the darkened flat to the woman and her son. One day the woman from the pharmacy rushed over to caution Deyun to lock the doors and windows, since there had been a rash of robberies in Wan Chai, reputedly carried out by masked pirates who had come ashore to harass the public. Deyun grabbed her man's sleeve and begged him to stay the night, but he fought her off, thinking she wanted to drag him off to bed, and walked out the door.

Having once introduced herself to Qu Yabing, the elderly neighbor woman returned and knocked, woodpecker-style, on his door with her fan. Yabing still did not invite her in.

"There's wisdom in the saying that a man must take a wife and a woman needs a husband." Catching him off guard, she nudged the door all the way open with her fan. Not a soul inside. "A bachelor, what a shame. As the saying goes, distant relatives are no substitute for close neighbors. You let your Aunt Yaxing find you a fine young woman from a good family."

She now took it upon herself to find a wife for Qu Yabing. The first candidate was the daughter of the proprietor of the Longxing Silverware Shop on Wellington Avenue, characterized as a goddess, sage and chaste.

"This looks like the perfect match to me. The Longxing Silverware Shop sells their goods to foreigners. Blue-eyed, redheaded foreigners come and go there, day in and day out, and I know you spend all your time at the guesthouse in the company of the foreign honcho. My nephew told me so." Aunt Yaxing clapped her hands. "Two families just made for each other!"

The reply came two days later. The Longxing proprietor was looking for a son-in-law with a pedigree.

What could Qu Yabing say?

Aunt Yaxing stroked her chin as she tried to come up with another plan.

"As the saying goes, a man hates choosing the wrong career, a woman hates choosing the wrong mate. Ah, I've got it. Here's what we'll do, we'll say you're a comprador working with foreigners for the emperor, and that you've recently been given a promotion, the first of many. Not only that, your family situation could not be simpler. Any girl who marries you won't have to worry about trying to please her in-laws, and will have all the freedom she needs—"

As soon as Aunt Yaxing started matchmaking for Yabing, he sensed that everyone was looking at him, so in order to give them a good impression, he was doubly careful in his speech and actions. Then, in order to keep a lid on the gossip, he went to work and knocked off early; on days when he was late getting home, he stopped as he passed Aunt Yaxing's house and played with the cat that lazed its days away on the bamboo chair, while complaining to her about all the demands the foreign honcho placed on him. Aunt Yaxing patted him with her goosefeather fan, complimenting him on his dedication to his job and assuring him that there were no limits to what he could accomplish.

On the eve of the Dragon Boat Festival, Huang Deyun was sewing a sachet for her son, which she filled with coins joined by a long thread.

"Tomorrow's a holiday, you don't have to report back, so come by a little earlier."

"What for?"

"We need to talk," Deyun said as she bit the thread in two. Then, worried that he might balk, she added, "The sister from the herbal shop is going to take him to watch the Dragon Boat races, so he won't be home all day."

But it was nearly dark when Qu Yabing finally showed up. The inviting smell of sticky dumplings wrapped in bamboo leaves drifted out through Deyun's door, which was hung with boughs of sweet flag. A platter of peaches and plums lying in the center of the dining table filled the room with a holiday aroma. Deyun had dressed up in pale blue matching pants and blouse, with sprigs of mugwort in her hair and a red pomegranate flower pinned fetchingly behind one ear. Without a word, she poured the man a cup of special tea. Seated stiffly at the table, his hands on his knees, Yabing assumed the pose of calm self-assuredness, the long, curved nails of his little fingers peeking out from under his sleeves. No sound was sufficient for him to raise his head, causing only an arrogant gaze through his lowered eyelids. If, at the moment, he'd been holding a water pipe in his hand, Deyun was thinking, and wore a queue coiled atop his head and kept in place by a skullcap, he would have been indistinguishable from a method actor playing an old master on stage. The old man who had married Liu Ruxian from the Embroidery Palace was, she knew instinctively, a rich but lecherous geezer old enough to be her father and had installed her as his seventh or eighth wife. With a sneer on her face, Deyun knew she had no reason to envy that other prostitute, for the person sitting across from her was a proper man of a proper age, someone boosted up the ladder by a foreigner, on his way to a bright future and burdened with no family entanglements; moreover, his native home was near Dongguan, not far in fact from where the conflict with the British had occurred. At the age of ten he'd been taken from his birthplace by his now deceased mother and brought to this tiny island, where he was left alone, with neither friends nor family, mirroring her own experience: remote and isolated. They were made for each other. Since he was forever complaining about how cramped his dormitory quarters were, why didn't he just move in with her? It made no sense for him to keep running back and forth.

"I've thought it all out," Deyun said as she wrung her hands under her apron. "I don't care about your problem in bed, that's something we can work out over time. . . . I took a vow in front of the marriage stone that, for better or for worse, I'm staying with you from now on."

Except for a slight movement in one of his pinkies, Yabing sat there like a statue, as if he were mulling over what she said to see if there was anything hidden beneath her words.

"Yes, I've thought it all out. You were the one who gave my son the name Richard. In two years he'll start school, and I already know that his schoolmates are going to ridicule him. But things would be a lot easier on him if he had a father at home." Having said her piece, one that she had practiced for so long, Deyun sat down on a stool by the door and covered her face with her hands, drained of energy. It had been easier than she'd thought. In her willingness to sacrifice desire in order for her son to have a proper surname, and for her to gain the status she'd longed for, Deyun had proposed marriage to him. This, after she had gritted her teeth and decided to take a vow before the marriage stone. As long as the man was willing to marry her, she would stay with him from now on, even if their marriage was devoid of intimacy.

A sense of unease had followed the vow, so she'd gone to the local temple to draw a fortune-telling lot. She felt better when she saw the couplet on the temple doors:

This is where wishes are granted
This is where prayers are answered

Deyun was waiting for Yabing to come over, lift her off the stool, and gently call her his wife. But she waited in vain, and as she climbed down off the stool, she interpreted his silence as acceptance of her proposal. She stood by the table waiting for a response—any response.

Neither of them moved. Deyun could sense that the man was looking at her, even though his head was lowered. That was his way: elusive, gloomy, cold. That coldness gradually infected her, starting from the soles of her feet.

On that rainy afternoon three years earlier, when he had stepped foot inside her flat for the very first time, Qu Yabing had brought with him an envelope inside a packet with the official seal of the Sanitary Board. The envelope had contained five *jiao* Hong Kong coins, which his superior, Adam Smith, had sent to help with her expenses. Standing there late in her pregnancy, she had glared contemptuously at the messenger and spat out the words, "Is the *guailow* dead, or have his feet rotted off? Why did he send a slave like you?"

Even if the Englishman was dead, his ghost lingered on. How could a thirty-year-old child in a man's body not be putty in the hands of this woman? He was reborn in the softness of her body, released from poverty and the grayness of his life; as Yabing opened wide his eyes, even the limestone walls appeared soft and inviting. But at the very moment he was reborn, he also fell into a state of misery he could not put into words. The woman in his arms had been a prostitute in Southern Tang Palace on Lyndhurst Terrace, but more important, she had been the mistress of his British superior, who had grown tired of her and sent him, his lackey, with a packet of money to tie up loose ends. In the end, he was now the one who climbed into her four-poster bed, he was the one to enjoy her body. His enjoyment was ready-made; he was to take over the woman abandoned by the Englishman, who had rented the flat he was to move into; sleep on the springy mattress in a four-poster bed bought by the Englishman at an auction in Central; even the food and tea on the table came from the dismissal money in the official envelope. Although the Englishman had left for good, traces of him remained throughout the flat; he was everywhere: his footprints were all over the red brick floor, either from the leather soles of his shoes or his bare feet, left there after making love and climbing off the bed. The tables, the chairs, the dressers, the cupboards were all covered with his fingerprints; folds covered the pillow on which he'd lain his heads on countless nights; and soft chestnut hairs from his head had intertwined with the lush black threads of the woman.

When Qu Yabing sucked the woman's lips, he was taking in the Englishman's saliva, and each time her body frightened him with its contortions in bed, she was merely reenacting scenes of passion with the Englishman. When she closed her eyes, it was Adam Smith she was seeing; she could not forget him. Even when Qu Yabing lied to her that Smith had been sent to Calcutta, she still could not put him out of her mind. Out of frustration, he reviled her time and again, but she would simply look at him out of the corner of her eye and say calmly, "Don't take your anger out on me. If you had any guts, you'd go settle scores with the Englishman." But now that Qu Yabing had received a promotion,

Huang Deyun no longer confronted him that way, was, in fact, somewhat intimidated by him. What tormented him was that he had no control over any of Huang Deyun's actions or thoughts. Everything she did, every look she gave him seemed to have hidden meaning, and gave rise to wild thoughts that led to uncontrollable jealousy and dark suspicions. The knowledge that he could never possess her completely nearly drove him mad.

Then one day the opportunity to get even presented itself. Residents of the New Territories had torched the Taipo provisional police station, sending the British fleeing in surrender, their hands in the air. Caught up in the intoxicating thrill of victory, Qu Yabing could finally crack his mighty whip and drive the Englishman away from her for good. Victory was his at last. The woman had said she was willing to spend the rest of her life with him, exchanging silks for cotton, saying she had long been a common housewife in all but name, and hoped to rectify that through him.

Unfortunately, in Qu Yabing's eyes, this woman in simple dress, who was content to stay at home, was still bewitching. Although originating in the soil of Dongguan, she had been nurtured by foreign winds and rain. Beneath her pale blue cotton blouse she wore a foreign brassiere, its straps precariously supporting her breasts, which jutted out shamelessly, straining to break free at any moment. She walked easily in feet that had never been bound, exposing herself to public scrutiny everywhere she went. Of even greater significance, Huang Deyun was unable to shed many of the habits she'd formed as a prostitute. She could hardly look at anyone without first casting a flirtatious eye. She was a woman who never shied away from doing what she felt like doing, and rather than follow the wishes of her parents and the advice of a matchmaker, she decided whom she would marry. Qu Yabing's ideal wife wore a shapeless blouse over binding that kept her underdeveloped breasts flat; she had tiny eyes and sparse brows, and walked with dainty, mincing steps. A proper woman from a good family, in the words of the matchmaker Yaxing—definitely not this woman. She was a blood-sucking snake, a soft-boned, writhing viper who could coil herself around him at will, or a taut band of silk that could wrap itself around his neck and render him immobile, prey waiting to be devoured.

Qu Yabing tipped back his head and drained the glass, then removed an official envelope from his coat pocket and laid it down on the table.

"The Englishman told me to give this to you. It's the full amount. Take it."

Wiping the last drops of liquor from his mouth, he walked to the door, saying before he left,

"I won't be back."

The matchmaker Yaxing did not disappoint Qu Yabing: she had found a proper woman from a good family, the daughter of a rice-shop proprietor in Central District.

"She's not quite young anymore, but definitely not old. And she has tiny bound feet that taper to a point like rice dumplings—"

This last comment was music to Yabing's ears. Marrying a woman with bound feet was precisely what he desired and deserved. His dream of having a wedding picture taken at the Xingchang Photo Studio, wearing his official skullcap and a pair of black satin boots, would be a dream come true. His eyes misted up. Mother, your son is going to give you a bound-foot daughter-in-law!

8

Life for Deyun took a turn for the worse after Qu Yabing left. Late one night a speckled capon she'd once kicked savagely suddenly began to crow, so frightening her she couldn't go back to sleep. Early the next morning there was a loud pounding at her door, which she thought was a pirate who had come ashore—the crowing of the rooster had announced his arrival—to rob her. Taking her son with her into the kitchen, she removed the lid from the rice vat and forced him to get inside and hide. The lid was no sooner back in place than her legs turned to rubber and she fell to her knees.

How much time passed she didn't know, but the pounding stopped. Mustering up her courage, Deyun walked into the living room, where she spotted a white envelope that had been slipped under the door. It was a signed notice from the landlord that the five-year period of lease, paid for by Adam Smith, was nearly up, and that he had other plans for the flat. She was asked to vacate the premises no later than the end of the month. Clutching the notice in her hand, Huang Deyun went out to the back yard, where her son had gone after climbing out of his hiding place in the rice vat, and held him tightly in her arms. They were now alone in the world, mother and son, with nowhere to go. A patch of green bamboo just beyond the fence out back had sprouted flowers, something that had never happened before, and she took this as a bad omen. It was time to move.

So Deyun put on her cloth shoes and went out to find a new place to live. With the bright sun overhead, she walked up and down the myriad streets and lanes, gripped by deepening anxiety. Without realizing it, she let her steps take her to the cobblestone street in Central. She gazed at the stone steps leading up to the Peak, where the rooftops of the brightly colored brothels curved upward like swallowtails; as if directed by a supernatural being, she had returned to the street with which her fate had been so intertwined. Seven years earlier, only days before being kidnapped by a trader in human cargo, she had been turning a waterwheel to irrigate crops in her hometown of Dongguan, only to wind up on the cobblestones of this very street, dragged along like a beast of burden by the kidnapper who had sold her to the madam of a brothel. Two and a half years later, the plague had struck, and she'd found herself sitting in a sedan chair hired by her British lover, Adam Smith, traveling down the cobblestone street in the opposite direction to be installed in a flat in Happy Valley as his mistress.

After seven long years, Huang Deyun felt that she had traveled as far as she could go. Lost in thought, she nearly jumped out of her skin when someone grabbed her by the shoulder. She spun around, and was face to face with a masculine-looking woman in a white blouse and black trousers, her hair combed into a single long braid.

"I've been watching you. You look familiar," the woman said in a gravelly voice. Then, looking down at Deyun's feet, she exclaimed, "Ai, cloth shoes and cotton clothing, that can't be her, I thought. If not for that beauty mark on your cheek, I'd have been certain you were someone else!"

The woman's strong grip was unmistakable. It had to be Aunt Liao Kou from Yihong Pavilion. Sold at the age of thirteen by the trader in human cargo as an adopted daughter to the owner of Yihong Pavilion, Deyun had been transformed into a classical beauty, but not before the madam had forced open her mouth with her strong fingers and examined her teeth as if she were buying a horse or an ox.

"You're Ah-yun, the girl from Dongguan, aren't you?"

After an emotional sigh, by way of acknowledgment, Deyun asked how Madam Yihong was getting along.

"Same as always." She made a gesture as if smoking an opium pipe. "She often asks whatever happened to little Ah-yun from Dongguan. She misses you."

That, of course, wasn't true, but just hearing it flooded Deyun's desolate heart with a mixture of sweet and sad feelings. The look in the woman's eyes changed. The person she'd been waiting for, she said, wasn't likely to show up, so why didn't Deyun come pay a call on Yihong? Once again the cobblestone street had entered Deyun's life and, as fate would have it, an unanticipated encounter had resulted. Thinking that Deyun would turn her down, the woman immediately accused her of being heartless.

"Just think how much trouble we went to back then, how we helped a little country girl bloom into a lovely flower. We didn't even want you to show your face; you were as precious as gold. Who would have thought we would never see you ever again after you walked out our door?"

Huang Deyun bitterly wanted to defend herself. She'd thought about making a return visit, had in fact entertained the idea of seeking refuge with Yihong, and would have if the face in her mirror hadn't looked so haggard. Otherwise, she might already be entertaining guests at Yihong Pavilion.

"The way I look now," Deyun said as she tugged at her clothes and shrank back, "she might not recognize me."

The other woman cast another glance at her cloth shoes.

"What are you afraid of, Ah-yun? If you were to shed these coarse clothes and apply some makeup, that beauty mark on your face is a guarantee that the money would flow again."

Beginning to be persuaded, Deyun looked around with a squint, and was struck by the unappealing surroundings. And so, when the woman tugged on her sleeve, she followed her up the steps, retracing the path she'd taken seven years earlier, the only difference being that then she'd had no idea what awaited her.

The years had taken their toll on Yihong Pavilion on Wellington Street, which wasn't nearly as lively as it had once been, having failed to recover completely from the disastrous plague that had swept the area five years earlier. Yihong was getting on in years and had not broken her addiction to opium, all of which had sapped her ability to turn girls purchased from traders in human cargo or girls born to residents of Buddhist nunneries into fetching beauties through diligent training and transforming dress and makeup—girls who were then offered up to wealthy clients willing to pay dearly for the pleasure of deflowering virgins.

These days Yihong Pavilion looked more like a private home than a brothel. Taking advantage of her longtime connections, Yihong lured concubines and mistresses of the very rich into working part-time for her in order to satisfy their own sexual urges. She swore she would protect their identity at all costs, yet she never hesitated to divulge to her clients that they were being serviced by concubines of the wealthy or to rake in the profits.

Huang Deyun was led once again to the black opium couch, which was as big as a small room. A dense cloud of heavy smoke filled the air, and a large fan hung from the curtain—nothing had changed in seven years, including the form stretched out on the sorrel-wood bed like a rigid bamboo plant enshrouded by a shifting cloud of smoke, feet covered in black satin shoes, with phoenixes embroidered on the tops and soles so clean they appeared never to have touched the floor. The opium smoker, on the other hand, had grown old and wizened; most of her hair had fallen out, and her purple undergarment could not conceal the sticklike shrivel of her neck.

Yihong invited Huang Deyun to sit down on the couch beside her and, with pretended intimacy, took her hand and spoke of the old days. The younger woman's callused palm told of a life of domestic hardships.

"My goodness, what has happened to you?" The shocked tone of Yihong's voice was palpable. "It breaks my aged heart to see you like this! Back when I first took you in, I wouldn't even let you get your hands wet to wash your face, and made sure that one of the maids patted you dry afterward, just to keep your hands soft and lovely. It truly breaks my heart!" She dabbed at her eyes, as if there were tears, with the sleeve of her green jacket. Deyun could say nothing as her eyes reddened, and she hung her head, so immersed in her own personal grief that she was oblivious to the scrutiny by the old madam, who peered above her raised sleeve.

Seven years had passed since this country girl from Dongguan had first stood in front of Yihong's bed. Now she was back, the frightened look in her eyes replaced by meekness. She had returned as a housewife with callused hands. As if she'd just awakened from a long dream, Yihong pulled back the curtain, while her onetime creation related the story of her life over the past seven years and described the scars they had left on her. Her full breasts were all the sharp-eyed Yihong needed to see to know that she had borne a child. Then, as the madam's gaze glided downward, it was as if she could see through the coarse clothing; what she visualized was a naked body, and by comparing that with her memory of the slim-waisted girl, she could see that she had thickened around the waist since becoming a mother, but that her skin had a greater luster than before, thanks to the increased fat content. Tauter than before, her skin had taken on a pink hue—different but no less attractive.

A few sentences were all it took to get Huang Deyun to relate the essence of her life since leaving Yihong. When she told how the Englishman had rented a flat for her, Yihong glared at her and said, "How much did you charge the *guailow* to cohabit with him?"

"It was during the plague, when everything was topsy-turvy—"

With a loud slap of her hands, Yihong cut her off.

"Stupid girl. Not only sleeping with a *guailow* but having his child! Is that how I taught you?"

Huang Deyun struggled to defend herself by saying that the Englishman had at least sent her money even after leaving her. But that only led to tears. More questions led to talk about the Englishman's subordinate, Qu Yabing, and, from the way she stammered, Yihong guessed the nature of their relationship, which had ended in her being cast aside a second time. With a frown and a sarcastic tone, she said, "The fortune teller said that Ah-yun was born to be the mistress of a respectable family, so as your surrogate mother, I burned incense and said prayers daily, hoping you'd wind up as a second wife to a rich man, one day being raised to the status of first wife, transformed from a lowly woman to the mistress of a household, visiting us here as your natal family and giving Yihong Pavilion a great deal of face."

As new sorrows joined old resentments, Huang Deyun fell into the madam's embrace and wept bitterly.

"All I want is a peaceful life and a chance to raise my son. . . ."

The words "peaceful life" fell on deaf ears, for nothing disgusted Yihong more than the path to normal domestic life, in which a woman helps her husband and teaches her children. "Ah-yun, if that is what you seek in life, then you've crossed the wrong threshold. Nothing worries Yihong more than being seen as a doddering old matriarch receiving the birthday wishes of a houseful of sons and grandsons."

Suddenly deprived of all hope, Huang Deyun dropped her hands and went weak at the knees. Yihong let her lie down on the opium bed.

"It isn't up to me, but my darling girl, it is wishful thinking to hope for happiness and longevity if your fate decrees otherwise!" But then, as an idea popped into her head, Yihong raised her voice. "It's strange, my darling girl, but you're so much prettier when you're lying down, which must mean that you were born to live this life. Becoming the mistress of a household requires a certain look. A moment ago, when you were standing there hanging your head, you weren't nearly as pretty as you are at this moment."

And so the decision was made for Huang Deyun to move back into her second-story room, with the same attendant who had served her before. She promised to return in three days, after vacating her Happy Valley flat and gathering up her possessions. Deyun declined Yihong's offer to have the maidservant go with her.

"Don't worry, I'll keep my promise to come back."

Embarrassed by the comment, Yihong gave Deyun a bottle of imported French lotion to soften her hands. "You say your Englishman was generous to you," she added, "so be sure to bring back all the jewelry and nice clothes he gave you. We can get you back to the way you were faster that way."

"I don't think those clothes will fit anymore, not after childbirth, especially around the waist."

Pointing at the space between Deyun's brows, Yihong replied somberly:

"Ha, that's what you say. But things will be different this time. Listen to me, and everything will be just fine."

9

Three days later, Huang Deyun returned to Yihong Pavilion, as promised. When the maid saw that she was carrying nothing, she assumed she'd left everything on the rickshaw she'd taken in order to protect her hands and volunteered to bring her things in for her. Waving her off with a smile, Deyun walked in and went upstairs to the room where she'd lived as a lowly woman. The curtains had not been drawn, even though it was broad daylight; she hurried over to open the curtains and expose the small, barred, prisonlike window high up on the wall. The iron bed had been replaced by an exquisite red bed with ivory inlays and thick bedding; all the other furnishings in the room were exactly as before.

Everything had been taken care of. Huang Deyun sighed softly. Yihong would supply room and board, as well as a maid, and Deyun would work independently, turning over half the money she earned with her body to Yihong Pavilion. Now that the conditions of employment had been worked out, it was time to give herself over to Yihong. The first order of business would be to shed her coarse cotton clothing, go to the wardrobe on which a pair of gilded mandarin ducks frolicked in the water, and take out a V-necked willow green jacket with tight sleeves. The jacket, which highlighted the contours of her full breasts, would be cinched at the waist with a scarlet pleated skirt. Then she would sit at the dressing table, remove the red satin that covered the mirror, and begin putting on her makeup. Would she, when she finished, be able to congratulate herself on recapturing a sensual appearance that was beautiful, whether she was angry or happy?

The words of encouragement uttered by Yihong three days before still rang in her ears: "My darling girl, now that you're back, you need to be clear on what is real and what is not. You will need to be more discerning than before. If one of your clients is particularly fond of you, exploit that until he's reduced to bloody pulp. The gold and silver that winds up in your hands, that is real."

The madam's final admonishment was that she must not divulge that she had a son.

Huang Deyun gazed at the red-lacquered ivory bed on which she would once again make her living. A pair of mandarin duck pillows rested side by side beneath the headboard.

"You are much prettier when you're lying down, my darling girl. That you must accept."

She hadn't accepted any of this as her fate before, unwilling to believe that she'd been born to make her way in the world in this calling. She'd wanted to run away. But every window in Yihong Pavilion, upstairs and down, had been sealed with iron bars, and a brawny, dark-faced man who looked like a door god never left his post. Even if she'd sprouted wings, she couldn't have flown to freedom. Now, seven years later, she'd willingly returned to Yihong Pavilion, an independent prostitute who would spend her nights lying on that bed, grinding her teeth in backbreaking labor.

Huang Deyun let her fingers run over the silver lock on the red-lacquered wardrobe standing in a corner. The Englishman who had put her up in the Happy Valley flat had fixed the same sort of lock on her wardrobe door. She had promised Yihong that she'd bring back all the clothes she'd worn for the sake of her Englishman, which could be altered to accommodate changes in her figure. That would save time and money. Yihong told her she would have to be responsible for whatever clothing and jewelry she wanted to wear.

Back home, when she'd opened the wardrobe, she'd gone first to the bottom, where she'd stored all the beautiful clothing, amid worries that mice and insects had already gotten to them; she would consider herself lucky if she found two dresses that were in good enough shape to be altered for her new clients. She'd cursed herself for having been short-sighted. Reaching into the trunk, she'd pulled out a pair of new cloth slippers that she'd finished not long before this reunion with Yihong. Haphazard though the stitching might be, it was all her work, and she'd held them lovingly to her breast, feeling a sense of pride and fondness. As her gaze traveled upward, she'd spotted several sets of blue cotton summer trousers and blouses that had been worn many times; the floral patterns had already begun to fade. Ah, how long ago that was! She had grown used to wearing such coarse, comfortable cotton house clothes, and she wondered if she really wanted to exchange them for a wardrobe of the lavish attire required by the life of a lady of the night.

Now, after struggling to extricate herself from that profession, how could she allow herself to return to it?

She knew she had to leave. As she was walking out of the room, Deyun turned for a last look at the dressing mirror. Oh, how I wish it could stay forever hidden by that red satin, so that the prostitute of former days would never again make an appearance!

Huang Deyun parted the curtains and walked out, feeling no regret at all. She sighed, as if a great burden had been lifted from her shoulders; each step in her black cloth slippers, which had lost their aura of inferiority, put that much distance between her and a life lived in that room.

Downstairs, she headed straight for Yihong's opium couch, the corners of her mouth rising in a self-satisfied smile. When the madam saw that she was still wearing the coarse cotton clothes she'd come in three days earlier, her face unadorned with makeup, she complained, "What sort of game are you playing with me? It's late. Now get back upstairs and get yourself ready! No one has died in Yihong Pavilion, so you can take off those mourning clothes. I've treated you like a mother, doing everything possible for you out of the kindness of my heart. I was concerned that since you just arrived, you might like to hear the accent of your hometown, so I sent someone running all over the place to find an old acquaintance you could talk to."

Curling her lip, Yihong continued, "My spoiled little darling girl has a short memory, and has probably never given a second thought to the comprador who put your ability to speak that barbarian language to the test, Wu Fu, who was as fat as a mountain. Does that ring a bell?"

The frown on Deyun's face expressed the revulsion she felt. Why is she in such a hurry? I barely step into the room and the client is right behind me. She took a deep breath to calm herself. She told Yihong not to worry, that she would leave as soon as she'd spoken her mind.

Yihong had been waiting for her return since early that morning. The maid came to tell her she'd arrived and had gone straight to her room. Perfect timing, the madam said to herself. Her beautiful and accomplished "lute girl" had returned to the nest, and she was ready to get the word out. She had no doubt that requests from clients, old and new, would fill the air like snowflakes, and the day that Yihong Pavilion would reclaim its former glamour was not far off. In order to keep a tight rein on this money tree that had appeared at her door, she planned to find a handsome pimp, whose sole task was to wait on her and report back on her activities. Once a bond was established between the two of them, the prostitute would not think of leaving. In a couple of years, when her looks began to fade, that would be the time to send her on her way.

"Leave? Do you think this is a place where you can come and go as you please?

Confronted with the madam's brows, which stood up like a pair of knives, Huang Deyun lowered her eyes.

"I am grateful for all your motherly kindnesses and the plans you've made for me. But I'm not up to the task."

"Are you afraid this place of mine is too high-class? Maybe you'd rather take yourself over to a whorehouse in one of Wan Chai's squalid lanes, where you can sit on a stool in the doorway just waiting for some pig butcher or coolie to pick and choose? Or maybe you'd prefer to work as a sex slave on one of those floating whorehouses, where they beat you black and blue and keep your clothes from you during the day so you can't go out?"

Rather than get angry, Huang Deyun actually smiled.

"You're speaking directly to my heart. A woman who returns to prostitution after being married is like a decomposing rat. She's guaranteed a hard life; as the years pass and her looks abandon her, she must then eke out a living by leading a blind masseuse to her clients. That is what I call a hard life."

She stared down at Yihong's embroidered slippers with their brand-new soles. "I wish I had your talents, but I am no match for you . . . besides, dragging my son along with me only adds to the problem. I plan to send him to school in a couple of years, and I can—"

"Hogwash!" Yihong leaned over and spat angrily into the cuspidor. "You're comparing yourself to me? How dare you! When I say something, I mean it. You'd pee your pants if I told you all the frightful things I've done.

"If that little bastard means so much to you, fine. You are no longer welcome at Yihong Pavilion, so get out! Go live your life as a filial mother!"

Huang Deyun straightened her clothes and bowed deeply.

"Once my son has made something of himself, he'll come pay his respects to you."

She took the bottle of French lotion out from under her clothes and laid it on the couch.

"I never opened the bottle, let alone used any of it. You can trust me."

Without waiting for the maid to open the door for her, Huang Deyun walked out of Yihong Pavilion and breathed a sigh of relief. She felt cleansed, cleansed and empty. She touched her hair to gather herself before starting off. Walking excitedly in her direction was a fat man who seemed as big as a mountain. It was none other than Wu Fu, the right-hand man of the comprador at Jardine's. Seven years earlier, he had just returned from collecting payment for opium in several provinces and presented Yihong with a gift of high-grade opium paste from Yunnan Province. He and Huang Deyun had exchanged a few words of English.

Now here he was, all smiles, having been invited by Yihong. The fact that the woman in the doorway was Huang Deyun, the one he had put on a pedestal seven years earlier, did not occur to him. He had been asked to stop by that afternoon to finally savor that which he'd been expecting for years. That is how the old madam had characterized the invitation.

As they passed shoulder to shoulder, he spotted the beauty mark on the woman's cheek. He turned and gazed at the retreating back, dressed in coarse cotton clothes.

10

The year: 1900. The eve of the Ghost Festival, midway through the seventh lunar month. After frantically running from place to place, drenching her shirts in sweat and wearing out the soles of two pairs of slippers, Huang Deyun finally found refuge for herself and her son in a shabby hut on a steep side street near Mount Taiping. She had left the huge four-poster bed with its springy mattress at the flat in Happy Valley; now, laying her meager possessions on the wooden bed and sitting down on a bamboo stool to wipe her sweaty face with a corner of her shirt, she was determined to start life anew. As she gazed at the squat door and windows, she complimented herself on her decision, for the big bed would never have made it through the doorway, even if she'd removed the double panels.

Finding a place to live had been much more difficult than she'd imagined. She had assumed that the angry departure of twenty thousand Chinese residents, who protested the colonial government's restrictive new housing regulations by returning to their homes in Canton following the most devastating plague ever to hit Hong Kong, would have resulted in empty houses all across the Chinese district on Mount Taiping. But that was not the case. As the plague raged through Hong Kong, the city's population actually increased, first by laborers from North America, Australia, and Southeast Asia, followed by refugee families heading south with all their possessions in the wake of the Boxer Rebellion. These new arrivals squeezed onto the stony island, which could boast no natural resources or fields to tend, then set about engaging in all sorts of occupations to keep body and soul together.

Huang Deyun hired a pair of rickshaws to carry her possessions that she had originally packed for her move back to her new living quarters in Yihong Pavilion. Her next-door neighbor, named Zhou, was a young widow whose husband had died in the plague of 1894. After burying her husband, she'd vowed not to remarry, and even after the mourning period ended, had continued to wear black clothing, She wore a constant frown and was not given to casual, light banter. She had no relatives in Hong Kong, but was a wonderful cook, specializing in dishes from her hometown in Canton, and was thus able to find work as an assistant chef at a Central District restaurant on Queen's Road.

Seeing that her new neighbor was about her own age, and that she had a small son but, apparently, no husband, Widow Zhou assumed that they were in the same boat, especially when she noticed that no relatives came calling and that the house was quiet all day long. A widow, just like her. And so, pretending she was returning a towel that had been blown off the clothesline by the wind, she knocked on Huang Deyun's door. As they got to know each other, Deyun learned that the other woman worked as a chef, and she wished she weren't so inept in the kitchen.

"I can help you look for work if you'd like. Not in a restaurant, maybe, since you don't seem to need that meager amount. You can just consider it extra money for flowers, and you'll have a place to go." Widow Zhou heaved an emotional sigh. "Time seems to stand still when you're cooped up in the house day and night."

That night, Huang Deyun lay in bed, still not quite used to sleeping on wooden slats, and mulled over what Widow Zhou had said. Since sleep was out of the question, she got up, pulled back a corner of the window curtain, and looked up at the muted light of the crescent moon. She let the moon's rays shine into every corner of the room.

Rain was falling outside, setting up a tattoo on the tile roof that lasted until daybreak.

When Widow Zhou came home after work the next day, she told Deyun that a pawnshop near her restaurant was looking for help, someone neat and clean who could read and write. Deyun asked what the job required, but Widow Zhou wasn't quite sure.

"If you're interested, come to the restaurant tomorrow, and I'll take you to see the woman in charge. You can ask her what the job is all about."

Actually, Deyun knew without asking that a job in a pawnshop was far from ideal, but she wasn't cut out for physical labor, and the only calling she had was peeling fruit and steeping tea for clients. Widow Zhou was not far off when she said that Deyun could use the money to buy flowers to wear in her hair. The coins left by the Englishman formed a small pile, and so long as she watched her money closely, there'd be enough for her and her son to get by on. When it was time to send Richard to school, she might have to sell off some of the jewelry she kept in her black-lacquered jewelry box decorated with a gilded phoenix, but that was still years away.

After so many years and the changes they had brought, in the end she was going to be a servant again. The more she thought about it, the less attractive it seemed, and she made up her mind to stay home after all. The next day she cleaned her new home, which consisted only of a living room and a single bedroom, from top to bottom. Since it was so much smaller than her place in Happy Valley, it didn't take long. Richard was off looking for playmates, so Deyun sat alone waiting for the sun to set. Finally, unable to sit there doing nothing, she decided to go see Widow Zhou at the restaurant. First she laid her clothes out on the bed, wondering what she should wear to make a good impression. She settled on an old but still presentable light blue blouse and pants, which, after many washings, had a baggy look that made her breasts look less prominent. Just before leaving, she removed the jade bracelet she normally wore everywhere. But going out with nothing to hold onto felt so strange that she picked up a pink handkerchief. Yet even that seemed somehow out of place for someone seeking a job, so she tucked it away as she stepped out onto the busy street, where rickshaws and sedan chairs vied for space with pedestrians coming and going in all directions. At the corner of Bonham Strand East, she spotted a peculiar, three-story building with a stone façade that gave it the appearance of a fortress, in part because it stood all alone. The word "Pawnshop" was etched above the doorway, and above the door hung a signboard that proclaimed Prosperity Pawnshop in the shape of a bat. The shop, standing proud and all alone, seemed to hold forbidden mysteries.

Huang Deyun skirted the screen wall in front of the door and stepped through a side door that opened onto the rear garden of the pawnshop proprietor's living quarters. From there, she passed down a long courtyard that ended in front of a dark room. Once her eyes had gotten used to the darkness, she searched for the pawnshop broker, a man in a long, padded and embroidered silk Chinese gown and holding an ivory fan in his hand. A little old lady sat cross-legged in an intricately carved armchair to the left of a black-lacquered altar table some three or four feet away from Deyun. The large figure of a female servant stood respectfully behind her. Not a sound disturbed the stillness of the dark room, except for the soft gurgle of the old lady's water pipe. Even on such a hot day, the armchair was covered by a thick woolen blanket, and resting alongside it was one of those silver-tipped canes preferred by Western gentlemen. The black velvet clothing worn by the old lady gave off a sort of luminescence that created a muted splendor around her. A row of shiny gold buttons ran down the front of her dress, each of them a gold fifty-cent piece brought back to China from San Francisco by an overseas Chinese. She held her water pipe in elbow-length white gloves, like those worn by ladies at an overseas ball. The gloves slipped easily over her rail-thin arms. Imagining the clawlike hands hidden by the gloves, Huang Deyun timidly moved her gaze upward to the old lady's cheeks, wrinkled as walnut shells, with spots of rouge at the tips of the high cheekbones. The same redness encircled her eyes, one of which sported a monocle, enlarging the eye behind it, which didn't so much as twitch. She was Lady Eleven, known to all pawnbrokers as the woman who had changed the course of the life of the proprietor of Prosperity Pawnshop, Mr. Li, by rescuing him from certain death.

The Li family of southern Canton had operated pawnshops since the early years of the Qing dynasty; business had never been better for the current generation, Li Quan and his brothers. Since the Daoguang reign, at the end of the Manchu dynasty, the coastal area of China had suffered repeated encroachments by imperialist powers, with nearly constant warfare and the resultant destruction of the area's agricultural base. The people were forced to pawn their belongings just to survive. So the Li brothers opened pawnshops in the marketplaces at Yuen Long, Sheung Shui, and Taipo. They had a thriving business, and the name Prosperity Pawnshop was known far and wide.

Following the Opium Wars, Li Quan, the third son in his family, crossed the water to Hong Kong, where he opened the territory's first pawnshop, and took the name of the family's businesses in Canton— Prosperity. The layout of the pawnshop was in accordance with age-old tradition: the bat shape of the signboard signified well-being and good fortune. The counter, which rose high above a person standing before it, was enclosed in a metal cage. The pawn slips, written in ancient, virtually unintelligible script, could be deciphered only by people working in the pawnshop.

Prosperity Pawnshop quickly established itself as one of the more successful businesses in the colony, and the Li brothers were so arrogant they spurned the fierce-looking police who came demanding bribes and left intent on getting revenge. Lawlessness reigned in the colony's early days, when pirates and highwaymen, petty thieves and small-time robbers disposed of their loot and stolen gains by taking them to a pawnshop to exchange for cash, free of any requirement to give their names or addresses; inevitably, a considerable quantity of stolen goods wound up in pawnshops.

Prosperity Pawnshop had taken in a gold Western wristwatch, which the police determined had been stolen from the home of an Englishman. As a result, Li Quan was dragged into court and accused of receiving stolen goods. The case got under way just as the Arrow Incident, the cause of the second Opium War, occurred. Worried that the Chinese would be provoked into a violent reaction against the British ruling class, the judge sentenced Li Quan to a fourteen-year stint as a conscript in Southeast Asia as a warning to others—killing the chicken to frighten the monkeys. Li Quan thus had the distinction of becoming the colony's first sacrificial victim to the colonizers' authority.

Li Quan protested the harsh penalty over such a minor offense, and demanded a lighter sentence. Six policemen dragged him out of the courtroom. Some time later, the Li family's Lady Eleven, who was the patriarch's sixth concubine, paid a bribe to the Chinese concubine of a senior official of the British colonial government; her efforts resulted in the official's intercession by reducing the sentence to two years.

Lady Eleven's great service was recognized even after Li Quan's death. Everyone at the pawnshop followed her orders.

By the time Huang Deyun met Lady Eleven, she was already a very old woman, and was no longer involved in the day-to-day business of the pawnshop. But, unwilling to change her routine, she got up early each morning, dressed in her finest, and, with the help of her servant, sat cross-legged in the armchair of the pawnshop to smoke her water pipe. Each time the proprietor was offered an expensive item, he sought the advice of Lady Eleven, in accordance with established custom. It was she who fixed the price. Most of the time, Lady Eleven passed the time reading the *North China Herald*. Six months earlier, she had lost sight in her right eye from glaucoma and had taken to wearing a monocle in her left eye, but reading a newspaper remained difficult even with its significant magnification. Since none of the women in the Li family was literate, Huang Deyun's job would be to wait on Lady Eleven by reading the Chinese newspapers aloud, filling her pipe with tobacco, pouring tea, peeling fruit, and fanning her. Deyun was hesitant to take the job, for even though she knew how to read, having been taught during her days as a prostitute in Yihong Pavilion, she was reluctant to be seen as a mere maidservant. The strange little old lady in the armchair seemed hard to please. But on the other hand, if Deyun passed up this opportunity, she could only return to her home near Water Moon Pavilion to gaze blankly at the shadows, with no one to talk to, since Widow Zhou didn't return home from work at the restaurant until after dinner. Twisting the handkerchief in her fingers, Huang Deyun was troubled by the thought of returning home to sit and wait for the sun to sink slowly behind the mountains.

A copy of the *North China Herald* lay on the table beside the armchair, held down by a magnifying glass, the handle still warm from the hand of Lady Eleven, who had just finished reading the newspaper. What did all those densely packed characters have to say that made the old lady so anxious to have a second pair of eyes read to her? Intrigued by the question, Huang Deyun took a look around the mysterious pawnshop, and before agreeing to try her hand at the job, informed them that she had a small child at home, which meant she needed to arrive late and return home early, and that she would wear whatever she thought appropriate, clear indication that she would not stand for being treated like a servant.

With her good eye, Lady Eleven scrutinized the woman standing before her; finding even that inadequate, she picked the magnifying glass up off the table, stared at Deyun through it, and asked in a stern voice if she had any other conditions of employment.

With a slight twisting of her neck and an adjustment of her carriage, Deyun said calmly, "Besides being able to read the *North China Herald*, I know a little bit of a foreign language. I can read the squiggles of the English alphabet."

That produced a far more respectful look in the old woman's eye.

The road to riches leads from a pawnshop.

As Hong Kong began to develop, money-changers and pawnshop brokers amassed wealth faster and more easily than most. Minimal competence was all that was needed to join the ranks of the very wealthy, which in turn earned them respect throughout society.

With little to do but relive her memories, Lady Eleven answered many of Huang Deyun's unspoken questions regarding pawnshop traditions, starting with the function of the screen at the entrance.

"Pawnshops are invariably located on busy streets, and the screens serve to protect the privacy of embarrassed customers, keeping them away from prying eyes." As for why the counter stood six or seven feet high, and was enclosed in a metal cage with two or three openings through which the customer could pass the items to be pawned, that was to protect the shop employees. "Some of our customers are desperate for money," Lady Eleven said, "and are often dissatisfied with what they are offered for their possessions. Once their anger mounts, they'd reach out and grab the pawnbroker by the collar if they could, and become violent. We cannot have that."

During the long summer days, Huang Deyun read the entire *North China Herald*, from the front-page headlines through the literary supplement, and was finished by early afternoon, when Lady Eleven took a long nap. When she awoke, Huang Deyun helped her over to her armchair, where she filled her water pipe and poured tea. Then the two women, who barely knew each other, sat in the darkened room gazing at the sky until the sun sank behind the mountains. Bored by just sitting there, Lady Eleven would begin reminiscing about events in Prosperity Pawnshop's long history, relating a host of interesting episodes to pass the time.

11

Huang Deyun saw Qu Yabing on one more occasion. She was passing by the Minru Teahouse on her way home after work, when she spotted his familiar figure entering the teahouse; she recognized him at once, with his black cloth shoes and foolish look. Those same black cloth shoes! She calmly turned away, feeling no pangs of regret.

He reasoned that she could only have wound up one of three ways:

Given her natural good looks, she could now be someone's concubine. That would be the best she could hope for.

A second possibility was that she'd returned to the brothel and a life of prostitution. After a few years, when her looks faded, she'd purchase a few girls and become the madam of her own brothel. The beauty mark on her cheek was an omen that favored this outcome.

The third and last possibility was that she had grown disillusioned with the mortal world and had entered a mountain nunnery to spend the rest of her days reciting sutras and subsisting on vegetarian fare.

What had in fact happened fell outside his prediction, at least for the moment. Qu Yabing could not have imagined that she would find proper work in a pawnshop. Given his suspicious nature, there were reasons for his conjectures.

If not for the fact that he had dirtied himself in a relationship with that whore, given his propensity for stirring up trouble and his training in making confidential reports on people, Qu Yabing would not have hesitated to reveal a secret to his onetime boss, that the man's illegitimate son, now seven years old, was living in a small room on a side street near the Water Moon Pavilion. The little bastard had gray eyes, skin whiter than his father's, and a mischievously upturned nose. Even without freckles, any sharp-eyed individual could see at a glance that the boy was a mirror image of Adam Smith.

Qu Yabing's latest news was that the whore was intent on having her bastard son attend a foreign school, to receive an English education. She had learned that a philanthropist by the name of Ho Tung, chief comprador at Jardine's, himself of mixed blood, had donated a piece of land for the construction of an elementary school, and had announced that students would be accepted regardless of race or religion. Huang Deyun went to register her son as soon as she heard the wonderful news, only to discover that the British colonials had adopted a policy of segregation, insisting that only white children could attend the school. Richard Huang's application was turned down. Reluctantly, his mother enrolled him in a Chinese school. Before his first day at school, she told him that if he was teased by his classmates over his high nose and deep-set eyes, or if they tried to bully him because he looked different, he was to say he had Manchu blood. He was not to reveal that his father was British.

Qu Yabing was well aware that the prejudice by the colony's white residents toward people of mixed blood was not limited to schoolchildren; after they grew to adulthood, they were restricted from membership in the Hong Kong Club and were not permitted to participate in any official athletic organizations. In a word, all realms of British society were closed to them. And where jobs were concerned, no matter how talented they might be, they received only half the pay given to British employees. In Richard Huang's case, not only was he of mixed blood, he also carried the shame of being illegitimate and the son of a whore. And so Qu Yabing could relish the prospect that the boy's future was bleak.

After Adam Smith returned from the New Territories to his old job at the Sanitary Board, he recommenced overseeing the cleaning of filthy streets in the Chinese districts. His shoes, with their mirrorlike shine, once again resounded on the cobblestones as he made his rounds, white-gloved hands clasped behind his back. But Qu Yabing had learned from his former colleagues that the Englishman had changed, was given to strange behavior and extremely moody. He would, for example, blow up at one of his assistants over a trivial matter, and on one occasion had even slapped a sanitation worker for moving too slowly, only to appear remorseful over his explosive behavior immediately afterward. Then, on the night before Easter Sunday, he summoned one of his Catholic workers and, in front of everyone, humiliated him by calling him "a local native who prays to the Guanyin Bodhisattva before going to church."

This gossip was not completely groundless, for Adam Smith was a man who found it more and more difficult to figure himself out and less and less easy to like what he saw in himself. One day his boss, Mr. Windsor, spoke to him about white slave traders in Africa, referring to the black natives as a race of savage cannibals.

"Sending those savages to Europe and America," Mr. Windsor intoned, stopping to puff on his cigar, "where they can learn from civilized and rational white men, eventually becoming productive members of the human race, is a charitable act."

Adam Smith listened with a look of agreement on his face, but deep down he questioned the validity of this view, held by most white colonials. As he left his superior's office with a bow and a sense of disgust, he abandoned Mr. Windsor as his model for a life as a well-bred gentleman and vowed that, except for the bureaucrats, he would have no more dealings with two types of British residents: evangelizing missionaries and rapacious merchants. From that day on, Smith could often be seen drowning his sorrows in the Hong Kong Club bar, all alone and often late into the night.

One night, an artist visiting Hong Kong happened to be in the bar with Smith. After a few drinks, the artist began talking about the Congo, where he had personally witnessed the barbarous activities of white merchants who plundered stocks of ivory and kidnapped natives as slaves.

"Not that this is the first time," the artist said as he sipped his whisky. "Centuries ago, when Columbus discovered the Americas, he claimed great quantities of gold and other riches as his own, to be presented to the king and queen of Spain."

Rather than respond, Adam Smith looked down and gloomily sipped his drink as the artist prattled on and on, painting verbal pictures of rafting through the jungle down the Congo and describing the strange customs of natives on the banks of the river. As they were saying good-bye, Smith suggested to the artist that he should take the Kowloon ferry the next morning over to the New Territories and spend the day painting the scenery there. He was sure that, like him, the artist would be captivated by the natural beauty of Chinese villages and would wander around the temples, the farmhouses, and the streams flowing beneath arched bridges, as if possessed. Then he could sit at the base of a wall and sketch the villagers as they smoked pipes and played chess beneath banyan trees or paint children riding bamboo horses on the temple grounds.

His eyes bloodshot from all the liquor he had consumed, the tipsy Smith felt himself transported to one of the villages, where he stood in front of a lantern shop, watching a village girl with a blue bandana on her head and a willow basket over her arm emerge from a narrow lane and walk toward him. Her pointed chin and the way she walked reminded Smith of the woman he had tried so hard to forget: she must have looked like that before she was kidnapped and sold to a Hong Kong brothel to be trained as a prostitute. Dressed all in white clothing with a flowered pattern, copper earrings dangling from her ears, and a fair complexion, just like this village girl. He conjured up a vision of a pristine village, with Huang Deyun sitting in a courtyard spinning yarn, while he sat in a wicker chair listening to the chirping of insects and sipping warm rice liquor. In his drunken state, he thought he'd found a place that resembled his hometown, some thousands of miles away, in Britain, where he could play the flute and recite lines from Tennyson's lyrical poetry.

If only he had met Huang Deyun in that village, ringed by mountains. Moreover, his dream of an appointment at the local police precinct, where he could stand on a balcony and look across at the hilltop where the Union Jack was lowered, was fading fast.

Smith raised his head and drank what was left in his glass. There was still one place he could go: the Qixiang brothel in Shek Tong Tsui.

On this night he would be holding a full-bodied woman and thinking about the laughable story of a territory opened by prostitutes and their clients, one in which he himself was actually participating. Smith wiped drops of liquor from his lips and had to laugh at himself.

Shek Tong Tsui had originally been a coastal mountain. The first to settle the mountainside were Hakka masons who came across the sea from Huizhou soon after Hong Kong opened up, making a living by selling granite from mountain quarries for building material. The mountain was leveled over time, until it was little more than a rocky hill near the ocean shore, exposing it to the menacing of pirates and causing a mass exodus by the masons; the area turned into a wasteland.

In 1903 the Hong Kong government completed a land reclamation project there, but, unfortunately, the vast new area remained undeveloped, owing to the proximity of Possession Street, with its taverns and brothels. Shek Tong Tsui could not compete. And so the colonial government devised the perfect solution: a decree was published that Possession Street was too small to accommodate the expansion of brothels in the overcrowded district, and the latest arrivals were given a deadline to shut down and move west to Shek Tong Tsui. In other words, the reclaimed land was to be developed as a red-light district.

The tavern and brothel proprietors, wanting neither to be in conflict with the colonial government nor to suffer a downturn in their business, had no alternative but to transport their customers to Shek Tong Tsui. Readers of Chinese newspapers frequently came across advertisements such as the following: "Rickshaws will be available at Possession Street every day from five in the afternoon to one in the morning for the use of our honored clients."

Thanks to the efforts of brothel and tavern owners, this desolate stretch of land was quickly transformed into a bustling district where music and gaiety filled the air nightly.

12

Huang Deyun had heard something about this "territory opened by prostitutes and their clients" and read one of the advertisements in the *North China Herald*. Such things were no longer part of her life, so she closed the newspaper, got up, and handed Lady Eleven a bowl of swallow's nest soup.

Huang Deyun had become a woman transformed.

She rose at the crack of dawn, dressed in clothes she'd laid out the night before, applied light makeup and a spot of lipstick, and, laying down her mirror, took her son to Granny Woo's house for the day. On the way over, she reminded Richard to be a good boy, then stopped on the way to buy two bunches of fresh flowers, both varieties of fragrant magnolia, which she wrapped in a cloth bundle to take to Lady Eleven. Once the lady had picked out what she liked, she'd pin the rest on her own lapel. Huang Deyun had barely stepped in the door of the pawnshop when the servant helped Lady Eleven over to her armchair and placed the day's *North China Herald* on the tea table beside her. From the moment Deyun opened the door, her world expanded; as she read the news from China and the outside world, her universe extended far beyond the confines of the dark room. Like a sponge, she absorbed the news, broadening her understanding and her knowledge of life.

An even greater source of knowledge came from Lady Eleven, who had lived a full life. During Li Quan's two years in prison, she had sat in her armchair, legs crossed, as she ran Prosperity Pawnshop; the degree of her success astounded Huang Deyun, who grew to revere the old woman.

When her curiosity got the better of her one day, Huang Deyun sat in the armchair while Lady Eleven was taking her nap; crossing her legs, she tried to imagine the almost magical aura that surrounded Lady Eleven, something she longed to possess herself.

On the hundredth anniversary of the birthday of the former proprietor, Li Quan, Huang Deyun gently helped Lady Eleven out of her armchair and over to Li Quan's portrait, where, aided by her silver-tipped cane, she went down on her knees. When Deyun helped her back to her feet, Lady Eleven had a dull look on her face, as if her deceased husband's portrait had taken her soul from her—as if she had gone to him, leaving behind only an insignificant human form. Slipping her hands under the old woman's armpits, Deyun had the sensation that she was holding nothing but clothing. In preparation for paying her respects to her deceased husband, Lady Eleven had dressed in a dark purple satin robe embroidered with coiled dragons; it was so stiff that Deyun was denied the feeling of flesh and bones in her hands.

What strength Lady Eleven possessed began slipping away after that day; no longer did she make comments as she listened to Deyun read the newspaper. Now she merely sat in her armchair, her good eye closed, apparently asleep. If she noticed no movement from the old lady for a long time, Deyun would quickly place her hand under her nose, wondering if she had died in her sleep.

Lady Eleven's breathing was as flimsy as gossamer, her body was wasting away, and she began to emit an unpleasant odor, the smell of impending death. Deyun noticed it as she wiped the old lady's lips dry of tea, and she began to grow fearful of being alone with Lady Eleven in the dark room, surrounded by the shadowy spirit tablets and portraits of Li family ancestors.

As Lady Eleven's naps lengthened, Huang Deyun got into the habit of walking upstairs to the patio for a breath of fresh air; there she would help the pawnshop apprentice, Yaming, air some of the fine clothing pawned by customers. The pawnshop practiced the traditional means of protecting clothing from rats and insects: once each spring and autumn, all the robes and jackets, silk dresses, and leather garments were taken up to the patio to be aired out. From snippets of conversation with Yaming, Deyun picked up sketchy details about the pawnshop operation. Driven by her natural curiosity, she listened with keen interest.

Lady Eleven's last waking moments were spent listening to a news report from Beijing in the *North China Herald*. The Boxers had wreaked havoc in northern China, and the eight allied powers had fought their way into the city of Beijing, where the foreign soldiers had sacked the local pawnshops, taking everything, including door and window frames, even floor tiles. They'd then burned the buildings to the ground, without exception.

"The bandits are coming, they're coming to plunder again. Run for your lives!"

Lady Eleven grabbed her silver-tipped cane with one hand and brushed off the wool blanket covering her knees, as if she were about to get up and run away. Her shoulders were heaving, but she was too weak to get up from the armchair. Deyun held her down gently and tried to console her. "Don't be afraid, there's no need to be afraid. That's happening far away, in Beijing."

"No, no, they're coming for us! They're coming in from the skylight. I can hear their footsteps on the roof. There's so much money in the pawnshop, and jewelry, that's what they want. . . ."

Back when Li Quan had come to Hong Kong from Yuen Long to make his fortune, he'd known that Prosperity Pawnshop would attract thieves and robbers because of its name alone, so he'd chosen this location on Bonham Strand and built the shop where there were no surrounding buildings. In addition to his fear of fire from an adjoining building, given all the valuable and flammable contents of the shop, this made it more difficult for thieves and robbers to do their handiwork. The most obvious means of entry would be the skylight, so he enclosed that with barbed wire and broken glass. Then he decided to build a vault for the most expensive items right in the middle of the central courtyard, far from the street, to keep it away from thieves who might scale the wall.

Lady Eleven had praised Li Quan's foresight many times in the past.

"It's a good thing my husband took those precautions," Lady Eleven said as she signaled Huang Deyun to come closer to share her secret. "The pawnshop itself was the last to be built, the masons working at night by lamplight. Not only did they use extra-thick bricks, they also constructed double walls to keep the thieves out."

Lady Eleven paused, as her breathing grew shallow. She leaned over to Deyun, frequently stopping to catch her breath, and divulged Li Quan's secret in his pawnshop plans, as if taking care of the last business of her life. When she had finished, her silver-tipped cane slipped from her hand and she slumped deep into the chair. It was her last waking moment.

Lady Eleven breathed her last soon after Qingming, and Huang Deyun spent the day weeping in front of the now empty armchair. Without being asked, she put on mourning clothes, as if she were the old lady's granddaughter.

Once Lady Eleven's funeral had ended, her son, Li Jian summoned Huang Deyun to see if she planned to leave or stay. Seeing that she was still dressed in mourning clothes for the departed matriarch, he hadn't the heart to send her away, so he told her to go speak with Manager Zhao instead. It was her first visit to the pawnshop itself. Manager Zhao was sitting behind the counter with his back to her, in the midst of determining what he would pay a customer for a bronze-colored satin gown embroidered with cranes and a gilded fan from Suzhou. In a high-pitched voice, the manager intoned: "Write a ticket." This he followed with a string of unintelligible chirps and squeaks, none of which Huang Deyun understood. But the clerk knew exactly what he was expected to write on the red-lined sheet of paper, which the manager took from him before the ink was dry and read as if it were a book from heaven, before making a series of rapid calculations on his abacus. Taking some money from the drawer, he handed it, together with the pawn ticket, to the customer. Meanwhile, Yaming, the apprentice, took the pawned items, tagged and wrapped them in lambskin after carefully folding the robe, then tied the bundle with a hempen cord and carried it upstairs, where he put it in a numbered storage bin.

Over the past half year or so, Prosperity Pawnshop had enjoyed unprecedented prosperity. People fleeing from the chaos of the Boxer Rebellion up north were pawning their valuables in order to start out anew in Hong Kong. A steady stream of customers entered through the pawnshop door. The manager manipulated the abacus with his right hand and kept his left hand in the money drawer, where the sight of all those shiny coins had a dizzying effect on Huang Deyun. To her, the money drawer was like a bottomless cornucopia; she spent half the morning watching the money leave the pawnshop amid the musical gibberish from the manager and the clerk and the constant clacking of abacus beads. She took a deep breath. The individual smells of used cotton batting; timepieces; jade, gold, and silver ornaments; and articles of clothing merged with those of coins and paper money, producing an odor that was unique to pawnshops.

She liked the place.

Manager Zhao wore a goatee on a face that had turned yellow from opium smoke. Originally a Xinhui farmer, he had suffered the loss of his land from flooding after a typhoon; still young, he was forced to flee to Hong Kong, where his first job was as a gold ornaments craftsman in a jewelry shop. His delicate workmanship and innovative designs caught the attention of the wives and concubines in wealthy families, and he became the shop owner's most valued employee.

The manager was the lifeline of any pawnshop. He alone set the price for pawned items, and his eyes determined whether or not the items were genuine or forgeries; paying premium prices for overvalued items was something every pawnshop owner feared. When Huang Deyun finally went to speak with Manager Zhao, he was just then pondering the authenticity of some old paintings, and he dismissed Deyun by sending her to help Yaming air out some clothing. When she was finished with that, she was to help out in the shop. At other times, when the shop was particularly busy and they were short-handed, he told her to take over for him or lend a helping hand.

Within three months Deyun had become the person everyone depended on to do odd jobs.

Word that Huang Deyun was studying the intricacies of doing business somehow reached the ears of Qu Yabing; his long, narrow eyes opened wide in a show of disbelief. No matter how much she'd changed, in his eyes she would always be a woman who'd sold her body. And if the goateed Manager Zhao had agreed to keep her on, it could only be a result of an illicit relationship between them. The very idea—a prostitute studying the intricacies of business! Convinced that he had been victimized by that whore, he believed he knew what she was up to, that her so-called studies were a smokescreen for her true intention of getting the manager in her clutches.

And Qu Yabing wasn't the only person who felt that way. Rumors and nasty gossip regarding Huang Deyun were making the rounds everywhere. Out in the courtyard, servants in the Li household doing their laundry talked about how she and Manager Zhao flirted: the two of them lay side by side on the opium couch, engaged in all sorts of shameless behavior, or so said a woman who swore she'd seen them when she went in to pour tea. Meanwhile, the clerk in the pawnshop spread word that the accountant, Yahui, unable to resist Huang Deyun's pestering, had taught her how to use the abacus. In delicious detail, he said, "At first everything was as it should be, with the woman toting up figures on the abacus. But before long, four hands started touching back and forth, and got all tangled up—"

But even as rumors flew, business at the pawnshop only got better. Meanwhile, there was a marked change in Huang Deyun's appearance and behavior. In order to make the trips up and down the stairs easier when she aired out clothing, she drew her trouser cuffs tight around her ankles and kept her collar fashionably low-cut, exposing her porcelain neck to view. The highest button was a United States fifty-cent gold coin, which, according to her, Lady Eleven had given her as a keepsake. But Lady Eleven's personal maid insisted that she'd stolen it, removing it with a pair of scissors when the old lady was drifting in and out of consciousness. But just as she was about to snip off the next button, the servant said, complete with hand gestures, Deyun heard footsteps and quickly put the scissors down.

Huang Deyun paid no attention to all this talk swirling around the place. Each day, on her way home, she stopped at the market in Central for some take-out food, which she and her son ate under a lamp. Then, when Widow Zhou returned home from work, the two women talked about what they'd seen and done that day, and some of the time, Huang Deyun related stores she'd read in that day's *North China Herald.* Just before turning out the lamp and getting into bed, she'd wash her son's feet and decide what to wear to the pawnshop the following day. She'd lay the clothes out over her bamboo chair, the sight of which brought home the reality that, at least for one more day, she'd have somewhere to go, and that kept the nights from dragging on interminably.

When business was slow, Huang Deyun waited on Manager Zhao on his opium couch, filling his pipe and pouring tea for him, infuriating the servant who normally carried out these duties. But even the jealous woman's cutting remarks had no effect on Huang Deyun, who concentrated on listening as the manager taught her how to calculate interest on pawned items. People who had pawned items knew that the standard calculation was "nine out, thirteen in." The interest was calculated monthly, based upon the lunar calendar. One day late meant another month's interest, and if the item was not reclaimed at the end of the specified period, the pawnshop had the right to sell the item and keep the profit.

Now Huang Deyun understood why her neighbor, Widow Zhou, called pawnshops "thunder and lightning." Visitors to the shop lost everything, as if demolished by a bolt of lightning. Like Huang Deyun, Widow Zhou was all alone in Hong Kong, and in order to give her husband, a victim of the plague, a proper burial, she'd been forced to pawn a pair of silver bracelets given her as an engagement gift. She never managed to reclaim them, and that remained a source of sadness. Widow Zhou's eyes reddened whenever she thought of it, but she was still pleased for Huang Deyun for being able not only to support herself but to actually thrive.

"It's not only poor people who frequent pawnshops," Manager Zhao said unhurriedly. "Many people take advantage of pawnshops as a means of keeping their fine clothes safe. When the days turn warm, they take off their padded jackets and bring them to Prosperity Pawnshop for safe-keeping. If there were a fire, or thieves, or an infestation of insects, not only would the pawnshop be responsible for the original cost, but we would have to compensate them for ruined items."

Yet people still referred to pawnshops as giant spiders just waiting for a tasty meal to fall from the sky.

At the end of the first year following the death of Lady Eleven, the pawnshop took stock of items that customers had failed to reclaim. As she was helping take inventory, Manager Zhao handed Huang Deyun a nearly new embroidered pleated skirt.

"It was part of the dowry of the young daughter of the licentiate from Wong Ngai Chung. Her husband brought it in to pay off some gambling debts. Like it?"

Huang Deyun stroked the skirt, made of fine Hangzhou silk, in fash-ionable rose red. Two sea-blue ridges of unequal depth ran down the front of the skirt; the delicate embroidery made it clear that this was no ordinary skirt. Embroidered patterns filled every pleat, giving it the appearance of scales on a fish. Women who love beautiful things called them "scaly pleated skirts." Huang Deyun could not resist holding the gorgeous skirt up to her waist.

"Take it home with you."

Deyun folded the skirt very, very carefully, letting her fingers linger against the soft material, and finally and with considerable reluctance, handed it back to Manager Zhao.

"It would be a shame to take such a fine skirt home, just so it could wind up at the bottom of a chest."

After that, Manager Zhao saw her in a different light. Sometimes, when the spirit moved him, he revealed some of the secrets in determin-ing the value of antiques or instructed her in the unique calligraphic style of pawn tickets. "Stained or ripped silk gowns, torn leather jackets, old padded blue coats—in order to keep the pawn amount as low as possible and forestall disputes when the owner comes to reclaim the item, whether the customer agrees or not, make sure you call high quality average, new items old, intact items broken, and valuable things common. All clothing must be 'tattered,' all furs 'moth-eaten,' all paintings and scrolls 'tattered,' all jade mere 'saltpeter,' chicken-blood stones 'soapstone,' pure gold 'mere alloy,' and sandalwood, redwood, and cedar 'assorted woods.'"

One afternoon, just before the shop closed up for the day, a crisp voice rose from the foot of the counter: "A silk painting of a lady wearing flowers by Tang Bohu of the Ming dynasty, how much is it worth?"

Manager Zhao pointed with his chin for Huang Deyun to take the scroll and snap it open for the manager to determine the value.

"Not so hard," the anxious customer complained. "Be careful, that silk is dry and brittle. If you ruin it, you'll have to pay. This has been passed down from our ancestors, and I plan to come back and reclaim it."

Huang Deyun paled in fright, but Manager Zhao took it from her, gave it a quick look, and rolled it right back up.

"Since it's an authentic Tang Bohu," he said as he pushed it back through the cage window, "you'd better take it elsewhere. It's too rich for our blood."

The man standing at the foot of the counter, deflated by the comment, asked, "If it's a forgery, what's it worth?" After waving the man away, Manager Zhao turned to comfort Huang Deyun, who was still rattled. People said that he put his hands on her breasts, which were quivering like a pair of hidden doves. The family water carrier swore to heaven he'd seen it with his own eyes.

Many ugly rumors like that reached the ears of Qu Yabing. By then he was a regular patron at the Minru Teahouse on Bonham Strand East in Central. He was finally given the opportunity to wear the skullcap and black satin boots he'd had specially made after being assigned as a special assistant by Colonel White, but not to attend a grand official function. The rulers, wanting to show the Chinese leaders that they were in favor of equality between the races, occasionally invited British-educated, well-mannered Chinese gentlemen to official dinner parties. He would never be invited to such occasions. But one day he did in fact put on his skullcap and his black boots—it was for the one-month anniversary of the birth of his son, presented to him by his bound-foot wife. Dressed in his finest and carrying his son in his arms, he knelt before the portrait of his deceased mother.

Feeling his status clearly on the rise, Qu Yabing swaggered upstairs to the Minru Teahouse private room, where he sat at a table against the inside wall and laid his hands on the surface. There was no need to summon the waiter, a man who both hated and feared him, to bring a pot of Yunnan Pu'er tea and several snacks to go with it. As he sat there sipping his tea, he opened his long, narrow eyes wide and took a look around. Keeping his ear to the ground and taking note of what people were thinking, he compiled regular reports, which he handed to the head of the Police Bureau, Colonel White.

Two or three fellow customers were whispering back and forth, so Qu Yabing leaned forward, pretending to add tea to his cup, to eavesdrop on the conversation, hoping to hear views of dissent against the ruling government. Imagine his surprise when what he heard was the hushed conversation about an adulterous pawnshop manager and a woman who worked there. Qu Yabing didn't know whether to laugh or cry, so he simply kept listening, and enjoying it immensely. He was not surprised by what he heard, for as he sipped his tea, he heard confirmation that Huang Deyun was still the same whore as always. Feeling especially pleased with himself for seeing things so clearly, he gradually lost sight of his reason for being there in the first place.

13

Rumors concerning the shady liaison between Manager Zhao and Huang Deyun went unabated. Then, on the eve of the first Mid-Autumn Festival after the Boxer Rebellion, Manager Zhao received a letter from his mother in the countryside at Xinhui. In it she said she was suffering from jaundice and dropsy and did not think she had long to live. She missed her son and hoped that he would return home to see her and, while he was at it, tidy up the ancestors' gravesites. Manager Zhao bought a boat ticket that very day and left for his home in Xinhui, leaving the pawnshop in the care of his assistant.

This occurred in the season when red coral flowers were blossoming on the kapok trees at St. John's Cathedral and on the embankments along the Causeway Bay coast. One afternoon that was pretty much like all others, the easily flustered assistant manager was seeing off a visitor in the main hall, the steward at the Liao Mansion. The preferred pawnshop customers were wealthy families that had fallen on hard times; their valuable heirlooms and expensive items of all types were the most eagerly sought goods. The scions of declining families, fearful of losing stature in society by showing up in person at a pawnshop, invariably sent their stewards or servants to pawn items. The pawnshop manager always treated these surrogates with courtesy, entertaining them in the main hall as honored guests and rewarding them with ample commissions.

After the assistant manager had seen his guest out, he returned to the hall to sort the pawned items with the clerks. By the time he held up the last item, a Buddhist rosary with one hundred and eight amber beads, night had already fallen. Huang Deyun picked up the oilskin umbrella she'd brought with her that morning to ward off the rain—when closed, the ribs showed up red; when opened, the umbrella was bright green— and was about to start off for home, when a commotion broke out in front of the shop, with a series of explosions louder and crisper than fire-crackers.

"Damn, that sounds like bandits! We're being robbed. Let's go, hurry!"

With a shout, the assistant manager and clerks took off toward the shop, as Huang Deyun's legs sagged, and she fell to the floor.

Bandits, just as Lady Eleven had said. Just as she'd said. With shouts and gunfire crackling up front, Huang Deyun got to her feet with the aid of her umbrella and grabbed hold of the assistant manager's pant cuff.

"Lady Eleven told me there are weapons in a false wall in the pawn-shop. The fourth brick on the left is movable. All you have to do is push it. Hurry!"

She then threw her arms over her head and hid alongside the old well in the courtyard. She heard footsteps on the balcony above her; that was the ideal vantage point from which the bandits could launch their attack, as Lady Eleven had said. Deyun was stuck, there was nowhere to run to, so she held her breath and squinted to see what was happening. A figure suddenly dropped from the balcony into the courtyard. The man was dressed all in black, and his face was covered, all but tiny openings for a pair of golden eyes. The dagger in his hand glistened in the cold moon-light. Backing up to find the best way out of the courtyard without stum-bling into a trap in the darkness, he was also looking for a target of his own. The way he stood, legs spread and bent slightly at the knee, made it appear that the courtyard was a stage and that he was performing a martial arts drill. Huang Deyun watched spellbound, wondering where she had seen the man before.

The man in black found what he was looking for—the vault for pawn-shop valuables. To protect it against robbers, the vault was sealed with a heavy metal lock, to which only the owner and manager had keys. The man in black attacked the lock with his dagger. At that moment, with no regard for her own safety, Huang Deyun flung herself at the black figure.

Hearing a noise behind him, the man nimbly stepped aside, and Deyun ran headlong into a door. She saw stars, as the man raised his dagger and was about to bring it down on her, when his hand froze in midair.

With a scream, Huang Deyun passed out.

When she regained consciousness she found herself sitting in the hall where the Li family's ancestor spirit tablets and portraits were arrayed. Deyun was seated in Lady Eleven's impressive carved armchair, surrounded by several people. The first thing to enter her field of vision was an ivory fan, held by a man in a long silk robe and silk-topped slippers. It was the owner of Prosperity Pawnshop, Li Jian. She noticed his protruding ears as he bent over her. She wasn't dreaming. Out on the street, word was spreading among people about how Huang Deyun had foiled a robbery at the pawnshop. Once again Prosperity Pawnshop had been kept safe by one of its women. That was all anyone outside was talking about.

Later on, Huang Deyun relived her moments alongside the well. She had been screaming when someone had clapped a rough hand over her mouth, and in the split second before passing out, she'd felt herself picked up and carried off to a dark spot, her limbs drooping weakly.

"Bandits! There's one in the courtyard. Go get him!"

Hearing the shout, the man had thrown the woman to the ground and jumped onto the ledge around the well. Grabbing hold of the eaves above him, he'd coiled his body and sprung up onto the tiles leading back to the balcony from which he'd jumped down into the courtyard. Quickly, he'd moved out of sight, leaving the roof tiles to return to silence.

Li Jian rewarded Huang Deyun lavishly. Leading her to the vault in the courtyard, he took out his key, which never left his person, and opened the lock, which had been mauled by the robber's dagger. He told her to go inside and choose any piece of jewelry she desired from among the unclaimed items.

That one soul-shattering shriek from Huang Deyun had preserved Prosperity Pawnshop's lifeline and had cost the brotherhood a source of riches. Rumors regarding the aborted robbery of the pawnshop flew, the most vivid of which circulated around a little dessert shop in a lane near the Central market. Word of what had happened caused the owner to think back to a day when Manager Zhao of Prosperity Pawnshop had honored his shop with a visit. He'd sat at a table carrying on a hushed conversation with a brawny man sitting with his back to the door. The shopkeeper described the man as having slanting eyebrows and bright eyes, a man with true martial bearing. A village relative of the shopkeeper's learned that Manager Zhao and Jiang Xiahun, a onetime actor in a Cantonese opera troupe who, it was rumored, had thrown in his lot with the bandit brotherhood, had been good friends in their days of wandering. While they were at the shop, Manager Zhao had intentionally let slip the location of the room in which the pawnshop kept its valuables. Then he'd taken leave to return to his native village, figuring that if he was absent from the premises when the robbery occurred, he would escape suspicion. The fact that he still had not returned only made the rumor that he'd been an inside member of the bandit gang spread like wildfire.

Huang Deyun emerged from the jewelry vault carrying her reward cupped in both hands. A single shriek had earned her a precious gem inside a little lacquered box. As she held it in her hands, a veil of melancholy fell around her heart. Could that really have been Jiang Xiahun? The stirrings in her heart caused by that pair of up-slanting, penetrating eyes poking through the mask still had not abated. On so many sleepless nights, when she hadn't known what to do with her arms and legs, those eyes had appeared in the darkness. Now, she thought back to having been picked up by the man, so close she could feel his breath on her. Cradled in his muscular frame, she'd felt safe and comforted; they were arms in which she could sleep forever.

But for now, Huang Deyun focused her attention on the jewelry box in her hands, for its contents would make it possible for her son, Richard, to attend Queen's College Secondary School and receive a Western education. She had it all figured out. Wrapping the box in a large blue hand-kerchief, she tucked it under her arm, walked out of Prosperity Pawn-shop, and headed home, remembering on the way to stop at a pharmacy to pick up some pills for Richard, who had developed a runny nose as the weather turned cold. Attending to it now, before the northern winds came, would keep it from turning into a full-blown cold.

The next day Huang Deyun returned to the pawnshop, attending to the same tasks as before: when the work piled up for anyone, from the manager to the accountant, even the assistants who wrapped packages, Huang Deyun pitched in to help. When anyone asked, she modestly told them she was still doing odd jobs at the pawnshop, which paid enough to put food on the table for her son. To pawnshop employees, from top to bottom, she was a woman who did not take advantage of her new status; she refused to behave arrogantly around the owner, and, without being aware of it, they began taking her lead in the way they conducted themselves.

The departure of Manager Zhao left Li Jian with a worry that the rob-bers might try again. So he began spending more time in the pawnshop, frequently in the company of Huang Deyun, whose various tasks often kept her at work well after dark. Some gossiped that she was given to showing off the beauty mark on her left cheek around Li Jian, with whom she was often seen in light conversation. The same people revealed the surprising news that they had witnessed the owner go out to the jewelry vault on more than one occasion and invite the woman to come inside and take whatever she wanted. The rumormongers received secondary confirmation from Deyun's neighbor, Widow Zhou, who said that her golden phoenix leather box, the one into which she had stored gifts from clients during her days as a prostitute, was filled to overflow-ing. Now this black-lacquered jewelry box, the size of a child's wash-basin and carved with a gardenia pattern, was already more than half full. Dating back to the Ming dynasty, it had been pawned by the stew-ard of the Liao family, which had fallen on hard times.

Rumors rose and fell endlessly, with fewer and fewer people nodding in agreement. Deyun continued coming to work at the pawnshop early each morning, as if nothing were amiss, except that now she penciled her eyebrows more heavily than usual and began adding rouge to her cheeks. Everyone at Prosperity Pawnshop was talking about her behind her back, remarking that she was looking more and more like Lady Eleven every day.

14

The next year, after the Lantern Festival had passed, news circulated among pawnshop owners that Prosperity Pawnshop had been purchased by Jardine's, the old and established British firm that had branched off from the East India Trading Company and made inroads into China by smuggling opium into the country before the Opium Wars, growing enormously wealthy in the process.

The comprador responsible for taking over the pawnshop was Wang Qinshan, whose father had been an errand runner in the hilltop home of Dr. Spencer, who worked at the Garrison Hospital. Convinced that the only way his son could have a future in the colony was to become fluent in English, Qinshan's father had managed to have Qinshan admitted into a church-run school, thanks to a recommendation from Dr. Spencer, where he received a full six years' English-language education.

After graduation, Qinshan worked for a while in a British-run auction house in Central; from there, thanks to his excellent command of English, he was hired as a British interpreter's assistant at the Hong Kong courthouse, where he met a renowned tea broker. All eleven of the tea suppliers in Fuchow could sell to Jardine's only by going through this particular broker, who recruited Wang Qinshan to be responsible for documents in English. Wang approached Jardine's manager, William Matheson, saying he could help them break into the Fuchow opium market.

After half a lifetime of serving his British bosses, Wang Qinshan finally managed to rise to the status of comprador. The company followed his recommendation to enter the opium trade. Several hours before each boatload of opium left Hong Kong for Shanghai, Comprador Wang ran to the manager to give the latest quote for opium prices in Shanghai. In a recent sale, an erroneous quote had cost the company a large sum of money, and Comprador Wang fretted day and night, racking his brain for another source of income that would put him back in the company's good graces.

Word reached him that business had fallen off for Li Jian, king of the local pawnbrokers, and that the pawnshop was expected to close, at least temporarily. Seeing this as a splendid opportunity, Comprador Wang sent his trusted subordinate, Wu Fu, to check with other pawnshop brokers to see if the news was true.

After receiving Wu Fu's report, Comprador Wang called upon his innate business sense and his experience in running a pawnshop to determine that taking over the old and established Prosperity Pawnshop, which had been operated by the same family for generations, would, if the shop was properly run, turn out to be quite profitable. In the past he had run three private banks for Jardine's, to move money back and forth between Shanghai and Hong Kong. Secretly, Comprador Wang borrowed money from the Hong Kong money exchange for his own business. Now, in consort with the taipan, Mr. Matheson, he planned to use the saved interest as capital to buy Prosperity Pawnshop, and have his most trusted subordinate run the business.

The first step in Comprador Wang's plan was to arrange for fire insurance from a capital-rich foreign insurance company and to strengthen antitheft measures, for which he was willing to put aside no less than 45 percent of the profits. Once he secured an expression of "deep interest" from the taipan, Comprador Wang wrote out a detailed business prospectus in beautiful English with a classical flair.

Soon after the prospectus was sent up, Mr. Matheson summoned Wang to go over the details, reminding him that since the pawnshop business was so lucrative, he would be facing stiff competition. Matheson, who took pride in his ability to speak Cantonese, personally named the enterprise "Moneybags Loans," which struck Wang as being inelegant, although he vocally applauded Matheson's choice of a name.

The first order of business was to lay off most of the pawnshop's old employees. Owing to her knowledge of the ins and outs of the business, not to mention her many achievements, which had attained legendary qualities, Huang Deyun was kept on. Through slitted eyes buried in layers of fat, Wu Fu stared at Deyun's softly rounded waist and told her she was to move into quarters at the rear of the pawnshop compound, making it easier for her to take care of business.

Huang Deyun wept on the day Li Jian moved out of the pawnshop. Kneeling for the last time before the spirit tablet of Lady Eleven, she seemed unwilling to ever get up. Li Jian, who was by then paralyzed, indicated that he was leaving the old lady's armchair for Huang Deyun, who sobbed in gratitude.

Then Huang Deyun returned to the Water Moon Pavilion to say good-bye to Widow Zhou and to thank her for introducing her to the pawnshop.

"There's no need to thank me," Widow Zhou said, a sad smile on her plain face. "With your strong will, you will climb to the top. It is your fate."

She refused the gift Huang Deyun tried to give her; it was, she could tell by the feel of the red wrapping paper, a pair of silver bracelets.

"It's just a modest token of my appreciation. I'm not sure if they're anything like the pair you used to have."

As if afraid she would soil her hand, Widow Zhou pulled it back. Huang Deyun tried to force the gift on her, but she steadfastly refused, unconsciously rubbing the spots where bracelets had once lain.

"I pawned them long ago, and they will never return. You have a good heart, but you surely know that some things can never be replaced—"

Huang Deyun let her hand drop, unwilling to force the issue, and the conversation turned to what some of their neighbors were up to, with Widow Zhou doing all the talking. With a sigh, she remarked how the wife of the hog butcher had come down with a strange illness, describing it in such detail that Huang Deyun's mind began to drift and she could muster no sympathy for the woman. She was all packed and ready to go; a pair of trunks rested on the bare bed, just as they had a year and a half earlier, when she'd moved in. In a while, she would hire a rickshaw and, along with her son, move out of this rundown room, with its adobe walls and low ceiling, leaving the artisans and laborers who lived in the neighborhood behind, severing ties with them once and for all.

Once seated in the rickshaw, she would ride through the temple grounds with her head held high on her way to the pawnshop on Bonham Strand East, where she would move into quarters at the rear of the compound. Wu Fu had given permission for her and her son to occupy Lady Eleven's rooms, which she had examined the day before. Everything was as it had been when Lady Eleven was alive, nothing had been moved out: the large bed, the standing closet, the dressing table, and the washbasin stand had all been specially ordered by Li Quan years earlier from a master cabinetmaker in Canton. Once the furniture was dusted, it would be as beautiful as ever, especially the exquisitely carved and meticulously cared-for bed, with its moon-gate canopy.

With these thoughts in mind, Huang Deyun interrupted Widow Zhou by asking her to invite the woman who dressed her hair to come and pick up the wooden bed as a gift. The bamboo furniture, kitchen cupboards and dishes, as well as some old clothes, were to go to an old lady named Yawang, who had been driven out of her house by her mean daughter-in-law and now lived alone in a tentlike structure by the side of the road.

Once everything had been taken care of, Huang Deyun took Richard by the hand, moved her trunks outside, in one of which was hidden her black-lacquered jewelry box, climbed aboard the rickshaw, and rode off.

Wu Fu was waiting for her at the pawnshop, stroking his double chin, caught up in his emotions. Twice he had missed his opportunity with this woman from his Dongguan hometown, both times at Yihong Pavilion. The first time, he recalled with self-loathing, he had failed to come up with the astronomical fee demanded by the madam for a chance to deflower this "lute girl" and had been forced to stare helplessly as the willowy girl walked out the door. Seven years later, as the trusted subordinate of Comprador Wang at a foreign concern, when he had accumulated enough money of his own through the sale of opium to visit Possession

Street and buy the first-night services of four or five young virgins, he did not want to turn down an invitation from his old friend Yihong. He went with breathless anticipation, his rolls of fat quivering, only to pass right by Huang Deyun at the door of Yihong Pavilion, the beauty mark on her cheek causing him to turn for a second look, but too late.

Two months earlier, when Wu Fu had gone with a broker to negotiate the purchase of Prosperity Pawnshop, Li Jian had received his guest in a reclining lounge and had Huang Deyun go over the books for the prospective buyer. So Wu Fu strolled into the main hall at the rear of the pawnshop compound, where a lightly made-up young woman sat in an imposing carved armchair, dressed in a narrow-sleeved jacket with buttons down the front and a gauzy black skirt, each with off-white piping. Tightly gripping an embroidered hanky, her hands rested on her knees, which were shaking from her nervousness. Full of his authority of a prospective buyer, Wu Fu stared lecherously at the woman of legendary talents who had frightened off bandits and kept the shop safe. A plan took shape in his mind: as soon as he was alone with her, he'd ask if she would like some news about her hometown, since he had returned from collecting opium in Dongguan only the month before.

This time she wouldn't get away.

Without so much as knocking, Wu Fu parted the curtains and stormed into Lady Eleven's—now, of course, it was Huang Deyun's—bedroom and gave her an exquisite abacus as a greeting gift. It was one of the New Year's gifts the Jardine Company had ordered to thank Chinese-run enterprises for their business. The frames, the rods, and the beads were all made of fine sorrel wood, the outer edges inlaid with nickel silver, while in the top center of the frame were inscribed eight words: A gift from the Hong Kong Jardine Company.

"Can you see what makes this abacus special?"

Wu Fu kicked off his shoes and sat down uninvited on the edge of the bed, like a mountain of shifting flesh that gave off a warm odor, reminding Huang Deyun of the smell from a recently butchered hog in the marketplace. Yet she managed to smile and, with a show of modesty, said she didn't know. "I'm afraid you've stumped me, Mr. Wu. We have one of those in the shop, but it's poorly made of bamboo, and cannot begin to compare with this one, though the bookkeeper treats it as a rare treasure and would glare at me if I so much as touched it." Deyun reached out and touched the beads with loving care. "How exquisite it is," she commented fawningly. "Is it really made to be used? I can't think anyone would want to."

With a smug laugh, Wu Fu signaled for Deyun to come up closer and took the abacus from her.

"An ordinary abacus has fifteen columns of beads, so you can only calculate up to four places. But our company deals in large amounts, for importing foreign machinery and exporting shiploads of Chinese products such as silk, tea, and porcelain, and fifteen columns isn't enough. That's why this type was invented. Here, give it a try, and tell me how many columns it has."

He had such bad breath that Huang Deyun had to hold hers.

"I count seventeen, Mr. Wu. Is that right?"

"It's those two extra columns that make it unique. You can add up massive figures." Wu Fu's chins were resting on his bulging abdomen as he clicked the beads with his fat fingers and stared at the beauty mark on her cheek, so close he could reach out and touch it. "For the grand opening of the new pawnshop, let this be a good-luck abacus for you to calculate large numbers. Now what do I get in return, hmm?"

Reaching out and putting his hand around the back of the woman's fair, slender neck, he pulled her toward him. But she slipped out of his grasp and avoided falling into his arms.

Still smiling, she thought back to the dream she'd had the night before: she was seated in front of a gigantic table, her left hand resting on an account book in a green cloth cover with plum-red stitching, her right hand flying over the beads of an abacus.

"I'm looking forward to learning how to use the abacus from Mr. Wu," she said, clutching the sorrel-wood abacus with its nickel silver lining to her chest. "We'll see what happens once I've mastered it."

"All right, we'll wait till later. There's plenty of time."

As he gazed at her thin wrist, Wu Fu was tempted to reach out and snap it. This time she wouldn't get away. He had nothing to worry about.

Not long after Jardine's took over the pawnshop, rumors about Huang Deyun again began to spread in the teahouses at Central. People said that every night the moaning of a woman emerged from the rear of the pawnshop compound, making the hair of passersby stand on edge. They said it didn't sound like the lustful moaning of bedroom activities. People who proclaimed a familiarity with the goings-on at the pawnshop made it known that Huang Deyun was possessed by ambition, and that she was willing to offer up her fair body to ensure that it was she who occupied Lady Eleven's elegant armchair and ran the pawnshop from behind the scenes. That was why she was willing to satisfy all of Wu Fu's perverse bedroom delights.

Rumors swept through the streets, even reaching the ears of Huang Deyun behind the stone walls of the pawnshop, but she would not lower herself to the level of rumormongers at the market. She had more important things to attend to, in particular the needs of Jardine's Comprador Wang Qinshan, the behind-the-scenes, but normally absent, manager of the pawnshop.

The moment Comprador Wang stepped into the pawnshop, Deyun saw that something was different, as if he'd turned into a stranger; something was missing. From where she stood, off to one side, she cast a furtive glance at him. He was dressed in a formal stone-blue patterned Chinese gown with side slits and embroidered silk slippers, and held a light-yellow snuffbox given to him by Wu Fu. It took Deyun a long moment to realize there was an empty spot behind his skullcap—his queue was missing. This was no trivial matter. Only by clapping her hand over her mouth did she keep from yelping in surprise.

Comprador Wang had just come from attending a solemn "queue-cutting" ceremony at the Chinese Commerce Association Assembly Hall, whose organizer, Guan Xinyan, had been one of Sun Yat-sen's fellow students at the Western Medical Academy. His mother had prevented him from joining the Republican Revolution, for fear of placing his family in jeopardy, so Guan did the next best thing: he promoted a queue-cutting movement to protest against the corrupt, alien rule of the Manchu government. He set the example by being the first to cut off his queue and then attending all sorts of formal occasions, queueless, in his Chinese gown. Now, in order to spread his influence, he had invited six hundred distinguished residents of Hong Kong, merchants included, to attend a major gathering at which a group of Irish musicians provided the entertainment. Each attendee answered the call to cut off his queue and then was photographed to mark the occasion. As the meeting came to an end, the attendees filed outside, where, led by the Irish band, they paraded up and down the streets to lessen the fears of the general populace of cutting off their queues.

Comprador Wang rubbed the back of his neck, where his queue had once hung, with something other than scruples on his mind. Fortune had smiled on him in recent days, as his business prospered. The money was rolling in from his work at the foreign firm, not to mention the business he undertook on the side. More and more people were smoking opium, one out of every ten Hong Kong residents, according to one estimate, with opium dens popping up all over the colony. The opium smuggled from Shanghai to Hong Kong provided enormous profits for Mr. Matheson and for him. Even the Hong Kong government benefited, since 30 percent of its tax revenue came from the sale of legalized opium.

At this rate, in less than two years Comprador Wang could build a villa, complete with flower garden, at Mid-Level. His dreams could take him there and no farther up the mountain, for Governor Nathan had implemented a segregation policy, passed by the legislative council, called the "Peak District Reserve Regulation," stipulating that the peak of Mount Taiping, from 788 feet above sea level, was reserved for Europeans, and that members of the yellow race, the Chinese, could spend the night on the Peak only with the permission of the governor. Nannies, rickshaw pullers, gardeners, maidservants, and others who served the colonials were, of course, excepted from this rule.

Ho Tung, Hong Kong's wealthiest merchant, a onetime comprador, received special permission from the governor to build a mansion on

Seymour Road at Mid-Level, with an ocean view. Painted red, it was an expensive estate named Red Residence, visible from the foot of the mountain, looking like a mountain castle.

Mr. Ho Tung received such special treatment only because he was of mixed blood—Chinese and British. But Comprador Wang was already planning to become a British citizen, with Mr. Matheson's support. He was confident that his flawless English would allow him to breeze through the oral examination. Then, once British citizenship had been conferred, the next step would be membership in the legislative council, and from there to chairman of Tong Wah Hospital. In the foreseeable future, he—Wang Qinshan—could rise to a position of leadership in the Chinese community, a vital link between the governor and the people. In order to break into the circle of the rich and powerful and set out on an official career, Comprador Wang attended the queue-cutting ceremony, at which he resolutely snipped off the queue he had worn all his adult life. He was imagining the scene the following day, when Mr. Matheson saw his new look: he'd give him a big thumbs-up, applaud his progressive attitude, and praise his ability to keep up with the times.

Not only were the times changing, even Hong Kong's topography was undergoing monumental transformations. The land reclamation project on the island had progressed without interruption since the British began running Hong Kong. When the queues hit the floor, the attendees filed out into the streets and paraded alongside the British Navy pier. Comprador Wang was astounded by the changes in the Central harbor district. After a decade of flying sand and shifting rocks as land was taken back from the sea, an unending struggle between man and nature, the work finally came to an end, with sixty-five acres of land reclaimed, a virtual cornucopia. Wang was impressed by the commercial vision of the reclamation project's director of planning, who had spotted the potential to expand Central and turn it into a gold mine. He calculated that the new land would generate revenues triple the size of the investment, and reckoned that the value of the land would just keep going up, and that the income from sales of that land might one day exceed that of taxes on opium.

Mr. Matheson saw early on that there was a great deal of money to be made in real estate, and intended to forge an alliance with the director of planning and create a real estate company. He predicted that this piece of reclaimed land would one day become Hong Kong's center of commerce.

"The Britons must be congratulated for how they moved a mountain to fill in the ocean," Comprador Wang said with an appreciative sigh, taking out his snuffbox to snort a thumbnail full of snuff. "In a few short decades, I've seen with my own eyes how Queen's Road gave way to Des Voeux Road, which in turn gave way to Connaught Road. So many buildings can be built on that piece of land. In the long run, land is where the real money is."

Huang Deyun was standing nearby, and Comprador Wang's comment did not fall on deaf ears.

Richard Huang was but a year away from graduating from the Chinese school when his mother dragged him up to pay his respects to Comprador Wang. The moment they stepped into the room, she commanded him to drop to his knees and bang his head on the floor to show his respect and beg for the comprador's support. Deyun said that her son had suffered throughout his childhood, looking neither totally Chinese nor totally European. The other children bullied him at the Chinese school he attended, but he had stuck it out this long, a year short of graduation, and his mother's fondest desire was that her bastard, fatherless son might have the chance to study at Queen's College Secondary School for foreign children. If Comprador Wang were willing to speak up on her behalf to his superiors at the foreign firm, who might then convince the headmaster to give the nod, it would be a turning point in Richard's life, and one day, when he amounted to something, he would do Wang's bidding as repayment.

After weighing the pros and cons of the matter, Comprador Wang went to see Wu Fu, having decided to grant Huang Deyun's wish.

On the day that Richard Huang, dressed in his Queen's College Secondary School uniform and carrying a paper fan in one hand, started at the new school, Comprador Wang handed him a Cantonese-English

topical dictionary, compiled for the purpose of "answering the communication needs of Cantonese and foreigners." One chapter, devoted to
common terms in commerce, was geared specifically to people who
wished to become compradors.

Huang Deyun told her son to get down on his knees and kowtow to
show his gratitude for Comprador Wang's generosity.

"The boy's still young, so I'll keep this book safe for him," she said as
she gently rubbed its cover. "Besides, I'd like to take a look at it when I
have a free moment. It's been years since I spoke the foreign language,"
she said with a sigh. "I've probably forgotten everything."

Huang Deyun was often seen sitting in her sorrel-wood armchair, lips
pursed as she struggled to pronounce words from the dictionary that lay
in her lap. She had set herself a quota of five pages a day, and was particularly interested in the section dealing with commerce. People who
saw her studying the book were reminded of Lady Eleven, the way she
pursed her lips, a sign of seriousness and diligence when reading the
North China Herald.

Closing the book, Huang Deyun conjured up an image of Richard
after graduating from the school and hiring on at one of the foreign
firms. He would be conversing with his superiors in fluent English, just
like an Englishman. A smile of contentment spread across her face.

Huang Deyun was a woman with considerable ambition, and it is easy
to see why, when she heard that Governor Nathan had issued a directive
that the brothels in Possession Street were to be moved to the seaside district of Shek Tong Tsui, so that the first settlers in this newly opened-up
area would be whores and their clients, the news had no effect on her.
Even if she were to meet up with Adam Smith, her British lover and a man
who had once set her soul on fire, she would never again lose control.

In the year since being promoted to head of the Sanitary Board,
Smith's comings and goings at the Qixiang brothel were spotted more
frequently than ever. At night he would embrace his drinking partner as
he waited, eyes bloodshot and clothes a mess, for the arrival of Jimmy
Xie.

This Jimmy Xie was one of Hong Kong's most prominent building contractors. His father had grown wealthy by buying up foreign shops and godowns that had failed through incompetent management. By the time Jimmy Xie arrived on the scene, he had accumulated enough capital to take aim at the districts where the foreigners built their homes, with the intent of breaking down the colonial policy of segregating Europeans from Chinese. Beginning on Aberdeen Street, he bought up Western homes and converted them into Chinese flats, partitioning them into small rooms, which he rented out to immigrants fleeing from troubles on the mainland.

As the Chinese population increased, the colonial government issued a new decree that placed stringent demands on construction in the Chinese districts, ostensibly to protect against another outbreak of plague; this led to the demolition of many buildings that presented a sanitation hazard.

Jimmy Xie's construction firm was in charge of the reconstruction. Regulations required that a space of three hundred feet behind each building was to remain vacant for the sake of proper ventilation; to make up for the loss of usable land, three extra stories were approved. Jimmy Xie, a profit-oriented businessman, planned to privately juggle the arrangement of those three hundred feet to his own financial advantage, while publicly taking up the cause of his fellow Chinese. He would do this by attacking the white colonials who sat in their bright, spacious offices, unmoved by the plight of ordinary Chinese and, with the stroke of a pen, set aside for ventilation purposes a vast amount of extremely valuable land, a testament to their wasteful habits. They had no idea that the Chinese districts were so overcrowded that the people were nearly living on top of one another.

Pleading the people's case, Jimmy Xie went looking for the newly appointed head of the Sanitary Board, armed with nearly finished blueprints and a petition from the people. He learned that Smith was a bachelor, which meant Jimmy Xie could not rally a wife to his cause by presenting her with exotic birds and rare herbs, as he'd been able to do with Smith's predecessor. His feelings of uncertainty vanished the moment he laid eyes on Smith, whose bloodshot eyes told him he was badly hung-over. Once his impression of the man was confirmed, he decided to handle the payoff the same way he'd handled it with the two previous department heads.

One year after construction was completed on rows of densely packed buildings, Hong Kong's population passed four hundred thousand, of whom all but slightly more than four thousand were Chinese. Then, on the eve of the Dragon Boat Festival, another outbreak of the plague occurred, throwing a panic into the populace. Governor Nathan had no choice but to appoint a commission to survey the public sanitation situation in the Chinese communities and determine whether or not building codes were followed in housing construction there. The commission reported back that Adam Smith and Jimmy Xie had conspired to monopolize sanitation facilities, enriching themselves at the public's expense.

A variety of stories circulated in regard to the dismissal of the Hong Kong government's Sanitary Board head, Adam Smith. One was that he had been pardoned by the governor and sent back to his home in England. On the eve of his departure, he sat in the Hong Kong Club bar, boasting to his British friends who were seeing him off that he would not for a single moment miss the colony, with its sailors, prostitutes, godowns, merchants, and gambling dens. He could leave with no regrets.

The second version had it that after the bribery scandal had been exposed, Smith had fled to avoid punishment but was eventually apprehended by the Royal Police on an oceangoing vessel at one of the piers. He had changed his appearance to avoid capture: he was barefoot and dressed in coolie shorts; his moustache had been shaved off, and he even sported a false queue.

Adam Smith's bastard child, Richard Huang, preferred to link his father, whose final whereabouts remained unclear, with the catastrophic fire that engulfed the racecourse in 1918, on Lunar New Year's Day, started by a fire in a Chinese food stand outside one of the horse tents during the annual British Derby. It spread unchecked, with a final loss of

life of over five hundred. Richard Huang wanted to believe that his
father was among the dead that day.

"A rail line! Just think, you board a train in Kowloon, pass through Taipo
and Shatin, cross the Lo Wu Bridge, into Shenzhen and the Canton
countryside, all on one line—"

The British did not begin developing the New Territories until the
blueprints for a rail line were completed. In 1898 Li Hongzhang had been
pressured into signing a ninety-nine-year lease of the New Territories to
Britain. Ten days after the signing, the British abrogated that portion of
the treaty dealing with the Kowloon-Canton Rail Line and forced the
Manchu government's minister of railways to sign a protocol ceding
authority to the British, who had far more grandiose plans, in which their
rail lines extended to the farthest reaches of Chinese territory.

During the celebration for the sixtieth anniversary of Queen Victoria's ascension to the throne, the power of the United Kingdom was at an
all-time high, extending to the Seven Seas; all four major continents fell
under the petticoats of the British queen.

After Mathew Nathan, a young, spirited, and upright engineer, took
office as governor, he put his experience to use by opening up a north-
south road north through Kowloon. Nathan Road was his legacy. He also
actively promoted the Kowloon-Canton Rail Line, approved, with mod-
ifications, by the Manchu court.

The rail line began operation at a ceremony on the eve of the 1911
Republican Revolution. Officials in formal attire boarded a train at Tsim
Sha Tsui in southern Kowloon and rode it all the way to Lo Wu, on the
northern border. On the mainland side, Cantonese officials, dressed in
formal Chinese gowns and short jackets, boarded a train going in the
opposite direction and traveled to Shenzhen, across the border from Lo
Wu. The two groups met in the center of the Lo Wu Bridge, signifying
the linking up of the two lines.

When the Canton train reached the Shatin Station, a crowd that
included old folks and small children milled around the iron dragon that

had raced across the earth, and marveled at the strange sight. Huang Deyun and her son, Richard, joined the crowd, after ferrying across the harbor to see for themselves. Wu Fu had told her that this iron dragon could take her back to her hometown of Dongguan, which she had last seen nineteen years earlier.

But Huang Deyun would not return triumphantly to her home, where the famed incense was still produced. Wu Fu, on the other hand, rode the train to Canton to collect opium revenues for Jardine's, and returned with local pastry and oyster sauce from Shenzhen.

"Ai," he said, animatedly describing the trip for her, "in the past, I had to take a boat, then travel on foot over mountains for at least half a month. Now, all a person has to do is board the iron dragon—they call it a train—and whiz past villages and fields without moving a muscle." As his double chins quivered, he described how the train arrived at Lo Wu and went no farther. The end of the line.

"Puffs of white smoke spurted from the dragon's head, but its body didn't move. To get to Shenzhen, I had to walk down a street in Sha Tau Kok called Sino-British Avenue, one side of which belongs to the English, the other still belonging to the Manchu court. Once a single village, Sha Tau Kok is now divided into two. Neighbors are not allowed to cross to the other side, even to exchange grain."

Wu Fu handed the oyster sauce he'd brought back to the owner of a general store on Bonham Strand East, urging him to move quickly to get a monopoly on Shenzhen products.

"In the future, when everyone sees how easy it is to travel back and forth on a train, these products could be available everywhere!"

To repay Wu Fu for this advice, the merchant revealed some news he had heard from his neighbor, the owner of a rice shop: soon after the Mid-Autumn Festival, the price of rice was going to skyrocket. The majority of Hong Kong's rice was imported from the Indochina peninsula, which had suffered from a series of Pacific Ocean typhoons over the past couple of years, which had led to nearly unending floods in the rice paddies of Siam and Annam, with devastating effects on their harvests; this was compounded by a severe drought in recent days, leading the governments to stop the exportation of rice to Hong Kong. That could only lead to drastic increases in the price of rice, and now was the time to corner the market.

After talking matters over, without informing Comprador Wang, whose permission would have been required, Wu Fu and Huang Deyun decided to divert funds from the pawnshop to stockpile raw rice, which they would sell on the sly when the price rose. As predicted, soon after the Mid-Autumn Festival, shiploads of rice stopped coming from the Indochina peninsula, and the price of rice virtually doubled daily until, in a matter of only a few days, it had increased tenfold, causing an uproar among the populace. In order to reap staggering profits, rice sellers pasted notices on closed doors that they had no rice to sell. People who had run out of rice at home crowded in front of the shops and refused to leave until they could buy what they needed. The colonial government, fearing a riot by starving residents, sent steamships north to Wuhu and Shanghai to bring back shiploads of rice to quell the disturbance. When Wu Fu heard the news, he began selling the rice they had hoarded, secretly splitting the enormous profits with Huang Deyun and paying the owner of the general store for his information.

One sunny afternoon, egged on by Wu Fu, Huang Deyun and Richard took the harbor ferry over to Kowloon to have another look at the train. As she walked down the streets of Tsim Sha Tsui, she noticed that since the last time she'd been there, the landfill projects in the Yao Ma Tei and Tai Kok Tsui districts had been completed and now comprised a broad flat area that had pushed the ocean far back. The newly reclaimed land was alive with laborers and craftsmen, vendors of salted fish and pickled vegetables and rice, as well as peddlers of all sorts of goods. There were also barbers, seamstresses who worked seated on grass mats, and stalls with signboards announcing the Return of Huatuo, the fabled doctor, where herbal medicines were dispensed.

Huang Deyun could see that the railroad would quickly make it possible for the area to become a commercial hub.

After Richard graduated from the Queen's College School, he took advantage of what his mother referred to as "English spoken like the English," aided by an introduction by Comprador Wang, to gain employment at Jardine's, serving Mr. Matheson but learning the business from the ground up. After years of moving up the ladder, he took his mother's advice and requested assignment in the firm's real estate management section, where he could study how to become a real estate broker.

Some years later, Huang Deyun went to her secret chest and took out the sizable savings she had accumulated; to that was added all the money she had made through the sale of jewelry over the years. She gave it all to Richard, telling him to invest it in real estate. With his mother's wealth in hand, Richard then borrowed a large sum of money from Mr. Matheson, at an annual interest rate of 10 percent. He risked it all as a down payment on his first purchase of land, a parcel of reclaimed land in Yao Ma Tei, close to the railroad, land his mother, who had acquired a keen business sense, had predicted would see significant development.

Now middle-aged, Huang Deyun, who wore her hair in a bun and dressed simply, was often seen on the arm of her son at the reclaimed site in Yao Ma Tei, walking into the sun toward the beach on her and her son's first parcel of land. The baohinia were in full bloom, their five-petaled flowers vying to be the first to open; everywhere mother and son looked they saw a carpet of bright purple, resplendent in the brilliant colors of the sunset.

PART

THREE

1

It was toward the end of World War I, in 1918, that Sean Shelley was transferred from Kuala Lumpur to replace Mr. Connelly, who had been the loan manager of the Wayfoong Bank, a stately white building in the ancient Greek style of architecture, for twelve years and was returning to London. Shelley was an enigma to people who dealt with him, a curiosity to his former colleagues, who often gossiped about him because he was such a loner. He had lived alone, deep in the jungle, in a big house with red tiles and green walls and a spacious balcony out front. The blinds were half closed the year round, exuding a sense of mystery. Every once in a while, on a weekend or holiday, his tall, slender figure would be spotted in a tailored, gray hunting outfit complete with a Panama straw hat, like any true English gentleman ready for the hunt.

But rather than hunt the rare and exotic animals that roamed the forest, only to display their mounted heads in his house, he was interested in flora, the people said, and foraged in the tropical forest to collect strange and rare plants to send back to the London Botanical Garden for study.

After being invited to Huang Deyun's house for the Mid-Autumn Festival, Shelley could not get her out of his mind. The unintentional matchmaker turned out to be Comprador Wang Qinshan of the Jardine, Matheson Company. Wang had accompanied the Jardine's taipan, Mr. Matheson, to a cocktail party hosted by the Wayfoong Bank to welcome Shelley. Instead of joining the array of stars encircling the moon, Comprador Wang stood off to the side, adjusting his tortoiseshell glasses, behind which his beady eyes rolled, while he planned how to win over the new foreign manager before everyone else. He had been contemplating buying and selling gold, which meant he would have to rely upon someone working for a foreign bank to gather information on the price of gold on the international market. He could then work with this person to buy and sell for profit.

World War I had ruined the economy of the British Empire. The Bank of England, which had manipulated the world's monetary exchange rate, lost its power; the value of the British pound depreciated daily, while the price of gold rose. All this made the Hong Kong dollar, which was tied to the British pound, depreciate. Comprador Wang had seen how the Hong Kong government did not interfere with those who profited from the purchase and sale of gold, except to collect licensing fees. He was thus convinced that now was the best time to deal in the commodity.

Wang had also heard that the owner of an old-style private bank in Central had bought a piece of land on Kennedy Road to build a mansion, after making a small fortune by hooking up with the foreign manager of a Jardine's bank to buy and sell gold. Wang Qinshan had been thinking about building a Western-style house with a garden at Mid-Level, and the new manager would be the perfect person to help him realize his dream. Therefore, armed with the knowledge that Shelley relied heavily upon his Chinese secretary for advice, he watched the Englishman closely at the party; he knew that at social events, Secretary Su followed his superior like his shadow, as if he were a rare commodity, protecting him so well that no one could get through without his permission.

So Wang chose to work first on Secretary Su, a native of Chaozhou. Taking advantage of the Mid-Autumn Festival, Wang paid the foreigner's confidant a visit with a basket of pears that had just been unloaded from a boat from Tientsin, plus two tins of moon cakes from Soochow. Secretary Su, who was nearly bald and whose index finger was adorned with a long, twenty-four-carat gold ring, came out to greet him, smiling broadly and insisting that, as an inferior, he did not deserve a visit from the Jardine's comprador.

A clever man, Wang immediately experienced a tinge of regret at coming, seeing beneath Secretary Su's humble attitude a smugness that came from working for a foreigner. Wang had lost status the moment he'd allowed a minor secretary to be his equal. But dealing in gold was a risky, boom or bust business. Aside from luck, success also depended upon the trustworthiness of the foreign partner. The purpose of this visit was to study Sean Shelley's character and personality.

Secretary Su, partly because he was unable to maintain his lofty airs and partly because he needed to show off, began talking about his new superior in his flat Cantonese without waiting for Wang to bring the subject up.

"Mr. Shelley says he wants to see the 'real' Hong Kong. So yesterday, at the crack of dawn, I went with him to Kowloon for morning tea and to watch teahouse customers show off their caged birds—what a strange man."

Wang also learned that Shelley, who was unaccompanied in Hong Kong, was staying in a suite at the King Edward Hotel on the corner of Ice House Road and Des Voeux Road. He was waiting for the Peak house to be renovated to his specifications before moving in. Secretary Su said that his superior was going to paint the house blue and call it the Blue House.

A brilliant idea came to Wang when he received this piece of information. Since Shelley lived alone and wanted to see the real Hong Kong, why not invite the Englishman to do as the locals do by celebrating the Mid-Autumn Festival? Wang was reminded of Huang Deyun's personal maid, Xianü, who was an excellent cook. Deyun would not object if he were to borrow Xianü to have her prepare a special meal. Wang had begun treating Deyun differently ever since checking the pawnshop accounts and discovering how clever and daring she'd been in dealing in treasures looted from the Qing palace; he had gradually turned important tasks over to her while helping her son, Richard, whom he'd sent to Jardine's to work for Matheson as soon as he graduated from high school. Huang Deyun repaid his kindness by having her maid cook for him whenever he visited.

Following proper etiquette, Wang personally delivered an invitation to Jardine's taipan, Mr. Matheson, knowing full well that Mr. and Mrs. Matheson, having lived in the colony for many years, were quite class-conscious and paid close attention to social hierarchy. As expected, after a glance at the invitation, Matheson said with an offhand gesture, "I appreciate the invitation. I shall urge Mr. Shelley to attend to admire the moon and enjoy moon cakes, since he is all alone and this will be his first Mid-Autumn Festival. Don't you worry."

The Huang household was turned upside down in preparation for this important guest. After the last Double-Ninth Festival, Huang Deyun and her son had moved out of the fortresslike Prosperity Pawnshop on Bonham Strand East in Central into their first real home on Bonham Road. It was a two-story brick house with a stained glass-studded front door that faced the street. Square red tiles covered the living room floor, from where a staircase led up to three bedrooms. The small garden in back was quite elegant, surrounded by seasonal flowering trees like tea roses, cassia, gardenia, and jasmine. Wisteria covered the trellis by the well, and up against the wall was a half pavilion, fronted by a pair of litchi trees. The garden, built along the rising hill, appeared to be hanging in midair when seen from below, with a green glazed tile railing encircling the steep hill. It was this garden that made Huang Deyun decide to make the house their home.

When Sean Shelley arrived, she personally greeted him and gave him a tour of her new house. In the living room, the Englishman admired the spaciousness created by decorative windows and could not stop praising the red sandalwood and teak furniture. In decorating her new home, Deyun had picked through the unredeemed hardwood furniture at the pawnshop, choosing an exquisite set of chairs and tea tables that, along with a marble screen, gave the house old and elegant airs.

She dressed for dinner in a short red jacket with silver threads that flickered in the lamplight. It was gathered at the waist with a rounded hem, which was all the rage. The sleeves were loose but short, with white Western piping that made her arms seem even more fair than usual.

During the meal, she got up several times to serve the Englishman, one hand holding back the other sleeve. When the predessert soup arrived and she bent forward to fill her guest's bowl, he noticed a yellow butterfly resting on the collar; not startled by her movement, it did not fly off. He could not tell that it was a button, knotted with yellow thread by Xianü's skillful fingers.

After dinner, Huang Deyun invited her guest to admire the moon in the small but tasteful garden, where a sandalwood table had been set up under the wisteria trellis. On the table awaited Soochow-style moon cakes and pears from Tientsin, both sent by Comprador Wang. Following the hometown tradition of smoking the moon, Huang Deyun stuck a stick of Dongguan incense into a burner placed on a water-filled plate to fill the moonlit area with fragrant mist. The night was given an unreal aura by night-blooming cereus, which bloomed only one night a year.

The entanglement between Huang Deyun and Sean Shelley began with a bath.

Surrounded by salty seawater, the residents of Hong Kong relied on the mercy of the old man in the sky for drinking water. When the wind blew in the summer and a heavy rain fell, the island's reservoirs filled up and the residents were spared a shortage of water. Otherwise, the reservoirs dried up and drought followed, which in turn prompted the Water Supplies Bureau to control the supply based upon the severity of the shortage.

In the summer of 1919 Hong Kong suffered through one of its droughts. After the Tomb-Sweeping Festival, the rain that should have fallen did not arrive, and five of the six reservoirs in Hong Kong and Kowloon were bone-dry. The Water Supplies Bureau was forced to implement second-stage water control, requiring the residents to fetch water on the street at hydrants. Before daybreak, long lines snaked through the streets, as people waited with their buckets for the Water Supplies Bureau to turn on the faucets. Friendly neighbors argued over a bucket of water, and sometimes police were called in to maintain order when fights broke out.

Huang Deyun's new house sat on higher ground, where the water pressure was low. On normal days they had to pump water up the hill. After second-stage water control was implemented, servants had to go fetch water; no one was spared, not even her frail old maid.

It was another sweltering afternoon. Huang Deyun had just awakened from a nap. Feeling listless, she leaned against the bed frame and listened to the tinny voice of the radio announcer summarizing a speech by the director of the Water Supplies Bureau earlier that morning. Third-stage water control would begin if drought conditions did not improve . . . every household would be allowed two buckets a day for cooking . . . police stood by to ensure compliance . . . residents would have to fetch stream water to do their laundry. . . .

The announcer's arid voice seemed to dry up Huang Deyun's mouth. Waving the rush fan in her hand violently as if to extinguish the fire in her heart, she began to seriously consider accepting Sean Shelley's invitation to bathe in his hotel suite.

He had said that the Water Supplies Bureau would not dare stop the water supply to hotels where British travelers stayed. If Huang Deyun wished, the Englishman said, his shiny white teeth showing innocently, she could bathe at the King Edward.

The drought continued into August, and it seemed inevitable that third-stage water control would be implemented. On a now common stuffy, windless night, Sean Shelley came to pay Huang Deyun a visit. As he talked about the loan procedures at the bank, she forced herself to concentrate, but she couldn't help but mull over how to broach the subject on her mind. She wanted to accept the Englishman's offer to enjoy a bath at his hotel, as she could no longer stand the sour perspiration smell that covered her. Trying a variety of phrases in her less than fluent English, she was unable to come up with the proper words.

Feeling Huang Deyun's eyes on him, Sean lowered his eyes to avoid her stare, while gently twirling the brandy glass in his hand. Taking a sip and licking his moist lips every once in a while, he looked up to smile at her so she wouldn't feel neglected. His face was creased by a sad smile, but the alcohol slowly relaxed him. The part in his hair seemed to lose its order and started to take on a look of messiness; Huang Deyun expected to see him smooth his hair, but he didn't. Sean Shelley had transformed himself from a banker into a self-exiled wanderer.

It was the messy hair that attracted Huang Deyun, giving her the impulse to rush over and hold Sean in her arms.

Before he left that night, Sean told Huang Deyun his room number.

"I'll have to trouble Mr. Shelley to come downstairs to meet me."

"Why?"

"According to the rules of the hotel, no Chinese, especially Chinese women, are allowed to enter. You just arrived, so you wouldn't know—"

The Englishman slapped his own forehead and apologized for being so thoughtless; he said he'd meet her in the hotel lobby. Followed by Xianü, who carried a bundle with a change of clothes, Huang Deyun turned at the corner of Ice House Road when she recalled what the Englishman had told her about his first day in Hong Kong. He'd just gotten off at Queen's Pier and hadn't expected to run into a labor strike. But the coolie who carried his suitcases, hearing the whistle for a union strike, dropped his suitcases in the middle of the road and ran off. Sean Shelley had no choice but to drag his luggage all the way to the hotel. Imagining how pathetic the English gentleman must have looked, dragging his luggage in a top hat and Western suit, made her laugh.

The Sikh doorman guarding the hotel entrance was nowhere in sight, probably taking a break. Hiding behind her mistress, Xianü trembled as she went up the steps and pushed the door open. The marble tiles on the lobby floor, arranged in geometric patterns, were so shiny they could have served as mirrors. Xianü curled her toes to keep from slipping, which made walking difficult. Huang Deyun was also struck by the imposing airs of the hotel; fortunately Sean made a timely appearance from behind a pot of orchids and led the women to the elevator. As soon as she saw the automatic door of the elevator open, Xianü trusted the bundle to Huang Deyun's arms, turned, and ran off, as if having seen a ghost. Trying to compose herself, Huang Deyun apologized for her maid's bad behavior as she followed him upstairs, where he pointed out the bathroom to her.

After closing the door behind her, Deyun sized up the bathroom. Water filled a semicircular white ceramic basin, which must have been a flush toilet, for there was also a semicircular cover above it. Comprador Wang had once joked about the time he'd taken someone from his home-town to use the toilet at the Chinese Merchants Club. The country bumpkin had knelt down and washed his face in the toilet bowl, which he'd mistaken for a washbasin. She'd heard the joke during the drought and found it difficult to laugh.

A shell-shaped tub against a white ceramic tile wall on the other side of the room was half filled with water. Apparently, the Englishman had saved water for her just in case the controls were applied to the hotel and kept Huang Deyun from enjoying a bath. Sensing his tenderness, she slowly undressed. With a long sigh, as if shedding a heavy burden, she experienced a sense of complete freedom as she stepped into the water. She lay back and let the warm water enfold her. Huang Deyun closed her eyes, relaxing every muscle and every joint.

A long time passed before she realized she had better get up. Assum-ing that the Englishman would not be in the room, she was surprised to see him standing looking out the window when she opened the bathroom door. Unconsciously she raised her hands to cover her face, believing that her makeup must have been smudged by the bathroom steam. She could not face the man looking like that. Covering her face with her hands, she retreated into the bathroom, where she looked for the mirror in the mist. After wiping it with a towel, she saw a face that required only light touching up. She picked up an eyebrow pencil and studied the barely visible crow's-feet around her eyes; but then she changed her mind, since putting on another layer of powder would only highlight the lines. She quickly washed away the remaining makeup on her face.

She wanted to appear in front of Sean with a brand-new face.

Sean handed her a glass of lemonade, finding it impossible not to look at this woman who had just stepped out of the bath.

"There'll be an opening party at the Repulse Bay Hotel. Will you do me the honor of accompanying me?"

He regretted it the moment the words were out of his mouth.

Although he was new in the colony, Sean could tell from the many invitations he'd been unable to turn down that the Britons in Hong Kong remained Victorian in how they acted and how they lived. How could he take this woman, to whom he'd just lent the use of his bathroom, into that status-conscious social circle, where she would be on a par with ladies and gentlemen who always kept their noses in the air? He didn't even know how to introduce her, since he knew nothing of her background. All he'd learned was from his visit during the Mid-Autumn Festival, when Richard Huang had pointed out the living room furniture and said they were heirlooms. Seeing her graceful manner and the shrewdness of her face, Sean found it difficult to place her in any particular social category. She was an intriguing woman.

Sean easily visualized the party at the Repulse Bay Hotel, which would be identical to those in Singapore or Malaya, where his fellow countrymen, the British colonizers, would play host in a land they had taken through military force. They would be absolutely unscrupulous, thinking that the world was still under the dominion of the British Empire.

The boredom he felt at such parties was assuaged only by the local color added by the Chinese gentry, who had been invited because the colonizers wanted to give the illusion of racial equality between the rulers and the ruled. He had met the local legislators, lawyers, and doctors, all upper-crust Chinese educated in England and more English than the English. Their wives were graceful and elegant, and they all spoke perfect English—neither too fast nor too slow, like ladies from good and respected families.

At home, these Hong Kong Chinese would eat with knives and forks; their wives played the piano excellently and sang "The Last Rose of Summer." At social occasions, they wore Western-style evening gowns with corseted waists and broad-brimmed hats decorated with flowers; they carried white parasols at outdoor parties. Sean missed the rare sightings of Malayan aristocratic women in their gold-threaded sarongs.

He knew that some of those Chinese women in their evening gowns and dressy hats would be among the elegant crowd at the hotel party.

Could he install Huang Deyun among her own people? He could not picture her dressed like an Englishwoman in a lace-trimmed hat, with a corset seemingly about to snap her in two at the waist.

Why had he invited a woman he barely knew, who was definitely no longer young and was a member of the yellow race, no less?

"When I first saw you," Sean would recall many years later, as he clasped her hands in his, "I thought you were Richard's wife, several years his senior. Isn't that a Chinese custom?"

Huang Deyun's age would always be a mystery to him.

At that first party at the Repulse Bay Hotel, Huang Deyun wore a black velvet dress embroidered with silver flowers, which made her stand out among the ladies in their elaborate dresses; she was the center of attention among all the guests, foreign and Chinese. Her appearance turned the heads of mistresses, who, covering their mouths with ivory fans or kerchiefs, commented on her from head to toe before whispering information about this new face that had shown up in their midst.

Huang Deyun was also seized with curiosity about this party, which was so heavily tainted with a colonial flavor. She saw gentlemen in dark attire greet and chat with each other in a manner befitting their upbringing. Their exchanges mostly concerned the current financial and political situation; more often than not they would also exchange views on that season's horse racing or a cricket match that had just concluded. The high-backed chairs alongside the bandstand were occupied by older, aristocratic ladies in silvery gray or pearl gray floor-length gowns. Their stiff posture made them look as if they'd just stepped out of a portrait. Occasionally someone would come up to greet them with a bow, to which they returned a ritualized ceremony of holding out their hands to be kissed.

Huang Deyun noticed several young women surrounding those ladies in high-collared brocade dresses or shimmering satin gowns. Some wore fresh flowers in their hair while others had golden locks hanging down around their faces. They were wearing pastel blue, pink, or soft yellow gauzy evening dresses with satin belts encircling their slender waists. As if by prior agreement, these properly dressed, well-behaved, unmarried young women cast imperceptible glances at her companion, Sean Shelley, the manager of the Wayfoong Bank, the colony's most valuable bachelor.

Later, when they had gotten to know each other better, Huang Deyun pointed out his ploy: "Now I know. You realized you'd never be able to accommodate those officials, generals and admirals, pastors and their wives, all of whom had wanted you to invite their daughter, cousin, or niece to the party so they could snatch you up. Not wanting to displease any of them, in the end you took me along as your shield. Isn't that right?"

He didn't respond, so she continued, "You weren't sure what kind of woman you wanted, so you didn't know whom to choose. You still can't decide—"

"Do you want to know what they say about you and where you come from? They believe you're an overseas Chinese from Indonesia, which is why they'd never seen you before. You're with me because . . . please forgive me, Butterfly. I'd rather not go on."

Her face flushed red when she heard the hesitation in his voice, but she didn't have the heart to press the matter.

"Butterfly" was the name he had given her so he could introduce her to the guests at the party.

She expected it would be her last party each time she left with her arm in his after the music had stopped and the guests dispersed. She'd wait for the moment: Sean would take her home, where he'd walk around to her side and help her out of the car, as always, then, at the door, bow deeply to thank her for serving as his female companion all these times so he could leisurely observe and, without alerting the young woman, find a mate whose background, interests, and moral standing all matched his. Huang Deyun would then retire, having completed her mission.

But that moment never came.

Instead, this man, who was several years her junior, pinned a large red flower on his lapel and attended her son's wedding, lowering his head and looking into the camera he held. She knew he enjoyed looking at her that way. After the newlyweds entered the honeymoon suite, their guests' good wishes in their ears, Sean Shelley surprised her by pulling her over to sit with him in the chairs recently occupied by the bride and groom. He then signaled for their picture to be taken.

2

The bride's name was Li Meixiu. Decades later, she would sit in her wheelchair and shake her head, lamenting over how the most important events of her life had occurred on the same days as Hong Kong workers' strikes: once in 1922, the day she was married, and again three years later, on the one-month anniversary of the birth of her son.

Li Meixiu came from a farming family in Xiangshan, Canton, where a major flood during the late Qing had washed away everything they owned. The family sailed to Indonesia for a better life, immigrating to Hong Kong when Meixiu was a teenager.

In 1922, on her wedding day, the first major workers' strike took place in Hong Kong, stemming from a demand for a 30 percent pay raise by Chinese seamen working for American, British, and Dutch shipping companies.

"If our demand is not met, the seamen will strike and their bosses will be responsible for the consequences."

After the companies failed to meet their demand and deadline, the seamen walked out en masse. The bustling treaty port died on the spot, with over a hundred ships crowding the harbor and paralyzing water traffic. Even the Star Ferry connecting Central and Tsim Sha Tsui was forced to discontinue its service. Left with no choice, the colonial government dispatched members of the British Navy to operate the ferry, but their unfamiliarity with the water currents sent it spinning in the water. Public outrage erupted, as the passengers nearly drowned.

Then the train and tram workers walked out in support of the seamen. Handcarts and sedan chairs that hadn't been in used in years were retrieved and brought onto the streets, where they ran around amid the shouts of their operators.

More than a month before her wedding, Li Meixiu's aging grandmother had arranged for rickshaws from a bridal and funeral service to parade her and her dowry on the street, before sending everything to Huang Deyun's house two days prior to the wedding. They had not expected that big hotels in Hong Kong would hire away the rickshaws by paying them several times more to carry incoming guests' luggage than they'd normally get at the bridal and funeral service. Even the gong beaters and drummers were hired away. The Li family was considering asking the matchmaker to relay a message to the Huang family that the dire situation required them to pay whatever the rickshaw pullers and others demanded, and that they could not scrimp on the tip, called "happy money," either. But before the message had reached the Huang family, all of Hong Kong's workers walked out on a sympathy strike, including postal and communication workers, employees of restaurants and newspapers, even household servants, sedan bearers, and cooks. All together, more than a hundred thousand workers left their posts.

While Huang Deyun consented that the dowry could be delivered later, she insisted that the auspicious day and time for the bride to enter her family not be changed. The wedding would take place no matter what, even if the Huang family could not find a traditional music troupe or an eight-man palanquin to carry the bride over.

Somehow she dug up a shabby bamboo sedan chair, with a coarse red cloth thrown over the top, to serve as a wedding sedan. Two listless sedan bearers deposited the chair at the door of the Li residence, thus concluding a silent wedding, a far cry from the eight-man palanquin covered with red silk and crepe fluttering in the wind that the Li family had expected.

Supported by a cane, Li Meixiu's grandmother shed many tears over the injustice inflicted upon her motherless granddaughter by the Huang family, with its backing by compradors of the foreign firms. The old woman had nearly bled herself dry over the marriage arrangements. From the beginning, the matchmaker, following ancient rituals and rules, had asked the families to exchange "visiting cards" listing the names of three generations of family members. But the Huang family never handed over theirs. The matchmaker, afraid she might lose the money, persuaded Li Meixiu's father to ask for the next best thing: a complete list of the Huang family properties and estates.

The response came quickly, along with the name and address of Comprador Wang Qinshan of Jardine's for the Li family to verify. Following the address the matchmaker gave him, Li Meixiu's father found himself standing before Comprador Wang's newly completed house on Seymour Road at Mid-Level. It was a garden estate that overlooked the ocean. He was so intimidated he didn't even ring the bell before turning and heading home.

When the bridegroom's family sent the matchmaker to discuss betrothal money, gifts, and braised pigs, Li Meixiu's grandmother personally purchased every item in the dowry. She also made arrangements for the dowry to be delivered to the bridegroom's family, including hiring the porters and making sure the procession would travel many streets to show off.

They had not expected the Huang family to send over a tiny sedan that wouldn't even be used to carry a concubine, let alone forego the music.

Li Meixiu cried as she climbed into the bamboo sedan chair that carried her to an unfamiliar place. After being helped out of the sedan chair, she crossed the threshold and entered the home she had tried to imagine countless times. She found herself in a dark room filled with black-lacquered, sorrel-wood, old-fashioned furniture. This was so different from the home she'd secretly hoped for. What she'd wanted was walls with mushy wallpaper with flowers and a green desk lamp on her dressing table. Ideally, there would also be a white organ in the corner. Back when she was a student at Sacred Heart College, she'd admired her music teacher, who sat stiffly at the organ and, with her head held high, played serene music to the words of the Psalms.

Now she sat sad and forlorn in this dark bridal chamber, where she saw nothing familiar to comfort her, as her dowry had yet to be delivered. She knew little about her husband, Richard Huang, only that they had exchanged a brief glance from the far ends of a table in the rooftop teahouse of the Sincere Department Store before she was whisked away by the matchmaker and relatives. Before leaving, she stole a glance at him just as a gust of wind sent his hand up to hold his felt hat. That hand seemed quite fair, particularly striking under the sun; she couldn't see his face clearly, since it was in the shadow of his hat, though he appeared to have a high nose and deep-set eyes, a more angular face than the average Chinese.

Her most tender memories of her husband were from the wedding night. When he took the red veil from her face, his first action was to part the bangs on her forehead; they were like a curtain that shaded her eyes. Richard Huang spread her bangs into swallowtails so he could have a better look at his bride. Holding her breath, Li Meixiu anxiously blinked her downcast eyes a few times.

Those same hands reached out for her on their first night. Squeezing her eyes shut, she kept retreating up against the wall, shaken by fear. Reciting the rosary silently, she tried to fight off the hands, as she envisioned the Virgin Mary in a chalky white veil and grayish white robe flickering before her. The Virgin Mary's eyes were downcast, as if to show sadness over the imminent loss of Li Meixiu's virginity.

After the engagement, she'd returned to Sacred Heart College, where she promised the sisters that she would carry out all the proper rites and rituals.

The second biggest day of her life was the one-month anniversary party for her son, William. It too fell on the day of another large-scale strike, in 1925, when the Hong Kong workers walked out to protest the May Thirtieth Shanghai Massacre.

Three years before, on her wedding day, Huang Deyun had reserved twenty tables at Prosperity Garden, which was famous for its bird's nest soup and shark's fins. The restaurant was a replica of Canton's Southern Garden, with flowers planted all over the courtyard giving it a quiet, elegant air. The spacious rooms were filled with splendid sandalwood furniture. Committed to sparing nothing for her only son's marriage, Huang Deyun was forced to cancel the wedding banquet, as the chefs and waiters went on strike. So she had no choice but to host a banquet at home. Worse yet, the strike had cut off transportation, which in turn resulted in shortages at the market. Pork, mutton, beef, chicken, and duck were scarce, as were fresh vegetables and fruit. She had to buy canned, preserved, and dried goods to cobble together two tables of food.

Li Meixiu's only memory of the wedding banquet could be summed up in one word: salty. Afterward, she favored lightly seasoned food and, after she took over the household, told the cook to use less salt. Later, when she immersed herself in medical books, she learned about the harm salt can do a person's body.

In order to make up for her wedding banquet, she persuaded her husband to lay out a big spread for their son's one-month anniversary and reserve ten tables at Heavenly Aroma. She even prepared the menu, all extravagant dishes, including the house specialty.

At first Li Meixiu had thought that the demonstrations would stop before long, since the massacre had occurred in Shanghai and had little to do with Hong Kong. She hadn't expected that the *China News*, after publishing a strike announcement from the seamen's union, would be accused of violating public security regulations by the colonial government, which sent police to shut the newspaper down and arrest the offenders. This caused such a public outcry that Chinese employees of foreign firms and shops retaliated by walking out. Workers at other firms also left their posts to return to Canton without telling their employers.

To mourn their Chinese compatriots who had been killed following the massacre, more than a hundred thousand people, including students, peasants, and soldiers, as well as the Hong Kong Chinese who had returned to Canton, took to the streets. When the protesters passed by Shaji, across the river from the British Concession, they were fired upon by British sailors on the shore and on warships. Fifty-two protesters died, more than a hundred and seventy were seriously wounded, and countless were slightly wounded. It was the infamous Shaji Massacre. When the news spread to Hong Kong, workers who had been wavering immediately walked out on a wildcat strike. The strikers ranged from telecommunication bureau workers and servants at foreigners' homes to restaurant and teahouse employees, barbers, sanitary workers, and marketplace fish and vegetable vendors. The number of strikers continued to grow until more than two hundred and fifty thousand people had left Hong Kong for Canton.

Li Meixiu's dream for an extravagant banquet for her son was crushed.

Among the servants working for the foreigners on the Peak or at Mid-Level, first to respond to the call to strike were the sedan-chair carriers and handcart pushers. No matter how much their foreign employers promised to raise their pay, they simply shook their heads and walked out. The foreigners had no choice but to hire carriers and pushers from the streets in Central, but within a few days they too refused to work. Watching them leave with empty vehicles, the foreigners could not believe their eyes. Just two weeks earlier, these carriers had been jostling for a fare on Pedder Street or fighting over a few pennies. How could they now actually turn down the money offered them and carry empty sedan chairs down the hill?

The spoiled foreigners had no choice but to get up early each morning and walk down the hilly path with a cane to catch the Peak tram to work. They looked up at the mountain range beyond Victoria Harbor, and nothing had changed; like the year before, summer was on its way in, a season of sweat and intermittent showers. They had seen so many Mays, each one the same. Except this year. Why was that?

Mr. Matheson of Jardine's congratulated himself for being one of the few automobile owners in the colony. Going to work in a moving machine not only saved him the trouble of dealing with the difficult carriers but also spared him the effort of getting up early each morning to crowd into the tram with civil servants and bank clerks.

But Mr. Matheson's gloating was premature. The strike spread like an infectious disease, and the dozen or so servants in his household, including the gardeners, the chef, and the cleaning crew, all quit under the pretense of going back to visit relatives in Canton, as if embroiled in a conspiracy. The only servants left in the enormous mansion were Mrs. Matheson's personal maid, the nanny, and a steward who was reputed to have served an aristocratic family in Scotland. All were from Britain. Normally these British servants, higher in the pecking order, would order the Chinese servants around and expect to be waited on by them. Now they were forced to do the menial work themselves.

Leaning against the second-floor veranda, Mrs. Matheson looked at her changed garden with tear-filled eyes, while massaging her aching abdomen. The playground on the northeastern corner had changed so much it was beyond recognition. The gardeners had trimmed the hedges to various animal shapes—giraffe, elephant, sheep, spotted deer—to the specifications of her children, who then gave the trees names. Following Mrs. Matheson's design, the gardeners had also planted shrubs to create a small maze for the entertainment of her children and their playmates.

Now the gardeners had thrown down their shears to join the strike and, after several rainfalls, the animal hedges had begun to grow out in all directions and lose their shape. Leaves and branches also grew at will in the once neatly trimmed maze, blocking the paths inside. When she looked down, all she could see was an overgrown garden and a misshapen maze that harbored green snakes.

Her children had chased two honking geese among the tall grass. Owing to neglect, the water in the pond had turned muddy, staining the white birds. Mrs. Matheson felt so sorry for her children: they didn't deserve this. But there were other, more unsettling things on her mind: after not being polished for a long while, the silverware had oxidized and turned an ugly black in the humid air.

One night, she asked her husband if she could return to Scotland, as she tried to tear her eyes away from the darkened candlestick.

"I want to leave on the next ship and take the children away from this godforsaken place."

Her hands, clutching a handkerchief, shook imperceptibly, for she had a darker fear, one she could not even bring up with her own husband. Mrs. Matheson sensed that this strike was different from previous walkouts and that it could turn into a riot. Pressing her knees together under her dark green satin skirt, she felt an impending sense of doom all around her. What if the Chinese servants, to exact revenge, joined the rioters and forced open the wrought-iron garden gate with their knives and clubs, then stormed in, tied up her defenseless husband, and turned their fury on her. . . .

The London *Times* had once published a letter from a missionary in India about a hair-raising assault on forty-eight British women in Bombay. They were tied to trees beneath a blazing sun and stripped naked; their faces were then painted black to make them look like untouchables before they were raped and tortured to death. All the British subjects, particularly the women, loathed and feared the black demons who had carried out the atrocity. As more letters, rumors, and eyewitness accounts spread out from India, Mrs. Matheson felt as if she'd experienced the same terrifying nightmares as the other women.

Later the British military in Bombay publicly repudiated the rumor, saying that the reports of rape were completely groundless, invented by colonizers who feared revenge from the local Indians. But Mrs. Matheson preferred to believe they were true.

"Please, I beg you, take me away," she begged her husband.

The strike continued, turning the once bright island into a dark, forlorn place.

After seeing his family off on a ship back to Scotland, Mr. Matheson was all alone in a virtually deserted house, pacing back and forth. He finally stopped at the window and parted the drapes to look out. The floral clock at the garden entrance was now overgrown with weeds; colorful daisies in the flowerbed had faded and withered away, leaving only rotting stalks. The clock had been not only the symbol of the taipan manor but also an icon of the British Empire. His guests called it the Greenwich clock, signaling world standard time, for the empire, with colonies on five continents, was surely the center of the globe.

But regrettably, after World War I, victory for the empire produced only superficial glory, for Britain had lost the maritime superiority it had enjoyed for over a century.

The empire was collapsing. As the guns sounded in Russia with the advent of the October Revolution, Asian and African colonies' resistance to British imperialism was on the rise; with colonized people clamoring for independence, "nationalism" was the new catchword. The empire on which "the sun never sets" was being threatened, and the great colonial enterprise was on its last legs. Even the tiny island of Hong Kong dared to question the authority of the British monarch.

Following the increasing importance of the local economy, the Chinese were now beginning to show their business acumen. Over the past two years, a fair number of overseas Chinese had come to settle in Hong Kong from places in North America, Australia, and the South Seas. Bringing with them management experience, they began to play an important role in the textile and food industries. Even in banking and finance, which had been monopolized by British groups, the Chinese, in addition to their traditional lending services, had begun to set up new-style institutions, such as the Canton Bank, hoping to carve out a niche of their own.

Times were surely changing. What puzzled Mr. Matheson most were the emotional ties these Chinese immigrants on the island had with the mainland. Whenever something happened over there, the Chinese here would not allow themselves to ignore it.

Earlier at breakfast, he'd read the six demands the Chinese had presented to the British government and nearly spit out his tea. The newspaper said the Chinese wanted the freedom to live anywhere they chose and to receive treatment equal to British subjects; they demanded that lashing and torture be eliminated, and that Chinese workers be allowed to send representatives to participate in writing the labor law—they were nearly ready to take over. Crumpling the paper in seething anger, he quickly contacted some friends who shared his views. They belonged to the Western Merchants Association, men who had all along favored tougher colonial rule through military force and criticized the wishy-washy way Governor Stubbs had handled the strike three years before.

Matheson recommended to the British government that, unlike the earlier diplomatic negotiations, it should concern itself with the interests of the empire and crack down on the strikers.

Following their advice, Governor Stubbs sent two urgent wires to London for reinforcements, only to receive a terse rejection from the prime minister: "London is deeply concerned over the difficulties in Hong Kong, but, owing to the larger picture, the government cannot send any troops at the moment."

The strike took a drastic turn for the worse, and things looked hopeless. Back when Hong Kong was ravaged by a plague in 1894, Matheson had left with his family, but he'd returned once the plague had passed. Now the idea of leaving resurfaced. His wife had already abandoned the taipan manor for Scotland. With his forehead resting against the windowsill, he wished it were all only a bad dream. Then he recalled the poetry by Kipling that he'd begun reciting before bedtime lately. Kipling's praise of the British Empire at its peak resonated within him.

The thought and inspiration of Kipling's poems lessened his pessimism. He knew he was invincible; he could see that in the eyes of employees of the firm. What troubled him, however, was the way Comprador Wang had begun dealing with him. The latter seemed more insolent and less subservient now that the Chinese were becoming more powerful. Matheson had never liked the traditional comprador system, because it encouraged the greedy, sneaky Chinese to deceive their bosses and manipulate the taipans. The compradors used their Western bosses' money and their influence when they sold foreign goods to Hong Kong and the mainland, while buying silk, tea, and china for export. They were not only the agents but also the sellers of the goods; they represented the foreign firms and meddled in every transaction, reaping tremendous profits from commissions in the process.

The foreign firms that provided the capital should theoretically have been the bosses of the compradors, their employees. But a foolish, softhearted taipan many years before had been convinced by the compradors' complaint that they made virtually nothing from the commissions. That set a precedent to allow compradors to run their own businesses on the side; now they had a legitimate store name and a marketing system, which gave them the opportunity to cheat, secretly using the firm's money to support their own businesses without having to pay interest.

In fact, the foreign firms' businesses had been changing and diversifying; they no longer needed to rely upon the compradors now that their businesses had expanded from import and export into insurance, shipping, and real estate. The compradors, however, had unfortunately become the leaders and representatives of Chinese stockholders, since the firms depended on them to attract Chinese investment.

The last thing Mr. Matheson wanted was for Comprador Wang to take advantage of the strike and profit himself. Without a second thought, he picked up the phone and ordered the manager at the Wayfoong Bank to reduce the amount Wang was allowed to withdraw to the bare minimum, just enough to pay for shipping, insurance, and other minor expenses.

Believing that he'd solved a long-standing problem, Matheson boarded a ship for Scotland, feeling absolutely unconcerned.

But he had just played into Wang's hands. Taking advantage of the economic depression brought on by the strike, Wang declared bankruptcy for Prosperity Pawnshop, making the investment by the foreign firm worthless. He then incited Chinese investors in foreign insurance companies to withdraw their investments and return to Canton, using Hong Kong's instability as an excuse. Upon hearing the news, Matheson called from Scotland and sent telegrams to Wang, asking him to reconsider and expressing his disapproval of the latter's intention to sever ties with the foreign firms. During the telephone negotiations, Wang insisted on leaving the firm, using old age as a pretense. In the end, he was talked into remaining as a consultant, but that was only to maintain enough control for him to recommend Richard Huang as his replacement down the line.

3

Once, long after Huang Deyun's death, Li Meixiu was interviewed by a newspaper reporter in regard to her devotion to charity work, exemplified by her years of tireless effort to raise money for orphanages, hospitals, and nursing homes in Hong Kong and Kowloon. She responded by saying that she had done it all out of a sense of repentance, hoping to please the Lord by being his worker. She'd finally realized why he had sent her to the Huang family; it was to temper her through suffering. Devotion to the Cross could then redeem Huang Deyun of her sins. Quoting Paul the disciple, she said, "Rich are the blessings where sins are the greatest."

Huang Deyun had indeed reaped huge profits from the 1922 strike. Social instability had prompted the governor to promulgate an emergency decree, which in turn allowed the colonial police to turn people's fears to their monetary advantage. Their targets were the lending services and pawnshops in Hong Kong and Kowloon, which were ordered to pay an exorbitant protection fee for a special alarm connected to the police station. If a robbery occurred, all they had to do was sound the alarm and the police would come to their rescue.

The lending services and pawnshop owners were only too happy to pay for the fee in exchange for a good night's sleep. All except Huang Deyun, who wanted to find a way to get her money back. After a brainstorm, she got the fat Wu Fu to talk every major pawnshop into posting a notice on its door—No Pawning, Redemption Only—under the pretense that it would prevent robberies during a time of uncertainty. The notice invited customers to buy back their pawned objects, while the proprietors turned away anyone who wanted to pawn their belongings.

During the strike, when countless average Chinese left Hong Kong for Canton, it was inevitable that they would lose their tickets in the process. They could not report their losses, and the pawnshops would accept only the original tickets. Others could not retrieve their belongings because their tickets had expired while they were back in their hometowns. The pawnshops were now at liberty to sell off the clothing and jewelry these unfortunate customers had pawned.

Li Meixiu recalled her shock over the mountain of goods she saw when she first walked into the Prosperity Pawnshop warehouse. She recalled that it was also the coldest year ever. The dry weather ignited a row of wooden houses on Shek Kip Mei Street in Kowloon one night, leaving several hundred families homeless. They were temporarily relocated to classrooms in a nearby elementary school, where they slept on the floor. Li Meixiu told the reporter that she led members of her church to the rear of Prosperity Pawnshop, where she asked the warehouse keeper to open the heavy lock. They then piled winter clothes that had not been redeemed onto trucks to be sent to the victims of the fire.

The warehouse keeper had indeed opened the lock and taken out the winter clothes, but the order was given by Huang Deyun, not Li Meixiu, and rather than end up on the shivering bodies of fire victims, they were sold at a market in Wan Chai. The money was then given to Richard Huang for expenses at his Happy Forever Money-Lending Service.

The reporter, after consulting the reference work *Major Events in Hong Kong*, discovered that Hong Kong had its coldest winter in 1923, but the fire had occurred in 1953. Exactly thirty years later. The reporter entered a large question mark on the notebook in which he recorded Li Meixiu's interview.

Throughout her life, Li Meixiu's greatest regret was her failure to persuade her mother-in-law to be baptized. The information Meixiu pieced together from neighbors' gossip worried her that the crimes her mother-in-law committed would condemn her to eternal suffering in fire and brimstone. But other than pray for her, Meixiu felt powerless, particularly because "the incidents" had occurred before she married into the family.

Business was booming at the pawnshop. Huang Deyun informed people that Wu Fu, unable to resist her enticements, had boarded a ship bound for Rangoon, after it had unloaded rice and grain. Not long after his departure, people with a keen sense of smell could detect a repulsive stench like that of a decomposing animal when they walked by the pawnshop at night. Gradually the odor got to the point that passersby had to cover their noses or take a detour. On a few occasions, Huang Deyun's personal maid, Xianü, was seen sprinkling water mixed with lime. And when she'd finished, she'd lean against the wall and try to stop vomiting.

The night of the winter solstice that year seemed cold and long. Tongues of flame leaped high into the air on the empty ground behind the pawnshop, lighting up the cold, starry night sky. A neighbor thought the ashes from the spirit money burned earlier had somehow rekindled and started a fire. He went over to knock on the pawnshop door, but drew no response. Before long the fire died out and the neighbor, not fully awake, went home to sleep.

On a bitterly cold morning soon after the Lantern Festival on the fifteenth day of the first lunar month, a line of people knelt outside the pawnshop, all clad in hemp mourning clothes, attracting a circle of onlookers. Someone had obviously informed Wu Fu's wife, for the woman, who had never left her hometown in her life, took a train from Dongguan with her children. Huang Deyun received them in the pawnshop, in the central room with its opium bed. Pushing aside the flaky pastry, her childhood favorite, a Dongguan specialty that Wu's wife had brought her, Huang Deyun told Wu's wife how she herself was concerned and had begun burning incense to pray for Buddha's protection after Wu Fu had been gone for a few months. As the litany progressed, she even dabbed at the corners of her dry eyes with a white handkerchief. Li Meixiu was told that Wu's eldest son had raised his balled farmer's fists in a threatening gesture but was pacified by Huang Deyun.

Another source told Li Meixiu that Wu Fu had contracted an embarrassing illness, from which he'd died suddenly. Worried about contagion, Huang Deyun had taken the liberty of sending the body to a crematorium. Prepared that sooner or later his wife would come from Dongguan to demand to see her husband, Huang Deyun handed her a death certificate she said had been issued by the hospital the moment she arrived. The eldest son, on the verge of creating a scene, sobbed and knelt to receive the piece of paper with trembling hands.

Huang then gave Wu Fu's wife the white handkerchief she'd used to dry her tears. The handkerchief unfolded before their eyes like a white flower, its stamen three glistening gold teeth. Wu Fu's gold teeth. But no one knew that he'd had gold teeth.

Holding the gold teeth, Wu's wife, followed by her children, all clad in mourning clothes, left the pawnshop to pay their respects at the cemetery to which Huang Deyun had directed them.

Wu Fu's disappearance remained a mystery, and the means by which the Huang family made its fortune remained the source of Li Meixiu's religious devotion.

After Wu Fu vanished under suspicious circumstances, Huang Deyun's wealth increased dramatically through the lending of money at an exorbitant interest rate. There were people who said she'd stolen all of Wu's wealth, except for the meager amount used to send his wife and children on their way. Wu's money was then used to open an underground money-lending service on Wing Lok Street in Central. After Richard Huang became the Jardine comprador, a real estate sign was hung outside the money-lending service.

That was in the early 1930s.

On a small island like Hong Kong, with its large population, every inch of land is precious and costly. Huang Deyun had seen how people were making fortunes by buying and selling real estate and realized that land was where her fortune lay. Her opportunity came during the strike.

A building boom had begun just before the strike, which then forced the builders into bankruptcy, as investors pulled out of declining prospects. The houses and other buildings were then auctioned off. When the strike was over, the price of real estate in Hong Kong plunged even further. The newly built flats in Yau Ma Tei and Causeway Bay remained empty, unfilled by people who had left Hong Kong for Canton. Even flats in the New Territories and Hong Hom built by the colonial government had but a 10 percent occupancy rate.

But that would soon change. Sean Shelley, the manager of the Way-foong Bank, revealed news he'd received from high-level officials: after his request for reinforcements was turned down by the prime minister, Governor Stubbs, in an effort to intimidate the strikers, had published a fabricated story in the *North China Herald* that the British government would send a hundred thousand troops to attack Tientsin to the north, Shanghai and Hankou in central China, and Canton to the south. Wealthy people on the mainland believed the false story and scrambled to flee the coming disaster. Fighting among warlords only added to the tide of refugees, who now flocked to Hong Kong, the new Eden.

With arrangements made by Sean Shelley, who served as their guar-antor, Huang Deyun and Richard Huang applied for a loan to buy sev-eral empty buildings in Happy Valley almost for a song. Shortly after the deeds had changed hands, the population in Hong Kong experienced a sudden upsurge and rents soared. The supply of available housing fell short of the demand, causing the cost of real estate to rise at an alarming rate.

This was the genesis of the Huang family fortune.

In the mid-1930s political upheavals on the mainland and Japanese encroachment into Chinese territory told Richard Huang that another wave of refugees would soon arrive in Hong Kong. Which meant that the already high cost of land would rise even higher. He convinced Comprador Wang Qinshan to come out of retirement to join in the for-mation of a construction company that Richard would represent in bid-ding for a land reclamation project on Tai Kok Tsui Road in Kowloon.

It was a formidable investment, requiring countless quantities of manpower, time, and money.

Huang Deyun, ticking away on her abacus, shook her head and com-mented that the capital for the land reclamation project was too high and that it would take too long to see a return on her investment. Where the exploitation of Hong Kong land resources was concerned, she had quite a different view. Geographical limitations placed upon the natural environment meant a scarcity of new land. She would rather invest in existing buildings than spend a huge sum of money and contend with the ocean. If she could grasp the right moment to buy and then wait for real estate values to go up before selling, she could sit tight and enjoy a tidy profit without having to lift a finger. She'd then invest in larger buildings, her income snowballing all the way to the bank.

She was surprised and worried about her son's plan to work with the Hong Kong governor. She'd never liked the colonial government; she trusted it even less. Ever since the day she was kidnapped and brought to Hong Kong, she felt she'd never enjoyed a sliver of care from the government, let alone real security. After setting out in the real estate business, she was even more incensed over the government's land ownership system. When she signed the contract for a piece of land she'd paid for with decades of hard work and savings, she was informed by a legal consultant that every inch of land in Hong Kong belonged to the British Crown. Those who paid for the land didn't actually own it; they only enjoyed the right to use it. They were, in fact, renting the land from the British Crown, and there was even an expiration date. They had to pay taxes on the land, but when their lease expired, they had to return the land to the crown.

Why, she wondered, did her own son not only not keep a distance from this kind of government but even be willing to work with it in its land reclamation project? The closeness between mother and son appeared to have dissipated since his marriage, and, now that they held different views in regard to the future of Hong Kong's real estate, a rift began to develop between them.

4

The first piece of land Richard Huang sold was a prime property located between Des Voeux Road and Li Yuen East Street in Central. It was a memorable day. He had barely taken over as the comprador at Jardine's when he stumbled upon his first pot of gold. The agreement he'd made with Mr. Matheson called for a 10 percent commission, a huge sum, all his. The contract was signed in the morning, but even that afternoon he could not contain his excitement. He was so happy he could barely keep his mouth shut, and he chose not to take the pedicab home when he got off work, feeling that the cramped seat could not contain his suddenly enlarged body. Bathed in excitement and self-satisfaction, Richard swaggered toward home.

It was a pleasant, late-spring evening. The exhilaration heated his body to the point that he had to take off his Prussian blue suit jacket. He believed it was that jacket, now draped over his arm, which had brought him luck. He'd tried his best to rid himself of the comprador image, refusing to look like Comprador Wang, who wore an old-style Chinese robe and looked forever sluggish and listless. Once he was promoted to the position, Richard decided to follow Western customs, coming to work each day in a neat suit and leather shoes and changing his hat style with the season.

The tailored suit he was wearing that day made him appear springy and radiant. As the saying goes, a happy event is invigorating. Thrusting out his chest with confidence, he found himself standing outside the house on Bonham Road. He stopped and lowered the hand poised to push open the door. He didn't feel like going home. Today was the first day in his life worth celebrating. He imagined pushing open the door and walking up to the second floor to the dark room at the end of the hallway, where Meixiu, the woman his mother had arranged for him to marry, would be waiting for him. He was certain she would be on her knees before the ivory image of the Virgin Mary at the window, muttering a prayer.

Shaking out his suit jacket, Richard put it back on outside the door of his own house. His mood that afternoon made him reluctant to enter a room decorated with pictures of saints, where he would be under the sympathetic scrutiny of St. Francis's gloomy eyes. He turned to go back to the street, where the lamps had just come on; there was a place on a narrow, hilly street in Central where he could go. He had fantasized about that place for a long time, yet never could muster the courage to go up and knock on the door. But on a day like this, it matched his adventurous mood. From the lewd gestures by bachelors in the firm's men's room and bits of gossip he had picked up, he knew that Brigitte, a blue-eyed blonde, would be waiting under a lamp at the far end of that alley. She would press those who dared enter her door into her snowy white bosom, singing tenderly to the face buried in her cleavage. Richard had heard that Brigitte was a singer from Liverpool who had come to Hong Kong as an entertainer, only to be abandoned by a Scottish soldier with whom she'd lived for a while. One night she was thrown into jail to serve two months for being drunk in a Wan Chai bar. On her release, she entered the oldest profession in a room at the end of the alley.

Richard soon found himself standing at the door, where he hesitated momentarily before gathering his courage to give the ring on the door a soft tap. Nothing happened; after a while he decided to leave, but a throaty, sugary voice came from the other side, "It's open. Please come in."

Throughout his adult life, Richard had pursued one type of woman, a blue-eyed blonde with a tiny waist, modeled after his high school English teacher. His first British woman, Brigitte, from the house in the dark alley, fit the description perfectly. His second British woman, Ingrid Baker, came from a respectable family in Birmingham.

It was at a light opera performance by a London troupe that Richard first met Ingrid Baker. Huang Deyun had turned down Sean Shelley's invitation at the last minute, saying she wasn't feeling well. In order not to waste a ticket obtained with great difficulty, Richard quickly changed into his formal wear to accompany the Englishman.

During intermission, Richard felt a gaze from behind, prompting him to turn and look. That was all it took to be captivated by the wavy golden locks framing Ingrid's face. Unconsciously, he tugged at his bowtie, afraid that in his haste to leave the house he might not have tied it right. Sensing his eyes on her, Ingrid turned to chat with her female companion, exposing a neck that was as fair as the finest porcelain. Richard was mesmerized.

After the performance, Sean Shelley stopped by the fountain outside the concert hall to greet Ingrid, who had rushed up from behind to see him.

"Good evening, Miss Baker," Sean said, touching his hat, a gentlemanly gesture. Obviously they had met at other social functions; her smile had not been directed at Richard.

Courtesy required Sean Shelley to drive Ingrid back to her place, Mrs. May's club for women. On the way, she was enthusiastic in her effort to get Sean to attend a party at Mrs. May's the following weekend. Richard was also invited.

"Thank you very much, Miss Baker. Unfortunately I know nothing about music and cannot play a single instrument."

"You're too modest, Mr. Shelley. I'm going to sing and would love to hear your comments."

After work the following day, Richard paced outside Mrs. May's club, imagining Ingrid to be the mistress of the white building while he, a wanderer, came to the hall and stood at the French doors, waiting for her to appear at the top of the stairs. She would be wearing a soft white dress with delicate piping, her hair glistening like satin. With an almost imperceptible movement of her long skirt, she would slowly descend toward him.

Reality did not match his fantasy. She was the wanderer: the white building had been designated by the colonial government as a residence for single British women. It was a not-for-profit hotel, where Ingrid had a room on the second floor. The downstairs dining room served meals and beverages and was equipped with a small bar. Regulations stipulated that the maximum stay for each tenant was two years; Ingrid, who had offered her services as librarian, lived free of charge for an extended period of time.

Her companion was George, a long-tailed green parrot with a red beak. In the morning she'd bring the cage down and hang it by the library window. Her job was to read novels newly arrived from England and check the contents. If there were too many explicit scenes of kissing or other expressions of romantic love, the book would be hidden in the dark basement as unsuitable for a female readership. The rules had been set by the club's founder, Mrs. May, who, back when she was the governor's wife, would sit in the library and check the contents of every book.

By observing the rules, Ingrid enjoyed the privilege of reading the books before anyone else.

Richard went alone to the party that night. He had already ordered two dozen yellow roses from a florist in Central. When Ingrid finished singing "The Last Rose of Summer," Richard's applause was the loudest. She forgave Sean Shelley for his absence and tried to use Richard to get close to that most eligible bachelor banker. But Richard invariably showed up without Sean, who remained the topic of conversation, until they had said everything there was to say. Richard would then change the subject and praise her voice. Finally finding an appreciative listener, Ingrid talked of her desire to be a singer. As a child, she'd been a soloist in her hometown church choir. Her school music teacher had discovered her talent and offered individual lessons after school.

"When will I have the honor of hearing you sing again, Miss Baker, so I can enjoy music as pretty as a lark?" Richard asked poetically one day, during one of his frequent visits to the club's library, on the pretext of borrowing books.

"My next performance? Who knows when I'll able to do that? I didn't practice enough last time and my voice was dry. Of course you couldn't have told if you weren't listening carefully, but I was dissatisfied with my performance."

Her room upstairs was big enough for a bed, an armoire, and a desk. Her neighbor was the head of nurses, an older woman from Wales who was stiff even without her uniform, like a stern governess.

"I daren't practice in my room. We share even the bathroom, so I must be quiet. Sometimes, when I can't endure it any longer, I shut myself up in the basement so I can sing as loud as I want," Ingrid said with downcast eyes, showing how she suffered the hardships of living under another's roof.

"That's so sad. But there may be a way——"

One drizzly fall evening, Ingrid closed up the library and picked up the cage. As she was about to leave, the telephone rang. It was Richard, who said he had a surprise for her. He'd found a quiet, private place where she could sing to her heart's content, a little green house surrounded by a thicket of cassia trees on a red hill at the end of Bowen Street. The owner, a retired engineer, had passed away a month before, and his nephew, who had come from Edinburgh to take care of funeral arrangements, had turned over the house to the court to be auctioned. As soon as Richard saw it, he knew it was the perfect place for Ingrid.

The fireplace, wallpaper, and Victorian mahogany furniture that filled the rooms reminded Ingrid of her home back in Birmingham. Autumn rains at dusk sent waves of nostalgia through her heart, prompting her to softly sing "The Last Rose of Summer."

As the melody echoed through the cassia trees, the rain stopped and pretty blue jays glided up and down on their bright blue wings, their vermilion beaks and claws flickering, as if they were dancing to Ingrid's singing.

Richard was captivated. When the song was over, he sighed. "Even the birds were charmed by your voice, Miss Baker. You're absolutely fabulous."

The little green house became Ingrid's villa, where she'd spend her weekends with George. One night, after making sure everything was taken care of, Richard ate the peanut butter sandwich she'd made for him, then picked up his hat, saying it was getting late and that he ought to let Miss Baker rest. She walked with him to the deck, where she tried to get George to say good-bye.

"Poor George, it's just you and me again." While still playing with the bird, she said to Richard behind her, "Mr. Huang, you probably won't believe this, but I have to lock George in the closet every night before I change—"

Richard was curious why she hadn't finished.

"Why?" he asked.

"If I don't, George gets excited when he sees my naked body. He jumps around in the cage all night long, making mating calls. It's rather annoying."

Without warning, Richard tossed his hat aside, grabbed her by her fair shoulders, pulled her toward him, and kissed her for the first time.

5

Much later, in her old age, Li Meixiu often hosted charity parties in her capacity as the wife of an honorary member of the board of the Tung Wah Hospital. In her welcoming addresses, she enjoyed showing off her medical knowledge, but after the applause died down, she would explain how she'd studied on her own in order to take care of her mother-in-law, Huang Deyun. In fact, she had always wanted to be a nurse, a lofty, honorable profession, even as a student at Sacred Heart College. She believed that Western medicine was far more effective than Chinese herbs.

But lacking the opportunity to be trained as a professional nurse, she had followed the other career choice popular among graduates of her college. She became a secretary for a foreign firm, which was why Huang Deyun had chosen her to be her son's wife, believing that Li could be Richard's helpmate.

After entering the Huang household, she recalled, she often heard Huang Deyun complain about her health. One morning she saw that the curtain was still draped over Huang's bed. Moaning softly, Huang showed her a rash on her palm, saying the itch had kept her awake all night. Li thought it must have been caused by an insect, so she shut the windows. But it was worse the next morning; Huang Deyun now had red spots, like little red spiders, all over her neck, her shoulders, and her chest. Shocked and frightened, Meixiu hired a pedicab and rushed to the dermatology department at Tung Wah Hospital, where she dragged the doctor back with her. But Huang Deyun would not open the door, telling Li to send the doctor back, that she was afraid of needles.

She tried again to get Huang Deyun to see Western doctors a few years later when Huang was suffering from an unknown malady. She'd been lethargic the year round, spending most of the day behind the bed curtains, preoccupied with her own thoughts. The family, worried about her prolonged bedridden state, sent an old Chinese doctor to see her. After taking some of the prescribed herbal medicine, she remained weak and listless. Li Meixiu sent for famous Western doctors from Hong Kong and Kowloon, all of whom Deyun turned away.

Eventually, a geomancer from the mainland convinced Richard that the *fengshui* of their hillside house was sapping the energy of the mistress. Based on the geomancer's instructions, a location was found on a small hill to the west of the island, where a bright light shone at night, as if lamps had been lit. Richard was puzzled over the source of the light, for there were no other residences on the arboreal hill. The geomancer clapped his hands and praised the location: "The midnight lamp comes from an underground cave, which means that the area has the best *fengshui* you can find."

A new estate, the future Yun Gardens, would be built there, shortly after the Wayfoong Bank had its second remodeling, in the year 1934. The classical structure was replaced by a twelve-story building using two types of Italian marble. Through Sean Shelley's connections, Huang Deyun was able to purchase marble from the same companies for the main room of her manor, Cloud Stone Hall. She was very particular about the colors, wanting them to match the mood of a middle-aged woman. After careful selection, she selected muted gold and silver gray as the dominant tones. Sean Shelley was pleased with her taste, the estheticism of the neoclassical mysticism.

When completed, Cloud Stone Hall was perfect for parties, even after the Japanese invaded the mainland and tension filled the air as people wondered what would happen next. There seemed to be no end to parties and balls for various charity purposes, from aiding refugees in Hong Kong to collecting money for the war against Japan; dance music played there nearly every night. Among the guests were senior Kuomintang officials and wealthy merchants who had fled to the south. As the national situation worsened, on the eve of the fall of Shanghai and Nanking, some of the highest-ranking figures in the KMT, including diplomatic and military personnel, went south. The Kung and Soong families both had villas in Repulse Bay, where the three Soong sisters held their reunions.

There was no sense of wartime in Hong Kong's high society. Horse racing, golf, polo, and garden parties were daily events. The people believed that the Japanese would not dare attack Hong Kong, the brightest jewel in the British Crown. Huang Deyun and Li Meixiu often found themselves in a quandary, unable to decide which party to attend. Richard Huang was also plagued by such uncertainties, wavering between playing cricket with the colonial officials and attending a yacht party hosted by the Japanese consulate general. His wife, Meixiu, led a dramatically different life. In the daytime she plunged into refugee work, traveling between charity organizations in Hong Kong and Kowloon. In the mornings she'd distribute food and winter clothes at a soup kitchen managed by the Church; in the afternoons she'd visit wounded soldiers who were passing through Hong Kong. Making use of every minute, she would appear at the army uniform sewing center in Kowloon to work at a sewing machine till dark. She would then pick off the threads in her hair and on her clothes as she walked to the family car waiting outside. She'd then tell the driver to speed back to Yun Gardens, where she would change into an evening dress and be off to a party.

In that autumn before the Pacific War broke out, a grand party was held at Yun Gardens. Custom called for Sean Shelley to lead Huang Deyun onto the floor for the first dance. She wore a garland of jasmine flowers in her still lush hair, which, with her silver-gray evening gown and gold piping, made her look exquisitely elegant and majestic. He couldn't look away. It was a look familiar to Huang Deyun; he had always looked at her with eyes filled with intense emotion, whether there were people around or not. He didn't care what people thought.

But that was all he could do, look at her.

After falling in love with Huang Deyun, Sean had visited all the hospitals in the colony under an assumed name and had undergone one examination after another administered by urologists. The diagnosis was always the same: there was nothing wrong with him physically; his sexual dysfunction had to be psychological. A young doctor at Western Garrison, an admirer of Freud, hinted that Sean Shelley might be in love with a woman he shouldn't love. Taking a look at his medical history, in which Sean had lied and said he was a married man, the doctor congratulated himself for reaching his diagnosis so easily: the patient was suffering impotence as a result of an extramarital affair. Guilt and an inability to adjust to his surroundings had induced fear and anxiety that in turn resulted in sexual impotence.

"It's probably temporary."

The young doctor winked and patted him on the shoulder as he saw his patient out.

Sean was comforted by the doctor's words.

Back in her house, once again he sat there rigidly, feeling uncomfortable. They were so close, yet she was out of reach. Behind the beaded curtain, the carved bed, which was barely visible through the bed curtain, so frightened him that he couldn't take a step forward.

He could only stare at her and lose himself in her beautiful, ageless face.

But that night Huang Deyun had failed to notice something else in his eyes, a look that entailed the sorrow of separation. When the music was over, he lowered his face to touch her flower-adorned temple and whispered in her ear:

"I'm leaving. I'm going back to England."

When the party was over, Sean Shelley walked with her arm in arm to the red-carpeted staircase, before leaving Yun Gardens forever. He was reluctant to say good night, yet did not see her upstairs. Instead, he stood at the foot of the stairs, watching her go up, one hand hiking her skirt, the other grasping the spiral banister. Slowly, very slowly, she rose, one step after another; gone was the lightness of earlier times, when she had come down the same staircase. As tears welled up in his eyes, he was tempted to abandon his upbringing as a gentleman and follow her up.

But he could not allow himself to do that. He just stood there, watching her back, lost in thought, until her skirt was swallowed up by the darkness.

Two days later, he boarded an ocean liner for London. Standing on the moonlit deck, he could not stop missing her. But he knew he had no choice.

6

Miss Ingrid Baker, Richard Huang's mistress, always said that her downfall commenced on that afternoon, as a typhoon approached.

On that day white waves surged in the ocean, as the force of the winds increased. The weather station had hoisted a force three alert, but there was no wind on the streets of Hong Kong or Kowloon, the typical calm before the storm. Leaving Jardine's earlier than usual, Richard was on his way to the money-lending service to check the books. His informants had told him that the manager had been gambling, incurring a formidable debt over the past month. Afraid that the manager, backed into a corner by his shortage of money, might decide to use the service's money to pay off his debts, Richard decided on a surprise inspection.

The moment he entered the bustling Chinese section with its myriad of odors, he regretted wearing his new beige double-breasted suit. It wasn't dinnertime yet, but smoke was already rising from every Chinese building, sending black specks of coal everywhere, including on him. He dodged left and right to avoid the barefoot children in rags running around among the vendors and food stands like little animals, while he kept his eyes to the ground, afraid to step into dirty puddles that would ruin his shiny shoes.

He showed up at the money-lending service unannounced and ordered the manager to bring out the account books. The first thing he did after settling in upstairs was to undo his tie and take off his suit, which he replaced with a China blue silk garment. He knew he wouldn't be leaving soon, so he kicked off his shoes and put on soft cloth shoes.

Rolling up the loose sleeves of his Chinese gown, he sat down at a sandalwood desk, immediately transformed from the comprador of a foreign firm in a Western suit into the young master of a money-lending
service in a Chinese robe.

Placing his left elbow on the blue account books, dotted with crimson
notations, he ticked away on the abacus with his right hand. But it wasn't
long before his thoughts began to wander beyond the carved window of
the building and flew toward that little green house at Mid-Level. It took
little effort to imagine the scene: the space behind the front door was like
a snow cave, decorated by his English mistress but under his instructions.
Richard was partial to the color white. White gauze curtains hung at the
window of the bedroom, where, on the sparkling white bedspread, his
white mistress lay, like a full-fledged white bird, waiting for him in all her
alluring charm. He'd pick up a white gardenia flower from the little garden and put it in the satiny hair behind her ears.

The crimson notations reminded him of her pink nipples, which
turned dark red when he caressed them . . . Richard couldn't sit there
any longer. Pushing the abacus and account books away, he stormed out
of the place, without even stopping to change back into his Western suit.
He ran like a wind out of the Chinese section, all the way to the little
green house, not to love her but to take her like a conquering hero. He
wanted her all to himself, this woman whom he kept with a house, a car,
fresh flowers, diamonds, and pretty scarves. But more and more he'd felt
he could not own her completely, from the way she looked at other men,
particularly those of her own race. He knew she was still looking, especially when she cast flirtatious glances from behind an exquisitely carved
ivory fan—one that Richard had bought for her—at navy officers in
their white uniforms.

She no longer looked at him that way. It was particularly hard for him
when she played her twice-weekly tennis at the club reserved for Cau-
casians, even though she only played with women. He could envision her
short skirt, one that fell above the knees, and how she ran around in front
of all the men, who cheered her on. Those men of her race surely didn't
care about the women's tennis skills; they had something else in mind.

Richard agonized over the fact that he had no way of stopping his mistress from exposing herself like that.

On that afternoon before the typhoon, he felt such an urgency to see his mistress because, in addition to increasing sexual desire, he wanted his visit to be unannounced.

Wearing his fine silk Chinese robe and cloth shoes, Richard soundlessly appeared before Ingrid in the white snow cave of her bedroom. She had just taken a bath and lay lazily in a white bathrobe, like a furry white cat, on her Victorian-style bed. With her elbows resting on stacked pillows, she looked down at the man rushing toward her, carrying with him a gentle breeze from the loose sleeves of his Chinese gown. Her mixed-blood lover, now in Chinese dress, had become Chinese only.

Ingrid found herself sexually excited by an unknown and yet excessive desire for the body beneath the Chinese clothes. Unable to control herself, she pounced on the man crawling onto bed, ripping open the cloth fastenings and lying on top of his flaccid yet alluring chest.

That was when she began lying on top when they had sex. She felt debased and ashamed of herself. She believed that that afternoon was the beginning of her corruption.

How had she ever taken herself down that road? Curling up in the untidy bed, she buried her face in the pillows as she recalled how Richard, the youngest and the most promising comprador in the history of Jardine's, would show up with a present in each hand every time he visited her. He'd tried everything to please his perfect woman; he was a regular at the Lane Carver Department Store, a connoisseur of current tastes, from nylons and perfumes to scarves and Cartier jewelry.

One day, Richard sent over a shiny white piano for her birthday. She had finally surrendered after caressing the ivory keys and singing "The Last Rose of Summer." That night Richard Huang had climbed onto the bed he'd built with gold bricks and silver ingots and had his way with her. She had been shocked by her actions, even though the possibility had occupied her mind whenever they were together. She had even subtly provoked him with a flirtatious glance or an audacious body movement, hoping he'd get the hint and take action. Now it had actually happened.

Ingrid Baker began dressing her lover, picking out the styles and patterns of his ties and selecting the shape and material of his cufflinks. Unhappy with the skills of the Shanghai tailor on Stanley Street, she took his measurements and sent them to England to have his suits made. She even promised that the next time she was in Europe, she'd order a brown camel hair top hat from the Parisian haberdasher where the Matheson family had bought their hats for three generations.

She dressed him from head to toe, even choosing the color of his socks.

"There are a few Chinese men who look presentable in Western suits, but it all falls to pieces when you look down and see white socks."

Her attention to detail helped Richard avoid making that mistake. In addition to turning her lover into a dignified Western gentleman, she began to pay attention to the ambience at the dining table. She would change into a white velvet, high-collared evening gown with long sleeves, light the candles in the candelabra, and instruct Richard to make as little noise as possible with his silverware. He was not offended; rather, he learned to hold a crystal goblet with three fingers when savoring his aged Bordeaux. He appreciated these candlelight dinners, fantasizing how he'd play a waltz on the gramophone after dinner, hold Ingrid in his arms, and dance with her in front of the French door drapes. How romantic and enchanting it would be when her long, silvery, tasseled scarf billowed.

The candlelight dinners stood in such stark contrast to their former trysts. In the past he'd never lingered in the living room; instead, he'd always headed straight for the bedroom. But no matter how low the candlelight dimmed or how late it got, he still had to go home. He never stayed overnight. Spring nights are short; even the daffodils on the table were withering as time ticked away. Desire rose in eyes staring across the table. Afraid to reveal her desire, she pressed her legs together tightly under her long skirt. He, on the other hand, was waiting for her to act first.

In the end, one of them did act first. Four lips were pressed together, four hands stripped away the clothes, and two people headed toward the bedroom.

She felt herself absolutely, hopelessly corrupted, and these feelings persisted until the day before Japan attacked Hong Kong.

As the national situation worsened, the farewell parties at the Japanese Consulate in Hong Kong for departing Japanese families were coming to an end. One by one, the Japanese guests failed to show up at parties at Yun Gardens. The Hong Kong Chinese claimed to see many signs of impending disaster. But the British did not take the threat of war seriously, believing that the defense lines built at strategic points in Hong Kong and Kowloon were adequate to intimidate the Japanese. They not only underestimated Japanese combat readiness but had also received a great deal of bad information. Not until the Japanese soldiers stationed at Shenzhen streamed across the border at Lo Wu did Governor Northcote began to panic. British women and children were ordered to leave for England. In the mid-1940s, all British subjects were provided with free passage to Manila, with the following stipulation: full-blooded British women and children could transfer to Australia from Manila, while the Eurasians were to stay in Manila, with the government providing living expenses.

The decision was greeted with an outcry. Many soldiers who stayed to defend the island criticized the colonial government for racial discrimination, as it gave special treatment to the families of high officials and wealthy businessmen. The Chinese were equally unhappy about the government spending their tax dollars to evacuate a small percentage of whites or Eurasians, while the majority of the Chinese women and children were left to fend for themselves. And the men whose wives were forced to leave were so upset they organized a "bachelor husband" club to protest the government decision to tear their families apart.

To avoid being sent away, some British women either took a timely trip away from the island or signed up for volunteer work as nurses, emergency aide team members, even document inspectors and code breakers. Ingrid Baker was one of them. Richard smugly bragged about how she had volunteered just to stay close to him.

Ingrid was assigned a volunteer post under the command of Dr. Hilda Stone, the highest-ranking female officer who had stayed. A born redhead, she was a radical member of the Labour Party. She'd come to Hong Kong with her husband, who was in charge of colonial medical affairs, and had been working for the Sanitary Board. A few years earlier she had organized a club with ladies from England to abolish the practice of prostitution. She was also the first to promote birth control in the colony, organizing fifty Chinese and Western doctors to spread the idea.

Considering herself a progressive, Ingrid had long wanted to join Hilda's group. Back when she was censoring novels at Mrs. May's club, she'd read about how the new women in London and New York were advocating women's liberation and feminist movements. She'd often associated Hilda with some of the characters in the novels.

The war made it possible to be a member of Hilda's little group, befriending women considered as antitraditional rebels by the conservative women of the colony. Among her new friends were revolutionaries who had tried to help with Indian independence, feminists jailed in New York for their advocacy of birth control, and others who were active in working for social reform and equality between the sexes. Before the British women and children were sent off to Manila and Australia, Hilda and her comrades were often the targets of criticism by the "gossip corner" across from St. John's Cathedral.

"Hilda Stone, that snobbish female doctor"—the wife of a whisky merchant fired the opening salvo—"wouldn't give us the time of the day and then debased herself by organizing a so-called Eugenic Society with that yellow woman, Madame Sun Yat-sen, or whatever her name is."

The wife of a minor official broke in:

"Speaking of eugenics, they have a new member, from New York, with a huge belly—"

"Oh dear, traveling under those circumstances," the owner of a tailor shop expressed her sympathy. "And how even her husband must have suffered."

"Do you really think a woman like that would be accompanied by her husband?" The wife of the minor official lowered her voice. "She came alone, and Hilda Stone met her at the pier."

The other women crowded up to her, but she held back until their incessant pestering made her reveal her secret in a conspiratorial voice: "The woman isn't married. Dr. Stone was her midwife. The two of them go everywhere together, so close you'd think something was going on—"

Covering their mouths, the women stared at one another, not knowing what to say.

Rumors like that never ceased at the "gossip corner."

After her training was completed, Ingrid went with Hilda to deliver medical supplies to the mainland, nearly accompanying her all the way to Hankow to visit the military hospital there. But Hilda complained after returning from Hankow about how hot and mosquito-infested her hotel in the French Concession had been, and how that had kept her from getting a good night's sleep.

Two days before the Japanese attack on Hong Kong, the British who remained in the colony were still attending horse races in Happy Valley, where surging crowds made the place as festive as ever. The Royal Scottish Orchestra crossed the harbor from Sham Shui Po to perform at the races, while the Welsh battalion went ahead with their cricket match. That night parties were held at big hotels; the governor, Sir Mark Young, had a hard time deciding which party to attend before finally settling on the Peninsula Hotel, where a charity ball was held to collect money for warplanes.

On the early morning of December 8, when thirty Japanese Zeroes, painted with a bright red rising sun, flew over Kai Tak Airport, Kowloon residents, who mistook the flight as yet another air-raid drill, did not even have time to sound the alarm. The Japanese planes came in at fifty meters and strafed the airport; within minutes, five aged warplanes and eight civilian aircraft on the runway were destroyed.

Five days into the war, the New Territories and Kowloon fell, but Hong Kong took eighteen days. During those days Hilda and her small group of women were held under siege at the hilltop St. Anne's Hospital. As bullets whistled outside, the women gave in to their anxiety and began fighting among themselves over trivial matters. Ingrid watched close friendships and camaraderie explode just like the bombs falling outside.

Three days before the fall of Hong Kong, Ingrid was sent to the Repulse Bay Hotel to tend to injured soldiers. Shouldering a first-aid kit, she left Hilda and her progressive friends-turned-enemies, climbed into a jeep, and heaved a long sigh of relief, feeling more relaxed than ever. She was certain she'd be the next to start a fight with the tiniest excuse had she stayed at the hospital.

Through the smoke and fire she could see that the hotel hadn't suffered any damage. She'd once hoped to spend her honeymoon at the hotel, with a room facing the ocean. In the early mornings she'd walk hand in hand with her new husband under the palm trees, then watch the sunset on the beach and dance the night away on the spectacular dance floor.

The honeymoon hotel of her dream had already turned into hell. Refugees weakened by hunger filled the hallways and staircases, while bleeding soldiers with missing limbs took up the beds in guest rooms. In the meantime the sound of rifle and cannon fire was getting increasingly heavy. The Repulse Bay Hotel fell on Christmas Eve. Japanese soldiers swaggered in, their hobnailed boots beating a tattoo down the long hallway, where they led away one ashen-faced refugee after another at gunpoint. Then they ran upstairs and kicked open the door, ready to bayonet the wounded soldiers. Ingrid, dressed in her nurse's uniform, found an unknown source of courage and stepped forward.

"You'll have to kill me first."

Stunned by the determination on her face, the Japanese soldiers lowered their rifles and backed out.

7

Three months before war broke out, Sean Shelley had boarded an ocean liner in London to return to the Far East. After disembarking, he went straight to Yun Gardens, where an overjoyed Huang Deyun could not stop crying. Later she put on a long yellow cheongsam with peacock blue piping and, carrying a beaded purse he'd brought back from Harrods, went to the Peninsula Hotel to host a welcoming party for him and to celebrate his promotion to governor of the Wayfoong Bank.

Sean moved into Yun Gardens. At her suggestion, he drove twice a week to Sha Tin in the New Territories, where he entered a house with green roof tiles in a peach grove. There an old Chinese doctor with a long white beard that made him look like an immortal taught him an ancient Chinese secret for restoring his manhood.

These visits were subsequently interrupted by gunfire from Japanese rifles. So Shelley hid in the bell tower of Yun Gardens, where he compiled lists of botanical specimens he'd collected in Hong Kong over the years. Deyun stayed with him night and day, until the sounds of war stopped after eighteen days of resistance. Sean walked out of Yun Gardens under Japanese bayonets and lost his freedom.

As governor of the bank, he, along with senior employees and their families, was housed in a shabby Chinese inn in Central, a row of second-story rooms separated only by thin plywood, with bad lighting and turgid air. Either because he was single or because they wanted to punish the highest-ranking employee of the Wayfoong Bank, the Japanese put Sean in a small windowless room in the middle, with bad lighting. Every morning he and others were sent off to work in shorts and T-shirts. The Japanese ordered him to lead the procession, which marched down the street whose name had been changed from Des Voeux to Showa. He was forced to lead the bowing when they encountered Japanese soldiers standing guard.

He and the comptroller would then be locked up in a secret room in the dome of the building, where he'd sign printed currency that the Japanese could exchange in Macao for goods to be transported back to Tokyo. Holding a special pen with ink that would neither fade nor smudge, Sean cursed himself for not destroying the currency—bills that were valid only with his signature, in accordance with colonial regulations—before the enemy took over, for now the Japanese would use the money to prolong the war. He felt he'd lost the sense of honor that a true English gentleman treasures more than life itself by not joining the volunteers in defending Hong Kong down to the last bullet. He had even disgraced the bank he represented.

Back when he'd first been promoted, he'd urged the colonial government to produce and circulate a great quantity of notes to bring the colony out of a money shortage. Now as he sat in the secret room, staring at the piles of paper waiting for his signature, he could not believe that the wide circulation of new currency would be his only accomplishment as governor of the Wayfoong Bank. Shortly after returning from London, he had come across a watercolor of the old Hong Kong mint. It had been built in the mid-nineteenth century, but the quality of its minting was so poor that production was halted and the building turned into a warehouse. Sean had planned to negotiate with the taipans to have the bank take over the mint and turn it into a museum of banking history in the colony and the history of commercial flow between East and West, for he had already sensed that Hong Kong's banking and financial future would play an important role in Asia.

But the war destroyed his plan. Instead, he was forced to sign the newly printed currency. Reluctantly he signed his name in the lower left corner, just below the date. His only means of resistance was to proceed at the slowest possible pace, constantly making excuses, such as poor eyesight caused by malnutrition, or a back pain that prevented him from sitting too long.

After signing the last piece of paper, he put down the pen and was immediately taken away. Accusing him of not showing adequate humility and respect when bowing to the image of the emperor, the Japanese guards, who never passed up an opportunity to find fault with him, sent him to a concentration camp in North Point to be interned with other British POWs. The camp had formerly been used by the Japanese as a stable; there was no water, no electricity, and no toilet. Mosquitoes and flies ruled the place. Sean came down with dysentery shortly after his arrival.

During the occupation the Japanese turned St. Andrew's Chapel into a Shinto shrine. To Li Meixiu, Hong Kong might as well have died in her heart. Dressed in black to mourn the colony, she locked herself up in the bell tower of Yun Gardens. She sent servants to collect the Japanese flags distributed to residents to parade in the street, then cut them into open-crotch pants for the servants' children in order to degrade the "rising sun." When the Japanese announced a plan to turn the Baptist church in Kowloon into a brothel for the soldiers, she could no longer restrain herself. Wearing a large silver cross around her neck over her black clothes, she went to St. Mary's Hospital to look up Hilda, who would introduce her to a Japanese pastor who would then take her to see a Japanese chief of staff.

Wearing the face of a martyr ready to die for her cause, she walked into the hospital. If the Japanese did not rescind the order, she would immolate herself on the church steps.

Hilda was operating on a patient at the time, so she sent a message to have Ingrid take Li Meixiu to see the Japanese pastor.

Never imagining having Richard Huang's wife appear before her like that, Ingrid was caught off guard. She nearly asked about Richard, wondering if he had returned from Macao.

Before the outbreak of the war, Richard had told Ingrid that he was going to Macao for a business associate's birthday party. Then the attack came and she left the little green house for volunteer work at the Red Cross. They lost contact. Richard, who was detained in Macao for two months and cut off from Hong Kong, turned the delay to his advantage by hoarding goods to sell at inflated prices.

Not until the war was over and Ingrid was back in Birmingham did she realize that she had chosen to stay in Hong Kong not to do voluntary work but to end her relationship with Richard.

In the end, the Japanese did not turn the Baptist church in Kowloon into a military brothel. Rumor had it that Li Meixiu, taking advantage of the fact that her husband was in Macao and Huang Deyun had locked herself up in her room, had decided to let the Japanese chief of staff use Yun Gardens to entertain guests in exchange for the church's integrity.

The Japanese moved all the furniture out of the rooms in the western wing, replaced it with tatami mats and sliding paper doors, and changed the place into a Japanese-style guesthouse named Thousand Year Hall. At night lanterns were lit and geishas were summoned to dance on the tatami. Drinking sake and singing, the Japanese men would not stop until dawn.

Meanwhile, the estate cellar was rumored to have been converted into a torture chamber by the Japanese. Ear-piercing screams from tortured resistance fighters echoed in the cellar for months. Reports that Yun Gardens was haunted inevitably started to circulate. One of the stories had a white shadow floating in the second-floor hallway when the moon was full. The shadow would glide from one end of the hallway to the other, then appear in the kitchen downstairs, followed by the noise of glass clanging against plates. The sight was interpreted as a hungry ghost cooking and feeding itself in the kitchen. In fact, it was only Li Meixiu, who suffered from insomnia, warming up milk. Clothed in a white robe, she sat on a stool with a glass of warm milk in her hands, neither drinking the milk nor letting go of the glass even when it turned cold. A soft morning light would seep through the windows and the roosters would crow before she went upstairs to her room. That went on until Richard Huang returned one dark night from Macao.

After Sean Shelley was taken away by the Japanese, Huang Deyun trod on every inch of floor, touched every wall and every piece of furniture over and over. She would sit in the bell tower, with its butterfly wallpaper, and stare at the botanical notebooks cluttering the desk and recall the tender moments they had shared. Sean's chair had been kicked off to the side and remained there, as if he'd just gone out for a moment and would soon be back.

Her days went by slowly as she reminisced, each day dragging on like a year. Standing by the window day after day, she waited vainly for Sean's return. Eventually, Richard was able to determine that Sean was being held at the concentration camp at North Point, so Huang Deyun, a dusty gray kerchief tied around her head, carried a bundle of cheese, oatmeal, and Italian sausages and went to see him. On the way, her personal maid, Xianü, anxiously cast looks all around, afraid that the food her mistress had paid an exorbitant amount for on the black market would be snatched away by starving citizens or robbers. The Japanese had sealed off the warehouses in Hong Kong and Kowloon, nearly cutting off food supplies altogether. Given only small rations of rice, nearly everyone was starving. Even rats were caught, cooked, and consumed, let alone cats and dogs. When army horses died, they too were slaughtered, their meat sold as if it were beef or pork. Housewives able to buy a small bag of rice at twenty times the original price on the black market could easily be knocked down and have their rice snatched away. Anyone carrying strings of tofu or vegetables might lose their food when a robber cut the string. All edible items would be consumed on the spot.

Rounds of barbed wire guarded the camp at North Point, where a Japanese flag fluttered atop a sentry tower. Huang Deyun asked the guard to inform General Aoki of her visit. Aoki had been a frequent visitor to Yun Gardens, and she was hoping to use this connection to see Sean. After a long wait, the guard returned to say that General Aoki had been called to an urgent meeting but had given permission for her to meet with the prisoner. The prisoner, however, had declined to see the visitor, citing bad health, although she was allowed to leave the food behind for him.

Questions and sorrow filled her head as she left the camp in tears. Afraid she would never see him again in this life, she collapsed as soon as she got back to Yun Gardens.

Overcome by despair, Huang Deyun stayed in the empty garden, her lover nowhere to be seen. She thought about returning to Dongguan, her hometown, where the sandalwood grew, a place that been appearing in her recent dreams. Kidnapped and sold to Hong Kong at the age of thirteen, she had come alone and would return alone after an absence of decades. Maybe she could find a spot at the Queen of Heaven Temple to spend the rest of her life in the sole company of a small lamp.

Making one last round of Yun Gardens, she caressed the tables and chairs, all of which were the fruits of her own labor but meant absolutely nothing to her at the moment. Covering her graying hair with the same dusty kerchief, she walked out with Xianü and a male servant as a bodyguard to join the homeward-bound crowd encouraged by the Japanese in their effort to conserve resources.

But rather than take the ferries provided by the Japanese, they boarded a train in Tsim Sha Tsui headed for Taipo. After the train ride she would have to cross mountain ranges for three days before reaching Dongguan. Shuffling along with the crowd, she saw that the road was littered with luggage and bundles left behind by their owners; she heard abandoned babies crying in the ditches and old folks cursing amid laboring breathing. Claiming to be guerrillas, bandits confronted the travelers with guns and knives and demanded that they hand over their meager possessions of money and jewelry. The bandits stripped Huang Deyun of the pair of jade bracelets she'd never before taken off, but she just stared impassively, devoid of feeling.

Then people in the procession began to whisper, and the closer they got to the border checkpoint, the more agitated they grew. Supported by her maid, Huang Deyun staggered to the checkpoint, where she waited in line for the interrogation. She was so exhausted she didn't have the energy to look toward her hometown. She just squatted on the ground, holding her head in her hands, waiting to pass the checkpoint.

The whisper had now turned into excited discussion. After another surge of agitation, someone behind her blurted out in a soft voice, "It's true."

Then subdued applause and cheering. Tearing her kerchief off, Huang Deyun listened as more talk followed.

"A prisoner has escaped from the North Point concentration camp."

"I hear it's more than one. All British—saved by the militia—"

Something seemed to stab at her ribs. Huang Deyun struggled to get up to hear more clearly. She asked around and got the same answer: "Prisoners have escaped from the camp. More than one, Britons—"

At that moment she decided she wasn't going back to Dongguan. She turned and staggered toward home. She wanted to go back to Yun Gardens, where she'd stand by the window to wait for Sean until he appeared before her. One of the prisoners saved by the militia had to be her Sean.

The militia had indeed rescued a few British POWs during a careless moment by Japanese guards. To prevent the recurrence of similar incidents, the Japanese labeled Sean Shelley an important prisoner and immediately transported him to a camp on the other side of the island. One look at the camp commander told Sean that he was the barber at the Gloucester Hotel who had tried to pry financial information out of him, using cutting hair as a cover. Rubbing the stubble on his chin as he lay on a gurney, Sean could not help but smile wryly at the spy.

Hunger, malnutrition, and inadequate medical attention told him that he would never walk out of the camp alive. When howling dogs on the beach woke him up at night, he would lie in the dark and recall the past. How had he fallen in love with his butterfly, a woman with whom he had nothing in common? She didn't even know that men and women used different kinds of soap. She had used his soap when she went to his hotel to use the bathroom and had walked out of the bath smelling like a man.

From the beginning, he'd known she would never be accepted by the colony's social circles. All those white ladies in their high-collared satin or silk evening gowns would invariably stop their conversations when they saw Huang Deyun and greet him in a manner befitting their upbringing, barely able to conceal their surprise and puzzlement. They would cast an arrogant glance out of the corners of their eyes at her, then nod in her direction without so much as turning their heads when he introduced her. The upper-class Chinese, those married to taipans and legislators, whom the white hosts used to decorate their parties, did not accept her either. Gathered in small groups, they would smile politely at this compatriot who had newly arrived at their gatherings, then resume their conversations in perfect English.

That was not how he'd fallen in love with her. So it must have been the time he took her to an afternoon tea at a tycoon's mansion at Repulse Bay. When he introduced his companion, the hostess was all smiles as she extended a rather overbearing hand to brush against Huang Deyun's fingertips by way of a handshake. Then she turned to chat with Sean, as if Huang Deyun weren't there. He was so upset by his host's arrogance that he left before the tea was over. He did not say a word until they were outside her door, where he held her hands tenderly and promised that he'd never again let anyone mistreat her.

Lying in his cot at the camp, he kept thinking about the past, telling himself that the afternoon tea that day had seen the beginning of his love for her.

For the next two years Deyun locked herself in the upstairs room, not setting foot on the stairs even once. During her days of waiting, a lack of fuel shut down the power plant, thus plunging the city into darkness, one that enveloped her. During the last days of her life, Huang Deyun was tormented by the hopeless prospect of ever seeing Sean again. She never did.

8

It was the late 1970s. Young people walked the streets of Causeway Bay or Tsim Sha Tsui chewing gum and humming Hong Kong pop music that expressed their feelings about Hong Kong in Cantonese. Long pointed shirt collars, like airplane wings, had gone out of fashion, as had bell-bottoms that created swirls of dust as they swept along the ground; straight-leg pants were gradually taking over.

The 1970s were coming to an end. The Cultural Revolution on the mainland had ended; the Canton-Kowloon Railway, after thirty years of interrupted service, had resumed; the harbor ferry waited for the whistle to sound before sailing to Canton; travel between Hong Kong and mainland cities had started anew; and the ferry to Shanghai had completed its first two maiden voyages. Hong Kong benefited greatly from the economic reforms on the mainland, resurrecting its role as a transit port; international businesses, realizing the potential of China's market, came to set up shops, thus helping the growth of finance, hotel, and travel industries in the colony.

Hong Kong was witnessing its most prosperous era ever; land sales continued to break records; the wealthy used gold for the bathroom faucets and toilet bases in their mansions. Customers thronged restaurants, big or small, never tiring of the delicacies. As the enjoyment of food and fashionable clothes reached its pinnacle, Hong Kong Chinese tried to change the island's image of "cultural desert." But at a place where commercialism reigned, the arts had no choice but to hitch up with commerce. The budget for the Hong Kong Centre for Fine Arts relied on donations from businesses, celebrities, and tycoons.

That was how Huang Deyun's great-granddaughter, Huang Dieniang, showed up at a fund-raiser for the Hong Kong Art Centre of the newly opened Shangri-la Hotel in Kowloon. Dressed in a dark purple silk evening gown with a plunging neckline, she stood conspicuously by the entrance, a purple figure that caught the eye of every guest who entered. The tailored gown seemed to a part of her tall slender body, hugging her curves. She was like a naked statue at a busy intersection, filling the eyes of every passerby. She returned their gaze boldly, searching for her prey among the crowd. No doubt about it, she was Huang Deyun's great-granddaughter.

But she lacked her great-grandmother's tact and grace. Once, half an hour late for a lunch date, without even waiting for the host to make the introductions, she blurted out, "Say, do any of your use laxatives? I've heard of one made of herbs and aloe oil, and was told it's quite effective. Has anyone tried it?"

The guests could only stare at each other, their appetites gone. But it didn't stop there; she prattled on about a poor lawyer friend of hers who had been constipated ever since coming to Hong Kong a year earlier. Enemas were his only salvation, but the doctor could find nothing wrong with him. So she had volunteered to help, asking everyone she met for secret formulas. Finally done with her litany, she apologized for being late: she had just returned from the airport, where she'd shipped some grapefruits to a friend in Shanghai. She was unable to contain herself: "Lucy has the same problem, you know. She has to eat a grapefruit every day or she gets constipated. This time she went to Shanghai on business, but her return was delayed and she already finished the grapefruits she took with her. She was worried beyond imagining—"

Her behavior offended many people. At parties, she'd barely have turned to leave before the backstabbing would begin, as people salivated over her family secrets.

"So what if her father is a magistrate? Everyone knows she's William Huang's illegitimate daughter. What's there to be so haughty about?"

"How did the Huang family start? Where did they get their real estate capital? From her great-grandmother, who earned it flat on her back, that's where."

"Do you know how her mother died? Killed by black magic! William Huang's mother knows sorcery; she cast an evil spell and killed her."

"I thought she committed suicide. But I heard somewhere that she's alive and confined in the Green Mountain Mental Hospital."

Rumor had it that Huang Dieniang's birth mother had been killed by Huang Deyun's personal maid, Xianü, on orders of Li Meixiu, Dieniang's grandmother.

All anyone knew about Zhu Rongrong, Dieniang's mother, was that she was a charming, petite, fair-skinned Shanghai woman. When the Communists took the mainland in 1949, she'd fled with her uncle, who was in the military, to Hong Kong. Before becoming a refugee, she'd spent two years at Shanghai's Sino-American Girls' High School, where she'd studied English with American nuns. No one knew how she met William Huang, who had graduated from the University of Hong Kong Law School and was applying to study at Oxford's Wadham College. Huang Dieniang herself was vague about their first encounter, except that William had fallen in love with Rongrong at a beach party. Noticing how the freckles on her pert, slightly upturned nose were increasingly visible under the autumn sun, he lost control and began kissing the freckles.

Then he took her by the hand and walked her into the thicket of trees.

That was something Dieniang was proud of, as she repeatedly crowed about her decadent gene, which manifested itself not only in the fact that she was an illegitimate child but also in that her parents had mated in broad daylight.

After the beach party William Huang set Rongrong up in the attic above the office of the Huang family's money-lending service in Central, behind the back of his fastidious, Catholic mother, who personally attended to every little detail of his life. The young lovers were careful and watchful; they waited until the employees left the office before sneaking into the attic with bedding, building their love nest behind a gilded screen. Still, he must have received tacit approval from his father, Richard, and when Li Meixiu finally discovered what was going on, her first thought was that her son and husband had conspired against her.

For a long time after the discovery, the Yun Gardens servants often saw her standing at the window in the veranda at midnight, her arms crossed. She spent many sleepless nights that way. When Dieniang was born, the rumors multiplied. Some claimed to have seen Li Meixiu show up at the Catholic Cemetery on Wong Ngai Chung Road more than once; there she would push open the heavy iron gate and pace back and forth in the shadows of ancient, tall trees, touching the pictures of the deceased carved on marble tombstones. It was about that time that rumors began to spread about how she had sent Xianü to the secret trysting room above the money-lending shop to cast a fatal evil spell on Zhu Rongrong, Huang Dieniang's mother.

9

When Huang Dieniang was little, her grandfather Richard Huang tried hard to bring her up as a lady. She began studying the piano, ballet, and horseback riding at the age of five. Richard asked the wife of a retired French diplomat to teach her social etiquette and hired a ballroom dancing teacher. Afraid she might be lonely, he invited children her age as playmates; he had mirrors installed in one of the west side rooms near the flower garden so the children could learn dancing and other proper codes of behavior. He even selected a boy called Spencer to be her dance partner.

"Grandpa was playing matchmaker. Spencer's father had been a ranking official in the Nationalist government." Dieniang wrinkled her nose and laughed whenever she told the story to friends. "Spencer's family left Shanghai in 1949 and came to Hong Kong to open a textile mill. Grandpa probably thought it was a perfect match for both families. He said the Shanghainese were more open-minded and worldly, unlike the Cantonese gentry families in Hong Kong, who cared so much about family background and social etiquette."

Richard preferred the new immigrants from Shanghai because they barely had time to learn much of the Huang family history. But they could not understand why Richard, a real estate tycoon with so much wealth, should be concerned that his granddaughter would not be a good match for local gentry. Could it have been that Dieniang's birth mother, who had never formally married into the Huang family, had come from a questionable background, as rumor seemed to have it? In fact, to get to the cause of his concern it was likely necessary to reach even further back, to his mother's reputation as a young woman. That must have been something he could not forget. It was also the reason Huang Deyun, when choosing a wife for Richard, had picked Li Meixiu, whose family had just arrived from Indonesia. The third-generation heir, William, earned a license to practice law in London, where he married an Englishwoman, a match that was blessed by his grandmother and his father. People found it hard to believe that, after all these years, Richard had exactly the same thoughts as his mother had when it came to selecting a husband for his granddaughter.

Dieniang admitted that she was a hopeless party animal. She loved being part of a crowd, where she was always animated and captivating. That, for her, was the true essence of life.

"There's also lovemaking, of course," she'd add.

She was a must-invite guest at postperformance cocktail parties at the Hong Kong Arts Centre. The annual Hong Kong Arts Festival in February was a major cultural event in the colony. Top performers would gather in Hong Kong, and invitations to consulates and major businesses flew like butterflies. Joining a group of wealthy, idle ladies who claimed to be cultured, Huang Dieniang dressed herself for volunteer work at the festival. She was in charge of taking care of overseas artists. Once she was asked to pick up a renowned pianist from Vienna and set him up at the Peninsula Hotel. As soon as he laid down his luggage, he ordered her to find a Steinway for him to practice in his hotel suite. Dieniang carried out her mission effortlessly, later telling people it was all because of her "investment" in the Swiss hotel manager.

One year she was charged with finding a Mercedes-Benz big enough to accommodate a three-hundred-pound Italian tenor. It took some doing but she managed to get the tenor to the music hall on time, before rushing home to change into an evening gown. Like a pretty butterfly, she flew from a preperformance cocktail party to a champagne celebration party, happily busy.

When the month-long festival was over, and there were no more farewell parties at various villas, private clubs, and yachts, she was sud-

denly plunged into inaction. Unable to endure the silence, she was forced
to attend a housewarming for someone below her social standing. The
host, an employee at an accounting firm, was still in his prime but beginning to go bald after years of hard work. He'd finally saved up enough
money for a down payment on a small Mid-Level apartment on Robinson Road. She'd met him during the festival, when he'd told her he was
a fan of chamber music. When she arrived, he flattered her by saying
how she'd lit up his humble abode before escorting her to the window to
show off the ocean view under twinkling stars. Most of the guests were
middle-management bankers, auditors, and stockbrokers, with a few
lower-level government functionaries. Although they wore Pierre
Cardin fashions, drank red wine, and talked about stereo systems,
Huang Dieniang could tell at a glance that they all came from poor,
lower-class families. Not enjoying the backing of family wealth, they
had acquired a university education with the help of scholarships. Some
had even gone abroad to study. Now, with a degree in hand and an abun-
dance of energy, they were working hard to climb the social ladder.

"My God! A houseful of vulgar middle-class professionals!" she mut-
tered to herself.

Huang Dieniang, catty as always.

In fact, the host and guests were all the products of Governor Mac-
Lehose's policy of nativization. Comprising the first generation of
Hong Kong natives born after the Second World War, and baptized by a
colonial or Western education, they dreamed of capitalist success. Having taken middle-management positions in government offices or private
businesses, they exuded confidence and took pride in the specialized
knowledge that underscored their ambition. This newly formed middle
class had begun to display a degree of intolerance toward the traditional
colonial government structure. Gradually becoming an entity of
increasing influence, they used their specialized knowledge to criticize
Hong Kong's economic policy and government leadership.

But Huang Dieniang didn't pick up her purse and leave after discovering that she was surrounded by vulgar middle-class professionals.
Curiosity made her stay to observe this group of strangers. They did not

socialize within strict boundaries of family background, an intricate kin-
ship system, schools, clubs, or churches. They were the latest group in a
consumer age; they worshipped designer brands, defining themselves by
the names of designers who represented them.

That night, Huang Dieniang met her first middle-class boyfriend,
Peter Fong, the promotion and expansion manager of a fast-food chain
in Hong Kong and Kowloon. Born in a shack on Kowloon's Diamond
Hill, he had received government loans to pay for tuition from high
school through college. Believing that he was literarily gifted, he began
earning money by submitting manuscripts to *Students' Weekly* when he
was still in high school. At the University of Hong Kong, he worked as
a paid research assistant for a foreign scholar in the economics department. During his student days, he participated in student protests and
was elected as a student movement leader. He promoted frugality and
praised poverty; took part in the Diaoyutai Island protest, as well as
movements demanding the replacement of English by Chinese; and
advocated anticorruption and social justice for all. After graduating from
college, he joined the newly fashionable fast-food business, quickly rising to the position of district manager for Kowloon.

Peter Fong told Dieniang that the job seemed to have been created
just for him. His mother had once pushed serving carts in a dim sum
restaurant where he had been taken along to work part-time as a youngster. He'd often ridden to the wholesale market on a truck to pick up food
supplies, which gave him an in-depth knowledge of the Mong Kok area
as well as the residents' buying habits. He later suggested to his superior
that they open a fast-food branch on Sai Yeung Choi Street.

"Back then, cafeteria-style food service wasn't popular. The older
customers would sit there waiting to be served, then leave angrily when
no one showed up. But the poor students were great customers; they
could eat what and however much they wanted, and the business flourished."

As the pace of life quickened in Hong Kong, fast-food restaurants
branched into Central. Peter's boss went public on the stock market,
allowing him to join the wealthy. To Dieniang, it all sounded like a fairy

tale. So she decided to get a taste of a fast-food restaurant, by going to the Everybody Happy in Central, where she lined up to buy Portuguese-style curried chicken with rice and free soup. Carefully holding her tray, she searched for a seat, when someone behind shouted for her to let him through, so startling her that she spilled the soup. Frustrated, she threw the tray into a trash can before storming out to enjoy a Western meal at the hotel next door.

Thus ended her adventure in a fast-food restaurant; her romance with Peter Fong, however, was just beginning. It was his first time, and he was madly in love with Dieniang, who seemed to have taken hold of him, body and soul. He kept telling her that he was prepared to die for love.

She held her hands before her, imitating the way Peter held his heart in his hands, for a friend from Taipei, one of the few people Dieniang found interesting enough to befriend.

"He said he'd spent two years studying the violin and that someday he's going to play outside my window to prove his everlasting love," she said. "Please, God, don't let him do that."

"I know you're taking advantage of the fact that he's new to this. How did you get him to fall for you? Let me guess—you played hard to get, pretending to be pure and chaste," her friend teased.

She nodded, her eyes smiling.

"After stringing him along, I decided it was time to reward him. But one time in bed, and he was ready to die for me. And in bed he's like a machine, effective but lacking passion."

She made up some strange sexual techniques when he came to see her, expecting to scare him into giving up.

"But instead of giving up, he was eager to try. That's the middle-class spirit of adventure."

Eager to rid herself of Peter Fong, Dieniang invited him to the Hong Kong Club. As soon as they sat down, he started to complain because she wouldn't go out with him on Valentine's Day.

"I was all alone. I felt so terrible, so I revisited the beach at Repulse Bay to think about you. But all I saw was couple after couple visiting the place in their cars. The more expensive the car, the prettier the woman inside. A BMW convertible had a pretty yuppie, but the woman in the next car, a fire engine-red Ferrari, was a beauty for the ages."

"So based on your standards, I must be the ugliest woman around," she teased.

"No! I bought a new car after we met. Didn't you notice?"

Huang Dieniang didn't feel like pointing out that he was still driving a Japanese car. She was reminded of the time they'd gone for a Western dinner at The Red Pillar. He'd picked a window seat. During the meal, his attention was divided between her and the view outside. It finally dawned on her that he was checking on his new car, afraid someone might steal it.

Changing the subject, she said, "Thanks for the white gladioli you sent on Valentine's Day."

Perhaps detecting the sarcastic tone in her voice, he quickly defended himself: "I didn't send red roses not because I don't love you. I picked gladioli because the cost was reasonable and they last longer."

She wanted to tell him that gladioli were only used for funerals in the West, but decided not to bother since she wanted to break up with him anyway.

Not noticing her silence, he continued with a smile, "The owner of the fast-food chain is going to give me a two percent stock option." He stopped to cut and eat a piece of steak. "We buy our beef directly from overseas and cut the cost by half. That's the secret of our success."

Huang Dieniang was getting impatient and could contain herself no longer.

"I'm the type of woman who rides in a Ferrari. My only ambition in life is to have fun. In the winter I like to go skiing in Switzerland and to the best spots in summer to escape the heat. This is our last dinner together, and it's on me, since only members are allowed to use their cards here."

His initial reaction was to beg for sympathy.

"If you leave me, for the rest of my life my heart will be like the lotus, forever carrying bitter seeds, or like a spring silkworm with its unbroken thread. . . ."

He went on and on with classical allusions that Dieniang could not understand. Finally she signaled for the check. The old waiter, who had served three generations of the Huang family, placed the check on a silver tray before respectfully carrying it over to Huang Dieniang.

"Magistrate Huang was here earlier, having lunch with a member of the British royalty," the waiter added.

That woke Peter Fong up.

"Now I understand that you are a woman who worships money and social status, just like all the other women out there. You're like a snake that chooses her victim before she bites him. I hope your next boyfriend is a fake!"

After wishing her good luck, he kicked the chair away and left in indignation.

10

There are more banks than rice shops in Hong Kong.

By 1979 there were 115 licensed banks, among which the Wayfoong Bank was, of course, the longest-standing and most powerful. It still controlled Hong Kong's financial lifeline, with the exclusive authority to sign and issue Hong Kong currency. Located on Queen's Road, the bank was a towering Greek-style building. Except for the two brass lions from Shanghai and the granite on the outside, all the other material had been imported from England and Italy. The mural on the dome was particularly magnificent and awe-inspiring; it had taken workers six months to install the forty thousand pieces of Venetian stained glass.

Huang Dieniang received insider information that the building was no longer big enough for the fast-expanding business of the bank, as Hong Kong was enjoying an economic boom with the ending of the Cultural Revolution on the mainland. The fifty-year-old building would soon be torn down to make way for a skyscraper. The inside scoop had come to her in bed, her new boyfriend's bed. She had been seeing a British manager of the Wayfoong Bank, Ned Atkins, who weighed over two hundred pounds and had a face like a half-cooked egg. He wore black knee-high socks, even when it was more than thirty degrees outside, even when they were making love.

"It's a habit from boarding school. I can't change it."

She just stared at his pink flesh, reminded of how he would lie on his stomach and pant after sex, like a Shar-Pei—a pedigreed Shar-Pei, of course.

Ned Atkins was from an aristocratic family.

He had come to the Far East for its traditional charm and fantasy. Huang Dieniang had heard that Ned, although a manager of the credit card department, was actually in Hong Kong to finish a book on Far Eastern botany.

Mrs. Atkins, Ned's mother, was a typical aristocratic lady, with a long nose and a stiff, straight back. Almost morbidly obsessed with cleanliness and order, she would even order the steward to put on white gloves and follow the cleaning ladies around to check the furniture and the fireplaces that had just been cleaned. Since childhood, Ned had been trained to control his emotions and adhere to the etiquette befitting his background. The family followed a strict schedule in eating, strolling, taking afternoon tea, praying, and going to bed.

Twice each season, the Atkinses would host a party at their residence in a London suburb. Mrs. Atkins would personally supervise the servants in decorating the dining tables, polishing the silverware, and arranging the folding screens. Once everything was done to her specifications, down to the last detail, she'd change into a silver-gray silk evening gown and put on a pearl tiara before gliding downstairs to gracefully wave her ivory fan and chat with her guests in a proper but friendly manner. She would look elegant and relaxed, so different from her usual self. But as soon as the party was over and she had seen off the last pair of guests, she would immediately wipe off the expression she had used for the evening and change out of the loving way she had treated her husband. They would turn their backs, paying no more attention to each other, and return to their own rooms. At dinner the following evening, they would sit at either end of the long dining table, returning the house to its cold, distant atmosphere.

"I hated their hypocrisy," Ned revealed. "To escape from that dreadful house, I spent all my time in the London Botanical Garden greenhouse. The towering coconut palms, the strangely shaped cacti, and the plantains with their large drooping leaves always stirred my imagination. I longed for the tropics, where the sun shines brightly and strange fauna bloom the year round."

He wanted to be a wanderer. Over the years he'd been to all the little countries in Southeast Asia.

Listening to Ned, Huang Dieniang had the eerie feeling that history was repeating itself. Her great-grandmother had also had a lover who was a wanderer and a collector of botanical specimens. But how different Ned was from the slender, slightly sad Sean!

Everything seemed somehow different.

Old Hong Kong was slowly disappearing. The bricks at the Hong Hom Station, the terminal of the Canton-Kowloon Railway, were quietly taken down, leaving a solitary bell tower at Tsim Sha Tsui to face Victoria Harbor and its past glory. The twelve-story Wayfoong Bank was leveled by cranes and backhoes. The Repulse Bay Hotel was also going to be rebuilt, and farewell parties were held for the soon to disappear old hotel, attended by guests wearing clothes from the 1920s and 1930s and dancing to jazz music.

Even the Hong Kong Club, the symbol of colonial power and authority for more than a hundred years, could not escape the fate of destruction.

Huang Dieniang went with an architect friend to the club to attend a meeting for historical preservation. The attendees belonged to a group of British professors who had spent a lot of time in Hong Kong. They asked everyone to sign a petition to pressure the governor into preserving the renaissance-style building, which had been erected at the turn of the twentieth century.

Sitting in the club, whose demolition date was already set, Dieniang felt a sense of absurdity as she listened to the Britons put forth reason after reason to preserve the building. When she walked out, a gust of wind blew over and she closed her eyes. When she opened her eyes again, she felt that the entire island had changed right in front of her.

A new Hong Kong was rising every day: there were the fifty-two-story Connaught Centre, the highest in Southeast Asia, and the modern looking Space Museum; a subway was operating; Ocean Park was open to visitors; fast-food outlets were everywhere; and low-income public housing had been built on the edge of town.

The deadline for demolishing the Hong Kong Club was delayed again and again, but there was no stopping it. An auction was held to sell everything: furniture, decorations, carpet, crystal chandeliers, tables, and chairs. Looking at the Persian and Turkish rugs that she had stepped on so many times, the high-back chairs in the dining rooms, the silverware and crystal wineglasses on fine linen, and the china embossed with the club symbol, she couldn't help but sigh. Everything had been turned into a number and bound in a thick auction book, waiting for a buyer.

"It was like a quartered beast. Just dreadful to look at," she said to a friend.

A few days later, the Huang family estate—Yun Gardens—was reported as slated to be torn down and turned into two-story, ocean-view villas.

11

Yun Gardens would soon be demolished.

Huang Dieniang had an idea: she'd give the place a grand send-off. She'd erect an outdoor stage in the front yard to connect to the second-story veranda and reenact the family history. She even thought up a dramatic opening: she'd play the part of the mistress of Yun Gardens, her great-grandmother, Huang Deyun. Dressed in a short-collared silk taffeta dress popular in the 1930s, she would lean against the second-floor railing to watch the sun set, until the last color disappeared in the evening sky before slowly walking back onto the stage as the light came on. . . .

Her idea was carried out, but not on the stage. A Hong Kong English-language TV station, to commemorate Yun Gardens, filmed a documentary, using Huang Dieniang as narrator to relate the estate's dazzling past. The show opened on a second-floor veranda scene.

The screen images took the audience back in time, showing Dieniang dressed up as a proper and elegant lady of the 1930s.

Her long, often unkempt hair was neatly gathered under a felt beret with a colorful feather; the skirt of her two-piece Coco Chanel suit reached several inches below her knees, showing off her slender waist. The dress was shocking pink, the color that had scandalized and captivated Parisian women in the 1930s.

Opening her full lips painted in mulberry red, she spoke in flawless English of Yun Gardens' glorious history, confident and composed, like an experienced actress; in fact, she had performed a few roles for small theaters in London.

As a high school student in a Catholic school, she had been caught smoking in class by one of the sisters. The Huang family, afraid she might ruin William Huang's future in the judicial administration if she continued that way, sent her off to London to study ballet. But she had barely arrived before being expelled for climbing out the window of her room at night to meet in a pub with a rock singer who wore black leather pants and rode a motorcycle. Richard Huang, thinking Dieniang could be trained to be a lady, spent a large sum to enroll her in a Swiss finishing school. She thought her grandfather expected her to marry a European aristocrat and become a real lady. Rather than acquiesce to his wishes, she attended an actor's workshop at a London avant-garde theater.

Dieniang's elegance and grace not only came from her dress and makeup, they were part of her inner qualities. It was common for people to focus on her outrageous behavior and ignore her background and upbringing. But one look at how she held her teacup in a white-gloved hand showed that she had been born with a silver spoon in her mouth.

With the cameraman's clever manipulation of the lenses, Yun Gardens, a fortresslike granite structure bathed in the dying sunset, reflected a sort of gloomy splendor. No broken fences or crumbling walls. To the producers of the documentary, it was as if the decay simply did not exist. The opening scene was a bird's-eye view of the estate, which, sitting atop a hill, looked as sturdy as a giant boulder. Then the camera followed a winding gravel path imprinted with the traces of time and entered the black wrought-iron gate. In the process, the surrounding areas were captured on camera: the tip of the bell tower stained red by the sunset, its ingenious corners, and the jagged-edged roof. Then the camera moved closer to record minute details in the design. The screen framed one slanting old wall after another, then the carvings on marble columns, a window in an intriguing style, a brick with animal patterns, a glass painted with flowers, a baroque trellis, a green-glazed railing spiraling up a stone staircase. Every shot was carefully planned.

Huang Dieniang, standing in the garden, points to a cluster of blooming dwarf palms and tells the audience that they were planted by her grandfather, Richard Huang.

The camera then follows her to the dried-up fountain, where she explains the allusion of the four Greek goddesses holding round funnels on the beige marble base. She makes a point of mentioning how the British designer adopted the notion that since water lilies represent purity in Eastern culture, the round funnels were to be styled in the shape of lily petals.

"East and West met here and produced a wonderful combination. In addition, there is also an authentic Chinese garden."

She leads the audience to a garden pavilion in the southeast corner, where she points to a pair of litchi trees and recalls the pleasure of climbing onto the stone table to pick litchi nuts as a child.

Then strains of a waltz, accompanying the lighting up of Cloud Stone Hall, create the illusion that couples are dancing the night away.

Then faded black-and-white photographs fill the screen.

"This was the first party after Yun Gardens was completed," Dieniang explains. "Note the red silk lanterns in the corners and the exquisite gold embroidery on the well-wishing screens. This photograph was taken on Christmas Day, 1937. The boy under the tree is my father—that is what Magistrate William Huang looked like back then. Standing next to him is my grandfather, Mr. Richard Huang. This one was taken at the 1939 New Year's Eve dinner. You can see three kinds of glasses on the long dining table, one for white wine, one for red wine, and one for champagne. A New Year's Eve party, with festoons twirling and the guests indulging in carnivalesque pleasure. That was just before the Japanese attacked Hong Kong, the last party at Yun Gardens."

That night, Dieniang's father called to congratulate her.

"It was nothing. I just showed the audience what they liked and what they wanted to see, so they could share in the sentiments. That's all."

"The cinematography was superb. I'm going to get a copy from the TV station, so I can recall the past after Hong Kong changes."

12

Eighty-seven years after the plague had taken so many lives, Huang Deyun's grandson, William Huang, sat on the magistrate's bench at the Supreme Court. Wearing a silvery white wig and a shiny creased red robe with a white silk bow tied around his chest, he was hearing a case of corruption and bribery that had occurred in the oldest and most revered institution in Hong Kong, the Victoria Club. The chair had been designed for a taller British magistrate; its back was too high for William, with his one quarter British blood, and left a considerable space above and behind.

The governor of Hong Kong had fallen in line with the trend to soften the British monopoly in high government positions. In the 1980s, amid a call for nativization, a few yellow faces appeared. The governor picked William from among three recommended lawyers to serve as magistrate of the Supreme Court, a decision that caused considerable commotion and discussion in Chinese legal circles. Everyone believed that the selection had as much to do with William's background and his British wife as with his qualifications.

No one knew quite how William got Elizabeth Noble to marry him. Huang Dieniang knew only that her father had been enamored of Elizabeth's British surname and that she would turn out to be the bane of his existence.

Except for an occasional trip to the Saigon Horseracing Ground to ride one of the retired old horses, the only activity befitting her noble name, Elizabeth refused to attend concerts or art exhibits with her husband. She did not like tennis, so on weekends or holidays, when she accompanied him to the country club, she simply put on her sunglasses and sat by the swimming pool, eating chicken satay and leaving her husband to run around on the tennis court.

"She was born into that environment and has seen or possessed everything," William once explained to his father. "Not like us, for whom everything is new and must be learned."

Elizabeth pushed her husband out of her world. When she fell silent and sniffled through her aquiline nose, William knew he'd done something wrong again. Dark circles would appear under her eyes the next day and remain there for as long as she was upset. With fear and trepidation, he'd ask what was wrong, only to hear, "If you don't even know what you've done, what's the point of my telling you?"

Brushing aside his pleadings, she continued to live in an abyss that was beyond his comprehension. As cold wars continued at home, she would storm around, pounding the floor with the heels of her leather shoes, her hands balled into fists, as if anticipating a battle.

To her husband, Elizabeth was a boring Englishwoman. Following his promotion, she tried to play the role of a magistrate's wife. She redecorated the house, top to bottom, and guests often filled the dining table, which could accommodate twenty-four people. Before dinner, she'd quietly and gently remind everyone not to bring up 1997, since the pressure on the magistrate had neared the breaking point.

After kissing the last guest good night, she would let go of her husband's hand as they went upstairs to their bedroom, where they would lie down on either side of the four-poster bed. They shared a dark green wool blanket, but the indentation in the center of the blanket represented the unbridgeable distance between them.

The distance grew larger following the progress of the talks on the handover between Beijing and London. When Prime Minister Thatcher tripped and stumbled on the stairs at the Great Hall of the People in Beijing, nothing would ever be the same again.

Elizabeth wanted to return to London for good. With downcast eyes, she finally forced out the words she'd practiced over and over.

After she left, the talks between China and Britain on the future of Hong Kong reached an impasse. Governor Youde invited a dozen or so local officials and merchants to Government House to gauge their feelings. William Huang was one of them.

A storm raged outside. William, who had come alone, noticed the sunken eyes in the face of the governor, who had been traveling back and forth between Hong Kong and Beijing. He'd become the twenty-sixth governor the year before and was dragged into the thorny issue of the handover barely months into his tenure. A mild-mannered career diplomat, Youde was thrust into this historical moment, caught between the British government and the six million Hong Kong residents who treated him as their protector.

The living room at Government House was like a boat, and on this night it was fraught with a surging undercurrent, as representatives of the six million Hong Kong Chinese cast their questioning gazes at him. The talks continued, but the residents of Hong Kong knew nothing about their own future, since Prime Minister Thatcher had insisted from the beginning that the contents of the talks be kept in strict confidence. Even the highest government office, the Administration Bureau, was kept in the dark. Hence, everyone, based on private logic, speculated on the intentions of the people who controlled their fate.

The capitalists, taking to heart Deng Xiaoping's message that investors had nothing to fear, as relayed by the former governor, Mac-Lehose, believed that China would not kill the goose that laid the golden egg, since a third of China's foreign reserves would come from Hong Kong.

For William and his friends in law, the 1842 Treaty of Nanking and the 1860 Treaty of Peking lacked legal standing since China had been forced to sign at gunpoint. The Communist government did not recognize these unequal treaties. To the People's Republic, 1997 was a trumped-up deadline and Hong Kong, along with Macao, could stay the way they were until China thought the time was right to take them over. If England continued to insist on legal grounds, it would be like picking up a rock to hit one's own feet. The political analysts who held this view urged the people to "forget 1997."

But when they woke up, the issue of 1997 was still there.

In the boatlike living room of Government House the guests cast looks at the helmsman, Governor Youde. Where would the six million Hong Kong Chinese go except where the helmsman steered them? They were frustrated over the fact that their fate was to be decided by others. Governor Youde, unwilling to meet those anxious yet solicitously questioning eyes, ran his hands through his hair, which grew thinner with each round of talks, and looked down at the whisky glass in his hand. He was trying to find the words to convey the fact that the British might not be interested in holding onto Hong Kong, that Prime Minister Thatcher was considering abandoning ship. This, even though prior to the opening of talks, victory in the Falkland Islands had emboldened her rhetoric when she first went to Beijing: "As the queen's prime minister, I am responsible for the residents of Hong Kong."

That was then; this was now. On the eve of abandoning ship, Governor Youde was charged with the task of sounding out Hong Kong residents to see how they would react to such a decision.

He downed the whisky before looking up, his marble-like blue eyes meeting the questioning gazes head on. Raising his chin, he asked in measured tones, "What are your minimum demands?"

The question sent a shock through William Huang's heart. He knew the end had come for Hong Kong.

The bold headlines proclaimed: MRS. THATCHER TO TURN HONG KONG OVER TO CHINA. Overnight, everything in Hong Kong changed.

Huang Dieniang walked along the streets in Central, rubbing shoulders with wave after wave of mainlanders, whom Hong Kong people called "country cousins." Dressed in the style of the 1950s, they raised ruddy faces that had been exposed to the sun for years of political campaigns and gawked at the bustling Central, oblivious to the disdain and hostile looks from Hong Kong Chinese.

Dressed in an old-style purple silk cheongsam with ruffled sleeves and double piping, she stood on the flagstone steps of Queens Road and cast a gloomy look around her.

Following in the footsteps of her great-grandmother, Huang Deyun, she walked on the street that had been so closely linked to her great-grandmother's fate. Kidnapped from Dongguan and shipped to Hong Kong at the age of thirteen, she'd been unloaded along with cases of cargo and had then climbed the flagstone steps on that street on firm and still-growing legs to the red-light district above, where she'd started life as a prostitute.

Dieniang came to Lyndhurst Terrace Street. She looked for the hillside brothel. Once inside, she would part the Soochow embroidered curtain onto copies of landscape paintings that hung on the wall behind the gilded screen. There would be an opium bed amid piles of trinkets, Chinese drum stools, and hardwood tables.

But tall buildings now reigned on the street; everything was different. She could not find the brothel or Madam Randall's house of pleasure. A seafood restaurant now stood where it had been. During the rampage of the plague, Adam Smith had stumbled into Huang Deyun's room, looking for the comfort of human companionship. The day before the Sanitary Board torched the infected area, she had climbed into a sedan chair sent by Smith and left the brothel to live in the Chinese-style house he'd rented for her near the Happy Valley racetrack.

Dieniang followed the parade route for Queen Victoria's diamond jubilee and arrived at the marketplace in Central, site of the first Chinese commerce center. The building had been renovated many times. This was where Huang Deyun had waited for Qu Yabing, after being separated by the lantern-watching crowd.

Automobiles sped down Bonham Strand East, where pedicabs had once vied with sedan chairs. Around the corner the three-story single structure still stood, seemingly as impregnable as ever, although the exterior showed its age. The mark left by the Chinese character for "pawn" was still visible, but everything else, including the name of the shop, was gone. Huang Deyun had walked through the door and into a dark room where Lady Eleven, whose fame had spread throughout pawnshop circles, sat. A few years later, Deyun had taken over the shop and become a powerful woman in the pawn business.

The last rays of the setting sun had disappeared behind the clouds. The fortresslike Yun Gardens, standing on the little hill, was no longer visible. Soon it would be turned into a pile of rubble by backhoes and cranes. It was a depressing thought. Night had arrived in a hurry; darkness came, just like that time years before, when a burlap sack, like a deep well, had dropped over a thirteen-year-old girl's head at the Temple of Mazu in the village of Dongguan. Before she'd had a chance to look up, she had felt darkness descend all around her.

Translators' Note

City of the Queen is three novels in one. In a perfect world, trilogies would never have to be condensed, either in the original language or in translation. That is certainly true here, for Shih Shu-ching's "Hong Kong Trilogy," a series of linked novels, is one of a scant few representatives of historical fiction that treat the fascinating history of Hong Kong. Yet, for a variety of reasons, it has been necessary to pare the three novels, published in 1993, 1995, and 1997 (on the eve of the Hong Kong handover), down to the single volume you have in your hands.

The trilogy spans nearly a hundred years, from Hong Kong's late nineteenth-century beginnings as a pestilential outpost in the British Empire to its peak as one of the world's great economic and cultural centers in the mid-1980s, when Prime Minister Thatcher's representative agreed to Hong Kong's reversion to Chinese control a decade hence. The story thus incorporates the lives of three generations of a family; in condensing the 700-page work, we have taken pains to retain not only the style and the narrative progression but also the approximate proportions of generational narrative in the original work. We have, however, found it necessary to alter the point of view in the final third, since in the Chinese original, the first two volumes are narrated in the third person, while first-person narration takes over in the last. Another concern had to do with names: people, places, streets. In the end, we decided to retain Hong Kong (that is, Cantonese) spellings for place names and some street names in the former colony (those with Western names retain them here), but to use pinyin spellings for everything else, including people's names.

We are grateful for the opportunity to make the essence of Shih Shu-ching's Hong Kong story, the only one of which we are aware that was written by a Hong Kong resident (Shih, a native of Taiwan, lived and worked in Hong Kong for more than fifteen years, eight of them involved in the research and writing of the work), available in English translation. We also thank her for her patience, her suggestions, and her approval of both the editing and the translation.